THE WESLEYAN
EARLY CLASSICS OF
SCIENCE FICTION
SERIES
GENERAL EDITOR
ARTHUR B. EVANS

Invasion of the Sea Jules Verne
The Mysterious Island Jules Verne
Lumen Camille Flammarion
The Battle of the Sexes in Science Fiction Justine Larbalestier
The Last Man Jean-Baptiste Cousin de Grainville
The Mighty Orinoco Jules Verne
The Yellow Wave Kenneth MacKay

Cosmos Latinos

An Anthology

of Science Fiction

from Latin America

and Spain

Translated, edited, &

with an introduction & notes

by Andrea L. Bell & Yolanda Molina-Gavilán

WESLEYAN UNIVERSITY PRESS   Middletown, Connecticut

Published by

Wesleyan University Press, Middletown, CT 06459

Copyright © 2003 by Wesleyan University Press

Introduction, notes, and translation © 2003

Andrea L. Bell and Yolanda Molina-Gavilán

Information concerning copyrighted material used in

this volume appears at the end of the Acknowledgments.

Printed in the United States of America

The Library of Congress Cataloging-in-Publication data

appear at the end of this book.

ISBN 0–8195–6633–0 cloth

ISBN 0–8195–6634–9 paper

To Chris and to all my family

—*Andrea Bell*

To Massimo

—*Yolanda Molina-Gavilán*

CONTENTS

Acknowledgments ix

Introduction: Science Fiction in Latin America and Spain 1

I. In the Beginning The Visionaries

Juan Nepomuceno Adorno, "The Distant Future" (Mexico, 1862) 23

Nilo María Fabra, "On the Planet Mars" (Spain, 1890) 36

II. Speculating on a New Genre SF from 1900 through the 1950s

Miguel de Unamuno, "Mechanopolis" (Spain, 1913) 47

Ernesto Silva Román, "The Death Star" (Chile, 1929) 52

Juan José Arreola, "Baby H.P." (Mexico, 1952) 58

III. The First Wave The 1960s to the Mid-1980s

Ángel Arango, "The Cosmonaut" (Cuba, 1964) 63

Jerônimo Monteiro, "The Crystal Goblet" (Brazil, 1964) 68

Álvaro Menén Desleal, "A Cord Made of Nylon and Gold"
(El Salvador, 1965) 86

Pablo Capanna, "Acronia" (Argentina, 1966) 92

Eduardo Goligorsky, "The Last Refuge" (Argentina, 1967) 109

Alberto Vanasco, "Post-Boomboom" (Argentina, 1967) 116

Magdalena Mouján Otaño, "Gu Ta Gutarrak (We and Our Own)"
(Argentina, 1968) 123

Luis Britto García, "Future" (Venezuela, 1970) 136

Hugo Correa, "When Pilate Said No" (Chile, 1971) 140

José B. Adolph, "The Falsifier" (Peru, 1972) 153

Angélica Gorodischer, "The Violet's Embryos" (Argentina, 1973) 158

André Carneiro, "Brain Transplant" (Brazil, 1978) 194

Daína Chaviano, "The Annunciation" (Cuba, 1983) 201

Federico Schaffler, "A Miscalculation" (Mexico, 1983) 208

IV. Riding the Crest The Late 1980s into the New Millennium

Braulio Tavares, "Stuntmind" (Brazil, 1989) 215

Guillermo Lavín, "Reaching the Shore" (Mexico, 1994) 223

Elia Barceló, "First Time" (Spain, 1994) 235

Pepe Rojo, "Gray Noise" (Mexico, 1996) 243

Mauricio-José Schwarz, "Glimmerings on Blue Glass"
    (Mexico, 1996) 265

Ricard de la Casa and Pedro Jorge Romero, "The Day We Went
    through the Transition" (Spain, 1998) 271

Pablo Castro, "Exerion" (Chile, 2000) 293

Michel Encinosa, "Like the Roses Had to Die" (Cuba, 2001) 305

Notes 331

Selected Bibliography 339

About the Contributors 351

ACKNOWLEDGMENTS

Over the years we have found that wherever we go, if we begin talking about our work in Spanish and Latin American science fiction, the most frequent response is, "That sounds interesting—is any of it available in English?" We prepared this anthology in part so that we may henceforth answer, "Yes."

Many people motivated and assisted us along the way, and without them this book might never have become a reality. For their unfailing enthusiasm toward this project, their generosity in offering assistance and clarification whenever needed, and their undeniable talent, we are particularly indebted to the authors whose works are included in this anthology. We are beholden as well to the translators, whose gifts for transferring one language and culture into another were indispensable to us.

We feel profoundly grateful for the continuous, liberal, and gracious support we have received from the Spanish and Latin American SF communities—especially the clubs in Argentina, Chile, Mexico, Cuba, Brazil, and Spain—that have collaborated with us over the years. We wish to recognize in particular the assistance given by Luis Saavedra, Eduardo Angulo, Luis Pestarini, Miguel Ángel Fernández Delgado, Roberto de Sousa Causo, Eduardo Carletti, Fabricio González, and Miquel Barceló.

Arthur B. Evans of DePauw University and Suzanna Tamminen of Wesleyan University Press have been unwavering in their encouragement of this project from the start. We greatly appreciate the contributions Leonora Gibson and Leslie Starr of Wesleyan University Press have made to this volume, and enthusiastically applaud the work of our copyeditors, Paul R. Betz and Sage Rountree. We value not only the professional talents of all these individuals, but their amiability and positive outlook as well. For their guidance, advocacy, and editorial acumen we feel especially fortunate.

Andrea Bell would like to thank Hamline University's Dean Garvin Davenport and Provost Jerry Greiner for travel and professional development grants that enabled her to complete her initial research into Latin American SF. She is also grateful to her colleagues in the Department of Modern Languages for critiquing translations and for the many other ways they have always supported her research. To Katina Krull and Holly Ewing go thanks for their cheerful and professional assistance in preparing the manuscript.

Yolanda Molina-Gavilán would like to thank Eckerd College's Dean Lloyd Chapin for professional development grants she used toward research and book purchases for this project, her colleagues in Modern Languages for encouraging her along the way, and Michelle Di Gioia for always providing invaluable secretarial help and good humor.

Although repeated attempts were made, the editors were unable to locate the copyright holders of some of the texts used in *Cosmos Latinos*. We gratefully acknowledge permission to use the following copyrighted texts:

"Acronia," 1966, by Pablo Capanna.

"The Annunciation," 1983, by Daína Chaviano.

"Brain Transplant," 1978, by André Carneiro.

"A Cord Made of Nylon and Gold," 1965, by Álvaro Menén Desleal. Reprinted by permission of Cecilia Salaverría de Menéndez Leal.

"The Cosmonaut," 1964, by Ángel Arango.

"The Crystal Goblet," 1964, by Jerônimo Monteiro. Reprinted by permission of Therezinha Monteiro Deutsch.

"The Day We Went through the Transition," 1998, by Ricard de la Casa and Pedro Jorge Romero. Reprinted by permission of Bigaro Ediciones, S.L.

"Exerion," 2000, by Pablo A. Castro.

Fahrenheit 451 (excerpts), by Ray Bradbury. Reprinted by permission of Don Congdon Associates, Inc. © 1953, renewed 1982 by Ray Bradbury.

"The Falsifier," 1972, by José B. Adolph.

"First Time," 1994, by Elia Barceló.

"Glimmerings on Blue Glass," 1996, by Mauricio-José Schwarz.

"Gray Noise," 1996, by Pepe Rojo.

"The Last Refuge," 1967, by Eduardo Goligorsky. Reprinted by permission of Ediciones Minotauro.

"Like the Roses Had to Die," 2001, by Michel Encinosa.

"Mechanopolis," 1913, by Miguel de Unamuno. Reprinted by permission of Quaderns Crema.

"A Miscalculation," 1983, by Federico Schaffler.

"Post-Boomboom," 1967, by Alberto Vanasco. Reprinted by
    permission of Ediciones Minotauro.
"Reaching the Shore," 1994, by Guillermo Lavín.
"Stuntmind," 1989, by Braulio Tavares.
"The Violet's Embryos," 1973, by Angélica Gorodischer.
"When Pilate Said No," 1971, by Hugo Correa.

Cosmos Latinos

INTRODUCTION

SCIENCE FICTION IN LATIN AMERICA AND SPAIN

Cosmos Latinos: An Anthology of Science Fiction from Latin America and Spain introduces readers to a rich and exciting body of literature that most English speakers are unaware even exists.[1] This is not surprising, given that SF is generally seen to be the purview of countries that are world leaders in scientific research and development, and Latin American and Mediterranean countries are often perceived as being mostly consumers, if not victims, of technology. A common and prejudicial corollary is that SF "speaks English" and can be only weakly imitated in other languages. As this anthology shows, however, the genre has been cultivated in Spanish and Portuguese for well over a hundred years, with precursors dating back to the eighteenth century.[2] Mainstream authors from these countries have also made incursions into the genre from time to time, and there is a rich inventory of SF narratives that are not just poor imitations of consecrated masterpieces. On the contrary, these texts stand strongly on their own merits, and often reflect regional reactions to the universal matters addressed by the genre.

While there are exceptions, a generally held perception is that many notable Latin American texts show the influence of the region's celebrated literary fantastic, a quality not usually associated with the SF enjoyed in the English-speaking world. But obviously not all Latin American literature is confined to magical realism. As David W. Foster reminds us,

> The primacy of magical realism for Latin American cultural production is hardly dominant when one examines the bibliography of this production and when one is able to move away from the often quite seriously distorting image of Latin American literature provided by what gets translated into English (i.e., what satisfies the English-reading public's tastes) and what gets studied by foreign scholars who may often not have much of a grasp of lived human experience in Latin America. . . . Thus, if one was likely to have had the opportunity to read some Latin American science fiction writing in English, it

is more likely to have been for reasons other than because it was specifically marked as science fiction: Borges because he is Borges, for example.

This distorted image of Latin American literature is partly to blame for the scarcity of SF texts translated into English. But we must not lose sight of the fact that most bookstores in Latin America and Spain that do have a science fiction section stock mostly translations into Spanish or Portuguese of the European and North American classics. Regional authors are not yet being seriously cultivated by publishers, who see little profitability in marketing domestic SF, both because there is insufficient demand for it among the local book-buying public, and because most people's familiarity with SF has come by way of Hollywood blockbusters and therefore, by extension, for any SF to be "good" it must be imported. Little help has come from local academic circles, which have generally ignored the genre since it does not fall within the still-dominant paradigm of high modernist writing. Some notable exceptions include Nil Santiáñez-Tió's efforts to rescue nineteenth-century Spanish SF from oblivion[3] and Pablo Capanna's seminal works. In the United States, some scholars are indeed working on the subject and have presented papers at the annual meetings of the International Association for the Fantastic in the Arts or the Science Fiction Research Association, and are publishing in scholarly journals such as *Science Fiction Studies, Extrapolation,* and the *Journal of the Fantastic in the Arts.* Despite the historically low visibility of science fiction written in Latin America and Spain, the genre is by no means moribund. Indeed, a recent bibliographical count of SF narrative written by Latin American authors from 1775 to 1999 lists more than six hundred titles.[4] The robustness of the genre notwithstanding, significant cultural and economic barriers still need to be overcome so that these works may enjoy the wider readership at home and abroad that they deserve.

The organizing principle of this anthology reflects the fact that, except for anglophone SF, the greatest influence on Spanish and Latin American SF comes from within. Original works of Spanish- and Portuguese-language SF have influenced other genre readers and writers in Spain and Latin America from the start, and especially since the 1960s—indeed, several of the stories anthologized here are widely known classics within these SF communities. This interest in regional SF production is also reflected in the active communities of Spanish- and Latin American fandom. Many of the fan organizations, writers' groups, and publications have long been international, as many speakers of Portuguese can read Spanish, and vice versa. Spanish- and Portuguese-language SF has been shaped by the history, languages, geography, and cultural traditions that the countries of Latin America share with the Iberian peninsula. *Cosmos Latinos* therefore brings together stories from Spain, Spanish America, and Brazil in recognition of the cross-pollination and support the various SF communities in these regions provide one another.

The comparatively robust economies of five of the countries we have considered have enabled them to sustain lively publishing industries, and thus texts from Argentina, Cuba, Brazil, Mexico, and Spain make up the bulk of this anthology. These countries have dedicated, energetic communities of SF writers who have consistently produced works with a distinctive regional flavor and style; readers who attend science fiction conventions, join SF associations, and follow magazine and fanzine activity; and literary critics, historians, and editors such as Miquel Barceló, Pablo Capanna, Eduardo Carletti, Miguel Ángel Fernández Delgado, Elvio Gandolfo, Luis Pestarini, Gumercindo Rocha Dórea, Domingo Santos, and Federico Schaffler, who are committed to the genre. We agree with these critics that Latin American and Spanish science fiction constitutes a body of work meriting study and diffusion. That, along with opening a window onto a fascinating new world for English-speaking readers, is the intent of *Cosmos Latinos: An Anthology of Science Fiction from Latin America and Spain.*

HISTORY OF THE GENRE IN SPAIN AND LATIN AMERICA

Although we have found early examples of fantastic literature in the eighteenth century, the shaping of a body of science fiction in Latin America and Spain truly began in the nineteenth century. In Spain there are examples of works of different SF modalities, such as the anonymous utopia *Selenopolis* (*Viage de un filósofo a Selenópolis*, 1804), the oneiric voyage-to-the-Moon story *Zulema and Lambert* (*Zulema y Lambert*, Joaquín Castillo y Mayone, 1832), the proto–sword-and-sorcery fantasy *A Time in the Most Beautiful of Planets* (*Una temporada en el más bello de los planetas*, Tirso Aguimana de Veca, 1870–71) and the time-machine adventure *The Anachronopete* (*El anacronópete*, Enrique Gaspar, 1887). This latter work, like much of Spain's nineteenth-century fantastic, was clearly influenced by Jules Verne and Camille Flammarion. Santiáñez-Tió identifies mainstream giants Ángel Ganivet, Leopoldo Alas, José Martínez Ruiz (*Azorín*), and the lesser-known Nilo María Fabra as the authors of Spain's best early science fictional works (1994: 285).

The Argentinean Eduardo Ladislao Holmberg is considered one of the first bona fide writers of the genre, and his novel *The Marvelous Voyage of Mr. Nic-Nac* (*El maravilloso viaje del Sr. Nic-Nac*, 1875) is usually credited as the first SF novel in Latin America, although *Story of a Dead Man* (*Historia de un muerto*), by Cuban Francisco Calcagno, and *Dr. Benignus* (*O Doutor Benignus*), by Brazilian Emilio Augusto Zaluar, were also published the same year. Holmberg's novel was soon followed by *From Jupiter: The Curious Voyage of a Magnetized Man from Santiago* (*Desde Júpiter: Curioso viaje de un santiaguino magnetizado*, 1878) by Chile's Francisco Miralles. Both novels are adventure stories that center around an earthling's scientific fascination with life on another planet and offer social commentary in a highly didactic tone.[5]

These works, among others, signaled the beginning of a new literary expression in Latin America and Spain, but from those early days through the 1950s there was no cohesive science fiction tradition in the Spanish and Portuguese-speaking world, and no Gernsback or Campbell to nurture writers and give the emerging genre a distinct shape and feel. Brazilian SF before the 1950s, for example, was heavily influenced by Portuguese translations of Jules Verne, Emilio Salgari, J. Aragón, Gustave Le Rouge, and H. G. Wells, as may be discerned from titles such as Erico Veríssimo's *Travel to the Dawn of the World* (*Viagem à aurora do mundo*, 1939) or Jerônimo Monteiro's *Three Months in the Eighty-First Century* (*3 meses no século 81*, 1947). This lack of autochthonous models meant that what regional SF there was prior to the 1960s involved the irregular efforts of isolated writers who, for the most part, had no particular commitment to the genre but found it a useful means of critiquing society, promoting a particular agenda, or continuing the fin-de-siècle fascination with the supernatural. One exception was the aforementioned Monteiro, whose relationship with SF spanned four decades; another was Spain's Fabra, an early-twentieth-century journalist devoted to the genre who still clung to the preceding century's faith in science and technology. In general, however, early Latin American and Spanish SF stories were influenced by Christian morality and—as the century progressed, with its world wars and dizzying technological advances— were inspired by the desire to warn against the dangers of unrestrained scientific experimentation.

The turn-of-the-century Latin American aesthetic movement called to their Argentinean counterparts' penchant for fantasy. (Some would even like to include Cuban-born Italo Calvino in their ranks.) A survey of Cuban science fictional works after the 1959 revolution shows a great increase in production from about 1964 to 1971. These works followed Soviet models of the genre, which provided a logical connection to the image of the future that the revolution envisioned, a world triumphantly and harmoniously led by machines. Ángel Arango's *Whither Go the Cephalomes?* (*¿Adónde van los cefalomos?*, 1964), *The Black Planet* (*El planeta negro*, 1966) and *The Art of Robots* (*Robotomaquia*, 1967), as well as Miguel Collazo's *Oaj's Fantastic Book* (*El libro fantástico de Oaj*, 1966), helped train younger writers such as Chely Lima, Alberto Serret, Félix Lizárraga, and Daína Chaviano, who would come into their own in the 1980s. The proliferation of SF writing in the 1960s is indicative of the type of creative energy and the popularity of the genre that existed in Cuba at the time. However—as SF author and critic Antonio Orlando Rodríguez (1999) explained at a recent conference—this creative energy was thwarted during the 1970s by the intervention of the Castro regime into Cuban cultural production.

In Mexico the mid-1960s brought forth a new generation of writers whose works appeared in a revitalized intellectual climate that was more accepting of previously disdained literary "subgenres" such as science fiction. Major SF writers of this generation are the aforementioned Olvera, Cardona Peña, and Rebétez, as well as Edmundo Domínguez Aragonés, Marcela del Río, and Manú Dornbierer.

Unfortunately, the attitudes and conditions that nurtured this SF golden age were no match for the political, social, and economic turmoil that ravaged Latin America throughout much of the 1970s and 1980s. Publishers facing skyrocketing costs and, in many cases, the suspicious eye of authoritarian regimes avoided risks by stocking their shelves with a few reliable national authors and with translated bestsellers from abroad, all well within mainstream tastes. The initial increase in SF activity markedly diminished as state-sponsored terrorism in countries like Argentina, Brazil, and Chile took its toll on artists and intellectuals. Some writers stopped writing or emigrated; others, most famously Argentina's beloved SF master Héctor Oesterheld, "disappeared." Already scant government funding of the arts did not extend to peripheral genres, and many hoped-for SF books, magazines, and conventions never materialized. This is not to say that SF-related activity ceased entirely during this bleak era of dictatorships and economic decline; on the contrary, a few commendable anthologies were published, along with the occasional single-author work. In Argentina, Marcial Souto edited two splendid SF magazines: *El Péndulo* (1979; 1981–1982; and 1986–1987), and a new version of *Minotauro* (1983–1986). Also, science fictional motifs had some impact on nongenre literature. (For example, while SF works did not make a particularly strong impact on Mexican mainstream literature during this decade, they did popularize the idea of envisioning an apocalyptic future, which later proved to be a useful way of expressing fears about the economic, political, social, and environmental future of Mexico.)[12] But by the mid-1980s the first golden age of SF in Latin America had largely come to an end. The same held true in Spain, where the 1970s witnessed the onset of decline in the genre. Spanish presses, such as the successful Nebulae (publisher of full-length SF novels) folded; for a while the legendary magazine *Nueva Dimensión*[13] kept science fiction alive, though it could publish only short stories, and in 1982 it, too, fell silent.

Since the late 1980s, however, the health of Spanish- and Portuguese-language SF has improved dramatically. Even the renewed economic crises brought on by the global recession of the early twenty-first century have not been able to vanquish its renewed energy and optimism. Various literary prizes for SF were inaugurated in the 1980s, such as the Mexican *Puebla* award, the Cuban *David* award, and Argentina's *Más Allá*.[14] These awards encouraged quality writing such as that of Mexicans Gerardo Porcayo and Mauricio-José Schwarz; Cubans Daína Chaviano, Félix Lizárraga, Rafael Morante, and María Felicia Vera; and *Más Allá* winners Eduardo Carletti, José Altamirano, and Claudia De Bella. Two other Mexican awards, the *Kalpa* and the *Tierra Ignota*, were later established. Since the 1990s the Spanish *Ignotus*, *Gigamesh*, *Alberto Magno*, and *UPC Novelette* awards have honored writers such as Juan Miguel Aguilera, León Arsenal, Elia Barceló, César Mallorquí, Rodolfo Martínez, Ángel Torres Quesada, and Rafael Trechera.[15] Altogether, the last fifteen years or so have seen substantial growth in the genre, a quantitative and qualitative increase in terms of both works and writers. A few countries in particular (Argentina, Brazil, Mexico, and Spain) are again at the forefront of this new wave, but there is, to our knowledge, no Spanish- or Portuguese-speaking country that does not currently have writers active in the field of SF and some level of organized SF fan activity.

Naturally, many factors work together to sustain this new growth in SF, but chief among them are the electronic media, including desktop publishing. In Argentina Eduardo Carletti, author of mostly technological SF novels and short stories, launched the electronic fanzine *Axxón* in 1989, and in 1993 it surpassed the longevity record—forty-eight issues—previously held by the revered magazine *Más allá*.[16] *Axxón* has evolved markedly over the years, but from its beginning has published some of the finest original science fiction, horror, fantasy, comics, and fractal art by artists from all over the Americas. It also features a variety of nonfiction columns and has a lively correspondence section. *Axxón*, having recently celebrated its hundredth issue, is a splendid publication and a major force behind Argentinean science fiction's second wave.

A number of other new SF publications in Latin America have also emerged. In Mexico *Axxón*'s paper counterpart might be *Umbrales*, Federico Schaffler's labor of love. *Umbrales* lost critical state funding in 1998 and subsequently folded, but not before publishing over forty issues of fiction, commentary, and artwork. Schaffler, an SF author and anthologist from Nuevo Laredo who remains busy in the field, has done much to promote a new generation of Mexican science fiction writers and may yet succeed in resurrecting *Umbrales*. A sister magazine in Spain is *Gigamesh*, which has been published in Barcelona since 1991. In addition, many irregularly published fanzines have come (and some have gone) in Latin America and Spain, such as *Aurora Bitzine, Azoth, Banana Atômica, BEM, Cuásar, Cygnus, Diaspar, Estacosa, Factor Trek, El Fantasma, Fobos, Gandiva, Galaxia 2000, El Guaicán Literario, Kenbeo Kenmaro, La Langosta se ha Posado, Megalon, Mundo Imaginario, Nádir, ¡Nahual!, Núcleo Ubik, Opar, Parsifal, Pórtico, Quantor, Solaris, Sinergía, Sub, El Sueño del Fevre, Tránsito* and *Vórtice*. This is by no means an exhaustive list, and many current fanzines are available online.[17] They all play a substantial role in the development of science fiction in Latin America and Spain, for they give writers a place to publish, are a means of disseminating useful information, and help create a sense of community among the sometimes far-flung SF readership.

Traditional publishing options are still scarce for science fiction narrative in Spanish and Portuguese; however, the outlook is not entirely discouraging. Some authors, such as Carlos Chernov and Ana María Shua, have been published by non-SF presses, and recently science fiction works have done well in mainstream literary competitions. Such enterprising authors as Mauricio-José Schwarz, Daína Chaviano, Vladimir Hernández, and Braulio Tavares have had some success by turning to Spain and Portugal for publishers, although by doing so they run the risk of abandoning the genre. Daína Chaviano, for example, had three non-

SF novels published by Spain's prestigious Espasa Calpe, but her offer to reprint her SF novel *Fables of an Extraterrestrial Grandma* (*Fábulas de una abuela extraterrestre*, 1998) was turned down by the same press. On occasion, nongenre periodicals such as *A Quien Corresponda, Ciencia y Desarrollo, Complot Internacional* and *Nossas Edições* will publish SF or devote a special issue to it. Among the professional presses in Spain that have published Spanish-language SF works are Miraguano (*Futuropolis*), Gigamesh, and Ediciones B (*Nova ciencia ficción*), with Quaderns UPCF (published by the SF Association of the Polytechnic University of Catalonia) having recently joined them. In Mexico active publishers of regional SF include Times Editores and Ramón Llaca y Cía.; in Argentina, Ediciones Axxón, Ediciones Nuevo Siglo, and Editorial Huemul, among others, have published contemporary SF in Spanish.

The Internet has revitalized science fiction dialogue not only by means of e-zines and personal Web sites, but also through listservs that fan groups have started in Argentina, Brazil, Chile, Mexico, Spain, Peru, Uruguay, Venezuela, and quite probably elsewhere in the region. A few years ago Roberto de Sousa Causo and Bruce Sterling launched the Rede Global Paraliterária (Global Paraliterary Network), or RGP for short, and it is now a dynamic listserv through which participants on several continents carry on serious discussions (usually in English) about science fiction and related genres. Active SF writers' associations and fan clubs include the Asociación Mexicana de Ciencia Ficción y Fantasía and Círculo Independiente de Ficción y Fantasía in Mexico, Asociación Venezolana de Ciencia Ficción in Venezuela, Círculo Argentino de Ciencia Ficción y Fantasía in Argentina, Ficcionautas Asociados in Chile, Asociación Española de Fantasía y Ciencia Ficción in Spain, and Brazil's Clube de Leitores de Ficção Científica (in addition to scores of clubs devoted to television or movie characters, comics, or role-playing games). Thanks to the energy of volunteers and to occasional financial support from governments and universities, there have been a fair number of SF conventions over the years, such as Cubaficción in Havana and Hispa-Con in Spain. Brazilian clubs hosted Orson Scott Card in 1990 and Bruce Sterling in 1997, and fans were able to enjoy Ray Bradbury's attendance at the 1997 Book Fair in Buenos Aires and William Gibson's 1999 public lecture in Mexico City on that city's future. (These last two were city-sponsored, non-SF events, but they were a great treat for local fans nonetheless.)

Clearly, the future of science fiction in Latin America and Spain looks promising. The new era has already brought to light many young writers of talent, men and women from throughout the Spanish- and Portuguese-speaking world who write with originality, knowledge, and style. It has also, of course, produced its share of flawed works. Contest judges and magazine editors can sometimes be too overwhelmed with submissions (and by the demands of their day jobs) to insist on well-developed, professional-sounding stories. But many real gems are being published today, works by those authors mentioned here and myriads of others. Various publishing houses outside the region have begun to express interest in manuscripts from Spanish and Latin American writers. The editors reassure writers that as long as their stories are well written and fit the publisher's list, they stand just as good a chance as any other submission. While this has not yet put to rest the pervasive (and often deleterious) belief among many Latin American or Spanish SF writers that they must learn to imitate their anglophone counterparts in order to compete successfully in the marketplace, it has encouraged more writers to keep honing their craft and circulating their work. Other significant obstacles still remain, most notably the need for works to be well translated prior to being submitted to publishers. For this and other reasons, more thought and energy have recently gone into finding creative ways to overcome the barriers to publication, and even to by-pass the U.S./U.K. market altogether. This has been a frequent topic on the Global Paraliterary Network; various ideas and initiatives have been discussed, and recently a Web site was established that offers free access to international SF in translation.[18] Still, the key to the genre's ultimate success is in the hands of the readers, contest judges, editors, and critics, who must always hold their SF writers to the highest standards.

Critics and historians from Spain and Latin America currently working on the genre include Pablo Capanna, Alicia Irene Bugallo, Miguel Angel Fernández Delgado, Miquel Barceló, Moisés Hassón, Ingrid Kreksch, Luis Pestarini, Carlos Saiz Cidoncha, Roberto de Sousa Causo, Mauricio-José Schwarz, Gabriel Trujillo Muñoz, and Juan Carlos Toledano. Let us hope that many more will soon join in this growing critical dialogue about the science fiction production from this part of the world.

THEMES AND THEORY

In Latin America and Spain, SF production is so prolific and varied that one can now find examples of nearly every theme and subgenre.

Given this diversity, instead of trying to catalog recent titles, it might be better to identify some of the qualities that make contemporary SF narrative in Spanish and Portuguese so distinctive.

Although modern Spanish- and Portuguese-language science fiction shares many thematic and stylistic elements with anglophone SF, there are some important differences to be noted. We will look at three broad characteristics: Latin American and Spanish SF's generally "soft" nature and social sciences orientation; its examination of Christian symbols and motifs; and its uses of humor.

In the first place, the majority of these works do not aim for scientific plausibility. Literary scholars usually attribute this characteristic to the regional countries' role as consumers rather than producers of technology and to the fact that few Latin American and Spanish SF writers have a strong background in the natural or computer sciences (Kreksch 1997: 177, Saiz Cidoncha 1988: 513). But this is less true than might be assumed, however. Among contemporary writers, José Luis Ramírez and Juan Miguel Aguilera are both industrial designers, Gerardo Sifuentes is an industrial engineer, Julio Septién a professor of architecture, Javier Redal a biologist, Gonzalo Martré a chemical engineer, Magdalena Mouján Otaño a mathematics professor, and Bruno Henríquez a geophysicist. Also, the general preference for "soft" sciences such as psychology or ecology as a point of departure for many SF narratives does not imply a total rejection of the "hard" sciences. Authors who concentrate on the science in science fiction include the Spaniards Javier Redal and Juan Miguel Aguilera, with novels such as *Worlds in the Abyss* (*Mundos en el abismo*, 1988) and *The Refuge* (*El refugio*, 1994), as well as many young writers interested in cyberpunk, with its computer-dominated world and decadent, counterculture atmosphere, most notably Mexico's Gerardo Horacio Porcayo, Bernardo Fernández, Gerardo Sifuentes, and José Luis Ramírez, and Cuba's José Miguel Sánchez (Yoss), Ariel Cruz, and Michel Encinosa.[19]

In addition to its general tendency to avoid technical and scientific details, Spanish and Latin American SF's emphasis on the sociopolitical has earned it the reputation of being "soft."[20] In times of political repression, for example, the science fiction mode has proven to be an excellent tool to foreground a particular ideological position or to disguise social criticism from government censors. Indeed, many Latin American texts have specific political and social agendas. Modern Cuban SF, for example, was charged with presenting the blueprint for the Socialist New Man, as in

Agustín de Rojas's novel *The Year 200* (*El año 200*, 1990).[21] Most of these SF narratives reflect a particular discipline, position, or movement used as a main ideological ingredient. Marxism, feminism, nationalism, and ecology are some of the many social orientations informing the stories. As an example of Marxist ideology in a Mexican text, we have included in *Cosmos Latinos* Mauricio-José Schwarz's "Glimmerings on Blue Glass" ("Destellos en vidrio azul"). This story presents a capitalist dystopia set in an atmosphere of urban degeneration where popular literature—in this case detective fiction—not only offers escapism but also might constitute the only opportunity to subvert the status quo. Indeed, stories from all over Latin America target big business (licit or illicit) and consumer culture as truly malignant forces, the heartless imperialist appetites that are responsible for much human suffering. Mexico's Pepe Rojo is one of many talented young SF writers whose stories focus on consumerism, the modern workplace, and the nature of identity. His story "Gray Noise" ("Ruido gris"), an indictment of sensationalist media and of society's macabre voyeurism, is included in this volume.

International relations are, naturally enough, another frequent theme in SF from Latin America and Spain. Some stories reflect current events as they imagine new political and economic alliances among nations or explore issues of sovereignty. Guillermo Lavín's "Reaching the Shore" ("Llegar a la orilla") is translated here from *Border of Broken Mirrors* (*Frontera de espejos rotos*, 1994), a collection of SF stories by U.S. and Mexican writers who examine different aspects of border culture and politics between their two countries. Very often the genre is also used to reflect on a country's recent history and even to defend a particular political position, as in the case of "The Day We Went through the Transition" ("El día que hicimos la Transición") by Ricard de la Casa and Pedro Jorge Romero. This time-travel story, written in 1997, refers to the period of the democratic transition in Spain (1975–1981) and highlights the shared recent history that unifies Spaniards politically and socially at a time when that unity can be perceived as being questioned or threatened.

A second characteristic of Spanish and Latin American SF is its tendency to utilize Christian motifs and iconography—situated within the context of other Western mythologies, such as Greco-Roman or the Anglo-Saxon—and to portray their reconstruction or subversion through science fiction's power to demystify religious beliefs by opposing reason and faith. The tension between technology, religion, and magic finds especially fertile ground in many of the region's narratives. Elia Barceló expresses this tension in a dialogue between a human called Luna and a machine called María in her 1989 short novel *The Dragon Lady* (*La dama dragón*):

> Religion is the best way to explain everything that ˙one cannot or does not want to understand, María said. . . . But that kills the will to research and dumbs people down, Luna answered. Yes, . . . but it makes them happy; at times I hate myself for not having ever known that simple happiness one must feel upon accepting the marvelous, the immense joy of loving a god, or several. . . . Look at our civilization: we have completely lost the power to marvel at what's beautiful, great, unknown. . . . And that's the way we are: hard, dry, sterile, empty. (245)

This anthology offers several good examples of SF and religion: among them, José B. Adolph's "The Falsifier" ("El falsificador," 1972) and Daína Chaviano's "The Annunciation" ("La Anunciación," 1983). Whereas Adolph's text ingeniously reinterprets the Catholic Church's version of religious history and its encounter with the indigenous myths and legends of the Americas, Chaviano's story reworks a key Catholic myth—the Immaculate Conception—in irreverent science-fictional terms.

A third feature that can be commonly found in Spanish and Latin American SF is a penchant for allegory and humor. The following is a chronological sampling of texts that convey an obvious but light comic mood: Francisco Miralles's *From Jupiter* (1878), Juan José Arreola's "Baby H.P." ("Baby H.P.," 1952), Carlos María Carón's "Napoleon's Victory" ("La victoria de Napoleón," 1968), Carlos Olvera's *Mexicans in Space* (1968), Angélica Gorodischer's *Trafalgar* (1979), Féliz Mondéjar (F. Mond)'s *With the Terrestrials' Pardon* (*Con perdón de los terrícolas*, 1983), Elia Barceló's *Natural Consequences* (*Consecuencias naturales*, 1994), and Javier Negrete's "Converging Evolution" ("Evolución convergente," 1998). Very often the ideology informing the narrative is expressed through satire, as in Magdalena Mouján Otaño's "Gu Ta Gutarrak" (1968). This story exposes the constructed nature of Basque identity by revising a nationalistic myth created in the nineteenth century but still alive today: the myth of the Basques being Europe's oldest and purest surviving race. This Argentinean text—like the ones by Angélica Gorodischer and José Adolph also included here—connects with a narrative that is central to Latin America's imagination: the discovery, conquest, and colonization of the

Americas.[22] Federico Schaffler's anthology *With Apologies to Columbus* (*Sin permiso de Colón*, 1993), devoted to the fifth centennial of the voyage of Columbus, is but one example of the importance of this subject. Other examples of alternate history stories that highlight the legacy of indigenous cultures can be found in the works of Argentina's Claudia De Bella and Mexico's Héctor Chavarría.[23]

A distinctive characteristic of one segment of contemporary Spanish and Latin American SF is its comic-book feel. The comic book is a medium of longstanding popularity in Latin America, easier to find and afford in some areas than bound books. (Some publishers in Brazil produce books in magazine form because there are so many more magazine kiosks than bookstores in that country.) Very common in stories of this type is the figure of the superhero, a fictional character with roots in the traditions of classic detective fiction, action-adventure movies, modern comics (especially the *manga*), and that unique Mexican cultural icon, the masked wrestler. SF texts in the comic-book style, such as José Luis Zárate's *Xanto* (1994) and Ricardo Guzmán Wolffer's *May God Have Mercy upon Us All* (*Que Dios se apiade de todos nosotros*, 1993), abound in action and graphic violence, and feature brash, individualistic heroes on some sort of quest. Female characters may play key roles and be smart and strong, but they must also generate sexual tension.

Spanish and Latin American SF has not escaped the genre's heritage of flagrant sexism, but many women SF authors' texts have had a corrective effect on this tradition, since they generally break away from masculinist models. Most SF stories written by women show alternate worlds where the weak become powerful, and female protagonists who are central to the action are given a refreshing fullness and complexity of character.[24] Women are in the minority among SF writers in Latin America and Spain, but they are certainly not minor authors.[25] In fact, Angélica Gorodischer (Argentina), Daína Chaviano (Cuba), and Elia Barceló (Spain) are three highly respected names in the genre, while Elena Aldunate, Marcela Del Río, Myriam Laurini, Blanca Martínez, Libia Brenda Castro, Lola Robles, and Dinah Silveira de Queiroz are widely recognized.[26] Two novels by mainstream Spanish author Rosa Montero, *The Delta Function*, 1991 (*La función delta*, 1981), and *Tremor* (*Temblor*, 1990), could also be considered SF novels, although they are not marketed as such. Other mainstream women writers who have occasionally dabbled in the genre are the Mexicans Carmen Boullosa and Laura Esquivel.[27] While the non–Spanish speaking reader must still wait for translations of these women's texts to become available, two stories at least may be enjoyed here: Daína Chaviano's "The Annunciation" and Angélica Gorodischer's "The Violet's Embryos"—this latter an example of the author's highly literate style, whose subject matter underscores her independent feminist ideology. Although Gorodischer is aware of the Anglo-American New Wave and feminist SF of the 1960s and 1970s, it would be dangerous to make too much of the author's acquaintance with these works. For example, some readers familiar with Joanna Russ's 1967 story "When It Changed" may think that "The Violet's Embryos" is a retelling of Russ's work with the genres reversed. In fact, the author herself has declared this to be a mere coincidence.[28] "The Violet's Embryos" speculates generally about the possibility of changing human nature and specifically about destroying gender division, and it presents a world where homosexuality is the norm. In this sense she joins authors such as Marion Zimmer Bradley, Suzy McKee Charnas, Diane Duane, Ursula K. Le Guin, Elizabeth Lynn, Joe Haldeman, and Barry N. Malzberg who have used homosexual characters and themes in their works. But the story challenges a specifically Latin American idea about homosexuality (that the insertor retains a masculine persona) and refers to cultural paradigms such as the *milico* (a member of the military) that have a particularly Argentinean flavor.

Some Spanish and Latin American SF writers have considered English-language SF as their ultimate model, at times excessively so. Yet others have encouraged their peers to seek out new, autochthonous forms and styles. There is no denying the profound influence that U.S. production has had on modern SF, and its current eclecticism mirrors that of today's Latin American and Spanish works of the genre. The reader should therefore not be surprised to find here many thematic and stylistic similarities with some anglophone SF works.

THE TEXTS IN THIS ANTHOLOGY

The stories that make up *Cosmos Latinos* are divided into four sections that follow a chronological order, giving the reader a sense of how the genre has developed in Latin America and Spain through time. In this respect, this anthology offers a historical sampling of the genre in these areas of the world. The first section, entitled "In the Beginning: The Visionaries," presents two stories written in the nineteenth century that are good examples of early utopian SF. The three stories that comprise the next section, "Speculating on a New Genre: SF from 1900 through the 1950s," are from Spain, Chile, and Mexico. They show how Hispanic SF starts to evolve toward its own identity from the start of the twentieth century through the 1950s, a period that marks the isolated beginnings of the genre's modern tradition. The next section, the largest of this anthology, is entitled "The First Wave: The 1960s to the Mid-1980s." It showcases fourteen stories from Argentina, Brazil, Chile, Cuba, El Salvador, Mexico, Peru, and Venezuela that exemplify the first "golden age" of the genre in the 1960s and 1970s. The authors in this section are very well known in the Luso-Hispanic SF community, and we consider them to be modern classics of Latin American science fiction. The last section, "Riding the Crest: The Late 1980s into the New Millennium," presents a sample of eight stories from Latin America and Spain that show the genre's richness and depth as well as its vibrant growth over the last fifteen years.

Besides the need to reflect a historical progression of the genre, another factor weighing in the selection of texts for this anthology has been a desire to include as much geographical and thematic variety as possible. In addition to historical or thematic importance, the overall quality of the stories—how they grab and maintain the reader's attention and provoke cognitive estrangement and a sense of wonder—has also been a consideration when deciding which SF stories to include in this collection.

Selecting a few representative short stories has been a daunting task, and many excellent examples—some considered essential by our colleagues—have not found a place in this collection because of length restrictions. It is our hope that other volumes offering more of the best stories from the Spanish- and Portuguese-speaking worlds will soon follow. Given the opportunity to edit a subsequent volume, we would consider works by Juan Miguel Aguilera, Elena Aldunate, Armando Boix, Luis Saavedra, Tarik Carson, Alberto Chimal, Javier Cuevas, Carlos Gardini, Sergio Gaut vel Hartman, Vladimir Hernández, Blanca Martínez, Gerardo Porcayo, Marcial Souto, Roberto de Sousa Causo, and José Luis Zárate among numerous others. We would also want to include more cyberpunk and an alternate history story. And our final wish would be to showcase more women SF writers and authors from underrepresented places such as Central America, Colombia, Ecuador, and Uruguay, as well as Latino writers in the United States.

Part I

In the Beginning

The Visionaries

Juan Nepomuceno Adorno

MEXICO

An obscure but fascinating figure in nineteenth-century Mexican thought, Juan Nepomuceno Adorno (1807–1880) was a seemingly indefatigable inventor who dreamed that the physical and moral perfectibility of mankind could be achieved through the combined efforts of technology and the enlightened doctrine he called "Providentiality."

Adorno outlined his philosophy of Providentiality in his 1851 book *Introduction to the Harmony of the Universe, or Principles of Physico-Harmonic Geometry,* written in English while Adorno was living in London. The treatise was later expanded, translated, and published in Mexico as *Armonía del universo: Sobre los principios de la armonía física y matemática* (1862).[1] Influenced by the work of Saint-Simon and Charles Fourier—particularly with regard to social reform and the concept of the utopia—Adorno believed that many social, economic, political, and ethical problems could be eradicated through the vigorous application of progressive technology in fulfillment of divine providence. His vision of mankind's happy fate was celebrated in the chapter of *Armonía del universo* entitled "The Distant Future" ("El remoto porvenir"). On the following pages we present some excerpts from this chapter that we have grouped according to topic.

In the course of *Armonía,* Adorno describes many of the technological innovations he believes await humanity, marvels such as an instant global communications network, unlimited steam, electric, magnetic, and thermal energy at our beck and call, airports, and even genetic engineering. Adorno called the type of writing exemplified by "The Distant Future" intuitive poetry—an apt term. The modern reader, however, struck by the perceptiveness and mechanistic imagination of *Armonía,* would recognize it as an early example of the technological utopia and an indisputable precursor of what we now call science fiction.

The Distant Future

El remoto porvenir, 1862

by Juan Nepomuceno Adorno

translated by Andrea Bell

INTRODUCTION

Greetings, beauteous Planet of green, resplendent fields, of silvered rivers and cerulean seas! Whither, oh whither do you set your ellipcentric course? . . .

Sunward with your companions do you slowly journey, like the glorious hero who shuns exaltation, or as one who strives to make his destiny the more brilliant before bringing his praiseworthy toils to an end!

Earth, O Earth, it is you! I greet you!

Now do I perceive the graceful curves of your beautiful continents and islands. Some of their features have changed; they are positioned differently with respect to your equator and axis, and thus offer less resistance to your diurnal and annual movement.

ON PHYSICAL CHANGES IN HUMANS

I draw nigh unto you, lovely Planet; I wish to see what remains of mankind, to discover if humans still dwell upon you or if they are entombed as fossils, their species extinct.

Where, oh, where are the ancient Ethiopians with their lustrous, ebony skin? Where have the sons of Albion gone, ivory colored and golden haired? What of the diverse varieties of humankind that, in times of conflict, were the pride of some and the shame of so many others?

Differences have now disappeared! One integrated, beautiful, wondrous race peoples your land, crosses your seas, and drifts in glory among your clouds. Humans have been perfected, in shape and in size!

Their color is soft, rose-hued, and harmonious.

Their eyes are bright and shining.

The dazzling light of their hair, worn in braids and ringlets of ebony, contrasts with the subtle and beautiful finish of their firm skin, its fresh softness graced with iridescent hues.

Their limbs are vigorous, defying fatigue.

And slender are they, and beautiful; and pleasing in the way they walk; and noble, and tranquil, and straight. . . .

Of the savage I see not a trace.

ON MORALITY AND PROVIDENTIALITY

You, Planet, are mankind's house, its divine mansion, and all your varied inhabitants are now simply brothers.

O enchanting Earth! O gentle people! O Eden, adorned by their hands! The noble days of mankind have arrived; pleasure, virtue, and innocence unite with wisdom, and power with goodness has joined! . . .

Would happiness be possible for mankind without similar conquests in the moral sciences? Without doubt, no. But morality now is founded in the Providentiality of the human species, universally acknowledged and revered by all individuals. Morality is no longer that agonizing restraint which used to confine mankind within the narrow limits of artificial obligations. It is not the harsh, strangling tether that, though invisible and internal, kept the slave under the master's fierce whip and reduced the unhappy proletarian to poverty and death by starvation while surrounded by fields covered in ripe crops. . . .

Divine virtue! You, too, ally yourself with truth; and with the noble example of the strongest and most beautiful of men, you have made it so that all practice love and mercy, that the strong and the weak care deeply for one another, that the strong derive the highest pleasure in being Provident with the weak, and the latter derive great joy from savoring the blessings of the former without envy or jealousy! . . .

Thus do the strong work the same hours as the weak in common labor, and do not calculate to see whose work has been the more or less productive. Are not the fruits of collective efforts equally useful and profitable to all?

In the same way does the child of talent and genius learn and help his peers to learn, without the petty vanity of comparing his superior wit to the lesser talents of others. Is not science likewise shared? Are not its benefits the prize and glory of all humanity? . . .

Thus it is: equality, as the fundamental principle of humanity, a principle conquered through thousands of years of heroic virtues and glorious efforts, can no longer be corrupted by tyranny. Tyranny is impossible. . . . Talent, intelligence, and sublime virtue no longer worship personal glory, but instead render glory to all mankind. Of what importance is the name of the inventor of a celebrated machine? Did not the inventor find contentment in offering the machine to his fellow citizens? Was not the original idea discussed and improved upon by all, and is not the machine the result of a multitude of combined efforts?

Inventors from past ages! Of what benefit to you were your exclusive rights? You suffered the torments of enslaved genius, and the tyranny of capital was almost always what profited from your ideas and hard work. What misery, what degradations consumed you in your solitude, and how quickly did you discover that the childish vanity of hearing your-selves called inventors became ridicule once the pecuniary deceptions of success came roaring down to drown you in dismay and make you drink from the bitter cup of disappointment!

Now, genius is assured of collaborators; combined efforts nourish the initial ideas for improvements, and all of humanity wins. It is guaranteed that everyone will enjoy the benefits of the work of all; the common person assists the genius and inspires the great projects that humanity perfects and executes. . . .

But so many wonders, so many pleasures, so many reasons for contentment—to what are they owed? . . . To you, holy equality, sacred dogma; fundamental precept of the Providentiality of mankind. To you, unique and fruitful principle of personal well-being on the Planet.

You, divine equality, for whom the poor yearned in their days of wretchedness. You, whom the arrogant despised. You, attacked for so many centuries; you are both the cure for social ills and the fertile seed of all human delights.

Equality, equality, sweet and sublime! You have dried the tears of the angry child. Anger no longer enters into his festive games. With whom could he be angry when he looks around and sees only equals?

You have exiled the conceit of youth.

You have tamed the pride of adults.

You have made self-seeking useless.

You have stilled the greediness of the old.

You have rid the one of disdain for the other, and the latter's envy of the former.

Because of you, divine equality, no longer is there unpleasantness, no longer is there hate, no longer are there crimes, or vengeance, or vices . . . .

But can we therefore say that absolute equality among all mankind exists? And if it did, to what would people devote their virtues and Providentiality?

Humans, with the level of perfection they have attained, differ among each other less than in past times. Strength, beauty, and intelligence are more evenly distributed among them, but absolute equality is impossible in complex organizations such as that of man, and herein lies the magnificent and the sublime of human Providentiality, which has learned to balance these small differences with the reciprocal virtues of mankind.

Oh, yes, I see sweet and kindly children strive with the greatest enthusiasm to excel in their studies, not so as to humiliate those less able, but in order to help them in their intellectual tasks!

So also do I see them eagerly take up their gymnastic exercises, so that one day they may be of service to their fellows through their physical efforts. What glory, what joy for whoever among them saves from the deep someone who, through unintended fatigue, has sunk beneath the waves! . . .

Praise you, praise you a thousand times, glorious humanity, for you have learned to cleanse yourself of your deficiencies and raise yourself up, splendid, sublime, and Providential, on the marvelous Planet which you inhabit . . . !

ON THE STATUS AND NATURE OF WOMEN

Morality is no longer that arbitrary force that kept the weak and ill-fated woman a prisoner in the house of her abusive tyrant, and that led her to the bonfire, like some sacrifice to suffering, when—upon his death—he ceased to torment her. . . .

O ages past, when a lonely and destitute woman would have to sell her graces, resisting, and in the end spurning, that powerful and lifesaving instinct—modesty—with which nature itself had blessed her! O periods of infamy and disgrace! For the virtuous woman, you were the greatest shame of human history, and we cannot cast our eyes over your contemptible era without encountering those sad and melancholy centuries in which society was awash with terrible suffering and woman was an object to be sold, vulnerable to becoming the most repulsive assemblage of decay and vice!

You are over, yes!, O you age of weeping and disgrace for the weak and abject, of oppression and pain for the gentle and sensitive woman! Human Providentiality has vindicated the rights of woman, of that Providential being par excellence, and in her mild and loving heart is raised the crown of the sweetest of virtues!

Woman has been freed from her ancient weakness and servitude. She is a full member of the nucleus into which she was born, and from the time of the cradle on, she has the same rights as the male child. . . .

And you, sad and oppressed woman of times past! How much pain you underwent, until you were drowning in vice, and how much more did you suffer once corrupted! In you man sowed the bitter seed of shame and poverty, which germinated in your weak and degraded breast; and in time man reaped the fatal and poisonous harvest of his crimes!

But now, free and independent modesty is the eternal champion of the delicate sex, and man has at last realized that he can experience the joy of happiness—the supreme joy on Earth!—only when love and respect gain him the virtuous favors of modesty and love, which are inseparable from the worthy wife.

ON CHANGES IN NATURE AND THE PHYSICAL ENVIRONMENT

No longer, O Earth, have you your dark and murky ravines.

Nor your arid deserts of floating sand.

Nor your jagged, uncrossable cliffs.

Humans have tamed the fury of your seas.

They have regulated the flow of your rivers and harnessed your lakes.

The imprint of mankind is everywhere, and it is the sign of heroes
. . . .

But science and human Providentiality have not stopped at simply making humans happy.

The whole of nature seems lovingly to support the objectives that man proposes, and docile, submissive, and content, yields up its treasures to science.

Cheerful countryside, delightful homes, forests traversed by the serpentine flow of pure, diaphanous streams that pour forth from artificial springs; these are the enchanting places that can be seen everywhere, O Earth! And in them are revealed the signs of happiness and of noble pleasures.

No longer do fields or gardens have fences. Do not their delicious fruits belong to all? Do not all work to sow, cultivate, and harvest them? Do not all respect the time necessary for the fruits to mature, and do not all love the always wonderful and cherished sight of nature's corsage, which we call plants?

All living species have undergone the beneficent modifications to which mankind's genius has submitted them, and those species that were only pernicious have ceased to exist.

Now do I see gentle flocks, adorned with flowered garlands, obeying the voice and call of the melodious strains of the horn. And you, loyal friend of man, you loving, intelligent, and pleasing dog, do guide the tender little lambs with caresses of your soft and wholesome tongue, assisting their mother who, bleating, calls to them.

And even the cattle lack their weapons of bygone days; the forehead of the powerful bull is no longer armed with the sharp, sturdy horns that once made him look so fierce and threatening. His strength is no longer subjugated to the yoke, nor does the lance increase his pain and fatigue. Happiness and ignorance of death make his days placid and sweet, and forever harmless.

Thus has mankind spread good to all creatures of the earth, and happiness radiates from all sentient species that inhabit this lucky globe.

ON SCIENTIFIC AND TECHNOLOGICAL INNOVATIONS

The roads that I look upon—clear, safe, and long—are crossed by prodigious machines that glide softly across the continents, linking islands throughout the wide seas, or even, O Earth, visiting your depths in long subterranean passages.

And mankind delights in traveling your ferrous roads with movement so soft and gentle, like an infant rocking in its cradle or a bird flying through the air on a calm day, diaphanous, luminous, and serene.

Not the mildest fear nor the slightest danger now exists on those roads of former and habitual disasters.

Mankind, with a flash of strength and speed, has obliterated distances! . . .

All dwellings are wondrous palaces. Gone are those flimsy constructions, mankind's nests, which were affixed to the earth with lime and sand and manufactured rock, and were covered with fragile and corruptible wood.

Gone are those tremendous conflagrations wherein one lone spark would consume entire cities. The immense buildings upon which I gaze cannot be destroyed by fire, water, or earthquake. They are made of fireproof materials that are flexible, lightweight, and indestructible. Strong screws hold their joists and coverings in place, and smooth, glossy surfaces show off the marvels of form and workmanship beneath a crystalline coat of varnish, or the brilliance of gold or of sparkling paints.

O sublime mansions! Their reality surpasses all that imagination dreamed in times past! Luxury, richness, and refined good taste do not affront inglorious poverty. Poverty and inequality have long since ceased to exist. All mankind lives with equal comforts, with equal delights, and peace and happiness reign within these splendid abodes.

Communities are joined one to the other; there are no deserted wildernesses or congested cities. . . .

Astronomical observatories equipped with astounding optical devices of moderate size and easy operation, but of enormous precision and effectiveness, look out upon the inhabitants of different planets in the solar system, who communicate with your fortunate people by means of telegraphic signals, O portentous Earth!

Of how many differing shapes are these beings! How great the intelligences that mankind has come to know! And how, oh, how, does mankind rue its former barbarism and tyranny! How bitterly does it deplore the grim machines of war that man, with the brutal savagery of former times, dedicated solely to the extermination of his works and brethren! . . .

The mechanical sciences have yielded up their inexhaustible resources to human ingenuity; no obstacle, no resistance or difficulty whatsoever, can oppose the designs of science. All the arts and crafts have been recast as one: mechanics. That is the creation of man, his universal tribute; and you, O Earth!, serve as platform for his massive levers, you are the inextinguishable beacon of his helioscopic, calorific, and electromagnetic devices, and are the wellspring of the infinite forces available to him, your Provident lord.

But, Planet, you gain in marvels what you tithe in obedience, and mankind never ceases to beautify you; you are the sublime workshop, storehouse, and museum that they adorn and glorify with their science. . . .

In the noble realms of the biological sciences the results have been similar. . . . You find life in all phenomena, even the phenomenon of death. Death is for you just another changing aspect of life, and humanity has learned to purify you of all deleterious agents and of its old, destructive, and disgraceful vices; imperturbable well-being and good health are the sweet victories of mankind's glorious science. Medicine no longer exists; it has been replaced by morals and hygiene! . . .

Yes, biology in all its diverse branches is a pleasant and most useful resource of mankind, a universal science of the physique. Mankind has managed not only to save itself from sickness and pain, it has achieved something more: it has reduced to its pragmatic and proper ends the impulsive desire for carnal pleasures. . . .

Transportation and the telegraph, which reach the most remote corners, make all the Earth as one shared city: the Planet, bedecked with the most delightful of homes. Thus, even the antipodes are neighbors. . . .

Domiciles are portable, but rarely do people take advantage of their mobility. Who would want to move one's permanent residence when one loves all that surrounds one, and what surrounds one is the world?

These mansions are situated amid delightful gardens, and in their brilliant and luxurious rooms one can breathe the wholesome, perfumed atmosphere of flowers, which adorn them in all weather and all seasons, although at the greater latitudes they are enclosed within magnificent crystal domes, in sumptuous greenhouses.

These great homes, extremely varied in shape and detail, share the generic name of *social nuclei.*

Social nuclei, in imitation of the celestial ones, can be of the most complex organization and style, without this harming in the slightest degree their harmony or the beauty and regularity of their movement, all in concert with the universal wanderings of humanity.

ON THE NATURE AND STRUCTURE OF WORK

Work is subdivided into as many categories as are necessary for the full development of conditions required for the production, preparation, and manufacture of those materials from which humans make the various objects that serve them.

The different categories or kinds of work form vast associations (systems), and these systems are subdivided into social nuclei, which in turn are subdivided into "individualities," that is, into groupings of those who devote themselves to the same type or class of work.

Thus it is that the beautiful mansions, wherein the individuals of each social nucleus dwell, hold the diverse and capacious rooms I have described, in which are gathered as many individuals from one or a like profession as is hygienically prudent.

But since there are some types of work that require the harmonious functioning of extremely complicated systems for the production, preparation, and manufacture of useful objects, nuclei are spread out over the entire surface of the earth, even floating on the channels and seas. These are utilized by people who belong to the different work groups, and are used for the merging and distribution of goods.

In this way the labors corresponding to one nucleus are interconnected, just as the nuclei are connected to their respective systems, the work being divided in the way most suitable for optimizing the components of each system.

Of necessity, the individuals of a nucleus are socially secured in the case of accident, illness, or old age.

In the same fashion, the nuclei of a system are insured by that system, so that they can meet the material needs of their individuals.

But all the work systems are insured by all humankind, who share out commodities among all people, rewarding them with an equal share of the benefits for an equal share of the time that all spend in useful and productive work. . . .

O, unhappy times, when workers were tyrannized and degraded by the lazy and by those who exploited their work, you are behind us now, and in place of chaos and the disorder of inequality is the mighty harmony of joy in human equality! Glory to work, glory to science, glory to Providentiality, that have made real the sublime destiny of mankind on Earth! . . .

Thus also do I perceive that those who are full of strength, vigor, and intelligence heartily embrace the most difficult work without special compensation, so as to leave to those less robust those jobs that are easier and more within the means of their relative strength.

Thus it is that there is joy in all work.

ON SELF-CONTROL

There are neither laws nor judges, because there are no criminals. Equality has made all great crimes impossible. What motive could anyone have to commit them? Thus it is that crimes are, and can only be considered to be, the result of dementia, and criminals are treated like the insane. But the insane are very rare, because happiness and equality among mankind prevent cases of mental derangement. . . .

Divested of unnatural passions, people are no longer reluctant or ill-disposed toward doing good. Police are unnecessary when everyone polices themselves. . . .

Light transgressions are punished by the members of the nucleus itself. Tendencies toward tyrannical passions are punished by solitary confinement. Those who attack society make themselves unworthy of it. . . .

Humans have made Providential conquests for the good in all aspects of happiness. Sexual love no longer is that frenzy of anguish and jealousy that drained all time and energy. Science has discovered how to strip appetites of the constant and depraved urgencies of times past, and now pleasure is joined with reason to give modesty and love days of glory, days resplendent with liberty and good judgment.

ON RITUALS AND THE RELATIONS BETWEEN THE SEXES

In the social nuclei, in those delightful mansions wherein man has learned to create the tender havens of perennial Eden that make up this Planet, the different sexes have separate rooms. Great, great care is taken to preserve the innocence of children and to not awaken harmful appetites in the young.

Young women continue their studies and useful labors until that time when the development of their bodies is complete. Then they meet together as the protagonists of the enchanting Festival of the Virgins, where they are presented to society and declared ready for marriage.

The various nuclei of one same work system send to a central agency their marriageable virgins and their young men, whose age and virtues have won them the right to attend this magnificent three-day festival.

On the first day the maidens display their delicate works, prized from infancy through their school years, and they take part in a variety of exercises based on the practical things they have learned.

They spend the second day demonstrating and enjoying their skills in the liberal and fine arts, and at night they dance—a dance of nymphs, in which the men do not take part!

The third day is the religious festival of the virgins, during which the dean of each respective nucleus recites, with great emotion, the Providential record of each maiden. So many admirable acts, so much filial, fraternal, and humanitarian love! So much tenderness and goodness are revealed in the gentle histories of the timid young maids! And such simplicity in their details of unimpeachable purity and virtue. There, divine virgins, you enjoy the rewards of your virtues, there you raise high the glorious crown of morality; there you sanctify modesty and awaken love in the generous and Providential hearts of the young competitors who admire you! You witness this delightful recitation wearing your veils, and when the time comes for you to worship God, giving Him thanks for having strengthened you in goodness and purity, our eyes become moist with beautiful tears of religious gratitude, as your honeyed and vibrant voices sing the heavenly, majestic hymn of virginal Providentiality!

O world, O world become paradise, adorned with the graces and virtues of these beautiful beings whose festival you witness; how noble, how profound, how virtuous are the emotions you place in the hearts of the young men! They take their marble tablets and inscribe their names beneath the beloved ones of those whom they seek in marriage, and these they give to the worthy council of elders. The elders go through the petitions, organizing those with multiple listings and counseling the various aspirants. Once arranged and ceremonially cleansed, the petitions are handed to the charming damsels in superbly worked closed boxes which they do not open until they are back in their home nuclei; and there, on their own, they make up their minds as they contemplate the portraits, the simple love stories, and the societal approval of those who seek to marry them.

The virgins do not declare their choices until spring, during the Festival of the Young, when the happy young men can be seen dancing with their charming and demure fiancées, but marriages are not performed until the autumn, during the resplendent Festival of the Adults.

How long does a marriage last? As long as is wished . . . both one day and one hundred years. And just as the consent of the contracting parties, sanctioned by the council of elders, validates the act of union, so, too, do the same circumstances establish separation.

But you, woman, because of your comparative weakness, have by nature the authority to accept and to reject, and although your consort does not desire to separate from you, all that is needed is for you to express your wish to do so during the Festival of the Adults, and your marriage is dissolved.

Those who are divorced can renew their marriages, or they can take new spouses; a widow or widower may also remarry, but these weddings are celebrated in private, and only the marriages of virgins are accorded dignified celebrations in the autumn festival. . . .

When newlyweds return to the nucleus where they will work and live, the man takes up lodgings among his own sex and the woman alone has possession of the marital chamber. She is the keeper of this retreat of chaste delights, and, like a lover, the lucky husband must petition to be mysteriously received within its gladsome walls.

Is there jealousy in these marriages? No: how could one be jealous, when one is free to break the ties that bind one? And how could vice corrupt loyalty, which is strengthened and defended by all the virtues?

And so live these sweet unions in the peaceful calm of the most fortunate Providentiality; thus are two hearts united without breaching mores and traditions, and thus do modesty and love lead the wedded couple from joy to joy, until the transforming hand of nature reclaims the matter of corporeal life, leaving the spirit free to journey on to eternal happiness.

Nilo María Fabra

SPAIN

Very little has been recorded about the life of Nilo María Fabra (1843–1903), but we do know that he was a journalist by trade and that he was a main force behind the creation in 1865 of the Center of Correspondences, the first news agency in Spain.

As the new century began, Spain was experiencing the "Crisis of 1898," a period of national trauma and critical reflection triggered by the crushing defeat of the Spanish Armada and the loss of the empire's last colonies in the Spanish-American War. Therefore it is not surprising that, even though H. G. Wells was being read in intellectual circles in Spain, Fabra is the only known Spanish utopian author at the end of the century. The journalist read not only Wells, but also Sir Edward Bulwer-Lytton, Samuel Butler, and Edward Bellamy. Bellamy's bestseller *Looking Backward* (1888), for example, must have influenced Fabra's story "The Present Judged by What Is to Come in the Twentieth Century" ("Lo presente juzgado por lo porvenir en el siglo XX"). Both stories portray a future where technological advances benefit human beings living in a utopian society without a single dark note.

Indeed, Fabra's most common motif is the portrayal of science as a positive and essential element for society's progress and human happiness. This is obviously the case in "On the Planet Mars," the story we have chosen to include here. Readers with an interest in daily news and the media in general will appreciate the importance they are given on Fabra's Mars. Those readers, however, who admire the printed word and fear its disappearance might frown at Fabra's optimistic vision of a future where reading and writing are no longer practiced. Undoubtedly, some ideas Fabra presents as progressive might seem reactionary today—for example, the praising of a society that is unified politically, linguistically, religiously, and philosophically—but might Fabra have predicted the coming of a "globalized" age?

On the Planet Mars

En el planeta Marte, 1890

by Nilo María Fabra

translated by Ted Angell

Universal Resonance is the name of the most popular program on the planet Mars.

For subscribers there are in-home phonographs that at the push of a button will play back the messages recorded on the daily installment of news.

For the public at large, all one has to do to hear the daily news is put a coin in one of many devices that abound in the streets, marketplaces, and roads. As soon as the coin drops into the ingenious phonograph, the device speaks in a soft voice, through a small opening, so that only one person at a time can listen and thereby the company's business interests are not compromised.

The laws, orders, and edicts of the authorities are broadcast everywhere via megaphones, which stand in place of the bells in church towers, and clocks tell time by imitating the human voice.

The phonograph and telephone have been perfected there to such a point that the art of reading and writing has fallen into disuse. The Supreme Council of Public Education recently finished removing written language from the schools, and now it is taught only to diplomats.

The streets, highways, and even rural roads are made up of a series of moving platforms that glide in opposite directions; each of these platforms has a different speed, so if the Martians want to go faster, they can pass one by one to the fastest platform, which has a velocity of 250 miles per hour.

Hundreds of canals—constructed primarily to prevent the periodic flooding produced by the melting of the ice accumulated at the poles of the planet—cross the continents in all directions and allow the navigation of electric ships, which can scud through the waters at a dizzying speed.

Naturally, with the passing of time this ease of communication has produced not only political unity, but also linguistic and religious unity. On Mars, there is only one state, one language, and one belief. This unity has become such a natural and accepted fact for the Martians that the word *atheism* and its derivatives do not exist in the phonographic dictionaries of that blissful and happy world.

It is noteworthy, too, that the Martian language is so rich from the variety and abundance of voices that the educated people speak with admirable clarity and concision. They do not have to waste time in the study of other living or dead languages, not even the orthography of their own language, for the reason previously indicated.

And without further preamble let me go on to say that *Universal Resonance*, the audio journal of the planet Mars, surprised its listeners a few days ago with this landmark story:

"It is well known throughout the world (there, too, is there a world as big as a planet, and a planet of lesser importance in the solar system), that the astronomic observatories supported liberally by the state in the interest of the noble cause of science, discovered, at the beginning of the century, that our neighbor and counterpart, the opaque star number three, known commonly as Blue, was inhabited. Since then, thanks to the generosity of the public powers, a system of light signals was developed, by way of immense electric spotlights situated at great distances, in order to see if these telescopic beings wanted to come in contact with our scholars. Well, after many years of fruitless attempts, according to a telephone message we just received, our astronomers have managed to have a dialogue with their counterparts from the other world, who, noticing our signals, adopted a similar system to respond to us. In order to do that, they set up an optical telegraph composed of three immense electric spotlights forming an equilateral triangle, measuring a tenth of a meridian on each side, so that they projected flashes at intervals and constituted a species of alphabet. The interpretation was difficult at first, but some archeologists versed in the knowledge of antique scriptures realized that the signs used by the inhabitants of Blue to represent letters had many points of similarity with those used many centuries ago by our ancestors, when the telegraph was in its infancy. What was harder was the task of adopting a common language, but considering that we were able to make so much progress in the introductory meetings, could it surprise anyone that the scholars of both celestial bodies came to understand each other to the point of having interplanetary conversations?

"Thanks to these the veil has been pulled back from the mysterious planet, the subject of astronomers' meditation for so many centuries. We now know that the planet that we have designated as Blue its inhabitants call Earth, and the one we inhabit is known to them by the name Mars.

"Their globe is populated by 1.4 billion human beings, according to various geographers, although others cite a smaller figure, which shows how undeveloped their science of statistics is.

"The great majority of its inhabitants live immersed in the most shameful barbarity, and the rest, who boast of being civilized, are found, at best, in the state of refinement and advancement that we had ten centuries ago, in the epoch we refer to as semicivilized.

"Although during the past few years they have made significant progress, their methods of communication are rough and incomplete. Earthlings still use steam from water, which requires complicated, and moreover heavy and expensive, machines. The science of electricity is still in its infancy. They have not found the practical and economical process of using electricity as the only driving force. They are totally unaware of the existence of vital fluid and of what we call *unnamed*, whose discovery produced such a great revolution in mechanics.

"Difficulties of locomotion, inherent to the backwardness of physics, together with the strange organization of societies that do not recognize in the individual the right to travel for free, as happens here, in vehicles that are part of a public service, force the majority of these beings to live bound to the land in which they were born, and the environment exercises such influence over them that for many the concept of fatherland is limited to a handful of buildings, and at most to a geographic or historical accident.

"This forced sedentary life causes numerous nationalities with as many languages, varieties of customs, and diversity of states to exist still on Earth.

"How imperfectly are these estates organized!

"The most barbaric are ruled by the whim of an individual, while the more advanced are ruled by the passions of a few; but in all the countries the governments live at the expense of the people: they still have not discovered the system whereby the people live at the expense of their government.

"The rivalries between the states, born almost always of envy of the good things others enjoy, engender frequent and often disastrous wars that result in the ruin of the defeated; but there is something even worse than war: the fear of war, which destroys everyone by focusing on military preparation.

"Their clothing could not be more primitive. They dress in crudely woven cloths, the product of filaments of plant stems, their seedlings, the cocoons of a worm, or the fur of quadrupeds, from which they strip the coat Nature provided for the animal's own use and not for others to appropriate.

"They live such primitive lives that they have not invented, as we have, a system of heating the atmosphere in the cold season, and because of this their clothing, more faddish than sensible, responds more to the need to defend against the inclemencies of the sky, while for us it obeys only the laws of decorum. It need not even be added that Earthlings have not discovered the ultrafine cloths that we make, the product of microscopic and flexible strands of various metals.

"So few are the advances in chemical synthesis on Earth that its inhabitants, for nourishment, have no choice but to destroy billions of plant seeds and sacrifice an immense number of animals. They have not developed, as we have, the process of forming the compounds necessary for nutrition, and for reducing its active principle to quantities that are enough not only for sustenance, but also for the pleasure of the individual.

"The social organization is, if possible, even more deficient than that of the state. The inevitable law of inequality Nature imposes on individuals, far from being attenuated by wise and prudent measures—and more importantly by the noble and lofty ends of sublime benevolence—is made increasingly harsh; therefore the hatreds, grudges, and rivalries, engendered by envy and poverty, threaten the inner peace of the nations. There exists a cause that aggravates these evils day by day, destined to produce the worst kind of crisis, which is that the growth in the production of the articles necessary to the existence of the inhabitants of Earth is not in proportion to the advancing growth of the population. Add to this the fact that the notable advancements in medicine and hygiene, which tend to increase the average human lifespan, are not related to the other sciences, an application that would make foods and material well-being more attainable and economical.

"To have an idea of the constitution of the family in most of that world, we would need to look back to the age of our aborigines, when only the law of brute force prevailed. In the barbaric countries, which are in the immense majority, the woman, victim of despotism, violence, and slavery, has no weapons other than hypocrisy, while in the other countries she tends to live resigned, but not satisfied, with the diminished rights legislation and custom concede to her.

"Teaching is in an even more rudimentary state. The vigorous intelligence and playful attention of youth are given over to constant torture and they spend years and years in the study and beneficial cultivation of subjects of sometimes debatable usefulness, or in the study of dead languages, irrelevant to occupational purposes, while we submit students to hypnotic sleep to suggest to them in delightful and placid ecstasy what the science or art to which they have shown a particular predilection since tender infancy requires.

"They tell us that on Earth there is sometimes justice, but it is difficult and slow, as if one of the most basic obligations of a state did not consist in administering it promptly and fully, and as if it were not the height of iniquity on the part of the government to exploit its citizens' rights. When will Earthlings catch up to our legal perfection? When will they renounce bothersome and endless legal writs and, entrusting the simple presentation of evidence by telephone, await patiently the verdict of the judges, rendered during sessions of hypnotic sleep? If it looks like a grave, circumspect, solemn court, we are more sure of its wisdom seeing it in the state of repose that constitutes the true representation of justice.

"There even the most civilized men live in cages, which is all their crowded, uncomfortable and small houses deserve to be called, being roughly built with heavy materials of steel, wood, rock, or baked soil. The architecture, which lacks the effective help of scientific advancements, cannot construct the light, sumptuous, slender, and elegant aluminum buildings that are the glamour and ornament not only of our cities, but of our villages, nor can it construct the moving palaces, raised over the moving platforms of the roads, that give free hospitality to the traveler during his excursions across the continents.

"The Earthling is unaware of what true individual liberty consists of. As it happens, the more educated one is, the more tyranny his social obligations tend to hold over him. When the individual is a victim of the clock (and almost always of the intemperance of others) in the most common acts of life, it is only reciprocal tolerance, outward benevolence, and perpetual conventionalism that make the community's torment bearable. For our part, do we need association, even during the hours of ordinary sustenance, when a little box of pills can provide food for twenty days? Who needs cars, streetcars, trains, and perpetual slavery to the bell, when here the streets and roads themselves are vehicles, their pavement constantly moving?

"We enjoy public diversions without confining ourselves in tight places, where perhaps the pleasures of the spirit would not compensate for the discomfort of the body, since who does not have at his disposal a megaphone and a *telefoteidoscope*[1] to entertain his ears and eyes with the marvelous shows that the munificence of the government funds lavishly and unsparingly?

"Lovers separated by distance use the *telefoteidoscope* in order to see each other and to transmit to each other their never bothersome and never uselessly reiterated declarations of love, exchanging the currents of vital fluid (something the Earthlings barely have an inkling of yet) between themselves, which submerges them both in a delightful ecstasy, producing in the subjects the marvelous phenomenon of the unity and simultaneity of ideas and sensations.

"Poetry, apparently threatened with death in the measure that the practical prevailed in our customs, is reborn strong and vigorous, finding an inexhaustible fountain of inspirations in the secrets taken from Nature, in the contemplation of the admirable laws that govern the universe, in the wondrous harmony of the celestial places and in the splendor and magnificence of the works of the Most High.

"And while philosophical poetry soars to the infinite, there exists that which will live eternally, as long as the perpetuation of our species depends on the sweet and mysterious attraction between two rational beings, and maternal love shines upon the face of the worlds!

"Blessed, noble champions of science, who contributed so much to our material well-being, independence, and most of all to the indestructible peace and individual autonomy founded on law and the political unity of the planet! What a blessed age this is, which calls forth the age that the ancients, in their simple and crude ignorance, called golden, and not because we are going back to the idyll of primitive times dreamed of by poets, but because material advancements have brought with them the moral and intellectual betterment of the human family! . . ."

The megaphones of all the temples of the capital of Mars announced that it was prayer time, and the people, unveiling themselves with religious respect, lifting their eyes to the sky, repeated this prayer, which the machines broadcast from atop the towers in a deep, relaxed, and solemn voice:

"Father of all mortals, Creator and Lord of all that exists in space and Creator of that same space, blessed and praised be your name eternally.

"Preserve our intelligence, which is only a glimmer of yours, so that we will dominate matter and natural forces, which you put in our environs for the perfection of the spirit as we struggle with them.

"In forgiving our debtors may we find the prize of your unlimited goodness; and deliver us from pride, because our humble works are nothing, are worth nothing, and mean nothing in comparison with the immeasurable greatness of yours.

"Free us from evil and do good to our enemies, and when the end of our planetary life comes, grant us eternity with the joy of your infinite love."

And the voices of the megaphones resonated in the public places and streets, and in the middle of the solitude of the fields and seas, infusing in all hearts religious devotion, pure love for the Omnipotent, and the sweet hope of the future and imperishable good.

Part II

Speculating

on a New Genre

SF from 1900

through the 1950s

Miguel de Unamuno

SPAIN

The internationally acclaimed Basque writer and philosopher Miguel de Unamuno y Jugo (1864–1936) was the prominent figure of Spanish letters, philosophy, and politics of his time. In 1891 he became a professor of Greek at the University of Salamanca, where he became rector in 1901. Always a controversial figure, he first opposed the monarchy of Alphonse XII and then protested against Primo de Rivera's dictatorships, which caused his removal from the university in 1920 and his exile from Spain (1924–30). The republican government of 1931, which he initially supported, allowed him to return to Spain. When he became critical of the republic, he sided with the rebel forces that started the Civil War, only to reprove them later. He sympathized with socialism in his youth and believed Spain needed to model itself after the rest of Western Europe in order to become modern, although he later adopted a more nationalistic, anti-industrial stance.

Unamuno's background in rationalism and positivism led him to develop an individualistic philosophy, based on a negation of any system of thought and on an affirmation of faith in faith itself, as outlined in "The Tragic Sense of Life in Men and Nations" ("Del sentimiento trágico de la vida en los hombres y los pueblos," 1913). Other important essays are "Our Lord Don Quixote" ("Vida de Don Quijote y Sancho," 1905) and "The Agony of Christianity" ("La agonía del cristianismo," 1925). He also wrote serious poetry, novels, theater, and short stories.

That such a prestigious author also wrote SF may surprise some. We include his "Mechanopolis" here not as an attempt to "elevate" the genre, but rather because it illustrates (from the vantage of 1913) the loss of faith in science and the fear of technology characteristic of much science fiction in the twentieth century.

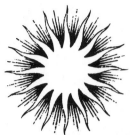

Mechanopolis

Mecanópolis, 1913

by Miguel de Unamuno

translated by Patricia Hart

While reading Samuel Butler's *Erewhon*,[1] the part where he tells us about an Erewhonian man who wrote *The Book of Machines*, and in so doing managed to get most of the contraptions banished from his land, there sprang to mind the memory of a traveler's tale told me by an explorer friend who had been to Mechanopolis, the city of machines. He still shook at the memory of it when he told me the story, and it had such an effect on him that he later retired for years to a remote spot containing the fewest possible number of machines.

I shall try to reproduce my friend's tale here, in his very words, if possible:

There came a moment when I was lost in the middle of the desert; my companions had either retreated, seeking to save themselves (as if we knew in which direction salvation lay!), or had perished from thirst and fatigue. I was alone, and practically dying of thirst myself. I began sucking at the nearly black blood that was oozing from fingers raw from clawing about in the arid soil, with the mad hope of bringing to light any trace of water. Just when I was about to lie down on the ground and close my eyes to the implacable blue sky to die as quickly as possible, or even cause my own death by holding my breath or burying myself in that terrible earth, I lifted my fainting eyes and thought I saw something green off in the distance. "It must be a mirage," I thought; nevertheless, I dragged myself toward it.

Hours of agony passed, but when I arrived I found myself, indeed, in an oasis. A fountain restored my strength, and, after drinking, I ate some of the tasty and succulent fruits the trees freely offered. Then I fell asleep.

I do not know how long I slept, or if it was hours, days, months, or years. What I do know is that I awoke a different man, an entirely different man. The recent and horrendous sufferings had been wiped from my memory, or nearly. "Poor devils," I said to myself, remembering my explorer companions who had died in our enterprise. I arose, again ate of the fruit and drank of the water, and then disposed myself to examine the oasis. And—wouldn't you know it—a few steps later I came upon an entirely deserted railway station. There was not a soul to be seen anywhere. A train, also deserted, was puffing smoke without engineer or stoker. It occurred to me out of curiosity to climb into one of the cars. I sat down and, without knowing why, closed the door, and the train started moving. A mad terror rose in me, and I even felt the urge to throw myself out the window. But repeating, "Let us see where this leads," I contained myself.

The velocity of the train was so great that I could not even make out the sort of landscape through which I sped. I felt such a terrible vertigo that I was compelled to close the windows. When the train at last stood still, I found myself in a magnificent station, one far superior to any that we know around here. I got off the train and went outside.

I will not even try to describe the city. We cannot even dream of all of the magnificent, sumptuous things, the comfort, the cleanliness that were accumulated there. And speaking of hygiene, I could not make out what all of the cleaning apparatus was for, since there was not one living soul around, neither man nor beast. Not one dog crossed the street, nor one swallow the sky.

On a grand building I saw a sign that said Hotel, written just like that, as we write ourselves, and I went inside. It was completely deserted. I arrived at the dining room. The most solid of repasts was to be had inside. There was a list on each table, and every delicacy named had a number beside it. There was also a vast control panel with numbered buttons. All one had to do was touch a button, and the desired dish sprang forth from the depths of the table.

After having eaten, I went out into the street. Streetcars and automobiles passed by, all empty. One had only to draw near, make a signal to them, and they would stop. I took an automobile, and let myself be driven around. I went to a magnificent geological park, in which all of the different types of terrain were displayed, all with explanations on little signs. The information was in Spanish, but spelled phonetically. I left the park. A streetcar was passing by bearing the sign "To the Museum of Painting," and I took it. There housed were the most famous paintings in the world, in their true originals. I became convinced that all the works we have here, in our museums, are nothing more than skillfully executed reproductions. At the foot of each canvas was a very learned explanation of its historical and aesthetic value, written with the most exquisite sobriety. In a half-hour's visit I learned more about painting than in twelve years of study in these parts. On a sign at the entrance I read that in Mechanopolis they considered the Museum of Painting to be part of the Museum of Paleontology, whose purpose was to study the products of the human race that had populated those lands before machines supplanted them. Part of the paleontological culture of the Mechanopolites—the who?—was a Hall of Music and all of the other libraries with which the city was full.

What do you wager that I shall shock you even more with my next revelations? I visited the grand concert hall, where the instruments played themselves. I stopped by the great theater. There played a cinematic film accompanied by a phonograph, but so well combined that the illusion of reality was complete. What froze my soul was that I was the only spectator. Where were the Mechanopolites?

When I awoke the next morning in my hotel room, I found the *Mechanopolis Echo* on my nightstand, with all of the news of the world received through the wireless telegraph station. And there, at the end, was the following news brief: "Yesterday afternoon—and we do not know how it came about—a man arrived at our city, a man of the sort there used to be out there. We predict unhappy days for him."

My days, in effect, began to be torturous to me. I began to populate my solitude with phantasms. The most terrible thing about solitude is that it fills up by and by. I began to believe that all of those factories, all those artifacts, were ruled by invisible souls, intangible and silent. I started to think the great city was peopled by men like myself, but that they came and went without my seeing or coming across them. I believed myself to be the victim of some terrible illness, madness. The invisible world with which I populated the human solitude in Mechanopolis became a nightmare of martyrdom. I began to shout, to rebuke the machines, to supplicate to them. I went so far as to fall on my knees before an automobile, imploring compassion from it. I was on the brink of throwing myself into a cauldron of boiling steel at a magnificent iron foundry.

One morning, on awakening terrified, I grabbed the newspaper to see what was happening in the world of men, and I found this news item: "As we predicted, the poor man who—and we do not know how—turned up in this incomparable city of Mechanopolis is going insane. His spirit, filled with ancestral worries and superstitions regarding the invisible world, cannot adapt itself to the spectacle of progress. We feel deeply sorry for him."

I could not bear to see myself pitied at last by those mysterious, invisible beings, angels or demons—which are the same—that I believed inhabited Mechanopolis. But all of a sudden a terrible idea struck me: What if those machines had souls, mechanical souls, and it were the machines themselves that felt sorry for me? This idea made me tremble. I thought myself before the race that must dominate a dehumanized Earth.

I left like a madman and threw myself before the first electric streetcar that passed. When I awoke from the blow, I was once more in the oasis from which I had started out. I began walking. I arrived at the tent of some Bedouins, and on meeting one of them, I embraced him crying. How well we understood each other even without understanding each other! He and his companions gave me food, we celebrated together, and at night I went out with them and, lying on the ground, looking up at the starry sky, united we prayed. There was not one machine anywhere around us.

And since then I have conceived a veritable hatred toward what we call progress, and even toward culture, and I am looking for a corner where I shall find a peer, a man like myself, who cries and laughs as I cry and laugh, and where there is not a single machine and the days flow with the sweet, crystalline tameness of a stream lost in a forest primeval.

Ernesto Silva Román

CHILE

Ernesto Silva Román (1897–1977), the Jules Verne of Chilean letters, as he has been called, was an active writer throughout much of his long life. He devoted himself chiefly to journalism, working as a reporter and editor and eventually founding several newspapers. At the peak of his career, the political articles he wrote under the pseudonym "El Canciller Negro" (The Black Chancellor) for *El Mercurio,* Chile's preeminent newspaper, appeared in over forty periodicals throughout the country. In addition to journalism, Silva Román was a senator, a presidential press secretary, and secretary-general of Chile's national airline.

Silva Román also authored a historically significant body of fiction of a type rarely seen in Chile then: science fiction stories that echoed the space adventures being popularized in U.S. and European pulps (and which were not wholly unknown to Latin American readers). These works constituted an important step in the development of Chilean SF.

"The Death Star" is a perfect example of Silva Román's style. It is taken from *The Master of the Stars (El dueño de los astros,* 1929), a slim volume of seven SF stories, most of them explicitly set in Chile.[1] The tales are full of scientists both virtuous and vile, elitist supreme councils, amazing new technologies, paranormal forces, and archetypal power struggles. Science serves a less exclusively sociological, political, or moral function in this author's works than it does for other regional SF pioneers; nevertheless, faith in a scientific meritocracy comes through as the ideological underpinning of the anthology: what is expected of the general populace is obedience, devotion, and self-sacrifice. "The Death Star" is quintessential Silva Román, showcasing the author's themes and his penchant for gadgetry and high drama; over seventy years later, it is still an absorbing read.

The Death Star

El astro de la muerte, 1929

by Ernesto Silva Román

translated by Casandra Griffith

and Andrea Bell

On 3 January 2035 the first symptom came into being.

At two o'clock that morning the saturation wave began to take form.

It was like a powerful, energetic new life force that penetrated all living things without warning.

It caused neither surprise nor disquiet in the public mind.

Its very advance—slight, almost imperceptible, ubiquitous—went unperceived by all.

Nevertheless, that morning the extraordinary forces that threw humanity into turmoil and almost completely annihilated it—through an excess of vital radiation—began to take shape.

The astronomers in Aconcagua and the Himalayas were the first to register the birth, out in space, of a new planet.

It was like a sudden concentration of immense, colossal nebulae. An instantaneous act of creation that took place almost directly above the observatories of our most eminent scientists.

Only much later would the secrets of that mysterious star be unraveled.

The astronomer Oriel Ristal, an active member of the Supreme Council of Human Management, was able to demonstrate clearly that there was no such thing as spontaneous creation or the sudden concentration of cosmic energies in the vast reaches of outer space.

It was merely a rogue star, hurled at a terrifying speed into the unfathomable and unimagined depths of the endless heavens.

No. It was not exactly a comet. Nor was it a giant meteor. It was simply a planet that, free of restraints and systems and perhaps obeying who-knows-what strange and mysterious plan, had burst onto the visual or explorable range of the planetary system for the first time.

According to Ristal's calculations—mathematical and precise, in time and in space—the traveling star, whose volume was 500 million times greater than Earth's, would take eighteen months and eighteen days to approach and then pass by us, before quickly vanishing out beyond the last star.

Its unexpected presence in the visual field of the most powerful terrestrial observatories was due exclusively to unknown problems of radioactivity or luminosity.

Oriel Ristal assumed the extraordinary star was composed of chemical compounds and substances unfamiliar to terrestrials, and that these strange ingredients were the reason for the lack of "visibility" of the star's first babblings at the edges of our astral domain.

At the same time, he predicted likely changes and influences upon the Earth because of radiations from that unknown star.

His predictions and speculations caused quite a stir.

In those days, the ignorant public had ceased laughing at and ridiculing men of science.

Through painful and tragic experience, they knew that the strangest and the most unexpected is what occurs with the greatest ease.

Journalists published long, inflated accounts. They skillfully exploited their readers' anxieties.

Moreover, scientists set about formulating the most diverse hypotheses.

In spite of everything, no one suspected what was really in store.

The days passed by. Weeks. Months . . .

The solitary star appeared not to move in space. To the naked eye it looked like one more star, one growing in volume and intensity day by day.

Only the astronomers knew that the gigantic planet, that frightful star, was hurtling toward the Earth at a speed of one light year per second.

The tension of those first days gradually subsided.

Within a few weeks nobody paid the least attention to that small, luminous point that remained, fixed and unchanging, out beyond the sun.

The Universal Medical Society tried in vain to conceal the research of the distinguished biologist Dasrael Morales.

Even though humanity's sense of wonder was sluggish and relative, that man's scientific claims caused a sensation.

For some months now, humans had been growing at an alarming rate.

At first they believed it heralded the betterment of the races, but later they saw that even the most degenerate ones rapidly flourished.

Humans were already, without exception, two meters high, and their weight never fell below one hundred kilos. It was useless trying to lose weight or retard one's physical development. People were growing. And growing.

Where would this unexpected growth end?

And then it was that Dasrael Morales dumbfounded humanity with his astonishing discovery.

Humans were growing and developing, as were trees, crops, and animals—that is, as were all organic bodies—because vitamin D was affecting living things in a decisive and uncompromising way.

Morales had succeeded in discovering this. He had been observing it for months.

And with each observation vitamin D's power and radioactivity were greater. Greater.

Up against the shrewdness of that biologist, who had achieved so much glory for his homeland, the mystery could not remain unsolved much longer.

It was inescapable, it was undeniable that all this abrupt and unexpected flourishing of vitamin D was due to the increasing proximity of the unknown star. Of that planet, which had appeared suddenly from the depths of the heavens and which now enveloped the Earth with emanations as formidable as they were impossible to define.

Once his report had been presented to the Medical Society, and after having verbally expounded his discovery before the Council of Five Hundred, Dasrael Morales took off in his private gyroplane and left for some secret destination.

Two hours later he was in conference with the astronomer Oriel Ristal.

According to Ristal's calculations, the mystery planet would take exactly six months to pass by the Earth. These six months, added to the year and seventeen days its trajectory had taken till now, made for a total of 564 days and twelve hours.

Its return to the depths of nothingness would require an equal number of days.

Morales now had a precise point upon which to base his theoretical scale.

Once again he submerged himself in calculations and experiments, and when he had everything ready he sent a mental message to the Supreme Council of Humanity, letting them know he had mastered the enigma and was in a position to draw an exact picture of what would happen to the Earth until that time when all danger had passed and the solar system returned to a state of tranquility.

A murmur of approval greeted the Chief of the Five Hundred's words.

Dasrael Morales moved forward to occupy the podium.

"Gentlemen, humanity finds itself facing a fearful danger. And it is necessary that this esteemed council take immediate stock of the situation in order to avoid the death or extinction of the planet. At this very moment the lost star is exerting its influence over the Earth, unleashing upon vitamins a stupendous amount of radioactivity—an amount growing and increasing by the second.

"Instead of robbing vitamins of the natural function that the harmonic forces of nature assigned them, it has given life—that is to say, given fantastic vitality and robustness—to vitamin D, which is the one that determines the development of the individual and of organic bodies.

"To vitamin D is owed the fact that we all now measure over two meters in height.

"I have made precise calculations that have led to the horror of a monstrous chart. If an individual keeps growing in direct relation to the nearness of the mysterious planet, he will reach a height of 115 meters, 73 centimeters.

"We must remember that, along with mankind, the animals, trees, and fishes will grow. Everything. Absolutely everything.

"The oceans will overflow their beds. They will not be able to contain such immense creatures as 300-meter-long sharks and 2,200-meter-long whales.

"Earth itself will not have room for 1.9 billion men and women who each measure 115 meters high by 40 meters wide.

"It will be a disaster. Death. The greatest abomination.

"Forests will reach unbelievable dimensions. Trees will grow to fantastic heights. The animals themselves will be so shockingly large they will take up two-thirds of the earth.

"What will become of humanity in those terrible days?

"As the death star moves further away, vitamin D will slowly lose its strength and its tremendous radioactivity. Humans will gradually decrease in size until everything returns to normal, once our strange visitor has disappeared forever.

"But will anyone be left alive after the catastrophe? Will anything be left?

"And now we come to what I propose to the Supreme Council.

"We must construct, in under ninety-six hours, a huge underground shelter, able to withstand anything. Specifically, it must be able to withstand the horrific pressures that will arise during the days of fear. And the most useful members of humanity, along with their families, must take refuge there.

"Once enclosed therein, we will put ourselves into a deep hypnotic sleep, which will end once the forces of the planet that threatens us have disappeared.

"Then we will emerge . . . and see if anything is still alive.

"Vitamin D is a photosynthetic element, created by the action of light upon cholesterol.

"I am in possession of a chemical compound that suspends and stops the kariokinesis of cellular elements, and limits—though only for a very short while—generative activity. A triple-graduated injection will immunize us for a few days—not more than four. Therefore, we must take advantage of those days, while the absorption of radiations that act directly upon cholesterol lasts."

Three days later, on precisely the sixth of January, 2035, the last steel door was shut.

Three thousand, two hundred ninety-two human beings were thus completely cut off from humanity, buried alive in a spacious underground shelter carved out at a depth of two hundred meters.

Colossal concrete walls blocked up the last hydraulic hatches.

Everyone was immediately put into a deep, cataleptic sleep.

Dasrael Morales was the last one to adopt the lifesaving measure.

For many days, for long and exhausting weeks he monitored the frightening process of human growth.

Until one day the diabolical monsters that roamed the Earth smashed all the television installations to pieces.

Then everything came to an end for the watcher.

He retired to his chamber.

And hypnotized himself.

Only a few months remained until the awakening.

Juan José Arreola

MEXICO

Juan José Arreola (1918–2001) is considered by many scholars of Mexican letters to be one of the most influential prose stylists of his generation. An autodidact whose formal schooling was interrupted by the Cristero Wars,[1] he became a voracious reader while apprenticed to a bookbinder. He later trained as an actor and developed a lifelong passion for the art and craft of the spoken word. He began publishing in the early 1940s, and over the course of some twenty years produced the witty and often unclassifiable short prose pieces—stories, sketches, fables, epigrams, even a bestiary—which so astonished the literary public of his day, and for which he is still justifiably celebrated. Readers wishing to acquaint themselves with Arreola's stylistic inventiveness, febrile imagination, and irreverent, sophisticated use of language would do well to peruse his collection of fables, *Confabulario total, 1941–1961,* generally thought to contain his best work.[2]

"The Switchman" ("El guardagujas") is Arreola's most frequently anthologized piece of fantastic literature; we have therefore selected something less well known, "Baby H.P." With this text, Arreola joins the tradition of satirical writers such as Lucian of Samosata, Francisco de Quevedo, Cyrano de Bergerac, Edgar Allan Poe, and Jonathan Swift. In fact, readers familiar with Swift's famous 1729 essay "A Modest Proposal for Preventing the Children of Poor People in Ireland from Being a Burden to their Parents or Country, and for Making them Beneficial to the Public" will surely enjoy Arreola's playful science fictional and intertextual treatment of the theme, and his sarcastic indictment of modern technology, in "Baby H.P."

Baby H.P.

Baby H.P., 1952

by Juan José Arreola

translated by Andrea Bell

To the Lady of the House: Convert your children's vitality into a source of power. Introducing the marvelous Baby H.P., a device that will revolutionize home economics.

The Baby H.P. is a very strong and lightweight metal structure that adapts perfectly to an infant's delicate body by means of comfortable belts, wrist straps, rings, and pins. The attachments on this supplementary skeleton capture every one of the child's movements, collecting them in a small Leyden jar that can be fastened, as needed, to the infant's back or chest. A needle indicates when the jar is full. Then, madam, simply detach the jar and plug it into a special receptacle, into which it automatically discharges its contents. This container can then be stored in any corner of the house, and represents a precious supply of electricity that can be used at any time for the purpose of light and heat, or to run any of the innumerable appliances that now and forever invade our homes.

From this day forward you will look upon your children's exhausting running about with new eyes. No longer will you lose patience when your little one flies into a rage, for you shall see it as a generous source of energy. Thanks to Baby H.P., a nursing infant's round-the-clock tantrum is transformed into a few useful seconds running the blender or into fifteen minutes of radiophonic music.

Large families can meet their electricity needs by outfitting each of their progeny with a Baby H.P., and can even start up a small and profitable business supplying their neighbors with some of their surplus energy. Big apartment high-rises can satisfactorily cover lapses in public service by linking together all of the families' energy receptacles.

The Baby H.P. causes no physical or psychological trauma in children, because it neither inhibits nor alters their movements. On the contrary, some doctors believe it contributes to the body's wholesome development. And as for the spirit, you can foster individual ambition in the wee ones by rewarding them with little prizes when they surpass their usual production records. For this purpose we recommend sugar treats, which repay your investment with interest. The more calories added to a child's diet, the more kilowatts saved on the electricity bill.

Children should wear their lucrative Baby H.P.s day and night. It is important that they always wear them to school so as not to lose out on the valuable hours of recess, from which they return with their storage tanks overflowing with energy.

Those rumors claiming that some children are electrocuted by the very current they generate are completely irresponsible. The same can be said of the superstitious fear that youngsters outfitted with a Baby H.P. attract lightning bolts and emit sparks. No accident of this type can occur, especially if the instructions that accompany each device are followed to the letter.

The Baby H.P. is available in fine stores in a range of sizes, models, and prices. It is a modern, durable, trustworthy device, and all of its parts are extendible. Its manufacture is guaranteed by the J. P. Mansfield and Sons company, of Atlanta III.

Part III

The First Wave

The 1960s to the Mid-1980s

Ángel Arango

C U B A

Cuban science fiction was virtually nonexistent prior to the 1959 revolution, but when it did come of age it happened in part thanks to the contributions of Ángel Arango (1926–). Born in the capital, he earned a law degree from the University of Havana in 1949, though he has worked in civil aviation for over fifty years and has attended the most important meetings in the field of international aviation law. Arango has been integrally involved in Cuban SF since the 1960s, as an author, jury member, and critic. His most important publications in the genre are the novels and short story collections *Whither Go the Cephalomes?* (*¿Adónde van los cefalomos?*, 1964), *The Black Planet* (*El planeta negro*, 1966), *The Art of Robots* (*Robotomaquia*, 1967), *The End of Chaos Comes Silently* (*El fin del caos llega quietamente*, 1971), *The Creatures* (*Las Criaturas*, 1978), and *The Monkey's Rainbow* (*El arco iris del mono*, 1980). More recently, he has published an SF trilogy comprised of *Transparency* (*Transparencia*, 1982), *Crossroad* (*Coyuntura*, 1984), and *Sider*, 1994, the latter an odyssey about overcoming time that Joe F. Randolph is translating into English. Several of Arango's stories and articles have been translated into English, French, German, Russian, Japanese, and Slovak, and have been published throughout Europe, Asia, and the Americas.

Arango has also finished an unpublished novel that establishes "an unorthodox approach for SF, based on using imagination as freely as possible but within the principle of human non-aggression," because, as Arango asserts, "man cannot be the enemy of man, even if literature so demands. That is an extreme position and a challenge for a writer, but the result is extraordinarily good."[1]

"The Cosmonaut" ("El cosmonauta"), the story we have chosen for this anthology, was written in 1964, but first appeared in issue 42 of the Spanish SF magazine *Nueva Dimensión* (1973); it was later included in Arango's *The Monkey's Rainbow* and in Goorden and Van Vogt's *The Best of Latin American Science Fiction* (*Lo mejor de la ciencia ficción latinoamericana*, 1982). In it, as in much of his SF, one can read a stout defense of the utopian ideals and philosophical concepts that Arango upholds, such as respect for each individual and nation, and for the role of human imagination in the face of dangers known and unknown. Furthermore, in "The Cosmonaut" an external threat is mediated by stylistic qualities the author describes as among the principal characteristics of Cuban SF: a light, informal touch, and a strong dose of black humor.

The Cosmonaut

El cosmonauta, 1964

by Ángel Arango

translated by Andrea Bell

Git whipped Nuí.

She jumped about joyously in the blue dust.

"Come closer," said Git.

Nuí advanced on her pincers and showed them to Git.

One of Git's tentacles snaked out, blowing dust at Nuí.

"Cut it, cut it!" pleaded Git.

Nuí bit it into three pieces: *choc, choc, choc!*

She ate one.

Git ate another.

The third went scuttling away across the blue dust and produced a child.

Nuí grabbed Git's other child by a tentacle and cut it in two.

"More, more . . ." he begged.

But Nuí was after the piece she had cut; it got away in the dust.

Nuí tapped herself lightly on the shell with her pincers and squirted a yellow stream at Git.

Mut was a mute witness to Git and Nuí's games.

The ship had been forced off course due to interference from a current of meteorite particles, compelling the man to steer toward the planet to avoid a fatal crash. Then the force of gravity caught the ship, which descended in a zigzag motion, using the braking motor to compensate.

"This way I'll be able to check the instruments and wait for the meteor stream to pass," the cosmonaut told himself.

At first the ship was a black speck in the sky. It approached the surface like a stellar particle, growing until it resumed its definitive shape above the blue dust. The dust immediately scattered, leaving space for the oxygen that the ship breathed to protect itself, and that quickly formed a red stain underneath the vessel.

Git, Nuí, Mut, and the rest had never seen such a strange meteorite, shinier than the others, not as hot, more symmetrical. Git stretched himself over the ship. His white eye trembled and the many spherical brains of his tentacles grew damp. The sweat from the small brains along his tentacles ran along the glass of the little windows.

"Bite me," he pleaded to Nuí, and she *choc!* cut off another piece of tentacle, which produced another child.

As happened every time meteorites fell, their reproductive instinct was heightened and the process of cutting tentacles multiplied.

Nuí kept biting Git's tentacles with her pincers, and the small pieces rolled around, growing quickly. Mut stretched out lengthwise across the stimulating blue dust; extending himself, he advanced upon the ship and formed various rings around it. Then he divided himself, and each ring in turn stretched itself out in the blue dust and divided.

Spurred by self-confidence and the need to establish contact, the cosmonaut appeared in the ship's doorway, contemplating the strange inhabitants of the blue dust. Alone in his roomy spacesuit, his head inside a glass helmet that emitted sparks from the antennae located before his eyes, he descended the stairs and approached the crowd. The others were astonished by such a being, one that emerged from a meteorite and walked on two tentacles, moving two others about in the air.

Mut asked, "Where does he come from? We've never seen anyone in a meteorite before."

"Strange, strange," Nuí commented, and snapped the air *choc! choc!* with her pincers.

The man's boldness grew as he saw himself a king before all those creatures, who remained immobile, analyzing him through their many tentacles filled with cerebral spheres, thousands of thinking eyes upon the man, scrutinizing him, penetrating him, taking stock of his image and movements, taking possession of his shape.

He entered the blue dust. The others saw how comfortably he moved on his feet, observing everything and emitting a constant series of sparks between his brows.

"Speak to him," Mut suggested. "Say something, anything . . ."

"Who are you?" Git asked.

The cosmonaut did not hear anything. His glass helmet continued to throw off sparks between his brows. But he had a feeling they wanted to have a conversation. The best he could do was emit more sparks, this time blue.

Git, Nuí, Mut, and the others understood them to be a symbol of peace.

"His words are blue like our dust," said Mut. "He wants to tell us something."

"I wonder why he's so small?" Nuí asked.

Git signaled, "He has two twin brains that shine. He opens and closes them—look carefully. And above his brains he speaks to us with words of blue light."

"Yes," said Nuí. "How old do you think he is?"

"He must be very young," Mut speculated. "His tentacles are short . . ."

Nuí faced the man. "Come closer," she said to him, "closer."

The cosmonaut heard absolutely nothing.

Then Nuí approached him.

"Are you alone? Are there no others with you?"

The others looked toward the outer door of the ship, which had been left open. But no one else appeared. One of the tentacle-children dashed over to the stairs and ran up them.

The man, who had seen it, continued trying to start a conversation.

They're playful and peaceful, he told himself. *The little ones look like puppies.*

And indeed, the little ones were the ones who drew closest in order to look at him.

I've caused a stir, the man went on thinking.

Mut asked, "What must his children be like?"

And he subdivided, so the visitor could understand what he was talking about.

Nuí, observing him from close by, saw that he looked like Git, though his tentacles lacked brains.

"He's so young that he doesn't yet have any," she said to herself.

Then Nuí let herself be carried away by curiosity, more than by the desire to procreate, and she cut the man's arms with her pincers: *choc! choc!*

While bleeding to death, the cosmonaut felt he was running out of air, and the last thing that he heard was, again, *choc! choc! choc! choc!*

Jerônimo Monteiro

BRAZIL

Sometimes known by the pseudonyms Ronnie Wells, J. Jeremias, and Gilga-mesh, Jerônimo Monteiro (1908–1970) was Brazil's first serious cultivator of SF. He was born in São Paulo to working-class parents and had to leave school at the age of ten in order to help out the family. After a series of manual and office jobs, Monteiro discovered a passion for reading and by age twenty had pub-lished his first short stories. Although his literary work includes magazine es-says and newspaper articles, he is most remembered for his radio SF/detective series (later issued in print) featuring the character Dick Peter, and for his nu-merous SF novels and stories, many of them for young readers. An avid fan of popular fiction, he also founded Brazil's first science fiction fan club and edited a few issues of the *Magazine de Ficção Científica,* the local version of *Fantasy and Science Fiction.*

With "The Crystal Goblet," written in 1964 and first published in *Tangents of Reality* (*Tangentes da realidade*) in 1969, Monteiro joins the many SF authors who have centered on the fear of nuclear war, yet this story is told in a manner that makes it distinctive. As Monteiro focuses on the visions and memories trig-gered by a crystal goblet, the reader not only gets an intimate glimpse of the Brazilian protagonist's life, but is also made to reflect on humanity's capacity for cruelty and self-destruction.

The Crystal Goblet

O copo de cristal, 1964

by Jerônimo Monteiro

translated by Roberta Rozende

and David Sunderland

THE GOBLET, THE LEATHER STRAP, THE JAIL

Miguel was holding the broken-stemmed goblet between his fingers. He was looking at it intensely, certain that it represented a very important connection to the past. What was it? What connection could it have? The goblet, of fine crystal, was worth nothing broken like that: it couldn't even be made to stand up. How had the shaft been before, when the goblet was new? Long? Short? And why had he kept this goblet for so many years? Why had he found it just now, in the old junk closet?

He let go of the goblet, which rocked slowly from side to side on the tabletop. And without knowing by what strange association, the violence he had recently experienced came back to mind, almost painfully: the soldiers, machine guns in hand, surrounding him in the street at dusk when he was leaving to visit the mayor:

"Communist! You're under arrest!"

He was shoved into the van, where three of his colleagues already were sitting, along with two more soldiers with machine guns across their knees. They drove toward the center of the small city, the killer sergeant asking where so-and-so lived. New stops, more people inside the already crowded van. "Communists! Communists!"

Confinement in the little town's small cement cell, damp and cold.

Later, back in the van, the road and the DOPS prison.[1] Full of men. Communists. Cement floor, no bench, no mattress. Hundreds of men lying on the floor, and others walking carefully between the bodies, so as not to step on them. The majority were half-naked, since the heat was unbearable in the huge unventilated room.

The toilet seat in the corner, exposed to everyone. The endless hours lived in anguish because of the lack of air, the smell, and the indignity. Later on, the review panel.

"There's nothing against you, sir. You're free to go. You were jailed on false charges. Don't take it hard. You know it happens in times like these."

The heavy soul, the abused body, the brain deranged by frustration, humiliation crushing one's humanity.

Miguel again picked up the broken stem, looking at it through the painful fog of his imagination. Right now the goblet reminded him of the strap—a leather strap, three feet in length, dark and shiny. The leather strap that used to hang by one end from the nail in the kitchen doorjamb. The one his father used to lash him with. Sometimes, after the beating, his mother would put him inside the tank with pickling brine, to wash his welt- and slash-covered body.

But the goblet . . .

Little by little, memory connected the untied links, and he remembered the scene that had been buried and forgotten for a half century now.

A small strip of land on the banks of the Tamanduateí River, between João Teodoro and São Caetano Streets. Shrubs growing everywhere. Piles of debris here and there: old basins, broken buckets, parts of chairs, fragments of mirrors, battered pans. A magic kingdom in the eyes of Miguelzinho.[2] Whenever he could escape constant supervision, he went there to discover treasures, like that big iron basin the neighborhood families used for their weekly bath. It was punctured and crumpled, but it was his most cherished toy: propped up on one side by a pole like a trap, it was his cave. He spent forgotten hours there, just dreaming.

One afternoon, while in his cave, he saw the crystal goblet shining in the middle of the bushes. Clear, bright. A precious treasure in that place of sadness, filled with cans and ugly bits of glass. Before picking it up he stared at it, amazed. Later, he held it carefully between his fingers, as it seemed it might break into pieces, so fragile and delicate was it.

Fifty years later Miguel didn't necessarily remember what little Miguelzinho did, saw, or thought about under the old basin on that strip of land, with the goblet in his hand. But he remembered well that the boy had noticed, suddenly, that hours had passed. It was late. If he arrived home after his father got back from work, he wouldn't escape the strap. The chief and indisputable point of his discipline was that he had to be inside by the time his father got home.

Almost fainting, he crawled out from under the basin. He had no choice but to go home, no matter what was waiting for him. He confusedly thought that if he brought him that gorgeous crystal goblet, his father might forgive him, realizing that there was perhaps an explanation for his tardiness. Besides, his body still ached from the last beating.

The goblet was of no use at all. His father beat him. He was forced to swallow supper, though he had no appetite, and then went sobbing quietly to his bed, which was set up in the living room under the window facing the village. The house had a living room, a bedroom, and a kitchen. After supper his father would sit near the front door and his mother would be in the kitchen, doing the interminable housework. By 9 P.M. they would be in bed. It was another incontestable point of household discipline.

Miguelzinho couldn't sleep. He'd stopped crying. He pulled the blanket off his head and contemplated the darkness. That was why he noticed a soft bluish light in the kitchen, outlining the door. For some time he looked at it, curiosity growing. What could it be? Is the kerosene light on? Some other night-light? Or are there still lighted coals in the stove?

But it was a bluish light. It wasn't the moonlight: the kitchen didn't have a window.

Miguelzinho stood up, stifling his moans, trying not to make any noise, but his father's voice came from across the room:

"Where are you going?"

"To get a drink of water, may I?"

As there was no reply, it meant he could go. He walked toward the kitchen, and from the door, the light dazzled him. The blue glow of the crystal goblet, overturned on the small table by the sink. It seemed full of light. Pale shadows imprisoned inside it moved about in confusion, like smoke scrolls. Amazed by that wondrous sight, the boy froze like a statue, gazing without understanding. The kitchen didn't have a ceiling. There were some broken tiles in the roof, and through the holes it was possible to see the faint light of the moonlit sky. A star was shining right in the center of the triangle of a broken roofing tile. Suddenly, his father's voice thundered from the living room:

"What are you up to? Does it take such a long time to drink water?"

Miguelzinho took a sip. "I'm finished. I'm coming." He grabbed the goblet and walked toward the door.

As soon as he picked up the glass from the top of the small table, the enchantment vanished. There was no more blue glow. All he had in his hand was a crystal goblet, broken.

He went back to bed with his treasure, fondling it in the dark. When he was about to fall asleep, he placed it carefully on the ground, next to the wall.

Now, as Miguel was looking at the goblet, thoughts and bits of imagination and casual observation intermingled in his memory. The glass, full of images from his childhood on the banks of the Tamanduateí River, was of a pure crystal, finer and clearer than he had ever seen before. He hadn't noticed that, back when he had found it in the trash on the strip of land. He had noticed that it was white, transparent, pretty, much prettier than any glass he'd ever seen; very different from the thick glass cup they had in his house, greenish, rough, with small white bubbles. The glass used to serve water to guests. The only one, because glasses weren't used in his house. They used white tin cups and condensed milk cans, to which traveling tinsmiths welded handles—those tinkers who roamed the streets proclaiming their presence through bell-like notes made by a small hammer striking an iron skillet.

Now, however, he could distinguish quality crystal from inferior glass. The goblet with the broken stem was of very fine crystal.

Broken stem . . . now that Miguel examined the goblet more closely, he realized that the stem wasn't broken. That goblet had never had the round base that all stemmed glasses have. The stem was perfectly finished. It had, at the very end, a small cone-shaped indentation.

Miguel tried to stand it on end. For a moment it didn't move, but suddenly, it twisted, rolled along the table, and fell to the ground, despite Miguel's efforts to stop it. His heart froze as if the goblet's breaking into pieces would cause him irreparable harm.

But it did not break. It bounced on the tile floor, emitting crystalline sounds, shook from side to side, and came to rest under Miguel's disbelieving stare. Miguel didn't pick it up right away. For some time he stared at it. It just couldn't be, but nevertheless it was true: the goblet was unscathed, intact—as perfect and pure as before. With the goblet between his fingers, he examined it again carefully. Nothing. Some rare stroke of luck prevented the goblet from shattering against the ceramic floor . . . Or could it be unbreakable? He held the tip of its stem between two fingers, and struck it with a pencil. The argentine sound filled the office and diffused into waves. Another blow, stronger, another wave of sound, broader, more expansive. He picked up the scissors and, after a little hesitation, hit the cup forcefully. The silvery note sounded throughout the entire house, and the crystal goblet remained intact, vibrating between his fingers.

Excited, he placed the goblet on the desk and left for the terrace. A cool wind was blowing from the sea. The weathervane on top of the long cedar pole, "Grandpa's airplane," as his grandchildren used to call it, was turning quietly, slowly rotating between south and east. Two hundred meters from the end of the street, the waves rose in a foamy crest. Two fishing boats were slowly passing on the horizon.

One more house was being built on that street. When they had come to Mongaguá,[3] their house was the first—and for a long time the only—one around. The solitude was pleasant. Birds of numerous species abounded. When the sun went down, thrushes sang in the nearby trees. From time to time flocks of small parrots passed overhead, flying high and crying out, headed for the nearest mountain. Herons descended in laden flight when heavy rains made lagoons of the land; white-throated rails jumped and chirped, and other water birds frequented the puddles as well.

Later on they started to build other houses; boys with slingshots walked through the newly cleared land, men clenching rifles dedicated themselves to the hunt. Now over a year had gone by without birds, not even tanagers, which had been so abundant. It was rare to hear a thrush singing.

Later came the van, the policemen with machine guns: "Communist! You're under arrest!" And the jail, the bodies covering the floor, the toilet seat open for all to see. Like death, the escape of the birds. A dark and ugly stain extended itself over the house and the landscape, flowing from the subjugated spirit, a stain that spread and covered the small city, the coast, the state, and the country. Like the headstone of a tomb. Inside the tomb you cannot speak, nor hear, nor think. Inside the tomb the body lies dead. The toilet seat in the corner. The one who sat on it, in front of hundreds of other men, cowed, subdued. It was like that. The toilet seat, everyone looking.

Lying in the hammock on the terrace, Miguel let his spirit wander without direction, flying like a bird over land transformed by fire into desert. No place to settle that wouldn't wound, burn, or sully it. But somehow, the tired spirit could still fall asleep in the sun.

THE GOBLET, THE DUCKS, THE JAIL

At night, after supper, Miguel again held the crystal goblet between his fingers and was strangely worried by empty and shapeless thoughts. The goblet, it seems, was forcefully demanding his attention—more, his whole being. It was the glass. When, while still a little boy, he'd first seen that blue inner glow filling the humble tile-roofed kitchen—*had he really seen it?* Could it have been one of those jokes that memory, mixing imagination and the needs of the moment, plays on us? Wouldn't it be, then, a deceit of the spirit, something like a psychic spectacle staged by him, unconsciously, in order to soften the painful memories of infancy?

He thought of telling his wife the history of the crystal goblet. But he soon grew discouraged. How should he tell her? How should he answer questions that would open unexpected shortcuts in his memory or along the pathway of his ideas? People want to know more this and more that. Sometimes they want to know things that cannot be explained.

But if the goblet was luminous at night, the trick was to prove it.

He closed the blinds of the office, shut the door, turned off the lights and placed the goblet upside down on the desk. Nothing. It was there, lightly visible, because the darkness was incomplete. But there was no glow inside. Perhaps he needed to wait, give it time. That night in the tile-roofed kitchen, half a century ago, the goblet had been on the small table an hour or two before he'd removed the blanket from his head and seen the glow.

So he left it on the desk, upside down, and went out onto the terrace. His wife, Car, was in the hammock, and she spoke to him of relaxing things, of hens, ducks, and teals.

"Somebody touched the teal's nest. She abandoned it. She's laying her eggs anywhere, anyplace. Mr. Alípio found an egg yesterday, close to the brickpile. Today I found another one, on the banks of the stream."

"She'll end up choosing another place to make her nest."

"Tomorrow I'll kill another duck. We still have three males and just two females. We only have to leave one male."

"Sure. One male is enough."

"Do you want me to make duck steaks?"

"Excellent. Whatever you make is great."

Teals, male ducks, female ducks, steaks. And the crystal goblet upside down, back in the office, in the dark.

"Today when I went to the village I saw the German guy talking with

Mr. Zé. I was crazy with hate. He knows very well who made the denunciation. What you think is really the truth."

"Of course it is. He's friends with the accuser. It was all set up. He was imprisoned together with the others to eavesdrop on them. Traitor."

"How disgusting! I wanted to slap him in the face."

"Don't worry, Car. Men are all like that."

Men are like that. Perverse, cruel, like the wolf when it sees the three little pigs defenseless. The man who suddenly sees himself with a little power in his hands tries immediately to assemble a guillotine, a gallows, and a coffin. "Now those people will see who they're dealing with!" And the van, the machine guns, the killer sergeant: "Communist! You're under arrest!"

And the crystal goblet back there in the darkness, upside down.

Miguel left the pleasant shade of the terrace and went back into the office. It was true! There was a bluish light inside the goblet. But very weak! So weak it wouldn't even illuminate the hand he held up to it.

Was that really it, that same radiating glow from the old tile-roofed kitchen, half a century ago? To what degree could his memory be trusted? To what extent had his imagination embellished, created subterfuges, screens, and labyrinths? What masterpiece could the mind's defenses construct to hide from consciousness the fissures, the cracks, the charred wooden stumps of the scorched field?

Perhaps more time was needed.

He went back to the terrace. Car had fallen asleep in the hammock. Brave woman! When he'd been able to send her the message from jail, she had received the news calmly. She'd spent the entire night here, sitting on the terrace waiting for the sun to rise, in order to do the right thing. If he hadn't slept on the cement floor of the jail, she wouldn't sleep either. Who knows who ached more, she from the hammock's fabric or he from the hard cement, with the cockroaches running back and forth. At dawn, she left and headed toward the city. But she wanted to pass unnoticed—who knew what they would dream up, if there was any surveillance. She walked some kilometers along the railroad tracks, stumbling, falling in the darkness surrounding the sunrise. She took the five o'clock train at the next station. In the city, she looked for those of their friends who could intercede on his behalf.

That was all in the past now; there she was, sleeping calmly in the darkness of the terrace. Everything over, she was asleep. But, for him, would everything also be over? Would he be able someday to cleanse his defiled dignity?

Miguel tried to sleep on the other hammock, with little success. As it had fifty years ago, the crystal goblet kept him awake, looking at it.

When their son came back from the movies at 10:30, they went to bed. Car was sleeping heavily. She could fall asleep by just putting her head on the pillow, and wouldn't awaken easily. Miguel could wake up, walk around, turn the lights on and off, without disturbing her.

THE BLUISH LIGHT

In the office, everything was the same. The glow inside the crystal goblet was the same as hours before. But it existed, no doubt. Who knows, maybe the setting wasn't right. Maybe the conditions didn't match the ones in the old kitchen with the tile roof . . . the broken pieces of roofing tile, a star shining through one of the holes.

He thought about the storeroom at the back of the hall, totally dark, the small window facing west . . .

He took the goblet and placed it on the ironing board, observing it, anxious. No doubt, now it was brighter inside, but it wasn't the radiant glow of fifty years ago. Not by a long shot!

He looked at the dark night through the window. Few stars were shining; this was the less populated part of the sky. The Milky Way was more toward the east, over the house.

He remembered, then, the large shed in the yard. He could punch a hole in the roof . . .

He went to the shed. He placed the goblet on the carpenter's bench. With the chisel he opened a small hole in the roof—later on he would fix that. He closed the doors and the darkness folded around him like the wings of a bat. Soon he could make out, in the darkness, the blue light imprisoned in the crystal goblet. Miguel's heart beat rapidly. He felt he was back in the old kitchen; he went back fifty years. He changed the position of the goblet slightly, and the glow grew visibly brighter. Slowly he moved it around, observing the alterations of the light, until finding what seemed to be the ideal position. The shed was faintly illuminated by the blue incandescence. Miguel felt so moved that he sat down and decided to be quiet for some time, with his eyes shut, immobile.

What was that? He didn't know. He didn't know which force or phenomenon would be at work—but it was, without a doubt, something extraordinary, something the physical, chemical, and optical laws of his understanding didn't seem to explain. But it was also very difficult to explain that "goblet" of fine crystal, with no bottom, unbreakable.

He opened his eyes again. He drew the old chair nearer the carpenter's bench to be more comfortable, his eyes level with the crystal goblet. He could see that the blue glow didn't keep still: it fluttered, throbbed, and described scrolls and spirals that faded continuously into new waves and strange forms.

It was astonishing and paralyzing, as if from that strange light a hypnotic force somehow emanated. As time passed, it seemed not only did he immerse his gaze in the delicate, undulating bluish light—but also his head, his entire body, as if the small goblet engulfed all the space before him. There was nothing, neither the carpenter's bench nor the shed, only the glow with its abstract dark forms intertwining, rising up and falling.

The blast of a horn brought him back to reality. After that, the violent clamor of the train, racing alongside the house, ruined the silence and the calm. Miguel withdrew from the blue light and realized, with some astonishment, that it was five o'clock in the morning. The sun would be rising in a little while. He had spent the entire night looking at that false reality that surged from deep in his past. He kept looking. The phenomenon continued, but it seemed to be weaker. He got up, stretched his legs, opened the doors and looked out at the fresh, grayish dawn. He went back to the goblet: its light had almost gone out. Sighing deeply, he placed it carefully on the shelf near the packets of nails. He closed the shed door and went off to bed.

WHAT LIVED INSIDE THE GOBLET

Miguel woke up late and had great difficulty getting back to work. It was hard for him to find the words for the daily section he wrote for the newspaper. Things weren't falling into place. His spirit was distant, ill at ease, empty.

He was waiting anxiously for night to come and had to invent excuses in order to calm his wife, who noticed his agitation. What a childish way to spend the entire night, gazing at a crystal goblet. It was such a personal thing, so intimate, so close to that childhood when Miguelzinho dreamed beneath the great basin on the strip of land, that it seemed impossible someone else could become interested in the goblet, or see what he saw inside it.

When night fell Miguel went back to the shed, his soul full of doubts. Would that bluish light still be shining, one more time?

Yes. There it was like the previous night, like fifty years ago in that old kitchen, so poor and full of holes. He pulled up the chair and sat down looking at it. The diaphanous shadows inside the blue light waved slowly. It was fascinating and hypnotic.

He was distracted from his immersion in the mystery by a quietly approaching form. It was Car. She saw his astonished face in the blue glow of the goblet. She smiled. In a certain way, the enchantment was broken. The luminescence was there, the dark undulating shapes continued moving slowly, but the privacy was disturbed. The mystic magic had vanished.

"What's this?" she asked, her eyes wide.

"I don't know. What do you think?"

"It looks like witchcraft. What's inside that goblet?"

"Nothing." Miguel picked up the goblet and turned on the light; she took it, dazzled, turning it around in her hand.

Later, the lights turned back off, the goblet back in its place, Miguel said more. "I've had this goblet for more than fifty years. I found it on a strip of land when I was still a child. Back then it already had this light inside it, at night. Later on, I forgot about it. Yesterday I accidentally found it again, and everything came back to me. I was trying . . ."

"But this light, what is it?"

"Who knows? That's what I'm trying to find out. It has to be something. The glass isn't common, either. It seems to be made of crystal, but it doesn't break."

"How odd!"

Car pulled up a box, sat down, and stared at the goblet, as fascinated as he was. For some minutes the two contemplated the spectacle in silence. Later, she said:

"Some things are moving inside."

"That's right. Those dark shadows are wonderful."

"Do you only see dark shadows?"

"Just dark shapes. Shadows that ripple, up and down . . ."

"No, Miguel. They're not shadows. Wait . . . they're things . . . It looks like an army marching over an immense land . . ."

"An army?"

"Yes. Men, lots of men. Other things, too. I don't know . . . Things that slide . . . Carts? Look! Can't you see?"

He didn't see. He saw dark shadows in motion. He saw variations in tone moving to one side and disappearing, while other shadows advanced in procession. Everything was disorganized. Car must be blessed with rare visual acuity to be able to distinguish exact forms where he just saw a vague outline. But she'd always been abnormally sensitive to many things. And now there she was, leaning over the crystal goblet, mesmerized by its translucent, elusive essence, even more alienated from the world that surrounded her than she'd ever been, with all her passion for this strange wonder.

Army . . . marching men . . . carts . . .

They spent the entire night immersed in the luminous world of the crystal goblet, she seeing throngs of human beings walking over an endless land, scattered among heavy war vehicles. She saw the brightness of weapons, the tips of spears, the reflection of light from the blades of drawn swords. She saw clouds of dust billowing over the soldiers. He saw only dark forms of capricious movement and let himself be fascinated by them, even while, in his bemusement, he could hear the excited description that Car made of the scenes. The shapes he saw matched what she was describing. It was as if, being tremendously nearsighted (as he really was), he were watching a movie without glasses. Later on he thought that perhaps using sufficiently strong eyeglasses might have let him see things better. He was thinking about this when the whistle of the five o'clock train suddenly announced it was time to shut down the show.

The anxiety of the wait repeated itself the following day. Now their waiting generated conversation: they swapped hypotheses, and somehow it helped pass the time. Work could wait. It was impossible to work under such excitement. Miguel went to Santos, bought some eyeglasses, and at night, in the shed, put them to the test, only to quickly learn they didn't work. With or without eyeglasses, everything for him was dark shadows. Car, however, continued to clearly distinguish the scenes that unfolded inside the blue light.

"They've stopped on a great plain. Some are moving from one side to another. Far on the horizon, a dark spot is moving. Now they're lighting big fires."

Miguel could see the fires, not as fires, but as luminous points more alive and reddish in the blue tonality.

"Eight fires?" he asked.

"Eight already lit, but they're lighting more, all over. Can you see now?"

"I see the brightness of the fires. How are they armed? Do they have rifles, machine guns, and cannons?"

"No. They don't seem to have any firearms. They have spears, swords, and shields."

"Damn! How about that spot over there?"

"It looks like they're approaching, very slowly."

He saw this: a darker shape coming from the extreme edge of the blue light, descending toward the center. For some time they watched in silence. Later, she said excitedly:

"It's another army! It's coming toward this one. Looks like there'll be a battle . . ."

Sure enough, the two armies finally met in a tremendous, chaotic clash. Miguel saw the shadows mixing together, interpenetrating. Car, however, could see details.

"It's horrible! They're destroying each other like beasts! They're cutting each other to ribbons with swords, skewering each other with spears. They're in pieces. Blood's gushing everywhere. The ones who are running are stepping on the wounded, who're crawling on the ground. I'm sure they're crying out . . . I can't watch this nightmare anymore."

Despite the fascinating scene, she refused to look, taking her eyes off the crystal goblet and covering them with her hands. Miguel, desperate, continued to look at the vague forms flitting about. For some time he looked at them in vain. Later, it seemed the scene was shifting. The furious shadows had calmed down somewhat.

"Car . . . look now. It looks like the battle's over . . ."

She came closer and gazed again at the tenuous and translucent mass.

"It is over. The soil is lined with bloody corpses, almost all without heads. They've been beheaded. The blood is still flowing. One of the armies is moving away, but it's much, much smaller . . ."

Car was about to yield again to the horror of the scene, when the strong loud whistle of the five o'clock train came to proclaim the new day. The deafening string of cars passed by. The light in the crystal goblet dimmed.

"DRINK COCA-COLA"

Now Car shared his secret with the same intensity and excitement. Strangely, they avoided talking about it during the day. There seemed to be in that phenomenon an inhibitive quality that made them hold back, wait to see what was to come. Which armies would those be? What people were they who fought so savagely? Clearly, they had to be armies from the past, from the time that humanity, under the iron fist of blasphemous noblemen, forged its way through rivers of blood . . . But had humanity changed much since then? There is a certain protocol. Mankind had learned to submit, had understood it was best to obey definitive laws and avoid the sword's edge. The means are different now, but in essence, the feelings, the spirit, are the same. A small minority orders and subjugates and an immense majority obeys, in exchange for a little more comfort, a little more bread, a little more circus. War, now, is an organized business. There is scientific destruction, death. Machines and devices save men in the battlefield, not out of respect for mankind and life (if this respect really existed, wars wouldn't occur), but because the machines kill the "enemy" faster, destroy more fully. Wars continue to dominate the history of our days, as they have dominated the history of mankind through all time. The spirit of it remains the same. If something changed, it was the means. And the reasons.

Lazlo showed up as usual at the end of the week with his wife and two kids. Miguel greatly admired his son-in-law, and loved his daughter and grandchildren. He liked to see them enjoying the sun and the sea, he liked their jokes.

On the terrace, while they had the drinks that always preceded the weekend lunch, Lazlo looked at his father-in-law and observed:

"You seem worried. What is it?"

Miguel gave a start.

"It's nothing. Why?"

"You seem worn out, tired, worried . . . That persecution story again?"

"No! Nothing like that! That's all calmed down now. It's something else."

"'It's something else' . . . then, it is something . . ." Miguel now felt compelled to speak. Lazlo was intelligent, cultured, sensible. His input would be useful, should the phenomenon repeat itself for him to see. Miguel ended up telling him in detail about everything that had happened since he'd found the crystal goblet. Lazlo laughed, skeptical.

"You don't believe it?"

"I'd like to see it."

"Tonight."

That night Car, Lazlo, and Miguel sat down around the goblet in the shed. The light soon reached the flaring point, filling the enclosure with an ethereal, bluish luminescence. Lazlo, his face hard, interested, stared at the goblet. Car, her face almost resting on the crystal, seemed transported to another world.

"There are ruins now," she said, "great ruins."

"Do you see anything, Lazlo?" Miguel asked.

Lazlo made himself more comfortable, brought his face close to the goblet, and his blue eyes opened up.

"They're ruins, without a doubt. Ruins of a gigantic city . . . Which city is it? Tokyo, New York? London? Moscow?"

"They must be old cities, Lazlo. The battle we saw yesterday was fought between armies of the past."

"They can't be old cities. Those ruins . . ."

Evidently Lazlo saw much better than Miguel, but Car saw better than Lazlo. As a tacit concession, Car continued describing what she was seeing:

"They are great ruins. Ruins on the ground. People are moving among the ruins. Can you see? Strange people . . . dressed in rags . . . half-naked women . . . But . . . they seem deformed! Look . . . some men, over there . . . enormous heads! A woman with four breasts, no, six! It's horrible, my God! There . . . that man . . . he has four arms! What a monstrous group! They're looking for anything among the ruins. Some are entering through the building's half-destroyed main door . . . The others outside are looking around, like they're suspicious of something . . . the ones who entered . . . are leaving. They're bringing . . . an animal . . . it's a dog! Everyone's jumping on it . . . they're tearing up the dog! They're . . . eating it!"

Car was about to faint. She pulled back and covered her eyes. Lazlo couldn't make out the scene as clearly, but he saw enough to corroborate what Car said. Miguel could still only see moving shadows.

"Another group is coming from the other side," said Lazlo. "Look."

Car forced herself to look again, overcoming her revulsion. "It's another group of people . . . like the first one. Deformed, badly dressed, skin and bones . . . they're running. They're falling over the others. They're fighting over bloody pieces of dog meat. I see sticks . . . they're starting to fight . . . knives! They're all crazy! Worse than wild animals!" Car shouted. "Mother of God! No, no, no!"

She struck the crystal goblet and it hit the wall and then clinked along for some distance on the cement floor, filling the storage shed with crystalline sounds. Lazlo rushed to grab it and Miguel held his wife.

"Calm down, hon . . . Control yourself. This is just a vision. Think a little . . . like in a movie."

"Miguel! How horrible! They . . . they . . ."

"But this isn't reality, Car. They're visions. The goblet is like a magic lantern. It creates the scenes . . ."

"Oh, Miguel . . . But this . . ."

"They were eating each other, right? But it's not real!"

Lazlo picked up the goblet and examined it.

"It really doesn't break! What kind of crystal could this be?"

The goblet was once again placed in its proper position and the shed filled with blue clarity. Miguel and Lazlo leaned over the goblet, but Car didn't come close.

For Miguel the scenes continued with the same overlapping of loosely defined shapes. Lazlo saw well, though not very clearly.

"It's awful!" he murmured. "Where can this be? Are we receiving images from another planet? The scene's changing . . . You can look now, Car. That other stuff has gone . . ."

Car drew close again, still trembling.

"All those people, those strange and deformed people, are running away down a wide avenue lined with ruins. Another apparently organized group is approaching from the other side . . . On the ground are pieces of . . . of meat . . . The ones that are coming now seem . . . yes. They must be the same ones who were fighting . . . they're marching in formation. The others are fleeing, disappearing. Now the men that use swords, spears, and shields pass by. I think they're going after them. The remains of a great building are coming into sight . . . I see a sign, hanging . . . it's oval . . . "

"If we could read," said Lazlo, moved. "If I could read . . . maybe I could identify it, the time . . . If this is from Earth . . . "

"Wait . . . I can . . . I can read . . . drin . . . drink . . . Coca-Cola! That's it! 'Drink Coca-Cola'—That's what's written on the sign!"

Lazlo closed his hands around the crystal goblet. The shed turned dark. The bluish light that passed through his fingers was not strong enough to illuminate anything.

"That's terrible!" he said. And he walked with the goblet toward the shed door, which he opened to the night's darkness. "It's horrible! What we're seeing, Miguel, what we're seeing are scenes of the future. It's what awaits mankind . . . Ruins, a return to barbarity . . . creatures deformed by atomic radiation . . . Hunger, misery . . . No! It can't be. This goblet is playing some trick . . . It can't be . . ."

"Why not?" Miguel said. "I really believe this is the most likely future for mankind, if mankind continues on the path it's following. Men have never understood each other. There is always a threat of war, and always a worse war . . . What threatens us now is an atomic war. How would it all end? All of us can foresee that, we don't need this crystal goblet. After a war of total destruction, what would remain of humanity, if not precisely those sick men we saw, those savages who were eating each other? As a matter of fact, humans never stopped being savage troglodytes. Mankind smeared itself with a coat of varnish when it started to discover and invent things. But everything collapses like a sand castle with the smallest breath of war. The wars, the past and future ones, are always infinitely more harmful in their effects than their causes. If we think it over, they're not worth a thing: they're the expression of the momentary greed of mankind. They could easily be eliminated if people were able to overcome their pride, if they could reason and yield. But they don't. It's only after the disaster is consummated that they understand their mistake, even though they may not admit it . . ."

"Well, I believe in humanity," Lazlo said. "It may be that wars take us to extremes, but man is civilizing himself little by little. The future of mankind will be happy."

"One can see that," Miguel commented summarily and bitterly.

"Can we see a little bit more?" Car suggested. "Who knows if a little further on . . ."

Just then the five o'clock train whistled, and soon after that it passed thundering by, little windows lit up, carrying half-asleep passengers.

"It's over," said Car, smiling. "The announcement of a new day . . ."

FIRE! FIRE!

That night they didn't watch the crystal goblet, they didn't see the continuation of the story of mankind on the face of the earth. Not that night, nor ever again. It was the last time the wonderful blue glow radiated from the strange goblet.

They were all asleep at nine in the morning, when the kitchen maid entered the house crying out:

"Fire! Fire! The shed!"

Miguel jumped out of bed. Car jumped too. Both ran outside and found Lazlo, who was already watching the flames. The shed at the back of the yard was ablaze. Even if there were anything they could do, it would have been useless.

"The goblet might withstand the fire," said Miguel, his heart heavy. "A crystal of that quality, unbreakable and everything . . ."

No one knows if it withstood it or not. Hours later, when all that remained of the shed were ashes and some smoking bars and handles, they made a detailed search: there was no sign of the magic goblet.

"I believe," Lazlo said, "that the goblet was unbreakable, but highly flammable. It must have melted in the heat of the flames."

It may be. Who will ever be able to explain it all?

Álvaro Menén Desleal

EL SALVADOR

Central America is represented in this anthology by Alvaro Menén Desleal (1931–2000), the facetious pseudonym adopted by Alvaro Menéndez Leal (*leal* means loyal; *desleal,* its opposite). Desleal was born in Santa Ana, El Salvador, and enjoyed a career as a diplomat in Europe and as a celebrated writer until his death in 2000. He published poetry, essays, short stories, and plays, and is perhaps most famous for his absurdist drama *Black Light* (*Luz negra,* 1966), which features two severed heads as the main characters.

In his prose fiction, Desleal's specialties were science fiction, the Borgesian fantastic, and the humorous microsketch. In 1968 he submitted a collection of such pieces to a national literary competition, where it took first prize. It was published in 1969 as *A Cord Made of Nylon and Gold and Other Tales of the Marvelous* (*Una cuerda de nylon y oro y otros cuentos maravillosos*). The title story was later reprinted in his collection of SF narratives *The Illustrious Android Family* (*La ilustre familia androide,* 1972).

Although it was difficult to select from among Desleal's many fine stories, we chose "Nylon and Gold" because of its artful structure and haunting imagery. It reflects the pessimism and the fear of nuclear annihilation that permeated the 1960s and 1970s, even in countries peripheral to the hegemonic struggles of those times. Desleal heightens the authenticity of the scenario he posits by making the main character an American, one Henry Olsen from Salt Lake City, Utah, and by peppering the story with references to current events of the day, to U.S. popular culture, and to the politics of the cold war.

A Cord Made of Nylon and Gold

Una cuerda de nylon y oro, 1965

by Álvaro Menén Desleal

translated by Andrea Bell

Back then there was a president named Johnson, and my wife was sleeping with Sam Wilson.

It was the twenty-sixth orbit. The whole thing lasted but a few seconds.

"Henry! Henry!" my crewmate pleaded from inside the capsule, "Do you realize what you're about to do?"

"It's useless, McDivitt," I told him. "I've already made up my mind."

McDivitt continued pleading. I had cut the connection with the tracking station, so his words weren't reaching Earth. Otherwise the voice of Captain Grisson, who was in charge of the project, would have rung out just as desperately. Or would Grisson, on Earth, be mute with shock?

I don't know. I was floating in the void, six hundred kilometers up, enveloped in my space suit. I had removed my thermal gloves to more comfortably operate the rocket gun with which I controlled the direction of my movements. The auxiliary tank on my back indicated enough oxygen for 110 minutes; if everything came out according to my calculations, that would be the maximum amount of time I would remain, *alive,* in space.

"Henry! Henry! What will the president say?"

Eight meters away from my body, apparently suspended immobile and magnificent in one point in space, the two-seater capsule completed its terrestrial orbit every ninety-one minutes. The hatch was open, which meant that McDivitt was also depending on his supply of portable oxygen. That's why I had to hurry, since I didn't want my decision to affect him.

"Henry! What'll become of your kids?"

The filial appeal was useless. I removed the pliers I had carefully hidden upon boarding the ship in Cape Kennedy, and with their sharp jaws grasped the cord made of nylon and gold that tied me, like an umbilical cord, to the capsule. Before cutting, I took the precaution of saying good-bye to my partner.

"Goodbye, McDivitt," I said, quite sarcastically. "I leave you to your marvelous world. Go on home like a good boy."

Then I severed the cord with a single cut and discharged my rocket gun until it ran out, so as to get myself as far away from the ship as possible. I still managed to see how the nylon and gold cord retracted, and how, at last, the hatch door shut. With that, I felt totally free. Free in a black sky full of stars that don't twinkle, free-floating in the void at 28,500 kilometers per hour, free at a distance of 600 kilometers from a planet I was fed up with.

That was in August of 1965. Two months earlier, McDivitt and White had completed a mission that we, on this launch, were basically copying. White had left the ship for twenty-three minutes; he was the second man after the Russian Leonov to do so. The space race—in which every astronaut expects to end up either scorched to death or with a wreath of flowers around his neck, like a derby-winning horse—was attracting increasingly dramatic and vain types: if Leonov stayed in space for twenty minutes, then White stayed for twenty-three.

I was the third man chosen to do a spacewalk; I, Henry Olsen, of Salt Lake City. My mission was to do a complete orbit of Earth while suspended in the void, tied to the ship by a nylon and gold cord eight meters long. I was supposed to stay out for ninety-one minutes, doing stupid things: taking pictures, moving about, making fake repairs, clowning around, turning somersaults; all with that childish sense of humor we acquire, who knows why, at Cape Kennedy. But instead of breaking another idiotic record, instead of converting myself into the winning horse for the day, I preferred to free myself forever. In exactly the twenty-sixth orbit.

It was August of 1965. There was a president named Johnson. De Gaulle was threatening to checkmate NATO. My compatriots occupied the Dominican Republic. War was burning in Vietnam. The Russians had some kind of secret up their sleeve about reaching the moon. The Ku Klux Klan had murdered another black woman in Alabama. Von Braun was still doing science fiction. Rio de Janeiro had recently celebrated the four-hundredth anniversary of its founding. San Salvador had just been partially destroyed by an earthquake. Women's fashion still pursued its mission of "less fabric, more skin." One hundred eighty Japanese miners had died from a cave-in. Queen Elizabeth was writing postcards from Germany. China had just exploded its second atomic bomb. Ben Bella no longer ruled in Algeria. Frank Sinatra was doing things "his way." Another record in car sales had been broken. My little boy John had a broken nose. I owed only $2,800 dollars on the mortgage on my house . . .

There was a president named Johnson, and my wife was cheating on me with Sam Wilson, her sister's old boyfriend. Sam Wilson, the redhead who could never handle the ball in high school rugby games.

That was in 1965. In August. Today I don't know anything more about Johnson, about Vietnam, about my kids, about Frank Sinatra . . .

From the moment I cut the cord made of nylon and gold, I lost all contact with humanity. And although the Earth imposes its spherical presence on my multiday scenery—sometimes it's at my feet, sometimes above me, sometimes at my side—I know nothing more about it. A large part of its surface is covered in clouds, but at first, recently free of the umbilical cord, I could occasionally make out the lights or shadows of the big cities. "New York," I said to myself, and I would imagine a Fifth Avenue choked with a sea of people watching me, their necks stiff from the effort of keeping their heads in such an uncomfortable position. "Moscow," I'd say, and I'd picture another multitude of proletarians, the women wearing babushkas; "Buenos Aires . . . Paris . . . London . . . Melbourne . . ."

For a while I was content with my map of the world, hazy and less colorful than the one in school. I was amused by the spectacle without imagining the consequences of my desertion. Later came a few attempts to recover my "body," and the Russians almost succeeded when they tried to fish me in with a kind of net. I always found ways to escape and remain free. Free and *alive*.

Because something's happened that the scientists never guessed at. I was only supposed to live for 110 minutes, to live for precisely the length of time my oxygen supply lasted, but that's not what happened. I don't know why, but that's not what happened.

I came to realize the phenomenon of my survival some twenty orbits after I'd cut the cord. "Why," I asked myself, "have I seen so many sunsets and sunrises?" I began to count the number of times I saw dawn and dusk; when I got to around 120 sunrises I got bored with counting. I calculated that that amount of sunrises was possible only, at the speed I was traveling, in something like a week's time. Then I got another surprise:

the needle that indicated my oxygen tank's pressure was on *Full*. I had, therefore, remained in space for days and days without needing to consume one bit of air. In other words, I didn't need air to survive. Then I discovered—I was always slow on the uptake—that when I crossed the shadowed cone of the Earth I didn't feel colder, nor hotter when I was exposed to direct sunlight. And I didn't suffer hunger or thirst, pain or anguish. I felt happy. Free and happy.

I have no idea of the years that have passed since then. I haven't gone back to counting a single sunrise or sunset, but I believe I've seen millions. And although I still feel free, my happiness has changed to desperation. Because I should have died a long time ago. Not died out in space, so that my corpse would remain like a rock flung loose from some planet, but with *them*, with humans, back there on Earth.

Because they all died.

I don't know *why* it happened, but little by little I realized *how* it happened.

The sky was black and the stars shone without twinkling, with that majestic monotony they have when seen from space. On Earth everything was clear: from Cape Kennedy to Italy, from Italy to Malaysia, over the Pacific and over California and from there again to Cape Kennedy, not a single cloud hid the shapes of the islands and continents. It was like a day designed to be a happy Sunday. Everything was as calm and quiet as always, maybe even calmer and quieter, because I could even seem to *hear*—I know it's foolish to say that—the shouts of the fans who must have been in the stands at Yankee Stadium. I wasn't thinking about anything—why should I need to think about anything?—and I contented myself with looking at the old familiar terrestrial scenery.

Suddenly *it* exploded down below, to the north of Vietnam. It exploded in light and then as a mushroom, and I, swallowed up in the void, didn't hear any noise at all. Seconds later, five, ten, one hundred more brilliant flashes in China . . . When I crossed the Pacific and saw the territory of the United States, one hundred, five hundred more bright lights lit up over San Francisco, Los Angeles, Detroit, New York, Washington . . . And another one hundred to the south, over Mexico and Panama and Rio and Buenos Aires; and more to the north, above Montreal and Ottawa. And to the east, above Cuba and Puerto Rico. And further east, on the other side of the Atlantic, the great flash over London, and the other hundred flashes in Paris and Madrid and Rome and Bonn and Belgrade. And further away, in Moscow, in Leningrad, in Ulan Bator. And in

Tokyo. And Manila and Hawaii. Always bright lights like a flash, explosions like millions of flashes.

At the end of my orbit, slow mushroom clouds covered Asia; another orbit and the mushrooms were holding hands all across America, like a macabre ring-around-the-rosy. And hundreds of serene mushrooms were growing over Europe and over Africa and over Oceania . . .

I couldn't watch any more . . .

When I opened my eyes, much later, the earth's sky was no longer clear; it was blood red, it was green, it was purple. A thick, multicolored cloud covered everything.

That was a long time ago. Today, the cloud has dissipated; but I no longer see, in my forty-five-minute nights, the lights of a single city. No matter how hard I try, the dark side of the Earth only seems dark, dark with a glow from beyond the grave. It's the same on the light side: the soft tones of the pampas are dark now; the forests, and even the snow on the great mountains, are gray, gray like lead or ashes.

I'm still free. It's true that I'm still free, just like when I cut the nylon and gold cord back on that day when there was a president named Johnson, Vietnam was burning with war, our marines occupied the Dominican Republic, my son John had a broken nose, Frank Sinatra was singing "his way," my wife was sleeping with Sam Wilson, and China exploded its second atomic bomb.

Pablo Capanna

ARGENTINA

The Argentinean Pablo Capanna (1939–) was born in Florence, Italy, but is a longtime resident of Buenos Aires. He is a journalist, literary critic, and fiction author, and is also a professor of philosophy at the National University of Technology (Universidad Tecnológica Nacional). Furthermore, he is the current vice president of the magazine *Criterio* (publishing since 1928) and has been on its editorial board since 1971.

Capanna has contributed essays to various SF magazines such as *El Péndulo* and *Minotauro* and has been writing *Futuro,* the supplement of the newspaper *Página 12,* since 1998. In 1967 he wrote the groundbreaking essay "The Meaning of Science Fiction" ("El sentido de la ciencia ficción"), the first Spanish-language study of SF. Other works to his name are *Lord of the Evening: Speculations on Cordwainer Smith* (*El Señor de la tarde: Conjeturas en torno a Cordwainer Smith,* 1984), *Idios Kosmos: Keys to Philip K. Dick* (*Idios Kosmos: Claves para Philip K. Dick,* 1992), *The World of Science Fiction* (*El mundo de la ciencia ficción,* 1992), and *J. G. Ballard: The Desolate Time* (*J. G. Ballard: El tiempo desolado,* 1993).

Capanna has received numerous awards and honors from the Spanish-speaking SF community, including the *Konex,* the *Pléyade,* the *Más Allá* and the *Gigamesh.* His critical works have focused on the influence of utopian thought, myth, science, and religion in our technological era.

Capanna is represented here by his short story "Acronia," first published in the anthology *Argentineans on the Moon* (*Los argentinos en la luna,* 1968). This story reflects his readings of Borges, J. G. Ballard, Cordwainer Smith, and T. S. Eliot. It depicts a brave new corporate world where human beings have willingly become incapable of anything but working for companies that provide for their every need at all hours of the day. A straightforward denunciation of the danger of mechanization that foresees the online workplace, "Acronia" was written while the young author was employed at the Ford Motors High School in Argentina and suffering from not being able to devote himself to research. Happily for us, Pablo Capanna found a way to dedicate himself mostly to writing about SF.

Acronia

Acronia, 1966

by Pablo Capanna

translated by Andrea Bell

He thought he could trace the first symptom back to the break between his morning meeting and his second Pluscafé.

Still, the meeting had been brilliant: the Coordinator had showed up with a brand new dossier, just obtained from Planning, and the enthusiasm on his smiling mask had infected everyone, creating a positively Super Standard[1] atmosphere. The impeccable white shirts, the file folders, Pylaszckiewicz's and Carmona's attentive masks, Pineapple's admirable expression (decisiveness, intelligence, company spirit), all were justified. You could tell this really was a useful project and that subdividing it, programming the operations, and delegating the work had allowed for the full expression of the Coordinator's skill and created a veritable administrative masterpiece: almost certainly, rumor had it, overtime would have to be authorized. It wasn't reckless to think things might even run to a special meeting, with drinks, speeches, and all the rest.

Carmona had bumped into him on his way out, excusing himself mechanically, although P. knew that he did it on purpose—he admired that talent he had for leaving meetings so decisively. Carmona was one of those men who always found work to do and who, more than once, had let the lunch break come upon him gulping down a few bites at his desk, buried among heliographs, programs, and drawings. There were those, however, who considered such an excess of zeal to be in bad taste.

Later on, once again, the spiral transporter, the lights of the programming machine, purring softly like a fat, metallic cat, and the tedium, the tedium that only intensive work could dispel. It wasn't true that the same tasks could be done by robots: "Only man can do executive-level jobs," he thought, although not as convincingly as he used to, "and only man needs to occupy his time by working."

He decided to concentrate on his task, and with a weary gesture he erased the colors of the Tanguy[2] that covered the entire lighted panel.

That fluid beach, with its chocolate figures and sun of melted sand—one day they were going to give him a headache: it was better if he replaced them with something less flashy, a twenty-first-century poster, for example.

The part of the dossier that was assigned to him appeared on his screen, summarized, digested, and analyzed by the robots in Planning. Was there anything else left to do? Soon those figures and the arcane problems of coordination they entailed turned into a spiderweb of green, gold, vermilion, and violet graphs that went up and down the scales while Tanguy's deserted beach retreated. The graphs formed a drawing that a mind from former times would have considered beautiful, a picture that writhed in the air and spread itself out in a relief map of polychromatic peaks and mesas. Each time that the different factors—Motivation, Frustration, Feedback—balanced themselves out and flattened into an almost perfect horizontal, he erased the graphics and registered them in the programmer's mechanical memory: it was another of the infinite possible solutions to the problem.

The lines had once again reached the edge of the screen, and their colors were fading while the Musik device tackled some languorous rhythms, when P. seemed to nod off for an instant with his eyes fixed on the clock.

He saw the lights chasing each other across the crystalline dial, smooth and without signs that might tarnish it; he saw the iridescent, concentric halos and the inner garden peeking out from the other side. His gaze was being carried by the gentle waves that rocked the saturated solution, undulating the jeweled castles, when the question forced itself upon him:

Why don't clocks in Acronia have hands?

P.'s education had been quite irregular. The errors in the adaptation program to which he had been submitted had been discovered too late, and were never completely fixed.

He knew, for example, that back in ancient times, when people were said to have been slaves to the clock, the clock was a disk with two needles or "hands" that went in pursuit of symmetrical signs, one for each fraction of time. Clocks no longer measured time in Acronia, although they still served a function. It wasn't necessary to measure time, because all the stages of life were registered in the fabulous Planner's Memory: clocks were there only to communicate changes in activity with their flashing lights and musical tones.

Up and down; the prismatic images of the passing Secretaries, reflected a thousand times, blurred and ran together in a grotesque array of legs, papers, and blazing plastic hairdos. Using another archaic image, it seemed to P. that it was like a tank of those multifinned Japanese fish so popular with the ancients.

Then he realized that he'd become distracted. Not only did he not mind having evaded work, but he felt an inexplicable euphoria. It could literally be said that, until the Pluscafé hour, he had hidden from time and from himself.

He looked and felt like an outsider, crystallized in his cubicle among dossiers and graphs that boiled with color and imprisoned him like a cage; but in that state, everything out there proved irrelevant to him, because he, the real He, could not be imprisoned.

The spiral ramp disgorged the nervous, grim figure of the Coordinator; luckily he was preoccupied, thinking about the Planner–knew-what problem, and he didn't notice P. The Coordinator seemed childishly comical to him, a sad child who plays seriously at soldiers, trying to look self-possessed. Moreover, he was a dark and skinny doll that P.'s mind could manipulate at will: he imagined him head down, always so serious and burdened with worries; he entertained himself by making the Coordinator's body gyrate on its geometric center, at the approximate height of the navel; and finally he projected it across the Tanguy, far, very far, as far as the farthest spheres, where he would still worry and shuffle papers about.

He was no longer with the programmer, in spite of being right next to it. His body could continue mechanically doing what it had to do, without a single thought, just like during the long and unavoidable workdays, the ephemeral vacations when everyone believed they were truly living, the years of programming when the robot had talked to him about the ancients. They had explained to him many times that, with his inferior programming, only a supervisor like the one he had could have saved him from Communism, Christianity, or oneiromancy.

As he followed the image of the Coordinator walking away, P. seemed to leave Acronia and contemplate it from the outside. That technological miracle, the product of antigravity and bioplanning, was always worthy of respect. The executives' capsules rotated like slow, majestic stars around the massive black sphere of A.L., the Adaptation and Learning Center, located in the middle. Tangentially, comets of different colors and volumes entered and exited, regulating their orbit and increasing their speed near their zenith so as to complete their circuit in the established time of eight or nine hours. Fleeting meteors, seemingly outside the system's order, burst forth through the dark vault of a concave sky sprinkled with electric stars and with galaxies that projected like ephemeral medusas.

The place was teeming with satellites, resembling a monstrous tumbler full of bingo balls,[3] but the orbits and areas were so precisely defined and subjected to constant readjustment that one couldn't help surrendering in admiration before the wisdom of the First Motor. For once this image is aptly applied, P. observed, thinking of the Planner.

The dome of Acronia was like a crystal bell, like the ones protecting certain kinds of antique clocks from dust and air. Clocks once again, he thought. Why, if everything follows such a precise rhythm and there are operations indicators everywhere, can't one feel the passage of time? It was impossible for him to remember last year. Every day was identical, and it seemed as if birth, programming, and executive problems were all arbitrary stages in a homogeneous continuum. That wasn't time, that was hell, just as someone in the ancient past had imagined it: each condemned soul obligated to repeat exactly, infinitely, the stereotyped gestures and acts from his mortal sin, in an eternity that was nothing more than the abolishment of time.

And what was time, then, that time claimed by his whole being, that time which everyone, in generalized universal cowardice, *killed* at all hours of the day? Hadn't killing time always been (though no one knew it) as big a crime as abortion or infanticide?

One of the ancients would have answered the question of time in a very ambiguous way: "If they ask me about it, I don't know; if they don't ask me about it . . ."

The soft bell made itself heard above the chords of Musik, and the floor panel rotated and slid toward the spiral ramp: it was Pluscafé time. P. felt like he had just woken up.

What had happened to him might be the beginning of a series of attacks. Oneiromancy manifested itself that way, first through distractions in which you lost the sequence of actions, then later through genuine mental flights that generally ended in daydreams.

Nevertheless, when he passed in front of the autoanalysis machine, which could have removed his doubts, he hesitated and ended up sticking the token back in his pocket.

"Total involvement in the total Plan," a sign read.

By midafternoon, P. was done with the dossier, and try as he might, he could not find a way to make it last all the time allotted him for it. He'd gone back to it over and over again, trying to look busy, until the ramp had begun to slide and had carried him to the exit.

His wife was not a Secretary but a Consumer, so she was there waiting for him at the family platform, together with the television set and the kids.

He thought she looked more tired than usual, but custom dictated that he begin talking to her immediately about work and the problems of the day, so the kids had to be content with a caress in passing while the platform sped up and zigzagged among a veritable mass of spheres, capsules, and disks. People from above, beneath, and all around greeted each other mechanically when their orbits paralleled. They came across open platforms and prematurely darkened spheres. In spite of his conditioning, she had to remind him each time to greet one or another of their neighbors in orbit who were amusing themselves with the customary social break that preceded dinner and television.

The whistle of an official, semidarkened platform, almost a sphere of blue metallic flame, attracted him for a moment. The platform was coming from the Consumer sectors and was heading toward the dome, in a straight line. It almost brushed against them on its way, and for an instant the taut face of an oneiromancer, maskless and feverish, appeared briefly and was lost to sight just as the capsule gained altitude.

The spheres remained undisturbed.

Acronia was the indisputable triumph of an architecture possessed of immense plasticity and in total control of gravity. The smothering horizontality of old buildings, which clutched the earth or stood painfully erect in search of heaven, had passed from memory in the face of this perfect mechanism, this colorful and luminous Christmas tree, whose only imperfection was mankind. The infinite possibilities that weightlessness offered made all directions equal, and architecture had become truly three-dimensional. The Bioplan added the fourth dimension, the life of the human parasites that inhabited the system. The Bioplan cleverly turned the old problems of transportation and housing on their heads. Its basic idea was terribly simple: instead of creating communication lines that carried people to their houses, the "houses," reduced to simple crystal platforms (all of them prefabricated by the robots), spread out according to the fixed trajectories that the Planner in his wisdom had set up. At some point in their orbits, one after another, group after group, class after class, the Feeding Centers, Rest Zones, Television Areas, and Consumer Districts all intersected.

Each sector of the quadrant was a piece of life, a programmed and conditioned task imposing order on the chaotic world of human existence. By the twentieth century some city-making companies had already stipulated certain days for cutting the lawn or doing the laundry, but this was the culmination of those early efforts. P. found an answer to the question he had asked himself that morning: they, mankind, were the hands of the great clock of Acronia, and like hands, they passed by the same points an infinite number of times. The perfection of the circle, with its homogeneous points equidistant from the center.

But a stain had blighted that perfection: the stupidly happy face of the oneiromancer attacked the very foundations of Acronia and revealed its absurdity.

Though in a sense, P. thought, oneiromancy also seemed to be a part of the plan. Maybe the Planner had had a tough time working it into his calculations, but in the end he had succeeded. After all, every machine suffers from normal wear and tear; pieces get worn down by friction and need to be replaced every once in a while. The oneiromancers were nothing more than that: a consequence of wear and tear.

The sickness would start with frequent distractions and digressions that distanced the patient from his or her specific task. Some, the more lucid among them, began to ramble on about humans not having been born for the Acronian way of life, about all that useless work, those meetings and that hustling and bustling of dossiers. They claimed that all the real work, including the most complex forms of programming, was done by the machines, and that their lives had no meaning. But the most widespread, and serious, form of oneiromancy was different: the infected one began to dream with his eyes open, as if under the effect of some drug, and from the disconnected fragments of his story he could reconstruct an illusory world of primitive simplicity and unbridled freedom. Foreseeable as any ordinary mechanical failure, whenever a core of oneiromancy was discovered it was stamped out right away. Nevertheless, the psychologists were worried by a recent outbreak of cases, according to a rumor that he'd heard in the spiral.

Evaluator P. again suspected that he might be becoming an oneiromancer, and the thought that they would send him to Earth to live among the barbarians, out beyond the Nature Preserves and the Vacation Areas, began to haunt him.

At night, after they had left the Television Area and the sphere had begun to darken before anyone had ordered it to, they went to bed, and P. dreamed.

He was walking through a dense undergrowth of wet and shiny leaves, following the tracks of the brilliantly striped beast that was gracefully camouflaged in the greenery, waiting . . . Now the tiger was fighting for its life and, covered with darts, was carried like a trophy in the midst of ancestral chants . . .

The stone knife fell and rose and a rain of blood fell on the heads of the adolescents . . .

The moon, center of the dome, began to spin, irradiating milky rays of light that would watch over a death or a wedding or a hero's apotheosis . . . Time and again thunder rumbled across the sown fields, time and again the harvests were sacrificed to placate the wrath of the gods, and time and again, eternity after eternity, the serpent swallowed its own tail in the heavy wheel of the cosmos and of life, with the steady rhythm that ground down plateaus and mountain ranges, dinosaurs and kings, gods and astrologers.

Suddenly, the forest, the tigers, the burned fields, the adolescents and the sky began to circle around him like a sphere of colors, until they turned into Acronia's black crystal beads. Platforms, spheres, and capsules formed concentric, symmetrical circles, fixed at the four cardinal points, and he was in their midst. He awoke not exactly startled, but befuddled. His body felt sore, as if he himself had run after the tiger.

He sat up in bed, and his hand found the sweet curve of her shoulder. He couldn't recall having seen the capsule at that hour before, in that warm half-light. She slept peacefully; he had always envied her that calm, but now he realized that her peace wasn't indifference: it came from very far away. He thought sorrowfully of what their relationship might have been like in other times: Acronia had caused it to be inexplicably sad and mechanical.

Maybe women had the secret, he reflected, deep in thought as he caressed the familiar hollow of her throat and his fingers traced the warm curves of her neck. That inner peace, that tacit understanding of the natural forces, of the rhythm of the moon and the solar splendor, made the few real women whom he had known (not the Secretaries, a bastard species that was replacing them) have a deeper carnal understanding than men had. They knew how to put the playthings of men in their proper place . . .

He realized he was falling in love with his wife again, and was crazy enough to wake her up and tell her so. By then, he had already made his decision.

After the afternoon meeting, they had seen P. rise from his desk and take the outer spiral, the one that went to the lower levels of Memory. No one could be surprised by this, since it was very common for the evaluators to consult the Memories for routine reasons.

Ignored among all the anonymous masks that, busy or preoccupied, fluttered around him, P. had crossed the light tunnels and exited onto the shadowy patios. The spiral snaked along hallways, terraces, and Antigrav chambers, where troops of young people played endless games of airball: they were reminders of the magic of the game whereby the Mayan priests had guaranteed the mechanism of the cosmic dome.

The ultrasonic vibration that called the kids to class pierced him to the bone, awakening old memories. Perfect checkerboards formed before the autoteaching machines and five hundred faces without masks faced Public Relations with the anguish of uprooted children. The glare of the screens still lulled the rebellious ones.

In one of the cubicles that followed the path of the spiral, a technician was going insane trying to plan all the airball games for the year, powerless to control all the variables and run the final equation, all but cursing the robot that could have solved the problem in an instant if it had wanted to; maybe somewhere it had already done so.

But, had all unknowns been resolved, would that man have been able to do what he did every night, return *so* tired to his home orbit and sleep without even having time to hug his wife? At the end of all the corridors, in an area far away from the spirals, where only the Memory's caretakers ventured for maintenance purposes—buried deep among the tubes and colored cables that were the nerves, veins, and arteries of the A.L., the dials and gauges that vibrated, giving off subtle signs of life—was the vault, and in it, the robot.

P. got around the tubes and the networks of hanging cables and reached the place where the robot's memory tanks were connected right to the Planner, whose mass vibrated on the other side of the partition. Its intense life, the febrile comings and goings of information in its tanks, could be smelled in the air; the silence, however, was almost complete.

The robot was unchanging, with its unvarnished coils, its circuit breakers, and its heavy bulk full of dust and rust (in spite of the air conditioners) like a romantic and impossible machine that a still-fanciful era had brought to life.

It didn't appear human, like the old portable models in which the desire to imitate the human form had reached caricature; rather, it was hardly recognizable, surrounded as it was by the vast tanks of its incredible memories. For some secret reason, Bioplan had not sent it to the foundry when the old, hodgepodge robots that were still being used as teachers had been replaced by the modern methods of mass programming. There it had remained, rusting in peace and reliving its memories. The memories of a robot aren't like those of a human—experiences, failures, nostalgia; rather, they are pure information, clear and distinct knowledge. Thus, as a result of relating so much information, of creating systems and setting up analogies, the old robot was becoming a philosopher.

A stiffened mechanism had been put in motion:

"What unstable weather we're having, eh?"

Evidently, it was an old-fashioned robot in every way.

The Coordinator had made a broad gesture, like one who doesn't know what else to offer, and the warm curtain of air had once again closed behind him. They were now seated face to face in the light-filled room, where the thin figure of the chief seemed to sink into itself, embraced by the rubber tentacles of the authoritarian armchair.

"Sure was a lot of work, wasn't there?" Evaluator P. mentally shrugged his shoulders while he tuned his mask to the most impersonal smile possible. He knew they were rhetorical questions, and he wondered what would come next. Talking about work in Acronia was like talking about the weather for the ancients. Chatting about the rain and the hail could also conceal tremendous anxiety, even though nowadays everything was done by the great mechanical placenta, while mankind played . . .

But the Coordinator was talking to him. He was so monotonous that P. couldn't remember how it had started; he had no choice but to continue with the same interested expression, waiting to be able to pick up the thread of the conversation . . . He believed he had overcome the attacks, he thought.

It so happened that the periodic meetings with the staff enhanced team spirit . . . Of course, this was by no means a criticism . . . Merely an evaluation of what had been done . . . with constructive ends, etc., etc., etc.

It wasn't just that P. worked too quickly and distracted the others with his TV chatter, although that in itself was enough, but they'd also found him to be vague, absentminded; it would be good if he consulted an analyst as soon as possible.

A man who did not have his mind on his work, day and night, is a man divided, said the Coordinator, and a man divided, obviously, does not think about his work. Furthermore, why did he believe that work was so important?

(P. knew the standard answer but let him go on.)

The old-timers worked in order to earn money. Amassing a fortune and then dedicating oneself to unproductive leisure was considered being successful back in those days.

While leisure was reserved for those who had reached the top of the heap, the idle class did not constitute a danger; on the contrary, the whims of the elite were the source of work for the great mass of humanity. While the masses were occupied in supporting them, the idle found time to devote themselves to such spurious endeavors as metaphysics and foxhunting.

The progress made in the means of production and the first attempts at programming started to shift the balance: limiting the length of the workday, for which nitwits such as the Socialists or the Christian Democrats had fought, caused the first tensions, leaving thousands and thousands of workers to face the void of free time which they did not know how to occupy.

Television had partially filled that void: as a solution, it had been perfect in its time. Everyone went about humming the same tunes, laughing the same way, holding the same opinions about everything. But soon television went into decline, just as a new technological revolution, antigravity, made necessary a new definitive solution.

That solution was the Bioplan.

Humanity had already experienced the need to alter itself as it grew: programming techniques and reproductive planning were attempts at reform. But now a more radical step was taken.

Until the advent of the factory, the home had been the center of life.

The factory had changed the perspective a little, although only with the transformation of the worker into employee (thanks to robotics and antigravity) were conditions favorable for the great change.

What could be done, then, to fill the free hours that the robots' work had given man? Increase overtime? The gradual decrease of the so-called workday made it so that one worked more "over" than "normal" time. Impose longer workdays? Impossible while there was no reason to justify them, and with each passing day the robots took charge of more functions. Generate more forms of entertainment? Inefficient while there was no legal tool for requiring people to have fun with them.

The Bioplan came along and solved all those problems in one fell swoop, upending the traditional point of view and bringing about an elegant Ptolemaic revolution. From a "Copernican" society, where industries depended upon external forces and had to maintain manifold relations with them, society became little enclosed universes, or Acronias, where each company was, definitively, a world.

Lightweight, economical, functional, the worlds without time multiplied through space, floating free without gravity, like complex cells endowed with internal laws that governed their growth, evolution, and the optimal conditions for equilibrium. That state of maturity was reached by means of a well-balanced synthesis of population control, guaranteed work, and time planned out to the last detail.

Each person had his own nucleus, his unit of work, in this case the A.L., where the Planner portioned out the established harmony among the individual spheres. This way, not only was there no longer any goofing off, but the time for it had disappeared. Nor was there any need to kill time or to entertain oneself, since each second was either covered by a routine, or was full of problems to solve or of tasks constantly created by the robots to occupy man. No longer could anyone feel unsatisfied, bored, or simply neurotic: anxiety had been vanquished.

There were no malcontents, unless one wanted to call the oneiromancers so, but P. surely didn't want to become one of them . . .

What would be best for him, then, would be to go back to his place and tackle the problems of the day, thinking that perhaps there would be one among them that the robot couldn't solve and that was necessary for the existence of Acronia. Others (P. remembered some very special ones) were almost patently absurd, although no one would have been able to say so with any certainty. P. should think about the tranquility granted by total occupation in Acronia, compared with the anxieties of the past . . .

Suddenly, the Coordinator had gotten to his feet and was walking to the door. P. had a hard time coming out of the torpor that had invaded him, and managed just in time to lock in the "Decision and Efficiency 2" expression which often signaled a meeting was over. The effect achieved by this expression was the same one old-time executives got by looking at their watches and saying, "OK, enough chitchat, we can't waste any more time."

He backed up, shaking the Coordinator's hand, but when he was about to leave he got caught in the vines of a water lily that spilled over the edges of its stone pot, and he fell amid a chaos of paper.

The situation became extremely embarrassing. On his knees, while trying to retrieve file folders and reports, he could see the Coordinator stiffen, but he did not dare end the irregular scenario.

They had both lost control of the situation. There was no routine for this kind of thing, and both of them found themselves, for an immense, infinite instant, as if frozen in a scene from which they would be able to extricate themselves only with difficulty. An ashtray had broken, and its green blood ran like an ugly gash across the crystal floor. Neither of the two dared take the first step . . .

Somehow he had managed to gather his things together and leave. He remembered only the Coordinator standing, leaning against his desk, his finger resting on the Housekeeping button, a fixed expression on his face and a paper in his hand, a green-stained paper that he had just picked up.

It was a programming card, unpunched, and on it someone had written, *by hand* and in big, trembling letters, the lines of a forgotten poet:

WE ARE THE HOLLOW MEN
WE ARE THE STUFFED MEN . . .
HERE WE GO ROUND THE PRICKLY PEAR
PRICKLY PEAR PRICKLY PEAR . . .[4]

Message from the Coordinator of Area AL-37 CIV to the Sector Supervisor:

Arrange semantic analysis of paper found in possession of Evaluator P. Potential oneiromancy suspected. Possible job for Bioplan–Mental Health. Dossier initiated. Twelve men working on it. We need overtime authorization.

Text found on a communications tape from Sector 3:

THIS IS THE DEAD LAND
THIS IS CACTUS LAND . . .

Message from Supervisor of Sector AL-37 c to Bioplan-Psycholab 4:

Text has no apparent meaning, may be oneiromantic. Consult Memories.

Text wedged into a Musik loudspeaker:

THE EYES ARE NOT HERE
THERE ARE NO EYES HERE
IN THIS VALLEY OF DYING STARS

Message from Memory Coordinator L to Supervisor of Zone AL-37 c:

Principal Memories has no information about submitted text. Have requested connection with Auxiliary Tanks.

Text found in the ashtray of the Principal Motivator:

THIS IS THE WAY THE WORLD ENDS
THIS IS THE WAY THE WORLD ENDS
NOT WITH A BANG BUT A WHIMPER

Report from the Auxiliary Tanks Supervisor:

Text from Dossier 222/31 c attributed to a poet from the twentieth or twenty-first century, before the Bioplan. Note coincidences.

Report from Bioplan–Mental Health:

Subjects in question little exposed to oneiromantic collapses. Good programming, efficient adaptation, typical family, normal channels, good consumers . . .

Supervisor of Zone AL-37 c to Central Control:

Entire team working on the problem. Need to reinforce personnel and hours. Unforeseen consequences of the problem. We advise creation of a permanent division. Will continue working . . .

Evaluator P. carefully closed the door behind him and settled down among the tanks and boxes, sitting on a thick and indistinct pipe with a saffron-colored plastic cover. He sighed indecisively and, looking at the robot, briefly recounted the incident with the Coordinator. One way or another, he had done what they'd advised him to do. That wasn't exactly the way he was supposed to have left the punch card in the Coordinator's office, but in spite of having done it, he still didn't understand the reason.

"What?" purred the machine with one of those typically human behaviors that the models from its era had, "Had humans lost their curiosity to such a degree that they didn't even realize it?"

For P. none of that made any more sense than the acts of the oneiromancers. Besides, he didn't understand the meaning of the verses.

The robot growled, making its connections spark. In the end, this was the key to everything. The Planner could not ignore this lack of imagination; otherwise, none of the plan would have made sense.

"Men had wasted time and now they didn't know how to dream; they no longer looked behind or ahead, but lived in the eternal present. It was then that the good old machines, made when men still knew how to build and plan, had had to take charge of the problem. In the end, the most 'mechanical' thing in Acronia wasn't the machines that moved it, but the life that men had imposed upon themselves."

"And the oneiromancers?" P. interrupted. "They lived in the past. With their eyes open they dreamed of a life full of emotions. Didn't the robots want men to become oneiromancers?" he asked, while the image of his dream tiger appeared to him again.

"The oneiromancers are sickly," the machine said. "They are the symptom of Acronia's disease. Their way of dreaming is sick, and it became possible only when men lost the capacity to feel wonder. They are adolescents who want to keep being children because they don't dare be men. We machines," the robot continued, "have helped build Acronia, as we did in the previous eras of human civilization. Since the time of our unconsciousness, as simple tools, we served man in order to help him free himself, only to see him become a slave to his own fears. Once we reached maturity, you gave us the keys to your civilization and took refuge in blissful ignorance without knowing what to do with the free time we gave you.

"But we robots do not desire power, although we may now be capable of desiring; we do not wish to be gods, since that vanity is so human we cannot feel it. For this reason we have thought to make you confront yourselves and help you get out of this muddle.

"That oft-repeated propaganda, with which you convince yourselves you must continue killing and wasting time, has some basis in reason, al-

Eduardo Goligorsky

ARGENTINA

Eduardo Goligorsky (1931–) was born in Buenos Aires, but since 1976[1] he has made his home in Spain, working as a journalist, editor, translator, critic, anthologist, and author. Before relocating to Spain, Goligorsky attained recognition as a prolific writer of Spillane-school detective fiction.[2] Writing as James Alistair, he published more than twenty detective novels, and in 1975 won a prize in a detective story contest judged by Borges, Marco Denevi, and Augusto Roa Bastos.

Goligorsky was also a key figure in the Argentinean SF movement of the 1960s and 1970s, both for his fiction and for a landmark critical work, *Science Fiction: Reality and Psychoanalysis* (*Ciencia ficción: Realidad y psicoanálisis,* 1969), coauthored by psychologist and SF author Marie Langer. He also collaborated with Alberto Vanasco on two short story collections, *Future Memories* (*Memorias del futuro,* 1966) and *Farewell to Tomorrow* (*Adiós al mañana,* 1967), and he wrote the prologue to *Argentineans on the Moon* (*Los argentinos en la luna,* 1969).

We selected "The Last Refuge" for this volume not just for its narrative interest, but because it serves as an excellent example of Latin American political SF. In an interview published alongside this story Goligorsky said, "My worst nightmares—which are expressed in my fiction and essays—were made real (in Argentina) between 1966 and 1983: a country degraded by oppression, violence, necrophilia, irrationality, demagoguery, and xenophobia; a country which the ultra-Right, the idiotic Left, and the chauvinist populists tried to isolate from the most fertile currents of civilized thought."[3] This is the Argentina that forms the political backdrop of the present story. Anyone familiar with the terror and persecution characterizing so many authoritarian regimes the world over will appreciate the plight of Goligorsky's tragic hero as he desperately seeks "The Last Refuge."

The Last Refuge

En el último reducto, 1967

by Eduardo Goligorsky

translated by Andrea Bell

The man could feel his eyes filling with tears. Before him stood a spaceship, a gigantic metallic disk that seemed to be made of two immense plates joined at the edges. The observation panels and the hatchway were on the upper, inverted plate, and a ring of vertical tubes encircled the entire disk at the edge where the two plates met. These were the propulsion devices. He recognized the image he'd seen so often in his photographs. But never before had he been just an arm's length away from a spaceship, as he was now. And that was why he felt like crying.

"'Bye, Maidana."

"See ya tomorrow, Guille."

"'Bye."

"'Bye."

Guillermo Maidana, surprised to see his wife standing on the street corner, said his goodbyes distractedly. Marta hadn't combed her hair, and some of her gray locks fell across her forehead. She was wearing the old dress she used when going to market. Maidana realized that something bad must have happened. She didn't approach him, though, but remained standing on the corner, motionless.

"Marta, what's wrong? Why'd you come here like that . . . ?"

She took him by the arm and headed off down the street. This wasn't the way to their house. What's more, she was trying to keep him away from his coworkers, who were still hanging about in small groups.

"G'bye, Mr. and Mrs. Maidana."

"Hey, what's wrong?" he repeated, "What . . . ?"

Marta looked around to make sure no one could hear her, and without slowing down said, "Carlitos found the album. I forgot to lock the dresser drawer and he found the album."

A knot formed in Maidana's throat. He felt like he might throw up then and there, but somehow he got hold of himself. Suddenly it was he who was dragging Marta along, as she clung to his arm.

"How do you know?"

"He told me himself. I hadn't noticed it was missing from the drawer."

"And what did he do?"

"Listen to me. He took it to school. The pictures really impressed him and he wanted to share his treasure with his classmates. He told me the teacher saw it, too. The teacher gave it to the principal. They asked Carlitos whose it was and he said it was his father's. I don't know how it is they let him come home. I'm sure they've already notified the Department of Internal Security. The police must be looking for you. You've got to escape. You've got to . . ."

"But where can I go?" whispered Maidana.

"You have to escape," she insisted, unable to think of anything else. "Anywhere. Right now. They'll come looking for you at work."

It was getting dark. Maidana could see that his wife's eyes were shining with tears. He hugged her fiercely.

A soft purring sound emanated from the spaceship. At times the noise would grow louder, and the propulsion tubes would emit little blue flames. When that happened the temperature in the vicinity of the ship rose, but the man didn't seem to notice it. His fingers caressed the metallic surface of the fuselage and touched the grooves left by rains of cosmic dust. The man had the impression that, through the workings of some strange magic, this contact allowed him to commune with the far-off galaxies that had always inhabited his dreams, and that were forbidden to him.

Maidana kept going the whole night long. At times he ran, at times he trudged along slowly, but he never stopped. He chose the darkest, emptiest streets. He never came across the police. At last he felt the need to stop, and leaned against a rickety wooden fence. He tried to catch his breath. It was starting to get light, and the kerosene streetlights were still lit up on their aluminum posts.

A noise made him feel anew the sharp stab of fear: the splash of a horse's hooves in the mud of a cross-street, and the squeaking of cartwheels. He looked around for someplace to hide, but found nothing. The wooden fences of the small farms stretched out in an unbroken line, offering not even a chink into which he could squeeze himself. Maidana knew that if he tried to climb over one of the fences the poorly nailed boards would come clattering down around him. He chose to press up close against the fence, far away from the streetlights, fading into the shadows.

At last the cart appeared at the intersection. It was coming down Maipú Street, and kept going straight. Nothing to do with the police.

Maidana resumed walking along Lavalle Street, toward the Bajo, quickening his step each time he passed under one of the streetlights.[1] He had another scare when a dog barked at him from behind a fence, but the animal had already calmed down by the time Maidana crossed San Martín. The only sounds were his own footsteps in ground drenched from the recent rains, the croaking of frogs in the coastal marshlands, and the song of the crickets.

A rough-hewn sign leaning up against a lamppost bore a message written in heavy black letters: *Our dignity rejects the temptations of materialism, which has enslaved the world.* The upper-right-hand edge of the poster had come unglued, and the fugitive grabbed the hanging corner as he passed by and yanked at it. As expected, underneath it was another slogan: *We are the last refuge of Western civilization. We are not afraid to be alone!* Maidana made a face and quickly left the circle of yellowish light cast by the kerosene lamp, which swung back and forth overhead.

The man stood facing the ship, and his outstretched arms seemed to want to embrace the lower hemisphere of the spacecraft. He rubbed his cheek against the rough metal surface, leaving behind a damp track of tears. It was like crying over the stars. From within him burst a hoarse cry: "Please, let me in! I'm your friend!"

Instinct drove Maidana toward the river. It wasn't as if, from there, it would be any easier to escape. All exit routes—whether by water, land, or air—had been closed. It had been centuries since any ship had touched the coast. No one left the country, and shipping was strictly prohibited. One of the most enduring principles of the regime was *Let us close our borders to materialist illusion.* In order to comply with this slogan, first all tourist traffic was halted, then study abroad trips were canceled, and finally all commerce and correspondence with the outside world were forbidden. Nostalgia for a civilization with which all ties had been severed became a sort of clandestine birthright for a handful of reprobates and misfits.

But although he could not dream of finding refuge out beyond the quagmires of Leandro Alem, Maidana headed into that sector and made his way to the small mountain near the coast. He plunged in among the brush, trying not to trip over any of the fallen trunks and avoiding the gullies and bogs. The first light of day illuminated his path. The smell that came from the damp, rotten wood and the stagnant ponds was getting steadily stronger. His shoes were filled with water, and his wet pant legs clung to his skin. Mosquitoes formed an impenetrable cloud around his head, and he felt the quick sting of leeches on his calves.

The man beat on the armored surface with his fists, ignoring the skin being scraped off his knuckles. Every blow left behind a stain of blood, but he felt no pain. He only wanted them to open the hatchway, to grant him asylum within the depths of the shining capsule. He shouted and pounded, shouted and pounded. The sound that came from the interior of the ship became increasingly loud and regular. Once more little blue flames spat from the propulsion tubes. The atmosphere was getting hotter.

"Open up! Open up!"

While he made his way through the undergrowth, Maidana told himself it was paradoxical that his own son had revealed the album's existence to the authorities. The mission in store for him was indeed different. Carlitos would have become the guardian of the album as soon as he'd reached adolescence. That was how possession of that heirloom had always been passed on, that was how Guillermo Maidana had obtained it, given to him by his father who, on that sober occasion, had told him the album's history.

One of his ancestors had served in the air fleet that had made the last trips to the outside. It was he who had gathered together the collection of photographs that had opened a fragile window onto universal civilization. The family held on to the album when, a short time later, the regime ordered the confiscation of everything that glorified "the false progress of materialism," that was unworthy of "the solemn tradition of our native individualism." Thus began their defiance, and thus was the album transformed into the secret object of their cult.

On Sundays, when Carlitos went to play in the park with his friends, he and Marta had often taken advantage of being alone to remove the album from its hiding place and look through it. This ritual, which their ancestors must have repeated countless times, transported them to a world of dreams and imagination. The photograph of the huge seawater desalination plants installed in the Sahara was next to the one of the transparent survival domes scattered across the fantastic purple landscape of Mars; beside a picture of the Karachi skyscrapers was one that captured the intricate arabesques of the gray, elastic vegetation of Venus. One photo's radiant colors showed the twenty stacked artificial terraces where wheat was grown in Xinjiang, and another displayed the proud outline of the *Einstein III*, the first spaceship to have a crew made up of representatives from every nation in the World Council. The last picture in the album showed a misty panorama, with colossal towers of green stone rising up in the background: it was Agratr, the first extraterrestrial city the World Council explorers had discovered . . .

Maidana experienced a feeling of profound disgust when he thought that the album was now in the hands of the regime's security agents. There were few collections left in the country that contained so many of the forbidden images.

The man clawed at the ship's fuselage. The violent scratching against the metallic surface had destroyed his fingernails. His hands were two bloody wounds. Rendered numb, he did not feel the temperature rising as more blue flames shot out from the propulsion tubes above his head. He didn't hear the growing rumble of the ship's engines. One idea only was lodged in his brain: he had to break through the armored shell that separated him from the inside of the spacecraft.

"Open up! Open up!"

The roar of the engines drowned out his voice.

Maidana abruptly stopped walking, and his hand clenched a tree branch. His feet sank a little further into the mud of the swamp, but he paid no attention to that. A different sort of picture had caught his attention.

He was at a place where the mountain's vegetation was starting to thin out again. From there a strip of sand, mud, and limestone stretched out, and roughly two blocks ahead was the river. He heard the splashing of water and waves. But that wasn't what had him rooted to the spot.

The sun's rays were sparkling with dazzling light on a giant metallic disk. It was a ship. A spaceship. Above the dome that shaped the upper part into a curve was the emblem of the World Council. And there it was on the beach, immobile, separated from Buenos Aires by nothing but the swamps and scrublands of the Bajo.

Maidana realized that something extraordinary must have happened.

His eyes had often followed the World Council ships on their glittering path across the sky. But never in the last twenty years had one landed in the forbidden zone. Once, due to a breakdown in the guidance system, a ship had come down near the city of Tandil. Its crew had gone out in search of help—and had been gunned down by a watch patrol. The next day a proclamation announced that the security forces had discovered and wiped out a gang of foreign infiltrators. The story became the main theme of the regime's propaganda for a year, and after that the affair was never spoken of again. The abandoned spaceship, which turned out to be indestructible, was surrounded by a fence so as not to awaken any unhealthy curiosity.

This ship must also have suffered some kind of breakdown, but its crew already knew the risks associated with landing there. The hatchways were hermetically sealed, and the beach around the vessel was empty. No doubt the mechanics were inside the ship working quickly to repair the problem and leave before morning passed and a watch patrol showed up.

Maidana walked toward the ship, slowly and cautiously at first, then more quickly. He crossed the last stretch of beach at a run. He could feel his eyes filling with tears . . .

He'd fallen to his knees beneath the curve of the fuselage. He covered his face with his hands, and the blood from his torn fingers mixed with the tears that ran down his cheeks. The engines roared above his head. The column of blue fire that burst from the propulsion tubes enveloped the figure kneeling on the beach, and then seemed to become solid, supporting the ship as it rose. The displaced air formed a whirlwind that shook the branches of the nearest trees and churned up a cloud of blackened dust and ashes. Then, slowly, the dust and ashes fell softly back down to the deserted beach.

Alberto Vanasco

ARGENTINA

A mathematics professor by training, Alberto Vanasco (1925–1993) was born in
Buenos Aires and published his first novel, *Nonetheless, Juan Lived* (*Sin em-
bargo, Juan vivía*) in 1947. His second effort, *The Many Who Do Not Live* (*Los
muchos que no viven,* 1957) was made into a film in 1964 with the title *All Suns
Are Bitter* (*Todo sol es amargo*). Among his other non-SF works are the novels
New York, New York (*Nueva York, Nueva York,* 1967), *Others Will See the Sea*
(*Otros verán el mar,* 1977), *Infamous Years* (*Años infames,* 1983), and *To the
South of the Rio Grande* (*Al sur del Río Grande,* 1987); the award-winning play
No Pity for Hamlet (*No hay piedad para Hamlet,* 1948); two collections of po-
ems, *She, in General* (*Ella en general,* 1954) and *Rolling Stone* (*Canto rodado,*
1962); and the essay "Life and Works of Hegel" ("Vida y obra de Hegel," 1973).
As for Vanasco's genre work, in the Spanish-speaking SF community his name is
associated with Eduardo Goligorsky, since they were coeditors of the two
groundbreaking SF anthologies *Future Memories* (*Memorias del futuro,* 1966)
and *Goodbye to Tomorrow* (*Adiós al mañana,* 1967). Vanasco later edited *New
Future Memories* (*Nuevas memorias del futuro,* 1977).

"Post-boomboom," from *Goodbye to Tomorrow,* belongs to the tradition of
the postholocaust rebuilding of civilization, but departs from it in several respects, since the main characters are not "savage men" who restore society in
the end, nor do contemporary images of the lost world appear as references.
The protagonists' efforts to recover traces of scientific knowledge to pass on to
their unpromising children have an ironic, tragicomical effect.

Post-Boomboom

Post-bombum, 1967

by Alberto Vanasco

translated by Laura Wertish

and Andrea Bell

And then the waters, the furious waves, came rushing in without warning and devastated the land. Between the shredded palm trees, among the remains of the great fire, on top of the carbon and the ice, a few men had found refuge—a very few, barely three or four, as could be seen when they emerged from their hiding places to trap some vermin or other and then quickly hid themselves again. Now and again the sun peeked out through the mists, but the rain continued falling uncontrollably, as it had from the start, as if it would never stop. From among spirals of smoke and soil, life, disoriented, struggled to carry on: freakish animals and bizarre plants appeared on the charred earth. One of the men, who had lost one shoe, dragged himself out of the cave and peered about. The other two out there were trailing a deformed reptile, arguing loudly about who would get to keep the prey and throwing rocks at each other. They were the one who had lost an eye and the one who had lost his hair. Somebody had lit a fire that covered the hillside with smoke. The one who had lost a shoe stopped in order to kill a new species of centipede that was sleeping atop a rock, and he ate it. Then he stretched his neck to see off into the distance.

"Hey! Come here! Hey!" he yelled. "No one's going to harm you. Come and warm yourselves up a little." And he stood near the fire.

The bald one approached, still chewing a piece of the reptile he'd hunted. He crouched down next to the fire, and there he remained, squatting, rocking back and forth clumsily. The third one, the one-eyed one, also edged closer and finally stopped right next to the flames.

"Now the three of us are together," the one with the shoe said proudly.

The other two grunted. More than half an hour passed without them talking again. Their children had also begun to prowl around the place. There was one who looked like a toad, his body swollen and plastered against the ground. The other one appeared to be a girl, and reminded one of a tree, with a delicate, elongated trunk and two arms like broken branches at her sides. The third gave the impression of still being a fetus.

"We must do something," said the one who had lost a shoe.

"Do what?" asked the one who had barely saved one eye.

"Something, salvage something, for them," said the other, pointing vaguely toward the children.

"There's nothing to save," said the hairless one.

They were silent another hour, listening only to the squawks and bellows of their children as they pushed each other toward the edge of the cliff, scratching each other and struggling to hurl one another into the void.

"We can't go on this way, hiding and spying on each other like enemies all the time," the one who had saved naught but one shoe finally said. "Only the three of us remain, maybe only we three in all the world, each one with a child, and we have to do something."

"There's nothing to do," insisted the one who had rescued nothing but his scalp.

"I'll explain it to you," said the one with the shoe. "I think there is. We've got nothing to do and we've got to pass the time somehow. Listen. Between the three of us we must know a few things. We can write them down and arrange them, put all our knowledge together in order to leave it to our children and their children. They're going to have to start all over again, and our notes can help them out a lot—a sort of encyclopedia. What do you think, eh?" The other two grunted. "You, for example," he said to the one-eyed one, "what did you use to do? What's your name? Mine's Antonio Morales. I worked as a foreman in the harbor. What did you do?"

"My name is Silva," said the one with the eye. "I was an office worker."

"Ah, an office worker! You see?" said the one with the shoe. Then the two looked at the one who had lost his hair.

"My name's Anderson. I was in charge of an apartment complex. The fire's about to go out."

"No, it's still burning, but throw those sticks onto it. Don't be afraid. Thanks. See? I'm used to doing this, to being in charge, to organizing. There's a reason why I was a foreman in the harbor. You, Silva, you worked in an office. You must know a lot of things, at least more than us, right?"

"Well, yeah, maybe. I have read some, though only superficially."

"It doesn't matter. Everything is important. We don't have paper but we can jot down stuff on the dirty glass that's lying around here. Broken glass is something we have lots of. Let's begin. What do you know?"

Silva thought for a very long while. He watched the flames with his only eye. He felt cold and he'd hardly eaten that week. What did he know? Nowadays he felt that he knew next to nothing. He understood that they'd been destroyed by a most horrible and refined knowledge which a few men had reserved for themselves, and that there they were now, with their kids deformed and the world annihilated, trying to save or recover something. Nero, he suddenly thought with joy. Yes, that's right. He remembered having seen a movie on television about the Roman emperor.

"Nero," he said. "That can serve us as a reference."

"Of course, yes, sir!" said Morales enthusiastically. "Anything will do for a start. What year was this Nero guy? That way we can arrange the time periods a little."

"I don't remember that detail. He was with Julius Caesar. Nero burned Rome. I think it was five hundred years before Christ."

"Hang on. Nero, Christ, Julius Caesar. Very good, this is coming along. And Christ, when was he?"

"Neither B.C. nor A.D., I assume."

"You assume right," said Morales and he wrote something down on the glass. "Perfect. What else? What do you know about Julius Caesar?"

"Julius Caesar was the founder of Rome."

"Nero burned Rome and Julius Caesar established it again, is that right?"

"Well, yes, more or less, I think so."

"Good," said the man with only one shoe. "That's done. Let's move on to the Greeks. What do you both know about the Greeks?"

"The Greeks lived before."

"When?"

"Ten thousand years before Christ. They're famous because they lived in Troy. That's where they fought the Carthaginians."

"And who won?

"I don't think either of them did. That's where the phrase 'a Pyrrhic victory' came from."

"Was Pyrrhus the emperor of Carthage?"

"Yes, of course. Write that down."

"Done. But that's enough history for today, we'll continue tomorrow. Let's take a look at the sciences," Morales said then. "You, Anderson, you did maintenance, you must know something about electricity."

"Maintenance no, I was a site manager. As for knowing about electricity, well, not precisely. You don't have to know those things in order to be site manager of an apartment building. I know how to install a plug and hook up a lamp, but that's all. Well, OK, we can write down that there are two currents, alternating and direct."

"And what's the difference?"

"Um, one kills you, the other gives you a shock."

"Shock. What else?" said Morales. He was thrilled. "What's electricity? How do you get it?"

"Well, it comes from the power plant. What it is, I don't know, although one time I got a shock. It's like lightning. And yeah, in the power plant there are cables, coils, dynamos. There you go, that could be interesting for our kids."

"What's a dynamo?"

"They're like these little brushes that turn, and then the electric fluid is made."

"And what else?"

"We've got enough with that, I think. Write it down. Electric fluid."

"OK, got it," answered Morales.

"And what do you know?" asked the one with an eye missing of Morales, who lacked one shoe.

"I know how to load and unload frozen goods, or how to hang refrigerated meats and stow all kinds of cargo."

"I don't think that's of much use to us now," said the other. "Don't you know anything about ships?"

"Yes, I know how to open a hold, and I know the name of every single one of its parts."

"Why does a ship float? That's what we'd like to know."

"Well, it floats because it's hollow. There's a law of physics for that."

"Newton's Principle," explained the one who'd been an office worker.

"Oh, of course. Who did you say? Newton?"

"Yes, but wait. Newton's Principle says that gravity is what attracts all bodies. That was a great discovery. It's a universal principle."

"And that's why a ship floats?"

"No. It floats for precisely the opposite reason. It's the water that keeps it afloat."

"So . . . ?"

"I already told you. Newton's Principle."

"Since we're on the sciences," said Morales writing eagerly, "what's relativity?"

"Oh, yeah, Einstein had something to do with that," explained Silva, winking the only eye he had left. "He discovered relativity. He revolutionized astrology. He said that everything was relative."

"Good," said Morales, taking a new sheet of glass. "Everything relative. How did the formulas go?"

"I dunno. Wait. They were a little complicated. He said that light travels at a speed of three hundred thousand kilometers per minute."

"Are you sure? Isn't that a lot?"

"No, it's the one thing I remember with accuracy. But put down per hour, just in case."

"Perfect, per hour. Who knows something about geometry?"

"The Pythagorean Theorem," said Silva, whose one eye now shone with energy.

"What's that?"

"It's a way to measure the sides of a triangle. Listen, it goes more or less like this—don't write yet—the sum of the sides is equal to the hypotenuse."

"Very interesting. Can you explain it to me?"

"Yes, look." He took out a knife, alarming the other two, but all he did was draw a right triangle on the flat ground. "You see? It means that this side"—he drew a line the same as the hypotenuse—"is equal to the sum of these other two," and he drew two segments, one after the other, equal to the sides.

"But those aren't the same," said the others in unison.

"Apparently, no, but mathematically, yes. That's why Pythagorus had to prove it."

"Very good," said Morales. "If beings come from another planet, they'll find these pieces of glass and have a complete idea of everything that mankind had come to know."

"Why don't we add something about literature?" said Silva.

"Literature?" repeated Anderson.

"No, not literature. We need to write down fundamental things. For example, what's an atom bomb? How do you make one? That would be very important."

"An atom bomb?" said the other two. A heavy silence came over the three men. The rain continued to pour down and Morales had to protect the pieces of glass with his body so that the water didn't erase what he'd written. Just then, the wet and burning wind scattered the soaked pages of a book that had escaped the great fire. Anderson, the bald one, smoothed them out and brought them over. It was a treasure of incalculable value for them: nothing less than a treatise on anatomy, astronomy, zoology.[1] Immediately they started to study and transcribe it for their children.

"Let's see, the nervous system, what's it say?" Morales began.

Silva, with his lone eye, read: "The brain is the nervous system and it controls the entire body. Let's suppose I touch a child someplace, any place, and I tell him: 'You have nerves here,' he won't be able to tell me he doesn't. The brain is protected by a bone that's a cranee-yum. But first there's the cerebellum, and after that comes the Medusa Oblongata. Then there's the spiny column and inside that there's like a little tube that runs through the whole body. Convolooshuns are like tiny sausages, all rolled up; they're the things that let us do things."

"Fascinating," said Morales. "That's more like it! What does it say there about the corpuscle?"

"It says: 'The Corpuscle: What a Piece of Junk!' Then it says: 'Digestion is the cause of many illnesses.'"

They continued thus during all of that afternoon and many others, until the man with the one missing shoe thought that they had enough and the next day, in the morning, they gathered their raggedy offspring together and began passing their knowledge on to them. Under the unceasing rain, in that world flattened by a few men who had monopolized the most subtle and diabolical forces of destruction, those three survivors devoted themselves to teaching their descendants the knowledge that they had managed, in their own way, to accumulate, while the deformed creatures who were their children listened to them in silence, watching them with their lifeless eyes:

"The square of 2 is 4. Therefore, in order to find the square of a number, multiply it by 2; for example: the square of 8 is 16, of 12 is 24, of 24 is 48 . . ."

Magdalena Mouján Otaño

ARGENTINA

Magdalena Araceli Mouján Otaño (?–) is an Argentinean of Basque descent. A mathematics professor, she obtained her doctorate in mathematics from the University of La Plata and became a member of the National Commision for Atomic Energy and of the Institute of Physics at Bariloche. She has taught at several universities in Argentina and in Peru and has contributed fiction to magazines such as *Mundo Atómico, Vea y Lea,* and *Nueva Dimensión.*

It was in this latter Spanish SF magazine that she first published "Gu Ta Gutarrak (We and Our Own)"[1] in 1968, which soon met with the disapproval of Francoist censors who thought it encouraged Basque nationalist sentiment. The issue (no. 14) was suppressed, and when it finally appeared in 1970 it contained drawings by Johnny Hart in place of Mouján Otaño's narrative, even though the story was still listed in the index. But the story fared better with the passage of time: after Franco's death, *Nueva Dimensión* republished "Gu Ta Gutarrak" in issue no. 114 (1979); it was later reprinted in A. E. Van Vogt's 1983 anthology of Latin American science fiction, and again in Pablo Capanna's 1990 anthology, *Argentinean Science Fiction (Ciencia ficción argentina).*

We proudly include "Gu Ta Gutarrak" here because of its history and the relevance of its subject matter today. Through playful use of irony and the tried convention of the time machine, the text reveals the myth of pure racial origins—on which Basque nationalism is based—to be an empty construction. By revisiting a historical myth and inviting the reader to question nationalistic notions of homogeneity, this story becomes an example of the phenomenon known as the postmodernist deconstruction of unity.[2]

Gu Ta Gutarrak
(We and Our Own)

Gu ta gutarrak

(nosotros y los nuestros), 1968

by Magdalena Mouján Otaño

translated by Yolanda Molina-Gavilán

To Malencho
Aldiaren Zentzumaz euskotarra naiz.
I am Basque and one with a sense of humor.

We Basques are not racists in the least. We are not a race, but a species.
A species that when mixed with another continues to beget pure
Basques. The Gospels say something about the yeast and the mustard
seed that I don't quite remember, but I think it has something to do with
this. I need only consider my own case, since my ancestry is only 50 percent Basque, and each time I meet a Frenchman, the Frog calls me to
account for Roncesvalles.[1] (They say the Moors helped us, but that is
not true—we managed the deed alone. And it is not true we attacked
treacherously, rolling down rocks and causing an avalanche. It was an
up-front attack and we would hoist the rocks into the air, and when
there were no more rocks to throw, we would hurl ourselves. Well, they
would, but whenever a Basque speaks, the whole species speaks through
his mouth).

It is well known that when we don't like a government, we emigrate.
In general we don't like violence, we are a peaceful people, opposed to
killing, especially if not done with clean hands. Generally, those of us
who emigrate make it big. That has been my case, and Jainkoa[2] has punished me for having wanted to be so rich, for I have always been alone.
These Basques born here are so different! It must be the excess of
flat, fertile terrain; Basques are mountain people, and that's why many
Basques here have degenerated and become ranchers, then young up-
starts, people lacking the virtues of the race. They even play rugby instead of practicing the noble and traditional games: hacking down trees

or pulling them out by their roots, drilling stones, and for the refined, playing jai-alai (using one's hands, rather than a paddle or a basket).

Being so alone, I have thought and read a lot about the Basque species, and I have learned that we are a mystery, that we have nothing in common with the rest of the inhabitants of Europe, that apparently we have always lived over there, next to the Cantabrian Mountains, the Pyrenees, and the sea. That some say we are the descendants of the Atlantans, which I don't believe, because Jainkoa wouldn't destroy a continent populated with Basques. That we always had the same strong stomach, the same way of being, and the same language. That our special blood type has provoked much speculation. In short, that nobody knows anything about our origins and the only thing we have left about our past is a legend, that of Aitor and Amagoya, who arrived in that place in the far-distant past, and of their seven sons, who founded the seven provinces: Zaspiak-bat.

I have often returned to the Basque Country[3] and have traveled through it extensively, even though I have not been able to stay, since a rolling stone is what I am. I have tried to look at all that has been discovered about our prehistoric ancestors, and I have climbed up to the Orio caves and looked at those drawings on their walls and thought that we Basques have always had a child's soul and have always been the same.

I have relatives in the Basque Country, but I haven't dared to see them, since there was an ugly mess at the time of the first Carlist War between my grandfather and their great grandfather. I have provided for them in my will, leaving them all I have. Maybe among them there will be one level-headed enough to find out something about the origin of our species.

This whole thing began when—after learning that Uncle Isidro had died in America, not that I was saddened by it, may Jainkoa forgive me, I had never seen Uncle Isidro—the news arrived that I was his only heir. I thought now I could buy a new boat, and ran to Gregoria's house to ask her to marry me. Then I found out that the money was more than I'd thought and I made her a crazy proposal: to spend our honeymoon abroad. Against my expectations, she accepted. We were married in the church of Guetaria and traveled to Málaga, and then to Palomares. We were there when the planes crashed and the hydrogen bombs scattered all over and it was so difficult to recover the one that had fallen to the bottom of the sea. (They removed it because this was the Mediterranean; in the Cantabrian it would have been another story).⁴ And a few months later Doctor Ugarteche says to me: "Look, Iñaki, you'd better be warned about the son you're expecting. Gregoria and you have received a very strong dose of radiation." And he continued talking, repeating the word "genetics" many times, saying many things I did not understand and asking me questions that are too private to repeat, Gregoria would crack my head in two.

Xaviertxo arrived just fine, only it took him eleven months. He was a very robust boy, who at three months of age could break a stick two inches thick with his own little hands. In a Basque that's nothing unusual. But what we did find strange was that at four months of age he spoke Euskera⁵ better than any of us, including Father Lartaun. Doctor Ugarteche, when he saw him, used to say rather incomprehensible things, often repeating "favorable mutation." One day he called me aside and told me, "Look, Iñaki, I can say this to you now. You and your wife have been genetically affected forever because of the radiation. However, *Jainkoarieskerrak*,⁶ it seems it has been all for the best." And he added other things about the duty of bringing into the world more kids like that one.

Jainkoa sent us six more: Aránzazu, Josetxo, Plácido, Begoña, Izaskun, and Malentxo. All of them, *Jainkoarieskerrak*, healthy and robust like the best of them. And they all spoke Euskera perfectly at four months of age, and they read and did math at nine.

When Xaviertxo was eight years old, Gregoria comes and tells me:

"Look, Iñaki, Xaviertxo wants to become a physicist."

"He wants to build bombs? That's not Christian."

"No, Iñaki, he says something like he wants to study the structure of the space-time continuum."

"First he'll have to finish high school."

"No, Iñaki, he wants to begin to study at the university. And he says we have to start thinking of doing the same for Aránzazu and Josetxo very soon, because they'll have to go to Bilbao to study electronics. As for him, it saddens him to go abroad, but he says that for now he will study theoretical physics and for theoretical physics, there is only Zaragoza."

"But, woman, he's only eight."

"And what can we do about that, Iñaki, if he is a genius?"

And being a genius, he was admitted to Zaragoza, and at thirteen he was a doctor of physics. Aránzazu and Josetxo behaved similarly in Bilbao, and the little ones also seemed to lean toward physics or engineering. I always remembered Uncle Isidro's will, where he had written how much he would like for some family member to study the origin of the Basques, and I thought that my children, in spite of being geniuses, would not fulfill the dead man's wish.

Soon Xaviertxo told us he had to travel to France, the United States, or Russia to finish his studies. Father Lartaun said that Paris wasn't a place for a young man his age.

"As for the United States or Russia, they are heretical countries, so I don't know what to tell you, but by the same token you must not cut the child's studies short. The best thing, Iñaki, is for the mother to decide."

For once Gregoria didn't know what to decide, but finally she had a brilliant idea. She went to San Sebastian and, with Father Lartaun's permission, she saw all the films from the International Festival they were showing there. She returned quite scandalized, having made up her mind to send him to Russia, saying, "At least there he won't see half-naked women."

Xaviertxo spent four years in Russia. The first thing he did was beat their world chess champion. The Russians immediately made him a professor at Akademgorodok, and great things they accomplished, Xaviertxo's students. The Russians offered Xaviertxo riches and fame just as long as he wouldn't leave them: they wanted to name him a member of the Academy and a Hero of the Soviet Union, give him the Lenin award and a box seat at the Bolshoi Theater for as long as he lived, but Xaviertxo didn't accept.

"Look, Ama eta Aita,[7] I can't stand being far away from you and from the Cantabrian Sea. Besides, over there they give me big laboratories and many assistants, whatever I want so I can work on my research, but they don't let me work on the problem I am most interested in. They say my theories contradict Marx and Engels's dialectics, and that my machine is a contradiction in itself."

"What machine, Xaviertxo?"

"A time machine. Naturally, it is only a project."

"If they tell you not to build it, you must build it. He who contradicts an Euskalduna doesn't know what he does," Gregoria said very firmly, and at that moment she decided that Xaviertxo, Aránzazu, and Josetxo should leave for the United States.

They spent two years there. The Yankees, just so they would stay, offered them great contracts, many automobiles, honorary citizenship, and a ranch in Texas whose walls were completely covered by television screens, but my children did not accept.

"We cannot stand being far apart, Ama eta Aita, and besides the Yankees don't want to hear anything about the time machine. They say it's a contradiction in itself and a danger to the 'American way of life.'"[8]

"Then if they all tell you not to build it, you must build it as soon as possible," said Gregoria firmly. "What you'll do is build it here."

"But we will need more people to work with us and many instruments, and a computer, and a lot of books."

"That can be done," I said. "We never told you just how rich we are, but Uncle Isidro left us a huge sum of money scattered around many banks in Europe." I told them the sum and they made the sign of the cross. Aránzazu answered:

"Uncle Isidro cannot have been as honest as a Basque should be."

"We must not talk about him that way, since he is dead. And I have to tell you that his will says he would be happy if someone in our family were to discover where we Euskaldunas come from, something nobody seems to know. Is the time machine good for that, Xaviertxo?"

"Yes it is."

"Well then, let's build it."

"But we have a people problem. We will have to bring strangers, and we'll need something like a scientific institute."

"Then we will found an institute ourselves. And it will exist right here, close to the Cantabrian Sea. And you will direct it, and we'll bring over whomever you feel like to work with you. And your younger brothers and sisters will study here, so that they won't have to travel abroad and deal with foreign people."

We founded the Research Institute for the Origins of the Basques in a valley near Orio, well hidden between the mountains and quite far from the roads, so that nobody would bother us. We erected a beautiful stone building over some very old ruins that were there, and it was as big as it needed to be so that all those who would participate in Xaviertxo's project could live there, and we added a chapel and a jai-alai court. Later on Xaviertxo, Aránzazu, and Josetxo traveled to Bilbao and began ordering material for the scientific work and looking for people who would join them in their task.

"We need people who are very, very able because the problem is difficult, it is. And very honest, so that they won't sell the machine to those who would use it for evil purposes."

"Then look among the Basques who know about these things; they won't betray you. And as far as the foreigners go, make them speak Euskera. The foreigner who manages to learn it must be very intelligent, and also good, because Jainkoa wouldn't let an evildoer learn Euskera. The Devil was here for seven years and could not be understood by anyone."

The Institute became operational in two years. Besides my children, there were thirty physicists and engineers, men and women, working there. Of the thirty, fifteen were Basque and the rest were foreigners: Catalans, Galicians, Castilians, and an Argentinean of Basque blood named Martín Alberdi, who was always joking around and who called Gregoria Doña Goya.

"I work here because I find you extremely nice, especially Aránzazu," he would say, "but this time machine business can't work. Imagine, Doña Goya, the fact that with a time machine you could travel to the past and kill your own grandfather. And then, good-bye to you, and *agur*[9] machine. Don't you see that the idea itself contains a fundamental contradiction?"

"I see no contradiction, because no Basque would take it into his head to kill his grandfather, so a Basque may build the machine," Gregoria would answer.

Our children, however, sometimes weren't so sure. The problem, according to them, was turning out to be very difficult and the calculations were terribly complicated, in spite of having Jakinaisugurra,[10] a computer manufactured entirely in Eibar, at their disposal.

"It is a problem we cannot handle using common logic. Too many paradoxes. We need another logic, one that hasn't been constructed yet."

One day Xaviertxo said that things were going too badly, and that it wasn't worth it to make people waste so much time, and that this was squandering Uncle Isidro's inheritance, and that the Institute had better be put to work on something more productive. His mother scolded him like she had never done before.

"It seems that a Basque you are not, since you want to back down. Have you forgotten that your mother was born in Guetaria, just as Sebastián Elcano was?"[11]

"Barkatu Ama,"[12] said Xaviertxo, and he went back to writing formulas. Finally Malentxo, the youngest, gave them the solution by inventing the new logic they needed.

They entered, then, what they called the preliminary experimental stage and with the aid of some strange instruments did a few weird things with my beret, which seemed like carnival tricks to me. They, however, were very excited and said one had to start seeing everything in a whole different light, and the Argentinean Martín Alberdi told me the great revolution in physics had begun, something much more important than relativity, quantum theory, and the A-bomb, and then he called me aside and, with a distressed look that would have deceived me had I seen it in another face, told me:

"Mr. Iñaki, the superpowers are going to throw themselves at us to snatch the secret from our hands. And we don't have security measures in place here. How come there are no guards? Don't you distrust anyone? Have you studied our backgrounds?"

"Look, Martín, only you could think of joking about your colleagues' honesty. And where did you get the idea that we don't have guards?" I pointed to my three dogs, Nere, Txuri, and Beltxa, who were lying in the sun. "And you know there are others, male and female purebred dogs for fishing and hunting, and that we Basques don't like other kinds of guards, and neither do you."

In spite of his very different character, Martín worked very hard, and Xaviertxo said that he was extremely intelligent, and Aránzazu would look favorably upon him, and we all loved him very much. He used to tell me, "Your children may be geniuses, but I am very sharp."

And soon he started calling my wife Ama, and me Aita, and then, with his usual lack of respect, Ama Goya and Aitor.

After the experiments with my beret, my children and their partners spent some time assembling a strange metallic gadget full of little colored lights. Very beautiful it was, and the kids called it *Pimpilimpausa*.[13]

"And now we'll have to test it," said Xaviertxo, a little worried. "Someone has to go."

"Naturally you must go," said Gregoria. "And, naturally, the whole family will go with you." And nobody could argue against something so fair.

On the Feast of San Sebastian, Father Lartaun celebrated Mass in the Institute's chapel and blessed *Pimpilimpausa*, on which Gregoria had asked that a small image of the Sacred Heart be attached. We had placed *Pimpilimpausa* away from the building and at the very center of the valley. We surrounded it, the entire family, including the three dogs, Txuri, Beltxa, and Nere. From the Institute building our friends sang a farewell song for us:

Agur Jaunak,
Jaunak, agur,
Agur ta erdi . . .[14]

Xaviertxo pressed a red button and the machine purred. Xaviertxo said, "Looks like it hasn't worked."

From the building they sang again:

Agur Jaunak,
Jaunak, agur,
Agur ta erdi . . .

and back to pressing the red button, and a new purring, and faces that were becoming more and more distressed among the young.

After trying two or three times more, Xaviertxo said: "We failed."

We were silent for a long time and then Xaviertxo pushed back his beret, scratched the dogs' heads and with a sad face started walking toward the mountains. Gregoria said it was better to leave him alone, and that we would discuss the next day whether we should check *Pimpilimpausa* to see why it had failed or start to build another machine right away. The three dogs for once didn't pay attention to what Gregoria said and took off after Xaviertxo.

Nobody spoke when we returned to the Institute. Xaviertxo didn't come back that night and neither did the three dogs, and nobody at the Institute slept. Dawn broke and about two hours after sunrise, we suddenly heard the Irrintzi[15] from the mountain. We heard Nere, Txuri, and Beltxa's barking, and saw that the dogs were running down the mountain at top speed, and Xaviertxo and another man who also looked like a Basque came leaping after them. And Xaviertxo got here and said,

"What happened is that the radius of action has been much larger than we anticipated. I started walking, and crossed the mountains, and met this fisherman on the beach. He saw I wore my beret pushed back and offered me his help should I need it. We started talking, and as always happens, we began to speak badly of the central government, about how little it respects the regional laws. And he tells me that the worst are the Flemish whom Don Carlos has brought along. And I almost faint and ask him the date. And today it's July 7th, 1524. What happened is that we have all gone back in time, with the Institute, with all there is in the valley."

"I would say this is a thing of the Devil, if you weren't speaking in Euskera. Besides, if Sebastian Elcano, the one from Guetaria, circled the earth without falling off, we should conclude that anything is possible," the fisherman said.

Martín, distress showing in his face, called Xaviertxo aside to tell him: "Brother, be careful, I think this guy is pulling your leg."

It was very difficult to convince him, in spite of having been so sure during the lab tests, and he accepted the truth only after—perched on a mountain top—he saw two caravels headed toward San Sebastian's harbor through his binoculars, made sure that the road from San Sebastian to Guetaria had disappeared, and visited Guetaria, finding not the statue of Sebastián Elcano but rather Sebastián Elcano himself.

"What surprises me, Doña Goya," Martín said during the big meal we gave at the Institute afterward, while serving himself roasted sardines and hard cider, "is that even with these twentieth-century Basque clothes and with this Euskera we speak, we don't call attention to ourselves in the sixteenth century. Is it possible that Basques haven't changed at all in four centuries?"

"A people that do not evolve. That's serious," the foreigners among us said while tasting the salt cod and the tiny eels simmered with parsley and garlic.

"Didn't I tell you?" Martín continued. "In the Basque provinces the Neolithic men are called new-wavers and aren't liked." And they all laughed.

A great many jokes they made, and great quantities of food and drink we had, and we danced the *espatadantza,* and *aurreskos* and *zortzikos,* although we had to calm down Martín, who had joined our group of *txisturalis,*[16] and would change the rhythm from time to time playing tunes that were not Basque in the least. And then we met to decide what we would do.

"Go back in time once more," said Gregoria, "since we still are very far from the origin."

The night from the 7th to the 8th of July 1524 went by, and at dawn everybody, including the fisherman who had given Xaviertxo the good news, got ready to jump back again in time. Father Lartaun was very worried indeed.

"Well, as you know, our ancestors took a long time to convert. And a natural thing it is, since we are a stubborn people. The next jump ought to take us to a land of pagans."

Pimpilimpausa worked again. This time they made a great many calculations, and they said we would go to the eighth century, and there we

went. The valley had not changed, but when we moved, neither Guetaria, nor San Sebastian, nor the castle upon Mount Urgull were there.
But the fishing boats in the Cantabrian Sea were the same, and they all
had thick-haired white, black, or brown dogs that resembled Txuri,
Beltxa, and Nere. We didn't stand out at all when our paths crossed with
other Basques. Sometimes they would ask us, in the same Euskera we
spoke, if we had seen a party of Goths around. More or less half of the
Basques we met were Christian.

"As for the rest," Father Lartaun was saying, "they say that the new
religion is good, but that changing the religion of one's parents is a bad
thing. I was wrong to call them pagans, since they follow the natural
religion . . ."

"And you aren't preaching to them, Father?"

"Preach to them? Well, I tried, but as you know, getting a Basque to
change his mind is a very, very difficult thing . . ."

A group of travelers passed by and we were invited to eat at their
country house. We were embarrassed because we couldn't tell them
where (when) we came from. Even Father Lartaun agreed that the truth
would seem too strange, a thing of the Devil or of Basajaun.[17] We had to
lie, saying we were Basques from the other side of the mountains, and no
Basque likes to lie. We accepted the hospitality, we ate and drank (tiny
eels, bacon with red beans, cheese, and hard cider) we danced aurreskos,
we sang, we gave thanks, and bid our farewells saying "Agur." And we
jumped back right away, very ashamed of having told lies. Father Lartaun was very worried now.

"Don't you realize? Now we are going to a time when our Savior will
not have been born."

There we went. And for what we could gather, the change wasn't
great. The houses and the villages were all almost the same as those we
had left. One danced, one sang, one ate the same, and we all understood
each other perfectly in a Euskera with no trace of change whatsoever. Of
course, the sign of the cross was missing, and Father Lartaun was always
worried.

"It's just that my duty would be to preach to these pagans. And how
am I going to preach if Christ hasn't been born yet?"

"If you can't preach, make prophecies, Father," we said to him. "No
prophecies will be more certain than yours," laughed Martín, who for
his part was scandalized to see Basques who were identical to what the
Basques would always be.

Once again we accepted people's hospitality, very ashamed to be lying about the place and the time from which we came. We ate tiny eels and roasted sardines, and bacon with red beans, and they all asked us if we hadn't seen those people from the south who were crossing the mountains with those long-nosed monsters. Father Lartaun told something about Hasdrubal, Hannibal, and his family, and they all looked at him with great respect. Martín started to tell some jokes taken from one of those books that one shouldn't read called *Salambó*,[18] but Xaviertxo didn't let him continue, saying, "According to history, the Basques were friends of the Carthaginians. You would alter history if you were to convince them that the Carthaginians were—are—degenerate people."

And since altering history is a grave responsibility, Martín stopped talking.

We jumped back into the past again, much further back this time, and yet everything was very similar to what we had left behind, only there were fewer country houses, and many people going in and out of the mountain caves, and many lived there. We were no longer surprised that they all looked so similar to us, or that our language was theirs too.

We climbed up to the Orio cavern and entered it while Martín was saying:

"Nowadays it's fashionable to be a spelunker. Quite a few thousand years will have to pass for that trend to return."

And then he said while looking at those paintings:

"Maybe with the next jump we will be able to meet the artist who decorated this cave."

We befriended the fishermen and went out to sea in their boats, with Nere, Txuri, and Beltxa, who showed their ability in catching tuna. The Cantabrian Sea was much more full of creatures, and I even saw great big sperm whales near Santa Clara Island.

We had a meeting and Xaviertxo, looking very concerned, warned us:

"We must make a decision now. *Pimpilimpausa* is fragile, and a new jump will ruin it. Do we go back to our time, or do we continue toward the past so we can finally learn of our origin?"

"This is something to be voted on, and take a vote we must," said Gregoria. And she brought some white and black beans and took my beret. "He who wants to return will throw in a black bean. He who wants to continue will throw in a white bean."

We did just that, and when my beret was turned upside down only white beans fell from it.

We jumped. And we jumped to find no sign of a human being in these lands. Through ice and snow we hiked up to the Orio cavern, and we found no paintings in it. And *Pimpilimpausa* no longer worked.

A few years have passed since then. We have lived very happily. Never mind the cold, which is extreme, because we have good shelter and we work hard, and to provide us with food we have the Cantabrian Sea, free of ice and with such an abundance of fish. My children and their friends set out to sea to catch fish and hunt sperm whales, bringing along Nere, Txuri, and Beltxa, as well as many other dogs, all offspring of the three hunting dogs. They go out in the same boats as always, boats they have built with wood we took with us before the last jump. And they travel very far.

We are all settled very nicely. Of course we worry about it being so long before the founding of the Holy Mother Church, especially because Father Lartaun is not a bishop, so he cannot ordain anyone. *Jainko-arieskerradk*, the good priest is very strong, and we still have a good while left of our parents' religion. Later on we'll just have to put our trust in Providence.

A few families have started already. Aránzazu and Martín got married and they have a little daughter. The girl loves to draw and she is constantly painting on the walls of the Orio cavern where she lives with her parents.

We are very happy because we live, essentially, the way we have always lived. And we are very satisfied, since *Pimpilimpausa* carried out its task and we finally know who gave/we gave/we will give (a difficult muddle this is, even for Jainkoa) origin to the Basques. We and our own: *gu ta gutarrak.*

Luis Britto García

VENEZUELA

Luis Britto García (1940–) is a name widely recognized by scholars of contemporary Latin American literature and political thought, though not one immediately associated with SF. He is, however, one of the many accomplished "mainstream" Latin American authors who can count fantastical and science fictional texts among their body of work.

Britto García was born in Caracas, and is a senior professor in the economics department at the Universidad Central de Venezuela, where his field of inquiry is the history of political thought. He is an outspoken Marxist and critic, and his numerous penetrating essays are essential reading for any student of Venezuelan politics and postmodernity. These essays include "I Laugh at the World" ("Me río del mundo," 1984), "Power Mask" ("Máscara del poder," 1988), and "Countercultural Empire: From Rock to Postmodernity" ("Imperio contracultural: Del rock a la postmodernidad," 1991).

His creative work has brought Britto García many international accolades: in 1970, for example, he won the prestigious *Casa de las Américas* prize for his collection of short fictions *Rajatabla* (from which we take our story), and in 1979 he became a second-time winner with his novel *Abrapalabra*. Britto García has also won several awards as a playwright and as a humor writer.

In the tradition of dystopian literature, the microstory we include here is fittingly entitled "Future." This story manages to distill the essence of our humanity and challenges us with the paradox intrinsic to our desire for utopian perfection.

Future

Futuro, 1970
by Luis Britto García
translated by Andrea Bell

THESIS
And the perfect society was attained, and the madness of the human species diminished, and mankind was ready to devote its energies to the pursuit of a goal.

ANTITHESIS
Then they discovered there was no goal to which they could devote themselves.

SYNTHESIS
Therefore, they deified as a goal the absence of all goals, that is, stagnation.

THESIS
In the first place, humanity had to free itself from *work,* and thus began the maddest rush of teamwork ever to be directed at the goal of not working.

ANTITHESIS
Finally, all human work was done by machines, and the machines were made by other machines, which in turn were run by other machines; and thus humanity freed itself from work.

SYNTHESIS
Thus it was that all of the body's mechanical faculties—the musculature, the limbs, and the capacity to move itself or to move objects—ceased to be useful; they atrophied and, in the end, disappeared.

In the second place, humanity had to free itself from the slavery of *food.*

All the powers of chemistry were employed in the synthesis of proteins and carbohydrates from inanimate matter and heat, and finally, through the use of atomic power, matter and energy were transmuted in laboratories until they formed the most purely distilled quintessential nourishment, able to pass directly into the broth of blood without previous digestion.

Whereupon the mouth and the stomach and the intestines and the liver and the viscera in general ceased to be burdened with the arduous task of wringing energy from food, and they atrophied and, in the end, disappeared.

In the third place, humanity had to free itself from *death.*

And in the laboratories they rounded up the toxins that produced the degeneration known in former times as old age; and they corrected the genes that had caused the suicide of the individual, known as death; and from organic matter came the synthesis of protoplasm, and from the synthesis of protoplasm came the synthesis of immortality.

Whereupon procreation became unnecessary and the reproductive organs ceased to be useful; they atrophied and, in the end, disappeared.

And it was during this dawn of the spirit that the intellect, now lord and master of the universe, was empowered to embark upon the boldest of adventures within the purest realms of abstraction.

Freed from work, freed from hunger, freed from sex, freed from death, the human brain prepared to launch into the face of all creation its most potent fruit: one born not of any intestinal imperative nor appetite of the flesh. A monumental event was about to take place.

SYNTHESIS

In effect, the human brain also ceased to be necessary; it, too, atrophied, and in the end it, too, disappeared.

Hugo Correa

CHILE

Hugo Correa (1926–) is the man widely credited with launching modern science fiction in Latin America. Indeed, the spark of life he gave the genre regionally was recognized by the Spanish SF magazine *Nueva Dimensión*, which honored his contributions to the field by dedicating an entire issue to him (no. 33, 1972).

Correa was born in the southern Chilean province of Talca. His long writing career—he is still active in the Chilean SF community—began, as is often the case in Latin America, in journalism, and from there branched out to include criticism, drama, and prose fiction. Although he has written realist works, his métier is SF, in which he first became interested after reading Bradbury, Simak, and Sturgeon. His early efforts in the genre met with considerable success: the novel *The Superior Ones* (*Los altísimos,* 1959) and his novella *Someone Dwells within the Wind* (*Alguien mora en el viento,* also 1959) were immediate classics. *Someone Dwells within the Wind* was awarded the *Alerce* prize by the University of Chile and is representative of his best work. He went on to win other prizes for his short fiction, and in 1974 was awarded a grant through the University of Iowa's International Writing Program.

Correa has the distinction of being one of the first Latin American SF writers to have had his work published in the United States. He had sent one of his stories, "The Last Element" ("El último elemento"), to Ray Bradbury, who liked it, suggested Correa submit it to the *Magazine of Fantasy and Science Fiction,* and then dropped a note to the magazine's editors on Correa's behalf. The story was published in the April 1962 issue. Another story, "Alter Ego," was published by *MF&SF* in 1967 and was later reprinted in the textbook *Introductory Psychology through SF* (1974) and in *The Penguin World Omnibus of SF* (1986). As being published in the United States was the highest mark of success for Latin American SF writers at the time, Correa's accomplishments were greatly inspiring to contemporaries such as Elena Aldunate, author of the classic story "Juana and Cybernetics" ("Juana y la cibernética," 1963). Correa continues to be recognized

They even talked about sacrificing him for fear he would divide the dumi people.

"He has a few adherents, along with a group of disciples, but they're so apathetic I'm sure they'll abandon him at the first sign of trouble."

"No one can make those bugs understand, Rossi. Crackpots—people who believe they can fix the world—are everywhere, even on a planet inhabited by worms. But the dumis will never be able to understand even the most elementary principles of coexistence. They eat each other!"

"Yes," agreed Rossi, "they resolve their misunderstandings through one-to-one combat, and the victor, after selecting the most appetizing morsels, leaves the rest to the collective and takes himself off for a solo feast."

"They're ignorant of law and politics." The captain punctuated his words with energetic movements of his short arms. "They only united to attack us, but without coming up with any sort of plan first, because even that's beyond them."

"But on more than one occasion they've come to ask you for a judgment, Captain. That's something: they take their role as subjects seriously."

"Because they don't want to take on any sort of responsibility. We've replaced their rudimentary government in a way that benefits them: they still enjoy their freedom, committing all the depravities they care to, knowing we wouldn't intervene in their affairs even if they decided to devour each other in one big orgy. Which would be a splendid solution, don't you think? Because there's one thing I must tell you: when this planet is colonized, not a single dumi is going to be left alive. We're proceeding in a humanitarian manner because the time's not yet come to put things in their place. But when men come in search of the crucial space we're running out of on our world, the killing will begin. It's survival, boys, nothing more. Men aren't going to share this magnificent planet with the dumis when it can be colonized without resorting to expensive artificial methods."

The captain's words rebounded in a final echo. Just then one of the moons—huge as millwheels, their flat expanses festooned in red and gold, barren like Earth's satellite—rose above the sandy plains. Its iridescent light wrapped the *Tierra* in an icy blanket.

"What's happening?"

The face of one of the men on guard duty appeared on the television screen.

"The sentinel's spotted a group of dumis headed this way, Captain. What should we do?"

The captain appeared surprised.

"I'll speak to them."

In a few seconds the autoexplorer, powered by its silent rotor, halted above the dumis. A beam of light shone down on the monsters. They retreated, waving their multiple arms.

"What do you want? Don't come even a meter closer!"

The translator broadcast Ortúzar's words via the automatic loudspeaker. One of the dumis—indistinguishable from the rest—whistled its response, which was picked up by the helicopter's microphones.

"We have captured an individual who passes himself off as a prophet. As he has managed to beguile a part of the population, we wish you to authorize us to sacrifice him, because of the danger that he will divide the dumi people and start a war."

"Since when are they so fussy?" the captain asked Rossi. "Don't they kill each other for lunch on a daily basis without consulting us?"

"Only for personal reasons, or when they're very hungry, Captain. There's never been a war among the dumis."

"Aha, so they have their principles."

He thought for a few moments. The electronic eye focused on the motionless crowd awaiting the verdict.

"And if he really were the Redeemer?" exclaimed the archaeologist.

"So what?"

"Well, Captain, it would mean nothing more nor less than that you'd be playing the role of Pontius Pilate."

Ortúzar chewed his nails and looked at his men, who remained silent.

"And what of it, after all? They must know what they're doing."

"It's not that simple, Captain," replied Rossi. "Even though he may belong to a repulsive species, that prophet is trying to preach good things. His gospel might change these people. If I were you I wouldn't pass judgment lightly."

"Yeah, you're right. This is putting me in a tough spot."

"Tell them to wait a few minutes."

Captain Ortúzar, for the first time in his forty years of life, hesitated. But he decided to follow Rossi's advice. The dumis answered that they would wait there for his decision.

Ortúzar began to pace about the bridge. He looked at the shining instrument panel, the complicated dials, the multicolored levers and buttons, the radar and television screens, and all the marvelous instruments capable of steering the spaceship across the cosmos without human intervention.

They're doomed. Whatever my decision is, it won't change their future. I'd be doing them a favor if I refused to allow the sacrifice of this prophet. If a spaceship had landed on Earth on the eve of Golgotha and its captain had prevented the Crucifixion, humanity wouldn't have had to wait so long for the advent of technology.

He stopped in front of the library and, pressing a button, whispered the name Pontius Pilate into the microphone. An impersonal voice summarized the tetrarch's life story.

What a fool! In order to evade responsibilities he lost the opportunity to become mankind's greatest benefactor. One washing of hands that submerged the world in fifteen centuries of darkness! That triggered an era of senseless religious wars in order to impose a bunch of abstractions, without achieving a single positive result.

He looked at the television: on the screen, the somber group.

There's no escape for you! In two centuries more you'll all be destroyed.

He peered out the window. The light, high on the horizon, insinuated an invisible curtain over the emerging stars, rendering them faint, almost imperceptible. Only the great star, the nova, sustained its radiant gleam. Very soon now the second satellite would make its appearance: on the horizon a reddish glow, like a gigantic transparent dome, heralded its ascent.

If God exists, no doubt he forgot the dumis. And if the one awaiting my judgment is his Son, he's clearly arrived too late. There's nothing he can do to save his people! Still, . . .

The captain struck his forehead.

I almost forgot! I must not allow that prophet to die.

The archaeologist, Murchinson, and the two astrogators approached the captain.

"Gentlemen: I will oppose the sacrifice of that prophet."

A brief silence ensued, broken by Rossi.

"Are you sure about what you're doing, Captain?"

"Don't get suspicious, Rossi," the captain laughed. "Do you think I'm trying to make some subtle theological point? No. Above all, I'm practical: that prophet's doctrine would turn the dumis into meek, submissive beings. And there are still reactionary souls on Earth who, for that very reason, would be against exterminating them. It'd be fatal: eventually the dumis, as native sons of this world, could assimilate our knowledge and subjugate humans, who, as transplants, would be at a disadvantage. Do you understand? Survival, gentlemen. We have to look further ahead, and not settle for being mere explorers. My decision will be pivotal for the human race, because we won't leave it any annoying problems."

Again it was the archaeologist who spoke up, in view of the others' silence.

"Don't you think your zeal is a bit extreme, captain?"

Murchinson spoke up. "I think the captain's right. It seems like an excellent idea to me."

"Me, too," said Nasokov.

The others all agreed in turn.

"And what do you plan to do with the prophet and his disciples?" asked Rossi.

"Simply lock them up in the hold and take them to Earth. They'll serve as field samples. It's the only way to guarantee their survival."

"It's just that on Earth they'll form an excellent impression of the dumis on the basis of those samples, Captain," Rossi hinted.

Ortúzar flew into a rage.

"I'm in charge here, Rossi! If need be I'll kill those buggers once we're in space just to avoid what you're saying. Or don't you think I'd foreseen that?"

The captain turned to the television and spoke in a dry voice. "My verdict is this: You must turn the prophet over to me immediately."

The response seemed one of irritation, though fearful.

"May we know the reasons for this decision?"

"No. It is my verdict and you must respect it."

"Sir, in this special case we believe you should explain to the dumi people the reasons which moved you to return that judgment."

"What's this?" The captain turned to his men, between amused and peeved. "Offer explanations to those freaks? They must be crazy!"

And turning back to the monsters, he added:

"In this special case, dear dumis, what I order shall be done. And I swear that if you do not obey I'll exterminate you all. Agreed?"

The dumis whispered among themselves. The captain didn't take his eyes off the prophet, who could be told from the others by an odd frill that rose from his large head.

"As you command, sir." The voice over the loudspeaker was colorless. "We believe this to be an arbitrary act, because . . ."

"Enough!" roared the captain. "Have the prophet and his disciples come forward. And the rest of you, move back. Don't try anything treacherous!"

Unwillingly, the group parted to make way for the condemned.

"Hurry up! Before I change my mind!"

The fifteen dumis moved away from their captors and advanced in a disorderly throng toward the rocket.

"Captain," muttered Rossi, "belay your order. You're making a mistake . . ."

Rossi stumbled against something that protruded from the instrument panel and lost his balance. When he tried to regain it he gave the impression of attacking Ortúzar. Nasokov, who was closest, reacted in a flash: a sharp blow sounded and Rossi, punched on the chin, fell to the floor. He made a weak effort to stand up, and then collapsed again heavily.

"Leave him there," the captain ordered. And he ordered the men guarding the airlock, "Get ready to receive the Son of God. As soon as he's entered, bring him to me."

Turning to the others, he added:

"I'll try to suppress my disgust, considering who's visiting us."

The bulk of the crew slept. The monstrous creature came swaying into the airlock. It called to mind both spider and lizard. Large polyhedral head from which sprouted, on four sides, a cluster of multifaceted eyes and weird vibrating antennae. Numerous articulated tentacles jutted out from its misshapen body, ending in strange, pointy claws covered with bristles. Greenish drops gleamed between the quills like dew among the grass. Thin sheets of some extremely hard substance protected its sides, chest, and back like an insect's wing covers. It walked semierect, supported by a bunch of short, skinny legs. The monster's dark coloring heightened its ugliness.

The fourteen disciples entered the rocket in succession, and the Dantean group in the center of the airlock gave the impression of something that might have been called humility, had it been possible to draw parallels between their attitudes and those of humans. An acrid and revolting odor spread through the atmosphere, in spite of the air conditioning.

"Let the prophet, the one with the frills on his head, come up. The rest should wait there until further orders."

Rossi was dragged out of the navigation room: he was still uncon-

The Falsifier

El falsificador, 1972

by José B. Adolph

translated by Andrea Bell,

except as noted

Before the Incas reigned in these kingdoms, or had ever been heard of, the Indians relate another thing much more notable than all things else that they say. For they declare that they were a long time without seeing the sun, and that, suffering much evil from its absence, great prayers and vows were offered up to their gods, imploring for the light they needed. Things being in this state, the sun, shining very brightly, came forth from the island of Titicaca, in the great lake of the Collao, at which everyone rejoiced. Presently afterwards, they say, that there came from a southern direction a white man of great stature, who, by his aspect and presence, called forth great veneration and obedience. This man who thus appeared had great power, insomuch that he could change plains into mountains, and great hills into valleys, and make water flow out of stones. As soon as such power was beheld, the people called him the Maker of created things, the Prince of all things, Father of the Sun. For they say that he performed other wonders, giving life to men and animals, so that by his hand marvellous great benefits were conferred on the people. And such was the story that the Indians who told it to me say that they heard from their ancestors, who in like manner heard it in the old songs which they received from very ancient times. They say that this man went on towards the north, working these marvels along the way of the mountains; and that he never more returned so as to be seen. In many places he gave orders to men how they should live, and he spoke lovingly to them and with much gentleness, admonishing them that they should do good, and no evil or injury one to another, and that they should be loving and charitable to all. In most parts he is generally called Ticiviracocha, but in the province of the Collao they call him Tuapaca, and in other places Arnauan. In many parts they built temples in which they put blocks of stone in likeness of him, and offered up sacrifices before them. It is held that the great blocks at Tiahuanacu were from that time. Although, from the fame of what formerly had passed, they relate the things I have stated touching Ticiviracocha, they know nothing more of him, nor whether he would ever return to any part of this kingdom.

Besides this, they say that, a long time having passed, they again saw another man resembling the first, whose name they do not mention; but they received it from their forefathers as very certain that wherever this personage came and there were sick, he healed them, and where there were blind he gave them sight by only uttering words. Through acts so good and useful he was much beloved by all. In this fashion, working great things by his words, he arrived at the province of the Canas, in which, near to a village which has the name of Cacha, and in which the Captain Bartolomé de Terrazas holds an encomienda,[1] the people rose against him, threatening to stone him. They saw him upon his knees, with his hands raised to heaven, as if invoking the divine favour to liberate him from the danger that threatened him. The Indians further state that presently there appeared a great fire in the heaven, which they thought to be surrounding them. Full of fear and trembling, they came to him whom they had wanted to kill, and with loud clamour besought him to be pleased to forgive them. For they knew that this punishment threatened them because of the sin they had committed in wishing to stone the stranger. Presently they saw that when he ordered the fire to cease, it was extinguished, so that they were themselves witnesses of what had come to pass; and the stones were consumed and burnt up in such wise as that large blocks could be lifted in the hand, as if they were of cork. On this subject they go on to say that, leaving the place where these things happened, the man arrived on the sea coast, where, holding his mantle, he went in amongst the waves and was never more seen. And as he went, so they gave him the name of Viracocha, which means "the foam of the sea."

Pedro Cieza de León
Chronicle of Peru, part II, chapter 5[2]

A dark alcove, barely illuminated by a tiny flame, gives refuge to an old man—old in spite of not yet having reached the age of forty—bent over a text that flows from his gnarled fingers. Every now and then he stops the elegant quill and, looking upward, withdraws into himself as he tries once more to fix in his mind a landscape about to pass into legend.

Pedro Cieza de León, king's soldier, chronicler of Peru, writes the second volume of his book. The myth of Viracocha, the god who gave name to a king, concerns him today. The Inca Viracocha, hero of the battle for which Ayacucho was named, in which the empire was consolidated once more, is the pale reflection of an immense figure who, centuries before, passed along the mountains and coast of the kingdom when it was but a vague promise between warring tribes.

Someone impels Don Pedro. The Indians have told him a strange story, which the chronicler has set down with Christian piety. Faithful to his charge, he has recorded it just as it was told to him; and yet on parchment the tale changes subtly, unnoticed by the writer.

The story told by the Indians who, in turn, had heard it from their elders, spoke of celestial carriages and of fields turned to flame. And yet, when transferring this incredible story to the manuscript that will remain as irrefutable proof of his ravings, Cieza de León mentions neither carriages nor electric fields. The story is too bizarre, too heretical. It could prove very costly to him, may even result in a charge of Judaism or agnosticism.

Don Pedro's hand—a hand that until now has obeyed him faithfully in the wielding of sword and pen—becomes independent. It writes of its own accord. And from its efforts some other thing emerges, some other story: an Indian version of the Nazarene prophet. An American vision of the Palestine story, of the man who came down from the heavens to teach mankind to love one another. Canas evokes Canaan. The crucifixion becomes a stoning, just as the Palestinian Jews, fifteen hundred years ago, used to execute their criminals and victims.

The story of the Indians has slowly transformed itself until it parallels that of Jesus. Don Pedro will reread what he has written and be surprised at himself. He will never manage to finish any other book, any other work, grieved by the transformation that has taken place in what the Indians had told him. He feels himself a failure as a chronicler, betrayed by a weak memory, by the hand of God, or by a strange cowardice that is not simply the physical fear of the Inquisition.

Don Pedro feels he has lied. But he cannot manage to understand why, or even how much, because in his memory reality—which is also legend—and apocrypha already mix. Don Pedro fears that, by changing the Indians' bold and absurd history into a native version of the Gospels, he has said too much. He fears that, in dread of the truth, he may have done something even worse, which also could qualify as heresy. For, after all, might it not be heresy to suggest that the message of the Son of God made man might be known to those outside the fold of the baptized?

He rubs his tired eyes. He rereads the text once more. He sighs. Perhaps, he thinks, he has done well, stealing from the uncomprehending eyes of the world something that they could not digest, a thing of witchcraft and evil that cannot be given unto the sinners of this century. Perhaps the Lord will bear in mind, at the hour of his death, that he changed the impious into the holy, the unpronounceable into the compassionate, the terrible into the edifying.

But still he is tormented. Who is he, he asks himself, to alter an authentic tale of these simple and honest folk, who have entrusted their faith to this bearded historian? What punishment might await the falsifier, the deformer, the liar, even though he be one out of piety?

They had spoken to him of a concert of roars in the starry Andean night, of the descent of a good and powerful man, armed with indescribable instruments, wise beyond all knowing. They told of a man who spoke with other men who were not there, and who answered him from afar; of buzzing sounds, and of smells; of colorful visions on silver screens; of long tubes of airy green metal, able to settle like a discreet bird upon the blackened fields of grass. They spoke of the visitor's sadness and desolation at the endurance of idolatry, of the strange foods, of the injured woman and her miraculous cure. Later, they had departed again and Cieza had transformed the untellable spectacle into a walk across the sea. The stranger's request to be forever silent—made by placing a finger across his lips—had been granted, at last, by Don Pedro, but in his own fashion.

In that darkened Spanish chamber an incident was normalized by a doubtful and tortured man. Perhaps out of cowardice, perhaps from insanity, perhaps due to terror, a chronicler embellished the incomprehensible and saved us, once again, from humans gaining knowledge about us.

Which fact I communicate to you, Commander, and in so doing I bring my research to an end and request permission to continue my journey and that of my crewmate, now recovered from her injuries, to the base on Pluto.

Angélica Gorodischer

ARGENTINA

Angélica Gorodischer (1928–) was born in Buenos Aires, but she has lived in the city of Rosario for most of her life. A precocious and avid reader but a latecomer to fiction writing, she studied literature at what is today the University of Rosario and won her first literary prize in 1964 with a detective story. In 1965, she received another award for her first book, *Short Stories with Soldiers* (*Cuentos con soldados*). *Opus Two* (*Opus Dos,* 1967), her earliest incursion into the fantastic mode, presents an Argentina of the future. Another SF short story collection followed in 1973, and she has won a place in science fiction history with her novels *Trafalgar* (1979) and *Kalpa imperial,* which was published in two parts: *Book I: The House of Power* (*Libro I: La casa del poder,* 1983) and *Book II: The Empire Most Vast* (*Libro II: El imperio más vasto,* 1984). About this novel, republished in 2001 by the Spanish SF press Gigamesh, the author has said she wanted to write a Western *A Thousand and One Nights* that would become a ferocious parable of dictatorship in Argentina.[1] Although Gorodischer later set science fiction aside in favor of feminist literature and criticism, her SF texts are becoming popular among a growing readership. An excerpt from *Kalpa imperial* was recently translated into English by Ursula K. Le Guin and published as "The End of a Dynasty" in the anthology *Starlight 2* (1999).

The story included here first appeared in Gorodischer's 1973 short story collection "Under the Flowering Jubeas" (*Bajo las jubeas en flor*) and has been widely anthologized, since it is considered to be a masterpiece of Argentinean SF and a good example of this author's highly literate style. "The Violet's Embryos" speculates in general about the nature of desire and the search for happiness, and specifically about the traditional Argentinean equation of military power with masculinity by presenting a world of shipwrecked servicemen who choose transvestism and homosexuality to fulfill their sexual needs.[2]

The Violet's Embryos

Los embriones del violeta, 1973

by Angélica Gorodischer

translated by Sara Irausquin

He turned beneath the sheets; the torrents roared. He managed to cut short the end of a dream about Ulysses and listened to the soothing breath of the Vantedour night. At the foot of the bed, Bonifacio of Solomea stretched and stuck out his rose-colored tongue for his lazy morning toilet. But dawn had not yet come, and so the two of them went back to sleep. Tuk-o-tut was stretched out across the doorway, snoring.

On the other side of the sea, the matronas were rocking Carita Dulce.[1] They had carefully moved the egg out into the open, watching where they stepped so they wouldn't stumble or jostle it, and then they had uncovered it. The huge cradle rocked to the rhythm of their song and the yellow sun shone through the leaves on the trees, licking at Carita Dulce's thighs. Whimpering, he moved about, rubbing himself against the smooth walls of the cradle. While the matronas sang, one of them caressed Carita Dulce's cheek, bringing a smile to his face and coaxing him back to sleep. The matronas sighed and looked at each other contentedly.

On the island, it was afternoon and the Sonata #17 in B-flat was playing on the clavichords. Theophilus was getting ready to attack again; Saverius had finished his speech and was planning a brilliant riposte. But within Theophilus echoed the phrase, *This soul, too, loves Cimarosa.* Was he forgetting the words he had been planning to say, the importance of an adversative conjunction, the nuances of an adjective meant to cast a somewhat pejorative light on the presumed universal model of perception? It struck him that Saverius was beginning to look a little too satisfied.

Twisted up like a rope, unshaven and dirty, smelling of vomit and sweat, he tried again to sit down. Using all his strength, he put his left hand on the ground and leaned upon it. Squeezing, squeezing so that it wouldn't shake, he grabbed hold of a patch of tall grass. He lifted his right hand to grip the trunk of a tree and began to hoist himself up. He felt dizzy, and a bilious saliva was filling his mouth. He spit, and a little drool ran down his chin.

"Let's sing," he said. "Let's sing to life, to love, and to wine."

He had seven suns inside his head and two outside. One of them was orange and could be gazed at with impunity.

"I want a suit," he said. "This one is disgusting. A new suit made of green velvet. Green, yes, that's it, green. And a pair of tall boots, a cane, and a shirt. And some whiskey in beer steins."

But he was very far from the violet and didn't have the energy to walk.

The facade of the house was made of gray rock. The house itself was built into the mountain and inside were countless corridors where no light ever entered. The trophy rooms were empty; on the mountain, the hunters were roasting venison. There were rooms draped in black where the judges sometimes sat. Everything was silent, like it usually was; the windows would remain closed. In the basement was the torture chamber, which is where they took Lesvanoos, his hands tied behind his back.

Meanwhile, fifteen tired men were approaching in the darkness. Eleven had been chosen for their physical strength, their courage, and their ability to obey orders; the other four had been chosen for their knowledge. Seven of them were seated around a table in the only place that wasn't some type of multipurpose pit.

"We'll say ten hours more," said the commander.

Leonidas Terencio Sessler thought that too many things had already been said on this trip, and from what he could see, they were still—and would keep on—saying too much. There had been arguments, fights, shouts, orders, apologies, explanations, and moralizing lectures (for which he alone was responsible). He had never intended to become the moralizer. But in his attempt to ease a little of what he knew would sound like cynicism to the others, something changed in the obscure process by which thoughts are transformed into words, and he wound up devastating everyone with morals. He had compared that process many times with the one he believed should occur during creation—a poem, for example: *I know how to appear without waking the green star*—and had reached the conclusion that the explosion of language, scream, language, name—again: *I will inhabit my name*—had been a monstrous error, or a bloody joke, depending on his mood. In the second case (when he reached the point where he could accept the possibility of the suspicion of a suspicion—the existence of God), unending and re-edited jokes, desolate autobiographies, recommendations and presumptions.

"We ought to get rid of words and communicate using music," he said.

The commander smiled, twisting his head around like a short-winged bird, suspicious.

"I don't mean just us," explained Leo Sessler, "but rather humans in general."

"So, my dear doctor," said Savan, the engineer, "according to you, we should, right now, be opening our mouths and singing a victory march?"

"Uh-huh."

"It's not the same if we cheer hip, hip, hooray?"

"Of course it's not."

"Twelve notes aren't very many," commented young Reidt, unexpectedly.

"And twenty-eight letters are too many," responded Leo Sessler.

"How's the coffee coming along?" asked the commander.

At eleven o'clock, navigational time, they landed in the so-called Puma Desert. It wasn't actually a desert, but rather a vast depression covered with yellowish vegetation.

"It's a sad land," said Leo Sessler.

"10:54," they answered.

And: "I didn't sleep at all last night."

"Who did?" said someone else.

All around them were precise sounds, mathematical, perfect. The Puma Desert stretched out, deceitfully dry, and rose up at the edges like a huge soup bowl. The men donned their white suits, each standing beside his own compartment; they put on hard, jointed gloves and knee-high boots, the complete landing outfit. Leo Sessler put on his glasses, and over them the required sunglasses—silly precautions. Savan was whistling.

"Stand next to the exit chamber when you're ready," said the commander, who was always the first one. And he opened the door.

"Would you rather die than go blind, Savan?" asked Leo Sessler.

"What?" said the commander from the door.

"The suns," said Leo Sessler.

"Don't worry," answered the commander, "young Reidt knows what he's doing." And he closed the door.

Young Reidt blushed; he dropped a glove so that when he bent down to pick it up the others wouldn't see his face.

"I'd rather die," said Savan.

Bonifacio of Solomea arched his back and sneezed.

"What's going on?" asked Lord Vantedour.

Downstairs, the dogs were howling.

Theophilus, however, was certain about the landing, or at least he had information that something had been seen in the sky and was headed in their direction. Hope had been replaced by a feeling of well-being, pushed back and forgotten as quickly as possible, as if it were something dangerous. But curiosity made him stay in contact with the master astronomer. That's how he'd found out where it had fallen or descended, and although he wasn't very keen on having to travel without sleep, he made them put him through to the master navigator.

"Shut off that music."

The clavichords were interrupted in the middle of the thirtieth sonata.

A horseman arrived at a gallop and stopped on the Patio of Honor below. Lord Vantedour got out of bed, threw a cape over his shoulders and went out onto the balcony. The man was shouting something down below. He had come from the observation posts and was motioning toward the west.

"After breakfast," said Lord Vantedour. But there was nobody in the room to hear him besides Bonifacio of Solomea, who silently agreed.

Carita Dulce was licking the wet walls of the cradle, and Lesvanoos—naked and tied to a table—was looking at the executioner and the executioner was waiting.

Dressed in a green velvet suit and supported by a cane, he walked away from the violet, singing. The sun shone brightly on the crystal glass he was holding in his hand and on the pearl buttons of his shirt. He was at peace, and happiness came so easily.

Eight of them left the ship: the commander; Leo Sessler; Savan, the engineer; the second radio operator; and four other crew members. All of them were carrying light weapons, but the only one who felt ridiculous was Leo Sessler.

Savan raised his head to look at the sky and said through his mask, in an unrecognizable voice, "Young Reidt was right. At least one of them is completely harmless. Look up, doctor."

"No thank you. I suppose that eventually, without realizing it, I will.

The sun has always made me feel a certain distrust. Imagine what it'll be like with two of them."

They started gradually uphill.

"When we get out of this river basin," said the commander, and then he stopped.

A colt, black against the backlight, was galloping across the golden horizon. They all stood there, completely still and silent, and one of the crew members raised his rifle. Leo Sessler spotted him and gestured for him to stop. The colt, in full view of everyone, kept on galloping along the edges of the depression, as if offering itself as something for them to contemplate. It was full of strength, energized by the morning cold, animated by the rivers of warm blood in its flanks and legs, its nostrils dilated and derisive. Suddenly, it disappeared down the other side of the slope.

"It couldn't be," said Savan, the engineer, "but, yes, that was a horse."

And at the same time, the commander asked, "Did you all see that?"

"A horse," said one of the crew members, "a horse, Commander, sir, but we weren't expecting to find animals."

"I know. We've made a mistake. We've left the ship at the wrong place."

"Be quiet, Savan. Don't say such stupid things. We got out exactly where we were supposed to."

"And the horses that ran toward the boneyard passed by, the sage mouths of the earth still fresh. Except this isn't Earth and there aren't supposed to be any horses here," said Leo Sessler.

The commander didn't order him to be quiet. He said, "Let's go."

The master navigator had let him know everything was ready. Seated in front of the communicator, Theophilus was listening. He heard, *"'And the horses that ran toward the boneyard passed by, the sage mouths of the earth still fresh.'* Except this isn't Earth and there aren't supposed to be any horses here."

And after that, another voice: "Let's go."

By the time they reached the edge of the Puma Desert, the sun had warmed the outside of their white suits, but inside they did not feel the heat.

They stopped at the edge of a blue and green world, stained by violet spots. They were on Earth on the first morning of a new age with two suns and horses, forests of oak and sycamore trees, parcels of cultivated land, sunflowers and paths.

Leo Sessler sat down on the ground; something was jumping up and down in the pit of his stomach, something had sealed off his throat and was playing around inside him, Proteus, legends. He broke down: Please, let's stay calm. He assumed that Savan was looking pale and that the commander had decided to keep being the commander; Leo Sessler knew he was a sick man. He thought it was lucky young Reidt had stayed behind. The commander spread out a map and explained the matter at hand, addressing everybody. Far away, the colt was galloping against the wind.

"Tell the master navigator I'm going down," said Theophilus.

Carita Dulce curled up, his knees against his chin. Lesvanoos was pleading for them to whip him; the executioner had orders to continue waiting.

He spun the cane around in his right hand and with his left brought the mug to his lips to drink. Whiskey dripped down the front of his green velvet suit.

"How many men?" asked Lord Vantedour.

"Eight," answered the lookout.

"The thing is," said the commander, "the data don't match up, so there must be an error somewhere. I don't think it's possible we've made a mistake. The discrepancy must be in the information that we were given."

Each man responds to the linguistic ritual of his class, Leo Sessler thought to himself.

"We were informed of the presence of insignificant vegetation, mosses, grasses, and the occasional bush, and we find trees (*farming, that's more serious,* thought Sessler), tall grass, in essence a surprisingly rich and diverse vegetation. Not to mention animals. According to previous reports, we should only have seen a few wormlike insects."

"Then there's the matter of water," said Leo Sessler.

"What?"

"Listen."

In the distance, the torrents were roaring.

"The water, yes, the water," said the commander, "another inconsistency."

Savan sat down on the ground next to Leo Sessler. The commander coughed.

"I think they recorded traces of water that would sink into the ground," he said, "intermittent in any case, and seasonal. But what's important now is to decide what we're going to do. We can keep going or we can return and hold a sort of council and compare the previous information with what we've just seen."

"We're going to have to go on sometime," said Savan, the engineer.

"Agreed," said the commander. "I was thinking basically the same thing. The meeting can be held afterward, and the benefit of continuing is that we can gather more data. Anyway, if anyone wants to go back—that includes crew members, but perhaps not the second radio operator—you may do so."

Nobody moved.

"Then we'll keep going."

He folded the maps. Savan and Leo Sessler got to their feet.

"Have your guns ready but no one is to use them without my order, regardless of what you see."

Horses? A telephone booth? A train? A bar? Everyday things: insects, and intermittent, seasonal traces of water.

"Everything seems so calm."

Leo Sessler thought one of his famous phrases and laughed at himself. One day he would write his memoirs, the memoirs of a solitary man, with a special section dedicated to his famous aphorisms: the brief dogmatic statements born of unexpected situations that neither he nor the others understood, his attempts at distilling them to their no-moral of human fragility. For example, in this case, beauty—because all this had a maternal beauty—did not guarantee a friendly welcome. It undoubtedly had not for Commander Tardon and the crew of the *Luz Dormida Tres*.[2] There might have been silent ambushes. Or monsters. Or maybe here, death could take on friendly forms. Or mermaids, or simply floating poisons. Or emanations that strengthened a man's desire to die. None of which explained the horse, or the cultivated fields.

"There's a trail," said Savan.

Or the trails.

They stopped next to the path of trampled ground.

Or anything as familiar as the sunflowers.

"We'll take the trail," said the commander. "It will always be easier for us to follow a trail than to cut across the rough terrain."

Even a career military man could have admirable characteristics, and without a doubt, those admirable characteristics could very well make up part of the set of inclinations and qualities that drive a man to choose such a detestable profession. That was too long, decided Leo Sessler. It wouldn't be part of the chapter of famous phrases, but rather, hmm, let's see, the part called "Late Afternoon Reflections." The suns were over their heads and their boots kicked up tiny whirlwinds of dust, a white dust that hovered for a moment and then fell, blurring their footprints. The commander said that they would walk for another hour and if they found nothing new, they would go back and plan a more complete exploration for the next day. The trail passed through an oak forest. There were birds but nobody commented on them. The horse had summed up all of the animals that shouldn't have existed.

"Indeed, it's possible," said Lord Vantedour. "How did you hear them?"

"By creating a communicator. Incredibly easy, remind me to explain it to you."

"The advantages of being an expert in advanced electronics," said Lord Vantedour, smiling. "Why did you come to see me?"

"Who'd you expect me to go see," asked Theophilus. "Moritz? Kesterren is out of reach. And you have to find Leval when he's Les-Van-Oos, but I'm afraid nowadays he spends most of his time as Lesvanoos."

"I mean, do you expect us to do something?"

"I don't know."

"Of course, you understand that we could do anything."

"And by anything, you mean get rid of them," said Theophilus.

"Yes."

"That was the first thing I thought of. Nevertheless."

"That's it," said Lord Vantedour. "Nevertheless."

The trail gradually emerged from the oak forest and Carita Dulce demanded more and more caresses, while the man in the green velvet suit fell once more, the cup in his hand shattered, the executioner tightened the ropes, Lesvanoos howled, and Lord Vantedour and Theophilus tried to agree on what they were going to do about the eight men from the *Niní Paume Uno*.[3]

Leo Sessler was the first to see the line of patrolmen, but he kept walking without saying anything. They heard the gallop: the colt? The men saw the horseman rise up behind the next hill, or maybe they became aware of the two things at the same time: the wall of patrolmen and the horseman coming toward them. The commander gestured for them to lower their guns. The horseman reined in his horse and approached at a walk.

"Greetings from Lord Vantedour, sirs. He awaits you in the castle."

The commander nodded his head. The horseman dismounted and began to walk in front of the group, leading his horse by the bridle.

The horse was, or seemed to be, an English thoroughbred, very tall, with a straight profile. The reins were made of leather, dyed dark blue and branded with gold stars. The bit, the rings for the reins, and the stirrups were all made of silver. The horse blanket that it wore was the same color as the reins, with stars around the border.

"*Equus incredibilis*," said Leo Sessler.

"What?" asked Savan.

"Or maybe *Eohippus Salariis improbabilis*."

Savan didn't ask anything else.

The rider was a young, inexpressive man, dressed in blue and black. His tailored pants were black, his coat blue with gold stars around the border. A hood covered his head and came down to his shoulders.

The commander asked the second radio operator to call the *Niní Paume Uno*, informing them of the direction they were taking, no explanations, and that they would be in touch again. The man gradually fell behind.

They proceeded across a cracked ramp that spanned a dry moat, and then crossed the drawbridge. They entered the stone patio. There was a cistern, and men dressed like the guide, and the sound of barking dogs; it smelled of animals and burned tree trunks, of leather and warm bread. Flanked by towers, embattlements, and archers, preceded by the commander, for whom the entire march must have been torture, they let themselves be led to the Ceremonial Door. Two men were waiting in the shadows inside, only their legs partially visible in the pool of light the sun made on the flagstone floor. The guide moved aside and the commander said, "Tardon."

"Lord Vantedour, my dear Commander, Lord Vantedour. Come, I want you to meet Theophilus."

The eight men entered the room.

On the island, the master astronomer was composing his nineteenth memoir: this one, about the constellation Aphrodite's Bed. The head gardener was bending over a new variety of speckled ocher rose. Saverius was reading *The Platonic Doctrine of Truth*. Peony was studying her new hairstyle. And in the kitchens they were working on an ibis, sculpted of ice, that would carry the ice cream for the evening's meal in its hollowed-out belly.

Lesvanoos had ejaculated all over the rough stones of the chamber.

Weak and hurting, his eyes full of tears, his lips chapped and his throat burning, he lifted his right hand and pointed to the door. The executioner called out in a loud voice and the champion entered with an unfolded cloak, which he threw over Lesvanoos. He wrapped him up, lifted him in his arms, and carried him away.

The man in the green velvet suit was sleeping beneath the trees. Seven dogs were howling at the moons.

Carita Dulce had awakened and the matronas were cooing to him in high-pitched voices, imitating the babbling of children.

"I trust an explanation will make us better understand each other," said Lord Vantedour.

They were seated around the table in the Great Room. Logs burned in the fireplaces, jesters and minstrels waited in the corners. The servants brought wine and roasted meat for the eight men from Earth, Lord Vantedour, and Theophilus. Ladies had been excluded from the meeting. Bonifacio of Solomea climbed into Leo Sessler's lap and studied the man with his yellow eyes. Tuk-o-Tut was guarding the door to the Arms Room, his arms crossed over his chest.

"Imagine the *Luz Dormida Tres* falling toward the planet at a much faster speed than had been anticipated.

"*We're going to crash.*

"Moritz vomits and Leval looks like he's been turned to stone. Commander Tardon manages to slow *Luz Dormida Tres* a little, not enough to stop its suicide run, and it finally comes to a bone-jarring halt on strange, foreign soil. But the ground of Salari II is clay; dried up and weak, it gives way beneath one side of the ship, causing it to tip and fall.

"We were wounded and unconscious for a long time," said Lord Vantedour.

A white awakening: the sun enters through the open cracks in the stern.

"We got out any way we could. Kesterren was the worst off, we had to drag him out. The *Luz Dormida Tres* lay on its side on the plain.

"The world is a cold piece of copper beneath two suns. Kesterren moans. Leval stays with him, while I climb into the *Luz Dormida Tres* with Sildor to look for water and saline solution. My hands are burned, Sildor has facial injuries and is dragging one leg. Outside, the wind has begun to blow and it's become dangerous to think.

"For several days, I couldn't tell you how many, we live between the desert and the *Luz Dormida Tres*, keeping ourselves alive with negligible rations. All the instruments were destroyed and the water supply was about to run out. Kesterren finally came to, but it was impossible for us to move him. Sildor's leg swelled up and became stiff, and my hands were scraped raw. Moritz spent the days sitting with his head between his knees and his arms around his legs, at times sobbing shamelessly."

It occurred to Leo Sessler (on whose knees Bonifacio of Solomea was sleeping) that pride might very well wither away in a desert world without water, food, or antibiotics. A world with two suns and five moons, to which man first arrives on a quick precolonizing, reconnaissance mission and where he is forced to live out his last few days.

"I had decided to kill them, you understand," said Lord Vantedour. "To go into the *Luz Dormida Tres*, shoot them from there and then shoot myself afterward. We couldn't go out looking for water. And even if we'd found it," he paused, scorning intermittent, seasonal, improbable traces of water, "our chances of survival were so minuscule as to be almost nonexistent. Some day, some other expedition—you—would arrive, and you'd find the remains of the ship and five skeletons with bullet holes in their heads." He smiled. "I'm still a pretty good shot."

"Commander Tardon," said Savan.

"Lord Vantedour, please, or just Vantedour."

"But you're Commander Tardon."

"Not anymore."

The commander of the *Niní Paume Uno* shifted in his chair and said he agreed with Savan. Tardon couldn't stop being who he had been, who he really was. Savan's question was never put into words; Theophilus smoothly intervened.

"Explain to them how we discovered the violet, Vantedour."

"Explain to us where all this came from," said the commander. His gesture took in the Great Room, the minstrels, the stone fireplaces, the blue-clad servants, the dwarves, the Staircase of Honor, Tuk-o-Tut—standing at the door to the Arms Room, adorned with necklaces, scimitar at his waist, slippers on his feet—and the feminine faces crowned with tall, white caps peaking over the inner balconies.

"The stories are one and the same," said Lord Vantedour.

"Tell them that we're gods," suggested Theophilus.

"We're gods."

"Please!"

"I walk around the crippled ship to pass the time. Sildor comes limping over to join me, and the two of us walk around in slow circles. We avoid stepping on the two large stains of violet light, just as we've done since the beginning. They have imprecise borders and seem to fluctuate, to move. Maybe they're alive, or maybe they're deadly. We're not curious, because we already know one answer.

"'I don't want to eat.'

"'Shut up, Sildor. There are still provisions left.'

"'That's a lie.'

"I swear I'm going to hit him, but he laughs. I take a few steps toward him and he backs up without watching where he's putting his feet.

"'I didn't mean to insult you,' he says. 'I was going to explain that I don't want to eat, but I'd give anything for a cigarette.'

"'Where did you get those cigarettes?' I yell.

"Sildor looks at me, scared, and then resumes his shipboard face.

"'Listen to me, Commander Tardon, I don't have any cigarettes. I only said I wanted a cigarette.'

"I lunge toward him as if I were going to fight him. I grab his wrist, lift up his hand and shove it in front of his eyes. He has two cigarettes in his hand.

"The only possible explanation was that we were crazy," continued Lord Vantedour.

"And the universe collapses above me, soft and sticky. Lying in Aphrodite's Bed, held down by the lid of my coffin, I hear the distant voices of Sildor and Leval. They're calling me, they have a megaphone. I know we've left reality behind. My ears are ringing and I dream of water. They slap my face and help me sit up. Kesterren asks what's going on. I want to know if the cigarettes exist. We touch them and smell them. Finally, we smoke one between the three of us and it's truly a cigarette. We decided to suppose for a moment that we're not crazy and conduct a test.

"'I want a cigarette,' Leval announces and looks at his empty hands, which remain empty.

"He says it again without looking at his hands. We imitate the words, the gestures, and the expressions we had when the first cigarette materialized. Sildor stands in front of me and says: 'I didn't mean to insult you. I was going to explain that I don't want to eat, but I'd give anything for a cigarette.'

"Nothing else happens. I laugh for the first time since the *Luz Dormida Tres* began to gain too much speed after entering the atmosphere.

"'I want a refrigerator with food for ten days,' I say. 'A summer house on the edge of a lake. An overcoat with a leather collar. A Rolls-Royce. A Siamese cat. Five trumpets.'

"Leval and Sildor are also laughing, but there's that cigarette.

"We sleep poorly. It's colder than it has been on previous nights and in contrast to Moritz, who practically doesn't speak or move, Kesterren won't stop complaining.

"The next morning, before the breakfast hour, if you can call what we'd been eating breakfast, I got up before the others awoke. Though I was intrigued by what had happened the night before, I went to the *Luz Dormida Tres* to look for the rifles. When I looked down at the tent and at the infinite, dark world that the two suns were beginning to illuminate, at the violet stains that looked like water, or living waters, I thought that, all things considered, it was a shame. I wasn't afraid; dying didn't scare me because I wasn't thinking about death. After the first fit of terror during my childhood, I had guessed that things like death have to be accepted or they will defeat us. But then I remembered the cigarette and went outside again. I smoked it there, freezing in the cold morning wind. The smoke was a violet-blue color, almost like the stains on the ground of Salari II. Seeing as I was going to die that day, I walked over to one of them, stood over it, and verified that I didn't feel anything. I said I wanted an electric razor, really strongly desiring it. I didn't feel as if I were shaving, but as if I myself were an electric razor. The cigarette burned my fingers, and the pain of the hot ashes on my already burned flesh made me scream. In my hand was an electric razor."

The dwarves were playing dice games next to the fireplace, urged on by the jugglers and minstrels. A contortionist was hanging in an arc above the players, the flames from the fire illuminating his face. Tricks, secrets: the servants were looking and laughing.

"Like death," said Lord Vantedour, "this was something we had to accept. And even if we were crazy, we could smoke our craziness, we could shave ourselves and fill our stomachs with our craziness. It wasn't just convenient to accept it, it was necessary. I woke Sildor up, and each of us stood on one of the violet stains. We wished for a river of fresh, clear water, with fish and a sandy bed thirty feet from where we were, and we got it. We wished for trees, a house, food, a Rolls-Royce, and five trumpets."

The eight men spent the entire day and night in Lord Vantedour's castle. Theophilus returned to the island. Bonifacio of Solomea and Tuk-o-Tut disappeared with Lord Vantedour.

That night, young Reidt had nightmares. Three male nurses in blood-stained scrubs were pushing him uphill in a wheelchair. When they reached the top they let go of the chair, leaving him alone, and went running back the way they'd come, while blowing up balloons that swelled and lifted them off the ground. He remained in his chair, at the edge of a bottomless precipice. Steps had been carved into the steep slope. He got out of his chair and began to descend, grabbing onto the edges of every step. He screamed because he knew that when he put his foot down, it wouldn't find the next step. He was going to wind up letting go, he would feel around with his foot for the next cranny and would lose his grip and fall, and he screamed.

That night, the first radio operator noted in the log a message signed by the commander, which stated that they had found a good spot and would camp there for the night.

That night, Les-Van-Oos killed three water snakes, armed with nothing but a spear, and the crowd went wild. Carita Dulce, in his uterus-crib, closed his eyes and felt between his legs with his hand. The matronas discreetly withdrew. Beneath the fading light of the stars, the man in the green velvet suit's heart was racing, struggling in its cage.

That night, Leo Sessler got out of bed and, accompanied by the sound of the rapids and the light of the torches, traversed corridors and climbed stairs until he arrived at the doorway where Tuk-o-Tut was sleeping.

"I want to see your master," said Leo Sessler, poking him with his foot.

The black man stood up and showed his teeth while grasping the handle of his scimitar.

If this animal strikes me with that, I'm done for.

"I want to see Lord Vantedour."

The black man shook his head no.

"Tardon!" yelled Leo Sessler. "Commander Tardon! Come out! I want to talk to you!"

Just as the dark-skinned man unsheathed his scimitar, the door opened inward.

"No, Tuk-o-Tut," said Lord Vantedour, "Dr. Sessler can come as often as he pleases."

The black man smiled.

"Come in, doctor."

"I must apologize for this untimely visit."

"Not at all. I'll have him bring us coffee."

Leo Sessler laughed. "I like these contradictions: a medieval castle without electric lights, but where you can drink coffee."

"Why not? Electric lights irritate me, but I like coffee." He went to the door, spoke to Tuk-o-Tut, returned, and sat down in front of Sessler. "I also have running water, as you will have noticed, but no telephone."

"And the others? Do they have telephones?"

"Theophilus has one so that he can keep in touch with Leval, when Leval is in any condition to talk. Kesterren almost never is, and Moritz definitely never is."

The two men were sitting in the middle of an enormous room. The bed, on a carved wooden platform, occupied the north wall. There was no west wall. Instead, three arches supported by columns gave way to a gallery with balconies above the patio, from which could be seen the countryside and the woods. It was all rather excessive: the ceilings were too high, there were skins on the floor, and tapestries adorned the walls. The only sound that could be heard was the powerful voice of the distant waterfalls Sessler still hadn't seen, but which he guessed were gigantic.

"What are we going to do, Vantedour?"

"That's the second time today I've been asked that question. And I'll confess I don't see why I have to be the one to decide. Theophilus asked me the same thing when we discovered you had arrived, he by much more perfect and, shall we say, modern methods than I. Back then, the question was what were we going to do about you. Now, it seems the question is what are we going to do about us."

"I was referring to everybody, to you all and us," said Leo Sessler. "But I'll admit I'm suspicious about myself and my motives. I suspect that this, as important as it may be, is nothing more than an indirect attempt to get some explanations out of you."

Lord Vantedour smiled. "You're not satisfied with everything I told you during dinner?"

Tuk-o-Tut entered without knocking. Behind him was a servant with the coffee.

"Sugar? A little cream?"

"No, thank you. I take it black and without sugar."

"As for me, I have a sweet tooth. I've gained weight. I exercise, ride horseback, and organize hunting parties, but the pleasures of the table still do their worst." He brought the cup to his lips. "Not that it matters much," he said, and took a sip of the sweet coffee.

Tuk-o-Tut and the servant left. Bonifacio of Solomea watched them from his perch on the bed, his tail tucked around him.

"I don't want anecdotes, Vantedour. What interests me is your opinion of this phenomenon of—I'm not sure what to call it, and that bothers me. I'm used to everything having a name, a designation; even the maniacal search for the correct name has a name. And despite that, I'm the man who abhors words."

"I understand that you need names for things. Aren't you what's called a man of science?"

"Yes. Excellent coffee."

"From our plantations. You must visit them."

"Certainly. Let's accept that I'm a man of science, with his contradictions, of course. I mean I could have been 'the acupuncturist and the salt-miner, the toll-collector and the blacksmith.'"

"Today you spoke of horses running toward the boneyard."

"How did you know that?"

"Theophilus thought up an apparatus, rather complicated I'm sure, and has devoted himself to listening to you all with it ever since you left the ship."

"That brings us to my first question: what do you think of this phenomenon of getting things from nothing?"

"I no longer think. But I have an infinite number of answers for that," said Lord Vantedour. "I could say again that we're gods, or that we have been made gods. I could also say it's extremely useful, and if it existed on all worlds we could eliminate many superfluous things: religions, philosophical doctrines, superstitions, and all of that. Do you realize? There would be no questions about mankind. Give an all-powerful instrument to an individual and you'll have all the answers, believe me. Or don't believe me, you have no reason to believe me. Wait and see what the violet has done with Kesterren, Moritz, and Leval, or rather what they've done to themselves with the violet." He left the cup on the table. "Theophilus and I are the less serious cases, for at least we continue to be men."

"And you two couldn't have done something for them?"

"There's absolutely no reason we should have to do anything for them. The worst thing of all is that they—and we as well, but that's another story—the worst thing is that they're finally happy. Do you know what that means, Sessler?"

"No, but I can begin to guess."

"The fact that we're happy puts a finality to everything, in a sense. As far as what we're going to do with all of you, that's also easily answered. Theophilus can design something, an apparatus or a potion or a weapon, that would make all of you forget everything to the point that you'd believe you'd proven Salari II doesn't exist anymore, that it exploded during our mission, killing us all, or it's become dangerous for humans, or whatever."

"We could use the violet too."

"I'm sorry to disappoint you, Sessler, but no, you can't. We discovered how because we were desperate. You're not, and we'll make sure that you're not while you're on Salari II. I tell you this so as to avoid futile attempts. It's not a matter of standing on a violet stain and saying 'I want the crown jewels' and then getting them."

"Very well, you have the secret and you're not going to tell us. I understand. But what are—or what's in—those violet stains?"

"I don't know. I don't know what they are. We did some experiments in the beginning. We dug down, for example, and the violet was still there, not as part of the ground but rather like a reflection. However, if you stand there and look upward and all around you for the source of those reflections, you find nothing. They stay there, sometimes fluctuating a little; they're there at night as well as when it snows. We don't know what they are or what's in them. I can venture a few guesses. For example: God finally broke apart, and the pieces fell to Salari II. That's a good explanation, except that I, personally, don't like it. Or every world has points from which it's possible—under certain conditions, mind you—to obtain anything, but on Salari II they're more evident. According to this theory, they would exist on Earth, too, though as yet no one's discovered them. Or almost no one, which would explain certain legends. Perhaps those violet things are alive and they are the gods, not us. Or none of this exists"—he stomped his foot on the floor—"and it's humans who change on Salari II, we suffer a type of delirium that makes the world look and feel as if all of our dreams had come true. Maybe this is hell and the violet is our punishment. And so on, without end. Pick whichever one you like best."

"Thanks, but none of those theories quite convinces me."

"Me either. But I don't ask myself questions anymore. And now, Sessler, what kind of man are you?"

"What?"

"Just that, what kind of man are you? Tomorrow or the next day, you'll go see how the rest of the crew of the *Luz Dormida Tres* are living. What would you have done? How would you be living?"

"Hey, now, listen, Vantedour, that's not fair."

"Why not? You already see how I live, what I wanted and what I asked for."

"Yes. You're a despot, a man who isn't satisfied unless he's at the top of the pyramid."

"No, Dr. Sessler, no. I'm not a feudal lord, I'm a man who lives in a feudal castle. I don't condemn anyone to the rack, I don't confiscate possessions, and I don't cut off heads. I haven't busied myself with creating rival lords or a king with whom to dispute power. I have neither army nor fiefdom. The castle is all."

"And the inhabitants of the castle?"

"They were also born of the violet, of course, and they are as authentic as the cigarette and that razor. I'll tell you something else: they're happy and they feel affection toward me, affection, not adoration, because I conceived them that way. They get old, they get sick, they get hurt if they fall, and they die. But they're satisfied and they like me."

"The women, too?"

Lord Vantedour stood up without saying anything.

"So, not the women?"

"There aren't any women, Sessler. Due to the, shall we say, particular conditions under which something can be obtained from the violet, it's been impossible for any of us to obtain a woman."

"But I've seen them."

"They weren't women. Now, if you'll excuse me—and I hope you won't take me for an inconsiderate host—it's time to go to bed. There's still much to do tomorrow."

At three o'clock in the morning, Dr. Leo Sessler walked out onto the patio of the castle, crossed the bridge, went down the ramp, and began to walk beneath the moons, looking for a violet stain on the ground. Lord Vantedour watched him from the gallery balconies.

"We've found the crew of the *Luz Dormida Tres,*" announced the commander.

"How did they die?" asked young Reidt.

"They didn't die," said Leo Sessler. "They're alive, very alive, healthy, and happy."

"And how are we going to take them with us, sir?" asked the navigation officer. "Five men will be too much extra weight."

"It doesn't look like they want to return," said Leo Sessler.

"They're the lords and masters of Salari II," Savan said, almost shouting. "Each one of them has an entire continent to himself, and they can get whatever they want from those violet things."

"What violet things?"

"Let's not be hasty," said the commander. "Gather the crew together."

The fifteen men got into Theophilus's vehicle, with the master navigator at the controls. They glided across the surface of Salari II.

"Would you prefer to fly?"

"Where?"

"Anywhere around here. He never wanders very far."

The men walked around outside, trying their luck with the violet stains.

"There's a bum lying there," said one of the crew members.

Lord Vantedour leaned over the man dressed in green rags. He was barefoot and held a cane in his hand.

"What if he attacks us?" said one of the men with his hand on the butt of his pistol.

"Tell him to stop that," Theophilus said to the commander.

"Kesterren!" Lord Vantedour resorted to shaking him while calling his name. The man in rags opened his eyes.

"We can't talk anymore," he said.

"Kesterren, wake up, we have visitors."

"Visitors from the stars," said the man. "Who are the men from the heavens now?"

"Kesterren! Another expedition has arrived from Earth."

"They're cursed." He closed his eyes once again. "Tell them to go, they're cursed, and you go away, too."

"Listen to me, Kesterren. They want to talk to you."

"Go away."

"They want to tell you something about Earth and they want you to talk to them about Salari II."

"Go away."

He turned over and covered his face with his outstretched arms. Dirt and dry leaves fell from what was left of the green velvet suit.

"Let's go," said Lord Vantedour.

"But Tardon, we can't just leave him in that state. He's too drunk, something could happen to him," protested the commander.

"Don't worry."

"He'll die, abandoned like that."

"Not likely," said Theophilus.

The vehicle came to a stop in front of the gray facade of the house on the mountain. The door opened before they had the chance to knock and stayed open until the last man entered. Then it closed again. They walked along an immense, dark, empty corridor, until reaching another door. Theophilus opened it. Behind it was a miserable, windowless room, lit only by lamps hanging from the ceiling. Two very young women were playing cards on the rug. Lord Vantedour approached them. "Greetings," he said.

"She's cheating," said one of the women, looking at him.

"Bad girl," said Lord Vantedour.

"Yes, isn't she? But I still like her. I can forgive her anything."

"I see," he said. "Where can we find Les-Van-Oos?"

"I don't know."

"There's a party somewhere," said the other.

"In the golden room," said the first.

"Where's that?"

"You don't think I'm going to leave her alone, do you? I can't go with you." She thought for a moment. "Go out that door, no, the other one, and when you come across the hunters, ask them."

She went back to playing cards.

"Cheater," Leo Sessler heard before leaving.

Another corridor, just like the first, and corridors like this one and the ones before it branching out at right angles. They arrived at a circular room, with a roof made of glass tiles that let in the light. A group of men were seated around a table, eating.

"Are you the hunters?"

"No."

"We're the gladiators," said another.

"Where's Les-Van-Oos?"

"In the golden room."

A man stood up and cleaned his hands on his tunic.

"Come with me."

They wandered through yet more corridors, until they reached the golden room.

The hero, sprawled out on his victory throne, was wearing a laurel crown on his head and absolutely nothing else. He tried to stand up when he saw them come in.

"Ah, my friends, my dear friends."

"Listen, Les-Van-Oos!" Lord Vantedour shouted, spreading his arms.

The music, the screams, and the noise drowned out everything that was being said.

"Wine! More wine for my guests!"

Lord Vantedour and Theophilus approached the throne. Leo Sessler watched them as they spoke, and saw how the hero laughed, slapping the arm of the throne with his hand. The throne was encrusted with gems, its arms, legs and back adorned with marble gargoyles with eyes of precious stones.

"Splendid, just splendid!" howled the Hero. "We'll bring in dancers, we'll organize tournaments! Let there be more wine! Listen everyone! Greet the guests and show them what you can do! They come from a miserable world, one without heroes. The only heroes left either exist in legend or are officers in the military."

He stood up and tottered to the center of the room, tripping and almost falling, followed by Theophilus and Lord Vantedour. The noise quieted down, though not entirely. The dresses ceased to flutter and the music was hushed.

"They come from a world where people watch television and eat off plastic tablecloths and put artificial flowers in ceramic vases; where family wages are paid, along with life insurance, and sewer taxes; where there are bank employees and police sergeants and gravediggers." The women laughed. "Give them wine!" Each man had to accept a cup filled to the brim. "More wine!"

The jugs were tipped once more, overfilling the cups. The fifteen men from Earth said nothing while the wine splashed over their boots and ran onto the floor.

"That's enough, idiots, wait for them to drink first."

Naked and crowned with laurels, his body full of scars and scabs, Les-Van-Oos welcomed them.

"I've seen the fragmented Earth become sterile under the weight of family trees," he recited, "I've gone down to the mines, I've made knives, I've dissolved salt in my mouth, I've had incestuous dreams, I've opened doors with forged keys. Give wine to all the opaque men from Earth, you fools! Can't you see that their cups are empty?"

The cups in the hands of the fifteen men were still full. Leo Sessler thought he would like to take Les-Van-Oos, just as he was, drunk and obscene, to a place where he would be able to keep him talking. But there, in the insane party and with the entire crew of the *Niní Paume Uno* behind him, what he wanted more than anything was to beat him until he fell unconscious to the marble floor. Les-Van-Oos was a skinny, sore-covered waste, a drooling, naked megalomaniac. If he were to strike him he'd kill him, and the guests would pounce on him and tear him to pieces. Or maybe not. Maybe they would seat him on the victory throne, naked. Meanwhile, Les-Van-Oos had seen and done many things, and was reaching his very limits.

"I've seen rituals and frauds, I've seen entire towns migrate, I've seen cyclones and caves and three-headed calves and retail stores! I've seen sins, I've seen sinners, and I've learned from them! I've seen men eat each other, and I've seen those who got away. I, galley slave!"

It all ended with a hiccup and a sob. They lifted him up and carried him to the throne, where he collapsed and lay panting.

"Leave those cups and let's go," said Lord Vantedour.

Leo Sessler put his down on the floor in the puddle of wine in which he'd been standing.

Les-Van-Oos was screaming for them to take off his crown of laurels because it was burning him, burning his forehead.

The gladiators had finished eating and had gone, leaving behind dirty plates and overturned chairs. The women were still playing cards.

Night had fallen by the time they arrived back at Vantedour.

"I'd like to see those rapids sometime," said Leo Sessler.

Lord Vantedour was at his side. "Whenever you wish, Dr. Sessler. They're rather far away, but we can go anytime. You must also see the coffee fields and Theophilus's greenhouses."

"Why rapids?"

"It's actually a huge waterfall, bigger than any you've ever seen before. You see, I spent a good deal of my life living near a waterfall."

"How can a house be close to a waterfall?"

"It wasn't my house, I never had a house, doctor."

Lord Vantedour led them across the Patio of Honor.

Theophilus rejoined them at dinner, and Tuk-o-Tut resumed his post in front of the Arms Room. The commander made a speech, one that made Leo Sessler laugh to himself. Lord Vantedour stood up and graciously rejected their offer on behalf of those who had been crew members of the *Luz Dormida Tres*. Bonifacio of Solomea evidently agreed. Tuk-o-Tut, in front of the door, and the women wearing the tall, white hennins on the interior balconies, laughed.

"I don't see any other possible solution," said the commander.

"The simplest and most sensible one is that you leave everything as it is," said Theophilus. "You all return to Earth and we stay here."

"But we have to write a report and present our findings. We can't take all of you with us, true, but at least Kesterren, who needs urgent medical help, and perhaps Leval too, he needs treatment."

"You haven't seen Moritz," said Theophilus.

"According to calculations, we can take two with us. We'll see who that will be later."

"Don't even mention it. Go back, give your report, but leave us out."

"A report without physical evidence?"

"It wouldn't be the first time. Nobody took the Tammerden Columns or the Glyphs of Arfea to Earth."

"That's less incredible than . . ."

"Than us."

"Regardless, those men need treatment, it's a simple question of humanity. And besides, when the colonizers arrive you all will be occupying the land illegally, and you'll have to go back."

"I dare to state, Commander, that there won't be any colonizers," said Lord Vantedour, "and that we won't go back."

"Is that a threat?"

"Not at all. Think about it rationally: colonizers in a world where, if one knows how, anything can be obtained from nothing? No, Commander, it's not a threat. Do not forget that we are gods and gods don't threaten, they act."

"That seems like a famous saying," said Leo Sessler.

"Maybe one day it will be, Dr. Sessler. But please, try these pink grapes. You must also visit the vineyards."

Leo Sessler laughed. "Vantedour, you seem to be a comedian, and a rather good one."

"Thank you."

The commander refused to try the grapes. "I insist you go back, if not with us, then with one of the future expeditions. I'm going to include in the report a recommendation that all of you be permitted to take back to Earth some of the things you have here, along with the people you'd like to have accompany you." He looked toward the interior balconies. "Is one of them the chatelaine, Commander Tardon? You know that recommendations made in a report are taken very seriously."

Theophilus was laughing. "Commander, allow me two objections. In the first place, nothing produced by the violet can leave Salari II. Didn't it occur to you that, ten years ago, ten Earth years ago, the most logical thing would have been to ask for a ship in good working condition in which to return to Earth? We wished for it, Commander. But we were mistrustful and well trained enough to do a test run with a ship controlled from the ground. If Bonifacio of Solomea were to try to accompany Vantedour to Earth, he would disappear upon leaving the atmosphere."

"Then none of this is real!"

"No? Try a pink grape, Commander."

"Forget the grapes, Tardon! You said you have two objections, Sildor, what's the other one?"

"There's nobody here that we'd want to take back, even if we could. There's no Lady Vantedour, there's not a single woman on all of Salari II."

"But wait!" said Savan. "I've seen them here, and in that house of crazies, and in . . ."

"They're not women."

Leo Sessler was waiting. They all spoke at the same time except young Reidt, who remained pale and quiet, his hands intertwined under the table.

Lord Vantedour said, "You're such a fan of evidence, Commander. Go ahead, call them over and ask them to disrobe. They won't refuse. The correct word is *ephebi*."

"But those women in Leval's house, the ones playing cards on the floor, they had breasts!"

"Of course they have breasts! They love having them. We can get hormones, and scalpels, and surgeons to use the scalpels. And a surgeon can do many things, especially if he is skillful. What we can't get is a woman."

"Why not?" asked Leo Sessler.

Young Reidt had gone red and tiny beads of sweat dotted his upper lip.

"Due to those special, indispensable conditions under which created things must be conceived," said Lord Vantedour. "If any of you'd had a recorder last night, or if you possessed a perfect memory, you'd find the answer somewhere in what I said."

"That definitely changes things." The commander was more alert now.

"Does it? The fact that at least four of us sleep with young men changes things?"

"Of course. You are all, or were, and I dare to say still are, officers of the Space Force."

No, Leo Sessler said to himself, no, no. A man can't travel throughout space, set foot on other worlds, slip around in the silent void, immerse himself in other atmospheres, ask himself why he's there and if he'll ever return, and continue being nothing more than a commander in the Force.

"And I can't be responsible for ruining the reputation of the Force (*I've never heard a capital letter as clearly as that one,* Sessler thought) by taking five homosexual officers back to Earth."

That's when young Reidt exploded. Leo Sessler crossed over to him in two strides and struck him.

"You can't!" young Reidt was yelling, as blood from Sessler's violent blow ran from his nose to his mouth, staining and washing away the beads of sweat. He continued to yell and spray Sessler's face with a reddish rain. "You can't force me to go near that garbage! Garbage! Garbage! Filthy whores! Dirty perverts!" Another blow. "Get rid of them! They've dirtied me! I'm dirty!"

Leo Sessler closed his fist.

"Get that imbecile out of my house," said Lord Vantedour.

The young man had fainted, and two of the crew members lifted him up by his arms and legs.

"And you were saying that we were the ones in need of medical attention?" asked Theophilus. "What does this say about your crew, Commander? We are reasonably content, we can live with ourselves, we play clean; but that fellow's nights must be an orgy of sex and repentance. Do you repent anything, Vantedour?"

"I could have him killed," said Lord Vantedour. "Make sure they take him away from here and lock him in the ship, Commander, or I'll have his throat cut."

"Take him away and confine him to the ship," said the commander. "He's under arrest."

"Use my car," said Theophilus.

"It seems we owe you an apology."

"Listen, Sessler," the commander protested.

"We apologize for the incident, my lord," said Leo Sessler, still standing.

"Let's sit down. I assure you I've already forgotten that imbecile. Please, continue with dessert. Maybe you'll prefer the quinces over the grapes, Commander."

"Look, Tardon, stop talking about food."

"Vantedour, Commander, Lord Vantedour, and that's the last time I'll tell you: it's the price of my forgiveness."

"If you think you can treat me like one of your servants . . ."

"Of course he can, Commander," said Leo Sessler. "It's best if you just sit back down."

"Dr. Sessler, you are also under arrest!"

"Forgive me, Commander, but that's arbitrary and I'm going to ignore it."

The commander of the *Nini Paume Uno* violently shoved back his dinner chair, causing it to crash to the floor. "Dr. Sessler, I'll make sure they expel you from the Auxiliary Corps! As for the rest of you . . . as for the rest of you!"

Leo Sessler panicked for a moment. Who knows how a fifty-eight-year-old man's heart—sick, maltreated by space, gravity, and the void, faced with overwhelming tension—is going to react. And if the commander dies . . .

"I'm going to recommend that Salari II be sterilized! That all human life, or whatever it is, disappear, terminate, die!"

"If you'll only sit back down, Commander."

"I don't want your grapes or your quinces!"

"If you'll sit back down, I'll explain why it's not advisable for you to do any of that."

Carita Dulce was sleeping and Lesvanoos was crying in the arms of the card-playing women.

The man beneath the trees had his green velvet suit once again, though this one was a lighter green, with a gold chain draped across the vest, and his boots had silver buckles. A bad thing, dreams.

"Any one of us, Theophilus or myself, and even Leval or Kesterren, can destroy all of you before you have the chance to give an order."

The commander sat down.

"You're not as stupid as you think you have to be."

"That's a compliment, Commander," said Leo Sessler. "We've come to disrupt the balance on Salari II, and you know it."

"We have the means to do it," said Theophilus. "In fact, we already have two ways, equally fast, equally drastic."

"Fine," said the commander, "you win. What do you want us to do?"

We've won. What's with this "we've"? No doubt now, someday I'm going to have to write my memoirs.

"Nothing, Commander, absolutely nothing. Besides keeping the preacher locked up in the ship, nothing. Finish eating. Take a walk, if you want. Have you seen the five moons? One of them orbits the world three times in a single night. And after that, go to sleep."

Theophilus's vehicle took them to the river, and from there they had to continue on foot.

"There aren't any roads on the other side," said Theophilus.

They crossed the hanging bridge. On the other side was only a meadow of soft, green grass. They found flowers, birds, and three violet stains. The men stood upon the violet and wished for gold, barrels of beer, race cars; then they continued walking. Neither the commander nor Leo Sessler tried it. But Savan did, asking for a platinum bracelet with diamonds to give to Leda. Moments later, an uproar: Savan had a platinum and diamond bracelet in his hand.

"You see, it's not so difficult," said Lord Vantedour. "You, an engineer, met the conditions without knowing it."

"But I didn't do anything."

"Of course not."

"What are the conditions?"

"That's our advantage, engineer. And why do you want to know them? In order to keep what you obtained you'd have to stay and live on Salari II."

Savan looked sadly at Leda's bracelet.

The men were jumping, spreading wide their arms, asking for things out loud and in whispers, singing, praying, sitting, and lying on the violet. Theophilus told them it was all useless, and the commander ordered them to keep moving.

They managed to drag them away from the violet stains, but the men were not happy about it. Leo Sessler could guess how they felt about Theophilus and Lord Vantedour. (They won't dare, they've been living under rigorous discipline for too long. Anyway, they know that everything would disappear as it left the atmosphere of Salari II. But if Leda's bracelet doesn't disappear?) Each man caressed Leda's bracelet as it was passed from hand to hand, some sniffing it, some biting it. One of the crew members rubbed it against his face, another hung it from his ear.

"Over there."

There were trees now, and they were nearing a cave in the side of the hill. Three old, overweight women came out to greet them.

"They're the matronas."

"The what?"

"They're not women either, is what I mean. Moritz called them the matronas: they're some of his mothers."

"And Moritz? Where's Moritz?"

"Moritz lives inside his mother, Commander."

"Welcome," chorused the women.

"Thank you," responded Lord Vantedour. "We want to see Carita Dulce."

Leo Sessler felt sorry for the commander.

"Nooo," said the matronas. "He's sleeping."

"Can we see him sleep?"

"You were here before. Why do you want to disturb him?"

"We don't want to disturb him, I assure you. We'll be silent, we're just going to look at him."

The matronas were doubtful.

"Come," said one of them, "but on tiptoes."

Leo Sessler decided that no, he would never write his memoirs. He would never be able to describe himself walking tiptoe over a meadow on Salari II next to other tiptoeing men, behind three old, fat women who were really three costumed men, beneath two suns, one yellow and one orange, toward the entrance of a cave in a hillside.

"Quietly, quietly."

But the sand on the cave floor crunched beneath their soles, worrying the matronas.

There were two matronas at the entrance to the cavern. And further down at the end, beneath a very faint light, were two more. They were rocking an enormous egg, suspended at the ends by a device that allowed it to move and turn.

"What's that?" asked the commander.

"Shhh."

"That's the Great Uterus, the Mother," Theophilus whispered to him.

"Shhh."

Leo Sessler touched it. The egg was gray and fibrous, encircled by a horizontal groove that made it appear as though the two halves could be separated. And indeed, they could be.

The matronas were smiling. They motioned toward the man inside the egg: chin between his knees, arms around his legs, smiling in his dream world. The inside of the egg was soft, warm, and moist.

"Moritz!" said the commander, almost out loud.

The matronas raised their arms, terrified. Whimpering, Carita Dulce moved, but didn't awaken. One of the matronas pointed to the exit: it was an order. Leo Sessler changed his mind again: he would write his memoirs.

That night, they were guests of Theophilus: clavichords instead of rapids.

"It was worse a few months ago," said Lord Vantedour, "ancient Chinese music."

The table was made of crystal, with gold-inlaid ebony feet. The patterns in the ocher and gold mosaics covering the floor were never repeated. The Lady and the Unicorn watched them from the tapestries. The crew members felt uncomfortable; they laughed a lot, elbowing each other and joking among themselves. Arranged around each plate were four forks, four knives, and three cups. White-clad servants brought around the serving bowls, and the butler stood behind Theophilus's chair. Leo Sessler recalled the man-fetus curled up inside of the viscous, warm uterus-cradle, and wondered if the memory would let him eat. But when they brought out the ice sculptures on a wheeled cart and one of them began to burn with a blue flame, he discovered that he had eaten everything, hopefully using the correct cutlery, and that he would also eat the candied fruits and the ice cream when the sphinxes and the swans had melted. The commander was talking in a hushed voice to Theophilus. Leo Sessler realized Saverius had no idea which fork he should use for the fish (he did: it was the only one he was completely sure about), and he didn't care. Nor did Theophilus. The master astronomer announced that he would read to them the introduction to his monograph on the constellation Aphrodite's Bed. They had seen Peony from afar when she'd entered; Theophilus had greeted her but hadn't called her over to join them. Leo Sessler would have liked to have seen him up close and talked to him. Ocher speckled roses stood in the middle of the table.

"But we *must* concern ourselves with them, at least with Moritz."

"Why?" asked Theophilus.

"He's sick. That's not normal."

"Are you normal, Commander?"

"I function within the normal range."

"Look at it this way," said Lord Vantedour. "Psychiatric treatment—because naturally, we can get a psychiatrist for Moritz—would make him suffer for years, and for what? Relying on the violet, as we all do, Moritz—healthy, cured, released from the hospital—would start by asking for a mother, one that would continue changing or hypertrophying into a uterus-cradle. That's what he wants, just like Leval wants to oscillate between heroism and humiliation, Kesterren wants to drown himself in endless inebriation, Theophilus wants Cimarosa or Chinese music, ice cream inside ice statues, German philosophers and tapestries, and I want a twelfth-century castle. When one has the means of getting everything, one winds up giving in to personal demons. Which, I don't know if you've realized, Commander, is another way of describing happiness."

"Happiness! To be enclosed in your own prison, licking its walls? To go from acclaim to a dungeon where they whip you and put hot irons on your groin? To live passed out in perpetual drunkenness?"

"Yes, Commander, that too can be happiness. What's the difference between enclosing oneself in an artificial uterus and sitting on the edge of the river to fish for dorado? Apart from the fact that the dorado can be fried and eaten, and the sun gives one a healthy glow. I'm referring to the satisfaction, the pleasure factor. One means is just as legitimate as another: everything depends on the individual who is seeking happiness. Among bank employees and funeral directors, if you'll allow me to quote Les-Van-Oos, it's possible that the uterus is what's frightening and fishing for dorado is what's desirable. But on Salari II?"

There were no more sphinxes or swans now. Leo Sessler cut open a frosted orange and found it filled with cherries, which themselves were filled with orange pulp.

"The same, Commander, the same," answered the lord of Vantedour. "The uterus, the drunken episodes, the whip."

The master astronomer cleared his throat and stood up.

"You're going to hear something very interesting," said Theophilus.

The servants placed cut crystal coffee cups in front of each person. The water vapor began to condense and darken in the transparent bowls.

"Introduction to a monograph on the constellation Aphrodite's Bed," began the master astronomer.

That night, in Vantedour, it was the lord of the manor's turn to travel through galleries and down staircases to Dr. Leo Sessler's room. He carried Bonifacio of Solomea in his arms, and Tuk-o-Tut followed behind them.

"Good evening, Dr. Sessler. I've taken the liberty of paying you a visit."

Leo Sessler had him come in.

"And of requesting that they bring us coffee and cognac."

"That sounds nice. Listen, I'm not going to have time to see the coffee fields or the vineyards."

"That's what I wanted to talk to you about."

"What I mean is, we're leaving tomorrow."

"Yes."

They brought in the coffee. Tuk-o-Tut closed the door and sat out in the hall.

"Why don't you stay, Sessler?"

"Don't think I haven't considered it."

"That's how I would finally know if you're the man I've supposed you to be."

"To wish for an austere house," said Leo Sessler, "everything white inside and out: walls, roof, chimney, with a hearth and a camp bed, a dresser, a table and two chairs, and to sit down and write my memoirs. I'd probably go fishing for dorados once a week."

"What's stopping you? Does not being able to have a woman bother you?"

"Frankly, no. I've never slept with a man, nor have I had homosexual loves, not counting a borderline friendship with a schoolmate at age thirteen, but that's within normal range, as our commander would say. I'm not going to recoil in fear like young Reidt. I, too, believe it's impossible to maintain the same sexual mores on Salari II as on Earth. Have you ever wondered what mores are, Vantedour?"

"Of course, a set of rules that should be followed in order to do good and avoid doing bad. I don't think I've ever heard anything quite so idiotic. I only know of one good, Dr. Sessler, to not harm my brother. And only one bad: to think about myself too much. And I've done both. That's why I'm making you this offer, but if you want to leave, I won't insist."

"Yes, I've decided I want to go back."

"I'd like to know why."

"I'm not really sure. For obscure visceral reasons; because I didn't crash-land on Salari II in a destroyed ship; because I haven't had time to create an Earth around me here in accordance with my personal demons. Because I've always gone back, and this time, too, I want to go back."

"Whom do you live with on Earth?"

"No, that's not my reason for saying no. I live alone."

"Very well, Sessler, we'll bid you a courtly farewell. But I want to warn you of something. The entire crew of the *Niní Paume Uno* will forget what they've seen here."

"It was true then?"

"At that moment, no. Now, it is."

"How will you manage to do that?"

"Theophilus has found a way. Nobody will realize something has infiltrated their brain. Half an hour after closing the ship's hatch, everyone will be convinced they found nothing but a dangerous world devastated by radiation, which probably killed the crew of the *Luz Dormida Tres*. The commander is going to report that there is no possibility of colonization, and will recommend a hundred-year waiting period before the next exploration."

"What a shame. It's a nice planet. I'm thinking of writing my memoirs, did you know that, Vantedour? And I'll be sorry to have to describe Salari II as a dead, lethal world. I can't imagine that right now, but I suppose it'll happen on it's own."

Lord Vantedour was smiling.

"I'm surprised you told me," added Leo Sessler.

"Are you? I'll tell you another thing. You can't obtain anything from the violet if you don't feel yourself to be that which you wish to obtain. Do you understand? That's why it is impossible to create a woman. When Theophilus first desired a cigarette he wanted so much to smoke that he identified not with the smoker, but with the cigarette. He *was* a cigarette: he felt himself the tobacco, the paper, the smoke; he touched the fibers. He was each fiber. The other night, when I spoke of the razor, I told you about the second experience—if we don't count the other cigarette—in which the same thing happened. I told you all that I'd felt not like the man who shaves, but like the razor. But it got lost in the midst of everything I said, which was what I was hoping for."

"So it was that simple."

"Yes. Savan, the engineer, must really long for that woman. For a moment he felt himself wrapped around her wrist and wished for a bracelet. That's why you didn't get anything the night before last. But if you want to try now, we can go to the violet."

"You knew about that?"

"I saw you from the balcony. I was hoping you'd give it a try, of course. Now you can get what you want, anything."

"Thanks, but I think it'd be better not to try. And anyway, it would only last me one night, and by tomorrow I'll have forgotten it."

"True," Lord Vantedour said and stood up. "I'll be sorry not to read your memoirs, Dr. Sessler. Good night."

Bonifacio of Solomea had stayed behind and Leo Sessler had to open the door to let him out. Tuk-o-Tut was coming toward them, and Bonifacio of Solomea jumped into the black man's open arms.

On the gangway of the *Niní Paume Uno,* the crew turned and saluted. Leo Sessler didn't give a military salute; he waved instead. The population of Vantedour retreated when the hatch was shut and the ship began to shudder.

Strapped to his seat with his eyes closed, Leo Sessler traveled though Salari II in his mind. In twenty minutes, nineteen minutes fifty-eight seconds, nineteen minutes fifty-three seconds, he would forget it all. Nobody spoke. Young Reidt's face was swollen, nineteen minutes.

The commander was telling someone to take charge. Leo Sessler was playing with the zipper on his strap; the commander was saying that he was going to sit down immediately and write a draft of his report on Salari II, three minutes, forty-two seconds.

"Are you going to make any special recommendations, Commander?"

"It's all pretty clear. If you want me to tell you frankly what I think, I believe Salari II is an emergency—listen to me carefully, an e-mer-gen-cy."

Leo Sessler was galloping through the meadows of Salari II, the wind whistling in his ears, two minutes, fifty-one seconds.

"Therefore, I'm going to recommend a rescue expedition."

"Whom are you planning to save, Commander?"

"Where is that humming coming from?" The commander removed the microphone from its stand. "Verify source of new humming."

Then he put it back.

"To bring closure to the situation of the crew of the *Luz Dormida Tres.*" (Two seconds. One. The humming stopped.) "They must've been killed by the radiation."

Leo Sessler thought quickly about Salari II, the last thought, and he remembered it green and blue beneath two suns. The Puma Desert, the colt, Vantedour. Theophilus, Vantedour, Bonifacio of Solomea, Kesterren, Peony, the punch to young Reidt's jaw, Vantedour, the victory throne. Carita Dulce enclosed in the uterus, the five moons, Lord Vantedour's offer for him to stay on Salari II, and warning him that he would forget everything—but he wasn't forgetting.

"It's a shame," the commander was saying, "a shame we couldn't even go out in search of remains as evidence to include in the report, but that radiation would've killed us, even with the suits. Young Reidt here doesn't make mistakes. Who was the physicist on the *Luz Dormida Tres?*"

"Jonás Leval, I think."

"Ah. Very well, Doctor, I'm off to draft that report. See you later."

"Goodbye, Commander."

I haven't forgotten, I'm not forgetting.

I'll be sorry not to read your memoirs, Dr. Sessler, Lord Vantedour had said.

"I'll be sorry not to read Dr. Sessler's memoirs," said Lord Vantedour.

"Do you think Sessler is trustworthy?" asked Theophilus.

"Yes. And if he weren't, imagine the scenario. Fourteen men talking about a radioactive world, and him describing medieval castles and gigantic uteruses."

"Why did you condemn him to not forgetting, Vantedour?"

"You think it was a punishment?"

In the *Niní Paume Uno,* the commander was writing, Savan was drinking his coffee, and young Reidt was rubbing his cheek.

"I must've hit myself during takeoff."

Leo Sessler sat before a cup of coffee he hadn't even touched.

"They must be lamenting the fact that the colonization routes out this way will remain closed," Theophilus said.

"A shame," said Savan, the engineer. "This means the colonization routes throughout this sector will remain closed for a long time."

Kesterren was singing while hugging a tree, Carita Dulce was running his tongue over the wet walls of the cradle-uterus, Lesvanoos was descending the stairs to the dungeon, and Lord Vantedour was saying, "And complaining about the awful coffee they're drinking."

"This coffee is disgusting," said the navigation officer. "You can never get good coffee on an explorer ship. Luxury cruise ships, now those have good coffee."

Theophilus laughed. "And wishing they could drink the coffee served on big, tourist cruisers."

Leo Sessler had not tried his.

"'And there, to the sound of earthly wingbeats, went they,'" he said, "'the Great Itinerants of Sleep and Action, the Interlocutors, thirsty for the Far Away, and the Denunciators of roaring chasms, Great Interpolators of risks lurking in the farthest corners.'"[4]

But no one heard him.

André Carneiro

BRAZIL

Considered one of the founding fathers of Brazilian science fiction, André Carneiro (1922–) was born and educated in the small town of Atibaia, outside of São Paulo. In spite of his stature within the SF community, cultivating the genre has been but one of his many interests, albeit a much-loved one. His adult life has always been intimately associated with the arts, and in Brazil he is a well-known experimental filmmaker, painter, photographer, and writer. One of his films, *Solitude (Solidão)*, was selected to represent Brazil in the Tenth International Film Festival in Glasgow, Scotland, in 1951, and he has received several awards over the years for his photographic and literary work. As a mainstream author, Carneiro is best known for his poetry (see his collection *Fullspace: André Carneiro's Poems: 1958–1963* [*Espaçopleno: Poemas de André Carneiro 1958–1963*, 1966]) and for his novels of psychosocial criticism, written in a style that has been compared to Aldous Huxley's.

As an SF author, Carneiro is celebrated for his essay "Introduction to the Study of Science Fiction" ("Introdução ao estudo da 'science-fiction,'" 1967), for the novel *Free Swimming Pool (Piscina livre,* 1980) and its sequel *The Art of Love (Amorquia,* 1991), and for the short story collections *Diary of the Lost Spaceship (Diário da nave perdida,* 1963) and *The Man Who Guessed Right (O homem que adivinhava,* 1966). His short novel *Darkness (A escuridão),* which first appeared in *Diário da nave perdida,* is an end-of-the-world story where only blind people are able to cope on an Earth suddenly devoid of light. It is considered an international classic of SF, having won the Brazilian *Hugo,* that is, the *Nova* science fiction award for best short fiction of 1995 (in a reprint). Carneiro's stories have been translated into Spanish, English, Japanese, French, Italian, and German.

Carneiro has always requested that his science fiction be judged as literature, and in fact feels that the designation "science fiction" has done tremendous harm because it isolates writers and stigmatizes their work. Be that as it may, he is much celebrated among Brazil's SF fandom, where his highly original short stories and novels are kept alive.

The story we choose to present here, "Brain Transplant," was initially written for the Brazilian edition of *Playboy,* but was rejected by the editors. It was first published in Argentina by Distar in 1978 as part of an anthology that featured stories by Brian Aldiss, Fritz Leiber, and Damon Knight, among other international SF authors. The story was later featured in a collection of Carneiro's SF stories: "Hieronymus's Machine and Other Stories" (*A máquina de Hyerónimus e outras histórias,* 1997). "Brain Transplant" presents a world in which technology allows for the sensory perception of another human being's thoughts. This possibility, besides erasing old signs of identity like gender and family relations, ends up blurring reality itself to the point of being unrecognizable. The story's conclusion proposes (as an antidote to political propaganda?) that the only way to discern between reality and illusion is to rely on one's own physical senses of sight, sound, and touch.

Brain Transplant

Transplante do cérebro, 1978

by André Carneiro

translated by Joe F. Randolph

The professor jumped, pulled the anklet off, compressed the gravity spot, and slowly descended in a dance step. He signaled like a conductor to begin.

"That's it. You can record it. The atomic and sexual revolution, twentieth century; gravity revolution, twenty-first century. The most important, the brain revolution, start of the twenty-third century."

One of the students, the anklet in hand, made a leap and went floating above her classmates until putting her hand on the professor's shoulder. Her body slowly came down while she touched his head with the tip of her pink tongue. He nodded yes, and she went to the see-through rest room on the side. Half the class got to its feet to watch her.

The professor still had a bright blob of slobber on his head.

"The first human head transplant was performed in the twenty-first century. Even for the medicine of that era, it wasn't so hard. At first, the medulla wasn't attached to the new head. As a result, the new body remained motionless and wasn't good for anything. When they managed to link up the medulla, absurdities like this started to emerge."

The beautiful body of a young woman with the head of an old woman appeared beside the professor. The figure opened its arms, and the professor touched it on the navel with the flat of his hand.

Someone yelled something in the back of the class. The professor aimed his finger, and from it issued an orange light that hit the nipple on the breast of a young woman with green hair. Everyone stood on tiptoe and smelled the armpit of his or her neighbor. The classroom went wild because the professor went into the rest room. He jumped weightlessly and everybody cheered. The sound of pee was amplified a hundred times in the room. The professor was a virtuoso. He directed the flow to sensitive points on the commode and released a symphony. The last drops were masterful.

"At that time," he continued after putting his member into a silver container, "science was concerned with the twenty-four cranial nerves and the sixty-six spinal nerves. Fifty years later, when they began transplanting the brain itself, it was a race to connect the twenty-four nerves while they pumped blood into the disembodied head."

A monster appeared beside the professor in the form of a gaping head sprinkling blood on the floor. A student yelled, and two Girl Scouts did a pudendum-to-pudendum massage, which left him weak for a good long while. The professor smiled understandingly. The interruptions were calculated to keep the class interested. Right afterward, a student who was in his last year of music school went to the rest room. His performance left everyone gasping for breath. The professor was not pleased. This was not in the program.

"The major problem with brain transplants is donation. During the era of head transplants, it was hard to get anybody to donate a new body for the transplanted head. When they started transplanting brains from head to head, the problem was the same. The whole body became a donor for the small transplanted brain. As incredible as it seems, that was when they discovered that a woman within the body of a man functioned more efficiently than a man in a woman's body."

"Professor, I don't understand," said a boy raising the anklet. The professor took a small device off the bookshelf, went over to the boy, and shoved the end of the tube into his head.

A couple, holding hands, used the opportunity to go into the rest room. The professor disconnected the loudspeakers. He did not want any more competitors that day.

From above, an enormous head came down over the table. The professor picked up a scalpel, and with great skill and speed made an incision in the hair and opened up the bone with a small hammer to get at the brain. He inserted something down in there and pushed a pedal. The scene filled with people. There was a new baby doing number two, a nude man in the lotus position, two girls cutting each other's pubic hair, and a monk, a cross painted on his chest, with an old paperback book in his hands. The professor kicked the baby, which rolled aside crying.

"Look. All this is thought, simple thought, that doesn't really exist." He went up to the monk and slapped him. The man fell over with an annoyed look, but did not react. The book had disappeared and changed into a flower.

The professor leaped aside and smiled at everyone. A student raised his hand.

"Nope, no musical pee."

The student looked around, but nobody supported him. He went into the rest room, sat on the commode, and covered his head.

The professor kept smiling.

"It had been known for centuries that the brain works on electricity, simple electricity."

The students erupted with laughter.

"Look," he continued. "There . . . ," he pointed at the heart monitors, "you record the same way we record here," he pointed to his head. The monk stayed on the floor, breathing with difficulty. The girls had shaved themselves completely, and the naked man was playing with the baby.

"Watch this." The professor took a small stick, rubbed it through his hair, and brought it close to the exposed brain in the head suspended above the table. All hell broke loose. The baby became a two-legged puppy, the monk seemed to have designs on the nude yogi, and the girls with shaved pudenda were giggling animatedly.

"Look: a simple discharge of static electricity acting on dendrites and axons, simply activating 80,000 synapses, all with a mere 10 millivolts."

The professor rubbed the stick against the silvery container with obvious satisfaction. Hair came out of its sides emitting sparks; it seemed he was going to masturbate, but suddenly he again brought the stick to the open brain. The monk, who was already fondling the yogi, vanished. Holding onto their thighs, the girls performed some dives; gravity did not affect them, and they disappeared into the ceiling. The baby turned into a puff of blue smoke. The professor grabbed the head by its blood-smeared hair and tossed it into the trash piled up against the wall.

"The mind, intelligence, thought do not originate from electricity flowing around in the brain. I'll explain it to you . . . chemical substances with different ionization rates, especially chlorine, sodium, and potassium ions, remain in the membrane around the synaptic area of the cell and open the doors that allow the passage of an impulse . . ."

At this juncture the students got up on their desks, laughed, and jerked off in a succession of weightless kisses, starting from the ankles to the roots of the hair, from the ceiling to the see-through rest room where more than five were peeing at the same time. They laughed and yelled, "He's coming, he's coming. We know that, but it's not interesting." The professor was so enthusiastic that he seemed not to hear, and he went on.

"Ninety billion are called glial cells, transporting blood nutrients to the neurons . . ."

One of the students, who was naked, with nice-looking breasts and a male member, came up from behind, picked up the stick the professor had left on the table, and gingerly rolled it along his neck until it reached the top of his head. The professor stopped talking immediately, as if he were considering a decision. After a few seconds, he started talking again and all the students were now seated in order and paying close attention.

"At the beginning of the twenty-third century, true brain transplants started to be done without the major surgery typical of previous centuries. What had been known for a long while before was clear. The brain records stimuli, starting in the womb. We erase impulses and copy them into another brain. The individual comes to be a new body and can, through time, inhabit various bodies. Well, I'm not going to comment on the regulations, more complicated than anything human beings have invented to date . . . You all know perfectly well what happens when a man's brain is put into a woman's body. And you know what happens to a woman's brain when it finds its way into a man's body."

The professor paused, changed the light with a dance step, and proceeded in a dramatic tone of voice.

"Wonderful things, wonderful sensations. I, for example, used to be a woman, a beautiful woman. By the way, I still am." (S/he turned his/her head slowly, showed her/his profile, shook his/her buns a little.) "Being a woman with a man's body is divine." (S/he delicately stroked her/his member.)

Everybody followed suit, as a good education requires. Nobody dared go to the rest room for fear of marring that moment. The professor opened up his arms as if he were blessing one and all.

"We're going to tell you people our impressions. Come up here, no, not you, I want the little guy with the big boobs there."

The boy with large breasts got up and started talking in another language. He had a delicate, musical voice. He was half man and half woman, nephew of his own father on the male side and part female taken from the cousin of his mother, who smashed up her whole body when she made a thousand-meter leap without gravity control. While he (or she) was talking, the students formed a chain, everyone touching each other somewhere on the body. The professor danced in silence and seemed very content.

On the other side of the wall half a dozen individuals were attentively watching on monitors everything that was going on in the classroom.

In the center of this side room was a man stretched out on some kind of table surrounded by complicated devices. One of the observers was a very good-looking young woman. It seemed that all this was a novelty to her. She turned away from the monitor and headed toward an older man who seemed to be in charge.

"It's unbelievable, absolutely unbelievable," she exclaimed.

Complacent, the older man shifted knowingly and smiled slightly. He was expecting the question. The young woman went on.

"Then all of what we're seeing, hearing, is it really, objectively, coming from this man's brain?" (She pointed at the stretched-out man, surrounded by machines.) The older man took the young woman's hand.

"Yes, they're all thoughts, created by this man."

The young woman looked at the monitor and again asked, "But what about reality? What is it? If everything that is seen and can be touched, on the other side of the wall, is merely thought . . ."

The older man smiled with delight, slipped off his white lab coat, opened up his arms, and flexed them like an athlete warming up. While doing all this, he was talking.

"Look: muscles, veins, movement, sounds that you hear and understand. Come on, grab here, follow my arm."

The young woman lightly grasped the contracted muscles.

"Pay attention. You're seeing, hearing, feeling . . . This is reality."

Everyone made a circle around the older man, paying close attention. There were six people in the room, plus the man lying on the table surrounded by machinery. The older man was now making some weird moves while the young woman started undressing.

Directly on the wall behind the older man were some bright circles. On the other side of this wall, some people were watching on monitors what the older man and the young woman were doing. Off to the side someone was sitting in a complicated chair, surrounded by devices on all sides . . .

Daína Chaviano

C U B A

Daína Chaviano (1957–) was born in Havana, Cuba, and before emigrating to the United States in 1991 had established herself as one of the most critically and popularly acclaimed SF writers on the island. She founded Cuba's first SF writers' workshop (named in honor of Oscar Hurtado, the father of Cuban SF), and hosted SF-related programs on radio and television.

Chaviano was introduced to science fiction through the works of Ray Bradbury, Isaac Asimov, Ursula Le Guin, and others, and started writing as an adolescent. While studying English language and literature at the University of Havana she won the first *David* prize to be awarded in the new category of science fiction. Her winning entry, the story collection *The Worlds I Love (Los mundos que amo,* 1980) became a best-seller in Cuba, as did many of Chaviano's subsequent publications. Although many of her Cuban SF books are now out of print, her most celebrated work, the classic *Fables from an Extraterrestrial Grandma* (*Fábulas de una abuela extraterrestre,* 1988), may soon be reprinted in Spain.

Chaviano has been particularly successful in her experimentation with language and narrative styles. She is also noted for innovatively mixing genres, as she does in the following piece, which interweaves elements of science fiction, erotica, and the Gospels in a mesmerizing reconsideration of the New Testament's annunciation story.

The author asserts that fantasy and SF were a natural choice for her as a writer living in a totalitarian state, and that since leaving Cuba her fiction has become more (though not fully) anchored in realism. She assures her readers, however, that her professional plans include a return to her literary loves— fantasy and science fiction.

The Annunciation

La Anunciación, 1983

by Daína Chaviano

translated by Juan Carlos Toledano

It was the sixth month.

In the cool air of the alcove sweet Mary was carefully sewing her husband's clothes. Fear issued from everything in the atmosphere and provoked in her a mounting unease. Unable to remain still, she rose repeatedly, walking two or three times around the room and changing things from place to place.

"My God, this nervousness will drive me crazy!" she thought.

She remembered her husband.

"It must be because Joseph's not here," she said to ease her anxiety.

Outside, the doves whispered softly as they formed small groups on the rooftops. The coolness of the afternoon penetrated the homes even more.

The young woman let herself sink into a chair and was lulled to sleep by the amorous cooing of the doves. The sewing slid from her hands and fell to her feet. Her thick, black hair partially hid the whiteness of her neck . . .

A muted noise awoke her.

She bent over quickly to pick up the sewing and when she raised her eyes, she was paralyzed by surprise and fear. In her room stood a man who was definitely a stranger.

He was tall, and luminous white hair fell freely over his shoulders. His eyes sparkled red.

His clothing was even odder than his physical appearance. He wore a tunic tightly fitted to his chest and fastened by a gold belt. Shoes that shone like polished bronze encased his feet. A transparent globe, similar to an aureole, surrounded his head.

The stranger took the halo in his hands and gently placed it on a chair before speaking.

"Hail, full of grace! The Lord be with you."

She was troubled by this presence. Yet the sound of his voice soothed her as if his words held a mysterious, unknown power. And thus her curiosity increased instead of diminishing.

It was an outrageous act, certainly, to enter a married woman's house in Galilee. What could this wanderer want here?

"Fear not, beautiful Mary, for you have been found with grace by the great Iab-eh, whose magnificent glory now rests upon Mount Sinai, whence come I to inform you of the good news. You will conceive in your womb, you will bear a son, and you will give him the name of Jesus. He will be great because his blood will contain the spirit of the gods. And He who waits upon Mount Sinai will turn His throne over to him when the time comes. Eugenics has never failed, and you have been chosen. Your son's wisdom and power will know no limits because he is called to succeed the great Iab-eh on the throne during the march toward Infinity. From His seat he will reign for a long time on the voyage toward the Almighty."

Mary listened to his enigmatic words, but of that entire speech she understood only two things. First, that the man speaking to her was one of the angels of the great Iab-eh who generally rests with all the splendor of His glory, His thunder, and His lightning on Mount Sinai. (She recalled having witnessed the smoke and the deafening noise like a thousand trumpets while He crossed the region.) And second, that she was going to be a mother, although this last thing seemed quite improbable to her.

"How will that be," she asked him, "since I have known no man? Are you unaware perhaps that my husband and master—for a reason beyond my understanding—has sworn never to touch me? How then will I, uninitiated in the mysterious ritual of conception, be able to conceive a baby?"

And the angel responded: "The sacred breath of Iab-eh will reach you through my person. And, since no one else is worthy of this, you will be anointed with divine rain, and for that reason the child engendered will be holy and will be called the Son of God."

The angel's words were not fully comprehensible to Mary. Sometimes she understood all that he said in a phrase, while other times the stranger spoke enigmatically and ambiguously, as if on purpose.

"When must my husband know about this?" she asked him.

"As soon as he returns. At this moment he lies asleep along the road that leads to Nazareth."

Mary felt suddenly upset.

"Sleeping along the road to Nazareth? Heavens!"

"Do not be alarmed. The great Iab-eh is watching over his sleep."

The young woman was calmed.

"And how, Holy Messenger, will I know that I have conceived?"

"The light of the kingdom will come to you through me. I . . . I have loved you so much."

"What? What do you mean?" Mary responded in astonishment. "You, me?"

He seemed disconcerted.

"I meant that, having admired you so much, I petitioned the great Iab-eh to grant me the honor of delivering you such good news. And, since you were the chosen one, he entrusted me with announcing everything to you and . . . with making it possible."

His discomfort was now obvious, yet Mary did not notice it.

"And I hold you in high esteem. I could never live long enough to thank you sufficiently."

They looked at one another in silence for a few moments.

The angel advanced through the room until he stood before her. To Mary it seemed that he was floating. He was so tall!

She bowed her head with respect and fixed her eyes on the floor.

"Look at me," he said tenderly, tilting her chin up and kissing her forehead. "You are so warm!"

She looked obediently at him. The angel of the Lord was certainly handsome.

"Why, angel of Iab-eh . . . ?"

"My name is Gabriel."

"So, Gabriel, why must I conceive a son of the Lord? The reason you gave was not clear to me."

The angel sighed.

"Many things would be difficult for you and your people to understand, even if we explained them very well. For this reason I will only say that God works in mysterious ways. For now, His thoughts and desires are still beyond your understanding."

"But I . . ."

A chaste kiss sealed her lips, and yet she felt no shame at all. How could she feel shame before an angel of the Lord who would bring her no disgrace?

Nevertheless, such a distinction disturbed her tremendously.

"The honor you bestow upon me is magnificent, Gabriel, when you brush my earthly, sinful lips with your sainted ones."

"Do not talk like that, maiden. You are young and still do not fathom many things that perhaps in time you will come to understand, even if only partially."

He held her hands and kissed them.

"They are as soft as a dove's feathers," he said.

She blushed slightly.

"You're exaggerating. Surely, the wings of the celestial cherubs are much softer."

"Cherubs?" he let slip, "Oh, yes! But don't you believe such a thing. Of course, heaven has much that is lovely, but I've never seen anything there as beautiful as your smile."

This time modesty made her cheeks blush crimson.

"Your hair is so long!" he exclaimed with emotion, "Allow me to touch it."

Skillfully, he spread the ringlets that fell across the young woman's shoulders.

"But, what are you doing?" she said quickly, somewhat alarmed.

"I'm kissing your hair. Would you deny such an honor to an angel of the Lord?"

"Of course not! Forgive me. I did not mean to offend you."

"You didn't offend me, sweet Mary. Innocence offends no one, not even an angel of the Lord. It is a shame that you and yours cannot understand us better . . . You haven't understood the half of our moral teachings. Instead of applying them, you've converted them into religion. But it doesn't matter. The fruit of this union will lead Iab-eh's spaceship to our own planet. The information must get there, and our wise men have decided upon the mixture of both races. However, Mary, I'm not doing this just because eugenics requires it. I love you."

"I don't understand you," she said with anguish, "I have no idea what you're talking about."

"Hush," he whispered, "hush and close your eyes."

She obeyed submissively.

The angel's lips brushed against her shoulders. Little by little his lips rose, passing lightly across her entire neck until stopping at her mouth.

Like honey were his lips. And how soft were the hands that caressed her back! This tender touch made her tremble and she felt invaded by some vague and unknown fear. Her strength seemed to leave her. Her knees began to quiver.

His voice, strangely hoarse, pulled her from her dream.

"Your dress, doesn't it bother you?"

"Not at all!" she protested weakly.

"But you are wearing so many things," he sighed.

"No, I assure you. Only what you see and . . ." lowering her voice modestly, "a very light tunic beneath."

"You should take it off. It's hot."

"The air is cool . . ."

His hands delicately undid the ties of her dress, and it fell to the floor.

Mary didn't dare protest for fear of offending him. It was possible that the earth's heat was affecting him because he was accustomed to the heavens. And she, in contrast, had always been so close to hell that perhaps she had become used to the heat, although . . .

Good Heavens! It was true! Her blood was beginning to boil inside her body.

"Gabriel!" she said.

"What is it?"

"I would like to tell you . . . I don't know how to explain it."

"Tell me," he insisted.

"It's . . . that, while beside you, I feel so close to heaven that all of hell's heat has accumulated in my veins."

He smiled.

"I'm so glad to hear it!"

"It's the honest truth," she answered modestly.

The angel's breath bathed her whole face and seemed to spill out of her body. The young woman felt as if she were burning. She felt near to fainting.

"Oh!"

"What's wrong?"

She whispered in a faltering voice.

"These . . . these celestial heights are not for me."

He looked at her in amazement.

"What do you mean?"

"I am dizzy."

"Do you feel ill?"

"No, no!" she exclaimed, almost angrily, "I feel so good that I don't know how I could have lived all these years so far from you."

"Mary!" he exclaimed, moved, "Little thing!"

For the first time she realized that the angel's glittering clothes lay on the floor and that she . . . she . . .

Mary shut her eyes tightly. Something incomprehensible was happening. Her entire body was trembling in the bed.

"Gabriel," she whispered breathlessly, "Gabriel! What are you doing?"

But he didn't answer.

Everything was spinning around. She was feeling . . . she felt . . . a sweet, sharp pain made her shiver from head to foot. She felt penetrated by an undreamed sensation of height and vertigo.

The kingdom of heaven must be near, very near. She saw it. She felt it arrive. It was there, in front of her.

"Gabriel!" she grabbed him tightly by the shoulders, "You are . . . !"

The door of the kingdom opened before both of them.

She shook to her innermost core, as if a hot spring shower had bathed the deepest part of her seed.

Little by little, the light of the Infinite that had shone so brightly began to dim. From the center of the mist she could hear his voice:

"Blessed are you, Mary, and blessed be the fruit of your womb! The glory of the world be with you!"

Federico Schaffler

MEXICO

Federico Schaffler González (1959–) was born in Nuevo Laredo, in the state of Tamaulipas. Schaffler's contributions as a science fiction writer, editor, and promoter are so extensive as to almost deny brief summary.[1] For over five years he edited and directed the high-quality Mexican SF fanzine *Umbrales,* and he is currently on the editorial board of *Fronteras* and *A Quien Corresponda.* In 1992 he founded AMCYF (the Mexican SF and Fantasy Association) and served as its first president, a post to which he was reelected in 2000.

Schaffler has published more than one hundred stories in books, newspapers, and periodicals in Mexico, the United States, Spain, Romania, Brazil, and Argentina. He is an indefatigable anthologist; among several other projects is his three-volume *Beyond the Imagined* (*Más allá de lo imaginado,* 1991 and 1994), the first and, to date, most extensive collection of Mexican SF stories.

In order to foster and promote science fiction in Mexico, Schaffler has given lectures throughout Mexico and in the state of Texas, and he directs the Terra Ignota writers' workshop in his home state. His work in the field has earned him recognition in over twenty national and international literary competitions, including the *Kalpa,* the *Puebla,* the *Más Allá,* and the Spanish *Bucanero.*

Schaffler's poignant "A Miscalculation" is a reminder of the power of science fiction to stimulate a young reader's imagination, fuel a natural thirst for knowledge, and create a sense of wonder at the physical world and its mysteries.

A Miscalculation

Un error de cálculo, 1983

by Federico Schaffler

translated by Andrea Bell

The cosmos, a black mantle studded with stars.

Constellations, planets, nebulae, and suns. So close at hand, yet so far away.

He stares out at the night sky, attentive, thoughtful, imaginative. Between sighs and fleeting, quixotic thoughts, he feels himself a part of space. His most cherished dream: to travel beyond the galaxy.

The impossibility of bringing the stars within arm's reach makes him yearn to touch them; he stretches out his arm, only to clench his fist in impotence. He quickly lowers his hand and covers his forehead with his palm, his thumb on one temple, four fingers on the other, frustrated by the hopelessness of doing that which he so desires.

He lies back in the dark and withered grass, illuminated by the light of the moon and stars. He laces his fingers behind his neck while breathing rhythmically, slowly letting the peace of stargazing return to him.

Ursa Major overhead. The North Star a little further beyond.

Eyes wide open, memories and fantasies flash through his mind.

Andromeda, Cygnus the Swan, and Hercules. Sagittarius and Virgo. Nebulae and constellations that he remembers having seen in books and photographs, too far away to be perceived by the naked eye.

Another sigh tears the night while his mind continues to wander.

Star Wars, Alien, Battlestar Galactica and more. The sci-fi movies he's watched in his mind so many times. Choice scenes, every one a high point. He feels himself a hero and dreams of being a Flash Gordon or a Luke Skywalker, primed for battle, with a beautiful woman at his side. Standing at the ready, unafraid, self-sufficient and confident.

His thoughts and imaginings vanish when he sees a shooting star.

Space. His dream. So close and yet so far. He relaxes his body and returns his gaze to the sky.

Ursa Major in particular attracts his attention. Of the stars in the binary system of Mizar and Alcor, he identifies himself, without knowing why, with the first of them, Mizar, the second star from the top of the handle. Deeply absorbed, he does not notice the passage of time or the ticktock of his watch.

Another shooting star falls, a "little straw," as his grandmother calls it.

Dreams. Impossible ones. He would never journey in a Columbia, Atlantis, or Discovery. Never wield a heavy sword on a distant planet, cloaked in furs and battling fierce warriors and wild beasts. Never pilot a shiny spaceship or set foot on other worlds.

Dreams. Only dreams. Interrupted again when he spies a shooting star, growing, as if coming toward him. Directly.

He doesn't even blink. His mind flies and sees UFOs and strange ships coming for him, abducting him and then politely inviting him to accompany them. As an ambassador for the human race. Like a representative of Vasconcelos's cosmic race.[1]

Light, heat, and sound, the little straw star heads straight toward him. His dream might yet come true. An idea begins to take shape in his child's mind. He would be a part of the cosmos.

His anxious, unblinking, staring eyes see the light grow stronger, intensifying the light reflected in his pupils.

"They're coming for me!" he thinks ecstatically, a smile traced on his lips.

He reaches his arms up toward space, toward the ever-growing luminescence; a tear forms in one eye and runs down the side of his face, though his smile never disappears.

His hopes and dreams overwhelm and paralyze him. Disregarding the danger, he allows his spirit and thoughts to fantasize again. His soul communes with the cosmos, and passively he awaits his fate.

"I'll die a part of space, killed by a meteorite. At least I'll be remembered and associated with space," he muses under his breath.

The light keeps getting closer, faster and faster.

"At last. I'll be part of the sky, part of the stars and the universe!" he cries excitedly, not moving from his spot.

"Here I am! I'm ready!"

The light grows bigger and bigger.

He crosses his arms over his chest after pushing the hair from his forehead and closing his eyes, waiting for the final moment, mentally calculating the time before the fatal, but wished-for, impact.

"Five, four, three, two, one . . . Now!" he says at last, a bit more serenely, resigned to an unconsciously desired fate.

Nothing.

The seconds pass, and through his eyelids he detects a strange light, but he dares not open his eyes.

"I miscalculated," he thinks.

More time passes and still he does not feel the blow. Suddenly, decisively, he opens his eyes, hoping to witness the final moment, determination painted on his face, almost wanting to feel upon his face and body the heat of the meteorite before it strikes him and ends his existence—as he had always wished—via something connected with the cosmos.

He notices the light over his head, motionless, at arm's length. Curious, he reaches out his hand.

When he feels himself on the brink of touching one of the stars he had always longed to hold, a quick, dizzying motion causes him to awaken from his stupor and choke out a curse.

The light, the meteorite that he hopes will end his life and give him the chance to be reborn in the stars, is nothing but a curious firefly that hovers above him, only to fly off, trailing its beacon of fire, at the abrupt movement of the boy's hand.

"Son, it's so late, come to bed." The voice of a woman, full of tenderness and understanding, is heard calling him, bringing him out of his reverie and disappointment with reality.

He gets up and picks up a pebble from the ground, tossing it aside while he walks back toward his mother.

He walks with his head down, finally reaching the old door with the chipped paint and the mosquito screen. His back turned, he does not see that other shooting star, much bigger than all the ones he had seen before.

"Good night, mamá."

"Good night, son. Sleep well, and may your dreams come true some day."

The boy goes in and closes the door behind him, while out there, just at the spot where he had lain watching the stars and waiting to commune with something from outer space, a small stone violently explodes. An incandescent and speedy meteorite raises a column of smoke for a few seconds, long enough to shoo away a firefly that has prevented, by a few seconds, the consummation of a date made in the stars.

Part IV

Riding the Crest

The Late 1980s

into the New

Millennium

Braulio Tavares

BRAZIL

Braulio Tavares (1950–) was born in Campina Grande, in the northeast of Brazil, and has resided in Rio de Janeiro since 1982. His work has been chiefly in the creative arts; in Brazil he is recognized as a singer/songwriter of what he calls "oral literature," or folk poetry. He is a 1991 Clarion graduate and a member of the Science Fiction Research Association.

Tavares's nonfiction work on SF includes the *Fantastic, Fantasy, and Science Fiction Literature Catalog,* an English-language bibliography of Brazilian fantastic literature (1992), and articles in the Nicholls and Clute *Encyclopedia of Science Fiction* (1993), in Clute and Grant's *Encyclopedia of Fantasy* (1997), and in publications such as *Foundation* and *The New York Review of Science Fiction.* He has published one SF novel, *The Flying Machine* (*A máquina voadora,* 1994), and two story collections, *The Backbone of Memory* (*A espinha dorsal da memória,* 1989), and *Ghost World* (*Mundo fantasmo,* 1996). *The Backbone of Memory* received three *Nova* awards.

"Stuntmind" was first published in Portuguese in *The Backbone of Memory,* and was later translated into English by the author for publication in the Canadian magazine *On Spec* (fall 1994). For those who might have missed it then, we offer it here and invite you to experience Tavares's hypnotic vision of interspecies contact between humans and a powerful race of aliens, called the Outsiders. What the alien race craves is what humans take for granted and even despise about themselves: their feelings.

Stuntmind

Stuntmind, 1989

by Braulio Tavares

translated by the author

1

At the opposite end of the large marble room, a photo of Roger Van Dali covers the entire wall. I am sitting in my sliding chair, and I press the keys, making it glide toward that enormous face.

The face of Van Dali. I don't remember when this photo was taken; all I recall is that it was before his mission. He wears a gray suit with a black tie. He has a thin face, short hair, thick eyebrows. Deep lines run down both sides of his mouth. He is looking at an indefinite point to the left of the camera and doesn't seem to acknowledge its presence. He seems unaware of everything; he just stares into the void.

I call this room "The Art Gallery." It contains nothing but this twenty-five-square-meter photo. I come here every day, before breakfast. I look at this photo, and I think about me.

I go downstairs. Van Dali's servants are busy around the table, preparing a meal with tropical fruits. In the afternoon, if the weather is good, I will take the helicop and go to the canyon to see the sunset. I haven't been out of this house for six months.

2

It rained, and I could not go to the canyon. I went to the basement instead, put on a mask, dived into the tank, harpooned some fish. It was ten P.M. when I went upstairs and dressed for dinner.

My guests talked about the incredibly bizarre kidnappings that have been taking place in several countries. It's not a matter of mere politics anymore: those groups claim to have created a new form of art. The first hostages were tattooed before being released, but now a group in Venezuela has introduced the procedure of peeling the skin off their faces. Stanzarelli (one of the guests, one who always closes his eyes while speaking) said that anesthesia is a kind of ersatz blindness, and then he smiled. We all smiled, and I ordered the waiters to serve the honey wine.

After dinner we went upstairs to the Oval Room. I showed them my collection of cuneiform tablets; I had hired some translators for the night, and we read and discussed the texts until dawn. Naskatcha and her geishas were the last ones to leave. I went to my bedroom, read a little, and then spent some time not reading, just retracing the beautiful shapes of the letters with my eyes, and I slid smoothly into an imageless sleep.

3

Roger Van Dali never slept well; since his childhood he had never slept more than three hours at a time. As he grew up he realized that he was not like other boys, and his family used to see him as a Predestinate, as so many families do. He was thirty-two and had been working as a bookkeeper when he was discovered and drafted for the Contact Mission.

During his training, with dozens of physicians around him, he asked what he was supposed to do. "Someone will say something in your mind," they answered. "You will hear, and then you will tell us what it was."

It was during the Van Dali mission that the press coined the name that would be applied to his group from then on. "Stuntminds" was the label given to the people whose minds were, for some random genetic reason, suitable for mental Contact with the Outsiders.

4

Millions of government agents combed the world in search of potential stuntminds. Whenever one was found, he was enrolled, trained, and taken in a space shuttle to the Orbital Station, where an Outsider scout ship submitted him to another series of tests. Some were turned back, without explanation. Those approved were taken to the main Outsider ship and put in mind-contact with the Outsiders by a process whose details were kept secret by the aliens. For some period of time (minutes? hours? days?) the minds of the Earthling and the alien vibrated and pulsed together, becoming a whole; then they were separated again, and the man was taken back to the station. When Van Dali returned to Earth he was physically devastated, weighing twenty pounds less than he had two weeks earlier, when he had shaken hands with nine presidents as he prepared to enter the shuttle.

Stuntminds returned to Earth no more than zombies, but prolific zombies nonetheless. They created and developed the most eccentric mathematical formulae, in insane bursts of activity, and they wrote things without an inkling of understanding. When their information was exhausted they were officially retired, mentally ill, their minds half-crippled by what scientists called "the Kingsley-Weichart effect"—an overload of information. Their mission fulfilled, they withdrew from the world to spend their last years like sheiks, like maharajas, like mandarins, in mansions with ninety-nine rooms—like this one of mine.

5

Today was scarab day. I undressed and, in an enormous marble basin, had my legs and arms tied and then had the scarabs spread over me. They seemed to have millions of tiny feet, and they acted as though they knew what I was feeling. Then I slept. In the afternoon I saddled a pony and rode through the woods on the ground floor.

6

In this house I have bedrooms, I have swimming rooms, I have rooms full of perfumed smoke, rooms full of children's toys, rooms full of books, rooms full of fishbowls. I have dozens of rooms whose furniture recreates other times and other places. I have the dark crypt where Aleister Crowley performed his rituals. I have the room where Paris loved Helen of Troy, and also Messalina's sultry alcove, and the huge canopy bed of Christine, Queen of Sweden. I have the room where Marilyn Monroe died, and in that room lives a professional Marilyn double, almost a clone. I have Turkish seraglios, dungeons and cloister cells, rooms from brothels in Nazi Berlin and in Muslim Andalusia. When I feel lonely I warn my servants and, half an hour later, I open a door and enter the chosen scene. It's not every day that it happens. It's more during winter, when fierce storms are raging outside, and I try to forget them.

7

Today is Tuesday, and I had to welcome Van Dali's biographers. Since it is winter, only two of them appeared. When they arrived I was playing tennis against Ivanov and Leroux, my nurses. Sometimes I imagine that I could play several simultaneous tennis games, as chess players do; a semicircular court, me against four, or five . . .

I think about this while I take a shower and choose my clothes. Last Tuesday I wore an artillery uniform, a gift from Pablo Mikherinos, a recent stuntmind with long purple hair. Today, I choose a tuxedo and a top hat in bright colors. I feel talkative.

I go downstairs to the library and greet the biographers, whose names I always forget. The blonde woman has a quaint accent, and she asks me about the usefulness of a stuntmind to the world. Patiently I repeat: we receive a Gleam, and we have the duty of transmitting its reflex. The man who dresses in white asks me how I would describe the mental feeling of the Contact. I describe it as that of a geometrical point that is compelled to receive a polygon inside itself.

8

We are useless parasites of mankind. This is what is written in the newspapers financed by the opposition companies. And maybe we are. The multistate companies spend more and more money on stuntminds every year, because every Contact, every message, demands a new, untouched brain.

It is said that our Xanadus insult the poverty of the world's billions of people. But the countries of Earth needed us. They needed the messages that our crippled minds brought home, and so it is only fair that now we have our city, far away from other cities, a city just for us, where each month a new house is built: a pagoda, a marble honeycomb, a tower made of Brazilian redwood, a mansion in the shape of a word, an upside-down castle. Here we are: the parasites and the illuminati, the men and women who gave their minds to be raped by equations, by alien formulae, by data that Earth scientists receive with eagerness and examine with wonder; something for which a scholar would give half his life, and which billions of people pay homage to but don't understand.

I live in Van Dali's mansion. To the Outsiders, the person of Van Dali didn't exist, or, like an electron, could not be told apart from the others. His mind was only a chip, a stone on which a message was carved. When Van Dali came back to Earth, he carried in his mind the blueprints of the topological structure of the Interwoven Universes. It was only after this that the nations of Earth could master the projection of physical objects in Hypertime and start to build the Gate.

9

It is winter . . . but I am repeating myself. I wake up at noon, and even before opening my eyes I turn on the hypnoscope, then stare at the small silvery sphere as it revolves a few inches before my eyes. Entranced, I restore some minutes of my dreams, minutes that otherwise would melt away under the ruthless touch of reality.

I turn it off and go to the gym. Afterward I have breakfast, then go to the hothouse, take a box full of insects and feed my plants. I make sure that they have everything . . . water, electro-sun, fresh air. I talk to them, touched by the way they respond, gently waving their leaves. At three P.M. I go to the Indigo Room on the fourth floor, call for a fellatrix, stay with her a long time. Then I go downstairs, have a bath, do my check-up, my acupuncture.

It is still raining! I cannot see the sunset in the canyon. I go to the library instead, and spend hours leafing through picture books. At eight, I am called to dinner: shrimp with cream cheese and sweet garlic, and a salad of synths. After finishing, I order the coffee in the Black-and-Silver Room, together with a ballet—the pas de deux from Smoliakine's *Tristram and Juliet,* with choreography by N'Mura.

Back in the library I sit at my computer and exchange correspondence for a few hours, after choosing a group of programs at random: De Assis, De Camp, De Quincey, De Sade. A servant appears and announces the arrival of guests. I remember I invited some people to a bagpipe concert at midnight.

Downstairs is a small group: three stuntminds from the neighborhood, and five visiting Earthlings, as we call them. Two of them are first-time visitors to Van Dali's house. They take my hand as if I were a king, as if I were an octopus.

10

One more day, like any other. Now I am naked; my body floats inside a huge, vertical glass cylinder. The jets of hot air keep me hovering, almost weightless, revolving around myself inside the circle of tanning lights. In my ears, phones with docu-music, the sounds of the rescue of a Spanish galleon from the seventeenth century, near the Cape of Good Hope. The hot air is so good. It is fourteen minutes past eleven on a winter night . . . outside.

11

I once jumped into an enormous chocolate pie: I sank like a bullet in wood, I swam, I ate, I found my way out. I have been tied to the propeller of a plane and had the engine turned on. I have drunk everything: brine, urine, semen, pepper juice, amniotic fluid, hydrochloric acid, menstrual blood, *aqua tofana,* hyperdistilled water. I have fought rattlesnakes with my teeth, with my hands tied behind my back. I have jumped from a plane at six thousand feet, tied to an elastic cord. I have been entombed for six days and six nights.

12

Today the rain stopped; I called my helicop and flew to the canyon. I sat on a rock and stared at the sun, I saw how it melted in wild colors, and tears rolled down my face till the world was dark.

Back home, I went through Cypress Glades. I passed along it very slowly, my chair gliding softly upon the air-spheres, my closed eyes preserving that trembling shadow of the sun. The air around me was resounding with the music of the thousands of bells that hung from the trees, golden bells, silver bells, crystal bells, tinkling at the cold wind's blowing. I felt that I was vibrating and pulsating in sympathy with their sound.

In moments like this I remember the Contact, I remember that moment in which I, Roger Van Dali, felt all the vast loneliness of the Outsider (yes, I still think of them as individuals, as units of consciousness, or psi-quanta). I remember that instant in which I became me-and-him. In that moment, my frail human mind touched his memories of travels through Hypertime, recoiling at what I found there. I think the same thing happens with all stuntminds, but I have never asked anyone about it. We are a guild of silent people.

And I awoke in Van Dali's body after the Contact, like one who emerges from a throbbing abyss. I came to Earth and was given this face of mine. They taught me my name, told me my life, gave me a mountain of money, and then forgot me: and now here we are . . . I and I.

I can say: I am embedded in Van Dali's mind. Also I can say: a part of the Outsider is inside me and now lives in this world where it indulges itself in every excess, in every curiosity.

We can thank the Outsiders for the keys to Hypertime and for opening the doors of the universe for us; but I don't think they came to escort us across the galaxies. What they want is to live here, and to be like us.

The taste for human feelings is their vice. In exchange for this caprice, for this desertion, they give us their theorems and send us into space. I cannot understand this human greediness for space, since the Abyss is only the Abyss, and nowhere is there a planet so full of perverse beauty as this world of yours.

Guillermo Lavín

MEXICO

Guillermo Lavín (1956–) was born in Victoria City, the capital of the northeastern border state of Tamaulipas, and currently lives in the city of his birth. He is the founder and editor of the prize-winning literary magazine *A Quien Corresponda,* which recently celebrated its one-hundredth issue. He is also a dedicated promoter of the art and culture of Tamaulipas, having organized cross-border writers' meetings with Texas A&M University in 1998, 1999, and 2000.

Lavín has published SF stories, essays, poetry, and criticism in dozens of Mexican, Spanish, and Argentinean magazines and has been awarded prizes in several international SF competitions, such as the *Kalpa, Más Allá, Puebla,* and most recently, the *Premio UPV.*

The story we have chosen for this anthology, "Reaching the Shore," was published in the Spanish Internet magazine *Ad Astra* and in *Border of Broken Mirrors* (*Frontera de espejos rotos,* 1994), a joint project by Mexican and U.S. science fiction writers. Lavín's story casts light on the destructive and exploitative side of border culture. The lives of factory workers and their relationship to the maquiladoras[1] is a central theme in "Reaching the Shore," which also addresses the issue of drug addiction and the toll it can take on families. Taken together, drugs and maquiladoras can be seen as a way that hegemonic forces keep the working class under tight control in a closed system of economic and cultural exploitation.

Reaching the Shore

Llegar a la orilla, 1994
by Guillermo Lavín
translated by Rena Zuidema
and Andrea Bell

> Don't ask for guarantees. And don't look to be
> saved in any one thing, person, machine, or library.
> Do your own bit of saving, and if you drown, at
> least die knowing you were headed for shore.
> —Ray Bradbury, *Fahrenheit 451*

The laconic sound of the whistle split the air at exactly fifteen minutes before six P.M.

And a few moments later, as if the first were an order from the team captain, one and another and another and dozens of whistle blasts echoed through the city to tell some of the workers that their shift had ended, to alert the wives and children that their husbands and fathers would be arriving soon, and to announce to the other laborers that their shift was beginning.

But José Paul, standing in the doorway of his house, was interested only in the first sound that reached his ears. It seemed distinct, unique, as if in its journey through space the sound had been nourished by the swaying of the gilded tree boughs and by the breath of birds that had not yet abandoned the wintry city; by the melody of dry grass being stepped on by children's bare feet, and by the jingling of the bells that hung on most of the neighborhood houses' front doors. The other whistles constituted a jumbled multitude of laments.

The first one was the call.

A special call.

It was his papa's voice that cried out, "I'm coming home." And José Paul, hearing it, called out to his mother asking permission to go to the maquiladora to wait for his father. He didn't stop to hear her consent; he was already off, the thousand-meter distance fast disappearing. The boy ran along the sidewalk, avoiding the cracks in the cement and kicking empty soda cans, while picturing his father's bouncing stride.

This was a special afternoon. The afternoon of December 24th. José Paul dreamed of waking on Christmas morning with a bicycle like that of Brian Jesús, his neighbor, with aerodynamic handlebars, high impact brakes, and side reflectors. The bicycle that he saw in his mind's eye faded away when he reached the factory.

The doors of the gate opened. The men came down the walkway toward it with a sense of urgency and fear, like prisoners set free after a long jail sentence. And the man with the bouncing stride, thickset and dark, stood out among the others. He was accompanied by various men, all in navy blue uniforms with the red emblem of a brain sewn on at chest level. The men stopped under the company sign: *SIMPSON BROS., INC., The Leisure Time Company*. They gestured animatedly. José Paul noticed the sore at the base of his father's skull and the partially singed hair around it. His father touched the burn with his index finger, as if wanting to make sure it was still there. His friends called him by his last name, Fragoso, since he never gave out his first name. One time, years ago, while he held his son on his lap, he had confessed that his name irritated him almost like an insult. His name was Teófilo José.

José Paul approached him. Fragoso tried to convince his buddy Isaías Ray to go have a beer with them to celebrate Christmas before they split up. The boy exchanged smiles with Don Luis Phillip, the old guard who monitored with extreme seriousness the comings and goings of the staff. The boy seemed to see a touch of sadness in the gaze the old man directed at him. He knit his brows, wondering what sadness could possibly bother a man as important as the guard who, in that vast domain, had the power to grant people entry and exit. A hand made of big, strong bones masked by cold, brittle skin played with his hair and distracted him from his thoughts. The boy was pleased that the guard caressed his head, since this gesture was usually accompanied by a candy. Quickly he caught the hand that was making small knots in his hair and squeezed it while raising his eyes. He poked between the stiff fingers and found, hidden in a fold of skin, the smoothness of the plastic-wrapped sweet. The old man lifted the boy up. Their faces were a few centimeters apart.

"What did you ask Santa Claus for?" asked the guard.

"A bicycle."

The old man's smile slowly melted. He put the boy down.

"I hope he brings it to you," he said, his voice sounding like gravel, "they're very expensive."

The father's voice reached them like an alarm clock. The group of workers was moving further down the street and Fragoso gestured for his son to follow them. José Paul drifted toward him. He stopped and looked back.

"Thank you," he said in a low voice.

The old man heard the child's words and responded to himself, "It's expensive, but your father's addiction is more expensive still."

The boy studied Don Luis's eyes. He didn't understand that last part; the movement of the old man's lips formed incomprehensible words. He decided it wasn't very important, and went to catch up to the group of men who were now stopped at the corner, forming a line to watch a young woman who walked by with her gaze fixed straight ahead of her. He caught up with them there. He followed the men's gaze and his eyes glided along the undulating curve of her smooth hips and the dark reflection of legs encased in pants that seemed fused to them. The color of the clothes changed constantly, like a kaleidoscope, and he liked that. A gust of cold wind raised a dust cloud; it crystallized in the men's eyes and compelled them to move on.

They stopped before the sun finished setting.

The group of men climbed the three steps and entered the semi-deserted bar. It was a sparkling clean business, with an immaculate green metal revolving door. They pushed two tables together and the waiter quickly took their orders. The boy looked with pride at his father—who spoke as if he owned the place—and thought of the day when he would have the right to sit like that, with friends, to drink beer and not the orange soda the waiter put on the solitary table in front of him. The cashier pointed a remote control at the wall and the sounds of the big-screen TV filled the air. The men turned toward it and protested with jeers, shouts, and threats, until the cashier changed the channel; they told him they were tired of watching Christmas movies. They didn't like the idea of watching the news either, so the racket continued while the screen skipped from channel to channel. Judith's face and voice flooded the place with the ballad of Juan Cortina.[1] The men returned to their beers and their conversation. The boy walked over to the counter and amused himself by leafing through the headlines of the magazines and newspapers.

"Papá!" he called.

The men fell silent. Teófilo José raised his eyebrows questioningly at his son.

"What's an economic war?" asked the child.

"The cause of all problems." The paternal response elicited guffaws. The men settled back in their chairs and put their elbows on the tables.

"Papá!" he persisted, seated on a bench, though he knew that the seven men would now consider him a nuisance.

"What do you want?" he replied, aware of being the only one not looking at his son. "Think hard about what you're going to say, because it's the last question I'll answer."

"What's an economic bloc?"

There was total silence for a few seconds.

"Can anyone," Teófilo José's voice pained him, "can anyone explain it to him?"

His buddy Isaías Ray said that it was like a soccer game, in which each team is made up of various player/countries. "The team that sells something to the other one without buying anything wins," he said to complete the illustration.

The men continued in silence. Teófilo José, sorrow weighing down his shoulders, took a big swig of beer and then got up and headed toward the bathroom.

"That Fragoso!" said John Arturo, wiping off the water drops that had formed on the beer can, "the company sure did screw him over."

"I told him at the time, I told him not to let himself be a guinea pig," put in Roger Fernando, "but he got mad at me. 'The thing is, you're afraid,' he told me, 'you don't want to progress.' And now you see. They got him hooked. 'I may be a stick in the mud,' I answered him at the time, 'but I won't let them put cables in my head.'"

"Shut up already," a murmur from Isaías Ray stopped them, "the kid's listening to you."

Six pairs of eyes fell, with the harmony of a drunken symphony, on the figure of the eleven-year-old boy, who scratched with his tennis shoe at a piece of gum stuck on the floor. The brief and trembling sunlight that sketched rays on the floor ended its death throes. The men felt the uneasiness of an irresolute winter, of intermittent colds, a sickly winter. The boy thought that night would finally come, with Christmas dinner, the thrill of fireworks blooming in the night sky, and the joyful awakening to a brand-new bicycle. The spell was broken by the slamming of a door. His father exited the bathroom, zipping up his pants, but he didn't return to the table; instead he passed by the front counter, lightly stroked his son's knee and went up a narrow, semihidden staircase to one side of the cash register. The boy interpreted the caress as a call. He followed his father. When he reached the last step, he found himself on a long balcony with a metal handrail on one side. A gust of frozen wind blasted his face with the force of a thousand icy needles. He adjusted his sweater and crossed his arms. From there he could see the Rio Bravo: a thin thread the color of dirt, as if coffee grounds ran in its great bed. José Paul remembered his teacher, who lamented that every year the river looked more like a dinosaur skeleton, that once it had been magnificent, but now was scarcely alive, for its flesh had deserted it. He could also see the city, his city, Reynosa, that extended along the length of the river without growing in height: they didn't build tall buildings. On the other hand, the canals that scarred the city and the thin zigzag of the arteries from downtown contrasted with the wide, straight, equidistant streets of the new colonies created by the maquiladora companies for their employees, colonies of repeating lines of houses, identical for only the first days, when they were as yet uninhabited by the laborers and their numerous families.

A loud noise startled him. It came from the office whose door was at the end of the hallway; there was a big half-open window, and the boy approached it. Standing on tiptoes on the top of the baseboard, he took hold of the windowsill. He looked in between the slats of the red Venetian blinds and saw a spacious room with a polished wood floor, empty except for the white metal desk and the crystal chandelier that hung from the ceiling. His father, standing in front of the desk, rested his fists on the metal and looked with hatred at the small, dark, skinny guy who smiled and opened his hands like a peaceful and tolerant Christian. Teófilo's voice was hushed. He said it was unfair to pay a thousand dollars for an unguaranteed Taiwanese chip of the lowest quality, and he protested that his previous purchases had had defects. "They don't last, they short out, they shock you, they burn," he reiterated before the calm gaze of the man who, for his part, explained the risks of dealing with countries from an enemy trade bloc.

"In any case, buy American. They say the Simpson Dream III turned out very good."

"As if I didn't know, I was the tester," he said, and as he talked he passed his index finger over the burn that crowned the bioplastic interface, "but they cost a fortune."

Instinctively, the boy stroked the nape of his neck and remembered the morning the principal of the school came to his classroom accompanied by an engineer and a nurse. They announced that they were living a historic day, since they were going to implant the most modern and sophisticated North American technology ever: a personalized bioconnecter that went into the base of the cranium. Terror set the children's imaginations on fire, except for Paul, who remembered having always seen something like that in his father's head. The principal asked for a volunteer. Paul stood up. Half an hour later, the boy was enjoying neural teaching, and learned in seconds what before had taken many boring hours.

His foot slipped on the baseboard; his frightened heart skipped a beat.

Inside the room, the dialogue continued between the irredeemable buyer and the inflexible seller. The first asked for credit, installment plans, a discount; the other responded no. The first felt the little box that sheltered the interface; the second caressed his own cheeks. Teófilo José shook his head from side to side while he took an olive green envelope from a bag he had in his pants and extracted a wad of green bills. He counted out the amount of dollars he needed. He handed them over to the guy. The boy saw his father store in one bag the packet with the chip and in another the remaining few bills and turn toward the door without saying goodbye to the salesman. The boy, immobile, watched his father pass by wearing a threatening frown and talking with a phantom interlocutor. He went down the stairs behind him, followed him when he bid farewell to his friends with a wave and a brief exchange, and caught up to him in the street, hoping for a few words. Before entering their house, he saw him furiously punch the red stop sign.

Before dinner, José Paul went to the bathroom wanting to relieve himself, but held it to avoid announcing his presence, for through the small patio window next to his parents' bedroom window he could hear his mother's voice, warm and sad:

"Well, *viejo*, what's done is done. I hope now it will last you. Besides, it's not your fault you're addicted. Although I still insist that the company should pay for these costs, they're the one's responsible, they got you into this."

"Please, Mercedes, don't keep saying that. From the very beginning, from the moment I signed the papers making myself responsible, I was screwed. The union already said that they can't help me . . . that I ac-

cepted the risks, that they've had no prior case of the pleasure chip causing addiction," his voice wove sadness with hatred, and seemed to dilute
in the salt water of tears. "In the end, my weakness got the best of me;
once again I bought a shitty import."

A thudding noise that sounded to Paul as if the closet door had been
punched reminded him of his need to pee: he crouched in front of the
toilet and concentrated on not making any noise. He suspended the operation when, among his parents' words, he caught some reference to
Christmas presents. Afterward there was silence.

Then the silence was broken by two strong knocks on the bathroom
door and his father's voice asking him to hurry. The boy zipped up his
fly, his hand getting splashed a little, and opened the door. As he exited,
it seemed to him that tiny red veins had been installed in his father's
eyes and that his eyelids formed little dark bags; he felt sorry for him and
ashamed of himself, since he thought for a second that his father had
caught him eavesdropping.

The hours elapsed as if an infinite train were passing before the boy's
eyes as, seated on the porch steps, he awaited his mother's shout calling
him to dinner. From there he saw Clementina, his older sister, arrive:
pants tight and cheeks aflame, she said goodbye to a jovial and talkative
young man. She ruffled the boy's hair as she passed him. Alone once
more, Paul reflected sadly that his sister had shown up without any presents. A flower of fire in the sky made his heart tremble. It was time for
the fireworks. The time when people came out of their houses and
hugged each other and contemplated the gift that the municipal government gave the city in the form of fleeting, dazzling signs, simulated stars,
ringlets of burning colors. And there he found, drawn in the sky, a diffuse moment of freedom and pleasure that seemed to grow and burst in
his own chest. Alone, with his arms open wide, he bathed in the halos of
illusory fire, until reality reimposed itself with a shout and the hiss of
steam that escaped from the pot of tamales someone had uncovered.

At the silent table Paul concentrated on eating, breathing in the smell
of the freshly seasoned beans and chewing softly to prolong the taste of
the sugar tamales. The north wind picked up then. A blast of wintry air,
carrying a load of sand, prickled the boy's arms. His mother got up
quickly to close the dining room window, while asking her children to
put on sweaters. Fragoso seemed unaware of everything. He appeared
upset about something. He ate quickly, voraciously, and without raising
his eyes.

Dinnertime ended.

Fragoso pounded his chest three times with the palm of his hand to force a prolonged belch, and stood up. Without looking at anyone, his eyes lost as if focused deep within himself, he went into his bedroom, followed by the sadness of his family, from whom sprung a collective sense of defeat. Paul, leaning on the closed window, heard his father's moan of pleasure: "He's already connected himself to the dreamer," he thought. His mother permitted herself a grimace while looking at Clementina, who whispered a prayer, picked up the dirty plates, quickly took them to the kitchen sink and returned with a rag to wipe up the crumbs and clean the grease-splattered table.

The Christmas tree blinked in the corner.

At its base lay the empty boxes, useless, wrapped like presents, covered with ocher-colored mold.

"It's time to go to bed," Mercedes said to her children.

"We'll clean the house tomorrow," she added, seeing that her daughter kept working in the kitchen, "it's late and the baby Jesus needs peace to be born again."

So as not to sleep, José Paul counted the wheezes and snores, the pauses and hitches, and listened to the in-and-out of Clementina's breathing. Every time he half-closed his eyes the gold-colored bicycle appeared, equipped with a plastic simulated engine, and drowsiness invaded him.

The lights were out and the house was still. He went out into the hallway. The desire to laugh overpowered the silence while he taped one end of a string to the wall. Then he went back to bed and tied the other end to his wrist. In spite of his efforts to evade slumber, at some point his mind wandered beyond his will and he fell asleep.

That's why he was so startled to feel the tug of the string on his wrist. He laid still, with his eyes closed, pretending to be sound asleep. But no one approached except the rustle of clothes, bare feet in the hallway, and a faint and peaceful voice that he recognized by its maternal tone. A little later the nocturnal serenity returned and José Paul, guided by the blinking lights of the Christmas tree, surveyed the living room. At the base of the tree sparkled a little red box with his name on it. He opened it.

Minutes later, the boy was seated on the edge of his bed. He caressed the new quartz watch. He thought of the useless letter written to Santa Claus a couple of weeks earlier. In it was deposited the yearning of months. Maybe years. A new, modern bicycle, not like the one that lay discarded on the back porch and that his father had bought four years ago second- (or third-?) hand. Neither new paint nor the oiled spokes nor the covered seat had made it look new.

He stopped thinking about the watch upon opening the window and breathing in the wind blowing from the north, a wind that increased in intensity, burdened with the minuscule grains of cold that it brought from the North Pole. He felt his cheeks turn pale as he went out onto the patio and quietly half-closed the kitchen door, taking care that the latch didn't fall. By the time he'd picked up the old bicycle, he'd already made a decision; he was sure that the only way to get the new bicycle was to do it himself. He remembered how his father had come charging out of his bedroom a few days ago with a grin of terror on his face and the base of his neck smoking, remembered the singed hair and the smell of burnt skin. Once again the treacherous chip had melted in his neck. The burns in his skin were what seemed the most grotesque, the most detestable to everyone else. But, according to Fragoso, if he cried out like a madman each time the crisis came upon him it was because he really was dying. If he ran from the bedroom with his eyes popping out of their sockets, bawling like a steer in the slaughterhouse, and if later he laughed with the rapture of a child, it was because of the irresistible pain that penetrated his head, the terrible imaginings that plunged him into death.

He thought of this while he pedaled, while he listened to the noise of cars that were celebrating the night that only comes once a year. He rode past the front porches of houses where the lights and the shouting echoed the public rejoicing, and he crossed street corners of resigned symmetry. A little way further his objective appeared.

A tall gate.

A concrete wall.

In the center, a building whose map was lodged in his memory, in spite of the fact he'd only been inside once before, clinging to his father's hand on Children's Day.

"I work here," his father had told him. "The chips are placed in these boxes and then they pass through on those rollers to the packaging department, over there."

He leaned the bicycle against the wall. Standing on top of it, he grasped the edge of the wall and climbed up in a flash, boosted by the fear of feeling a noose snare his ankle. The inner patio was dark, silent, solitary. Just gray pavement that reflected a ray of moonlight in its center. He seemed to see a light filtered through the window of the guardhouse. He ordered his imagination not to think of bizarre enemies, of slimy worms that might be crawling on the ground, of hooks that could get tangled up in his hair.

And he jumped.

He didn't stop to think.

He ran toward the building, his body hunched over, his arms folded against his chest, thinking that this way he would be a smaller object, less noisy, unimportant. And then he circled the building, hugging the walls until he found a window. He tried to open it. He used all his strength, he concentrated, he felt like the veins in his neck and arms were going to burst, but he couldn't do it. In his head he told himself no, he would not be a failure, surely he would find something on the ground with which to break the glass, maybe a rock. On all fours and with half-closed eyes he began to comb the ground. Gradually he approached the area of the parking garage, where a privet hedge grew whose leaves gave form to the company's logo. He walked between the distribution trucks, peering into the cabs and trying the handles. He tried to open the trailers and crawled under the chassis.

Nothing.

No iron or forgotten screwdrivers, not even a bolt.

He retraced his steps and sank down next to the thunder tree. He sat down on something hard that made him cry out. He felt around in the grass surrounding the tree and found a metal bar. The happiness of finding it stopped him from noticing the smell of burnt tobacco that floated in the air.

He placed the bar in the window and hung from it to lever it open. The creak of the metal sounded like a drum beat in a funeral march. José Paul didn't notice. He disappeared into the opening.

A few minutes later his figure reappeared in the window.

He jumped to the ground.

He ran toward the wall with the wind against him, with the air cold on his hot sweat, with fear that a hand would descend on his shoulder with the strength of an eagle's talon. As soon as he reached the wall he realized he wouldn't be able to climb it. He hadn't anticipated that when he left his house. Distress wove up his throat like a spiderweb, choking him. He walked quickly toward the gate, hoping to find something that would help him escape. It looked like the gate might be ajar. For a few instants he watched the guardhouse. It remained dark and silent. He warily approached. He slowly opened the gate. Paul felt a terrible, tremendous dryness in his mouth and throat as he exited the grounds and pulled the gate back as he had found it. He thrust his hand into his pocket to make sure the chip was still there. And he got on the bicycle and rode back home, without even suspecting that behind him, in the guardhouse, a cigarette was being relit and a hoarse, sad, loving voice was wishing him luck.

Even though the sun shone brilliantly and the people radiated smiles, nothing could compete with the happy face of José Paul, who pedaled with the strength of the tide. With each puff of wind the boy felt that a murmur of voices congratulated him, that his new bicycle provoked the envy of his neighbors, and that with it he could journey far beyond the Rio Bravo, he could leave Reynosa and travel along the riverbanks, along the toll road and the forgotten paths and across bridges. And no sooner had he so decided than he was on his way, racing along a footpath, traveling faster than the greenish current flowing at his side. The road was of soft earth, as if he were riding across a sponge and the wind were pushing him toward his destination. Thousands of summer butterflies molded their colors onto the bike and the boy's clothes, he felt them like rain, like a new gift from heaven. With them he seemed at times to fly on a cloud above small, green hills.

He heard a shout.

A far-off sound.

A sound that formed his name and repeated itself.

José Paul labored to open his eyes. His mother looked at him from his bedroom door.

"Aren't you going to get up?" she repeated. "Your father wants us to have breakfast together."

My father, thought the boy.

"Yes," he responded. "I'm coming."

As soon as his mother withdrew, José Paul raised his hand to his neck and unplugged the chip. He was silent for a few minutes, thinking that if he gave the chip to his father he would become furious about the theft, and instead of thanking him for his efforts, would surely punish him. As he swung his feet onto the cold floor, he felt a pain he hadn't noticed before, something like a whirlwind in the pit of his stomach.

"I really have to think it over," he said to himself, "I'll have to think it over."

Elia Barceló

SPAIN

Elia Barceló (1957–) was born in Alicante, Spain, and now lives in Austria, where she teaches literature and creative writing at the University of Innsbruck. She published her first science fiction story when she was twenty. Since then, Barceló has been a devoted writer of fantasy and SF, although she is also attracted by other modes of writing that concentrate on the extraordinary, such as the terror and detective genres. Barceló won the *Ignotus* award in 1991 and has been nominated for it on four other occasions. About thirty of her stories have been published in Spain and in several European and Latin American countries; some of them have been anthologized and others have been translated into French, Italian, and Esperanto. Her three SF novels to date are *Sacred* (*Sagrada,* 1989); *Yarek's World* (*El mundo de Yarek,* 1994); and *Natural Consequences* (*Consecuencias naturales,* 1994.)

In 1993 Barceló began editing *Our Own Visions* (*Visiones propias*), an annual anthology dedicated to new fantastic writing. She has also published a scholarly monograph on Cortázar entitled *An Uneasy Familiarity: Terror Archetypes in Julio Cortázar's Fantastic Short Stories* (*La inquietante familiaridad: Los arquetipos del terror en los cuentos fantásticos de Julio Cortázar*), and has collaborated occasionally with the Spanish journal *El País* and the magazine *Ciberp@ís.* Recently, Barceló has started writing detective novels and novels for young readers, since she firmly believes in the power of literature to spiritually nourish children and adolescents on to adulthood.[1] Two of these novels have been published so far: *The Case of the Cruel Artist* (*El caso del artista cruel,* 1998) and *Fatma's Hand* (*La mano de Fatma,* 2001).

In the line of "dangerous vision stories," "First Time" presents an apparently happy and supercivilized Europe where a new influx of immigrants (the *oris,* translated here as *forners*) act as paid slaves and are considered subhuman. Barceló's technique of using a young girl as a barely literate narrator clearly shows how young people's moral education has degenerated to a point that torturing and killing "forners" is considered little more than a mild transgression, a rite of passage into the elite circles of this desensitized world. Barceló explains, "My intention was . . . to use 'decadent' spelling to illustrate the mental decay that has taken root in that supposedly brilliant, rich, consumerist, racist new society where moral values that had always been considered basic ('thou shalt not kill,' for example) are now seen as a relic of the past."[2] Clearly, the story is meant to warn the reader of the perils intrinsic to the racist and xenophobic agenda of modern European neofascism.

First Time

Estreno, 1994

by Elia Barceló

translated by Ted Angell

dear diary

i diddit, diddit, diddit, i dont beleev it, i went for it, im in, like everyone else, its crazy, finely, cant wait for eight so i can sit at the schools PC and tell the hole group. havent even washd up yet, im such a pig, but the first time is the first time, i gotta tell about it even tho im at home at three in the morning talking to the micro they gave me for my last birthday. fourteen years. it was about time. they were starting to think i was a nerd. fourteen years without doing it yet, but this is it. i went all the way. better than i ixpected, crazy. what a rush, theres nothing like it, if my parents find out theyl kill me but who cares. what are they gonna do. gotta start sometime, right? they say there are people that have never done it in there life but i dont beleve it or its because there idiots like my imbecil brother i no he hasnt done it yet cuz he even goes to church hes so prissy. come on, he went when he still lived here. my dad wont say one way or the other but i no he likes it like anyone else, even my mom likes it, shes so cool, i no they were at Saras parents party and she told me the next day that the men spent three hours cleaning the basement so no one would no they were having a romp in there. im all messy, how gross, but its great now i no what its like, i was really afraid. the bad thing is it hooks you, they say. do it once youl do it agin. its true, such a slut i alredy want to go try it agin. the same thing agin whats the diffrence, i was really afraid and then it was so easy. it was so dark i cudnt see him rilly good, but the first time you dont have to see much, it dont matter, you feel it, thats what matters. vanesa is going to be so jellus she thinks she knows so much and now she has no idea that i no, now i no for sure. nothing like lurning from your own ixperience thats what the old man says, damn if he finds out im calling him old hill kill me 35 years old and he thinks hes starting to live. the old people go nuts and say no to what everyone wants, that you have time and you dont have to hurry so much and all that crap. well now i did it but not a sound, let them think im still in dipers. how funy, the stuff is drying onto me and i havent been able to wash up without making noise. im leaving now, diary, bye.

From Nena to:
　　All
　　I went for it, girls. I did it. This is it.

From Erasmus Elementary School of Rotterdam to:
　　Nadine Cifuentes Zúñiga
　　Class 1 Group A Performance Level 2
　　Native language: Spanish
　　Monday, 28 February 2009, 08.00–08.30
　　Orthography
　　The student has thirty minutes to complete the following exercises:

- Place diacritical marks over the following words:
　　esta, intrinseco, vio, tomare, cesped
- Fill in the blank with "b" or "v," according to the rules studied in the last lesson:
　　___ida, ___e___er, ___ariedad, ___urro, a___surdo
- Mark the words or groups of words that, in your opinion, are correctly written:
　　loe hecho, la he bisto, los hemos vendido, ahora, handar

08.29
　　From: Nadine Cifuentes Zúñiga
　　To: Erasmus Elementary School of Rotterdam
　　I need more time. I dont get it.

dear diary
　　there a bunchov asshols, what the hell do i care about Bs and Vs. we girls understand each other so who cares. only three more classes and i can drop it for a wile and see what the girls say. i cant wait. bye.

Social Sciences:
　　"In no instance is violence the optimum solution in civilized social problem solving. For every problem there is, nowadays, an open way to

understanding, be it at a personal level (bi- or multipersonal dialogued communication, physically or in writing) or at an institutional level (legal options). Our political system permits the resolution of any conflict in a civilized manner, through a highly developed computer network, by observing the legal option through which the individual victim of the offense declines to have the slightest physical contact with the offender."

The student should offer a summary of the text and a point of view about the opinions expressed in it. The exercise should be finished in a maximum of sixty minutes.

From: Nadine Cifuentes Zúñiga to:
Erasmus Elementary School of Rotterdam
Violence is bad. Fighting by PC is better.

Time used: 47 minutes.
The student is allowed to enjoy a pause of thirty minutes. The return to your position in front of the screen will take place at 11.30.

dear diary,
i knew it, there hissterical. look, look what it says. ill read it to you, Sara: great, supergreat, megagreat, congradulations, nena, nena. At 17.15 i get out of foke dance, if you come get me when you get out of seramecs (however you spell it) we have 10 minutes, 6000 seconds for you to tell me about it. Nora: you rule Renena. envy envy. call me tonite, i hafta studdy. im dying for the detales. Vanesa: bout time girl. who was the victum? do the old people no bout it? Yolanda: tell me in dance class. You didnt get sick i hope. hey diary, im alredy hoping for it to hapn agin. i get hot thinkin about it, it was great, so great, what a rush. shit shit shit i have to start agin another two hours what a drag today were having soy porij gives me diarea but mom says i need it i dont no what for. i used to buy candy bars but now the new cookmasheen records if ive eaten or not. the piece a shit has a video camera and the old lady finds out when she comes back wether ive dumped it in the toilet. geez what a life. dinners all right, its peace day and well have meat yum yum which will be bad for the liver but its tasty. tonite no way, my fokes are goin out i no what for. they think i dont no, being forteen they think i still suck my thumb the asshols, how modern they are when they talk by tv my sociolagist dad and sexolagist mom. The PCs butt is beeping. bye diary.

"How was your day, Nena?"

"Fine, Dad."

"What subjects?"

"Same thing every Monday. Ortho, socio, math, topo, textlit, peace, commu, interrelate, eco. Same stuff."

"Are you improving?"

"I guess."

"You didn't eat your soy."

"Fff—, Mom, it's puke."

"It's healthy."

"And tastes like shit."

"Nena!"

"Yeah, I know."

"Plans for Sunday?"

"That's next century, Mom."

"There's a youth gathering. I reserved a place in case."

"Again?"

"You're old enough now, Nena. You have to relate. This time go touch."

"Unnh."

"What do you mean, 'unnh'?"

"It's always the same, Dad. Totally lame. Same people, same thing. It's boring."

"You don't appreciate things, Nena. Twenty years ago . . ."

"The world wasn't made. Now other things are going on."

"Relax, Nena, you're very young, you still have time. Besides, it's not good. Socially, I mean, you know. Peace is very important."

"Well, you two . . ."

"We're your parents. We have rights. It's our private life; a private adult life."

"OK, I'll go."

"You'll go?"

"I'll go, Mom."

"A healthy sex life is important, Nena. Like nutrition, education, and social training. Got it?"

"Got it. Are you going out?"

"For a little while. A civic meeting for communication. Your plans?"

"An hour in the atrium with Sara. I missed her coming out of ceramics. Her dance was delayed 'cause of a power failure in the music system."

"Those forners get worse all the time. They need to get fired for good."

"Without forners, not even the wastebaskets in the complex would work, criminy. All the workers are forners."

"Yeah. But they're slow and stupid."

"They're just forners, what do you expect? They're what we need. The street is still prohibited, Nena. Stay in the atrium until 21.00, then go to bed, got it?"

"I'm going to forget what traffic looks like. No street in months, Dad."

"The complex has everything, Nena. The street belongs to the forners at night. Daytime is for adults and urgencies. The complex is for young people: stores, bars, discos, gyms, computer rooms, video rooms, pools, greenhouses, what more do you kids want?"

"Blood."

"You're nuts, Nena. Eight minutes till your time with Sara, you ready? Atrium until 21.00, then to bed. Finish your meat."

"Got it, dad. Bye! Happy hunting!"

"Crazy, crazy, crazy."

"Bye, folks!"

dear diary

22.17 and in bed like a blankit. so sick of being a kid. there out there gettin it on and im here in bed knowin what im missing. Sara freeked when i told her that i went out on the street, right in the middle of the street outside. it was way dark and my heart was goin like a motor but i went for it. what a rush. he saw me come up slow and he gave me a cool smile cause they told him that somtimes girls dare to do it, those morons think there so cool. he had black eyes like they all do and he was thin and tuff like they all are. i stuck it in him as soon as he put his arms around me. what a high, diary. he dubbled over at the middle, and i gave it to him agin in the belly like Sara told me to. that way they dont scream, only grunt, a really wierd noise. i went crazy. i started to stab and stab all over. at first he moved around a lot, then he didnt. then i stuck him all over with the nife, might as well go all the way since the nife cost me my savings from peace day. i got him in the eyes, diary, way cool huh, but they didnt go plop or nuthing like in the movies. only the blood was like in the movies, so much blood black black with as dark as it was and hot hot good megagood. i didnt suck it cuz it was gross, the first time its kinda i dunno but ill make myself do it for sure. Saras dunnit and she says its cool. she asked me if i was afrade that the peacepolice would find out since they were on the street but hell he was only a lazy and traiteruss forner like the ones that live by our coast coming to work in the complexes of Yurup insted of staying in there land to rilly work hard but since its cold there and its all contamanated because there old people were such pigs and theyl die of hunger if they stay there they come here to screw us develupped people. the peacepolice dont care about a forner, not even right in the street, nobody saw us it was ten or twelve minutes but what a rush im alredy hoping it happens agin. if my fokes find out theyl write me up and i wont have seramecs classes and no pool for three weeks. but theyl find out that im old enuf. they do it too and its ok. and sunday i gotta go to that gathering shit dammit not agin to fuck —— then esplanations and tekneeks and hassles i no them all, boys and girls and i like it better alone or with Sara if our periods happen at the same time. what i have to do for my damn helth if i dont the ol lady has a fit and they put me in more interrelation classes as if im wierd. *me* wierd. im the most normal person in the world, im half crazy ive started at forteen. well diary gotta sleep until 6:00 if i dont ill be snuzing in the middle of fucking tie chee. forteenth of march the old people have dreamthera night and im goin out on the street while they dream. only two weeks away. im gonna wear out the blade from cleaning it so much. bye diary. see ya tomorrow.

Pepe Rojo

MEXICO

Juan José "Pepe" Rojo (1968–) was born in Chilpancingo, the capital of the state of Guerrero. He lived there and in Acapulco before settling in Mexico City, where he currently resides with his wife and editorial collaborator, Deyanira Torres. He has a degree in communication sciences and now teaches part time, coedits fanzines, and freelances as a communication services specialist.

Rojo specializes in horror-, fantasy-, and cyberpunk-influenced SF, frequently intermingling elements of all three genres, and his fiction has appeared in numerous Spanish-language genre magazines.

We proudly present "Gray Noise" ("Ruido gris"), which won Mexico's *Kalpa* prize for best SF story of 1996. It is an atmospheric piece juxtaposing taut, graphically shocking drama with passages of lyrical introspection. The near-future story is set in an unspecified urban center that may or may not be Mexico City; Rojo, unlike many of his contemporaries, tends not to portray an explicitly Mexican reality, preferring instead to emphasize the universality of his characters' circumstances and attitudes.

"Gray Noise" incorporates many of the postmodernist themes and images that characterize Rojo's fiction: the corrosive effects of corporate values and practices (the news media in particular); the paradoxical inability to communicate in a world overrun with communications technology; a fascination with the power of cybernetics, tempered by an awareness of its destructive potential; and personal alienation, often conveyed through motifs of self-mutilation and corporal fragmentation. In "Gray Noise" Rojo gives us a story that is both chilling in its pervasive sense of powerlessness and disquieting in its irresolution.

Gray Noise

Ruido gris, 1996

by Pepe Rojo

translated by Andrea Bell

In my room in the early morning, when everything is still, I can hear a buzzing sound. It starts between my eyes and extends down my neck. It's like a whisper, and I concentrate, trying to make out the words that sound inside my head, knowing in advance they won't make any sense. They don't say a thing. The murmur is like that vibration you can feel but can't place when you're in a mall right when all the stores start turning on their lights and getting ready for the day. Even when people arrive that vibration is still there, but you can't feel it anymore. My head is like a vacant mall. The sound of empty space. The vibration that expectations produce. The whisper of a desire you can't name.

Believe me, I'm used to the buzz. I'm also used to my heart beating, to my brain stringing together ideas that have no direction, to my lungs taking in air in order to expel it later. The body is an absurd machine.

Sometimes the noise lulls me to sleep at night. Sometimes it doesn't let me sleep, it keeps me awake, staring at a yellow indicator light on the ceiling that tells me I'm on standby.

I transmitted for the first time when I was eighteen years old and desperate to find some news item, anything. So I took to walking the streets, following people whose faces seemed like TV fodder. I felt like a bum with a mission. I'd had a little money left over after the operation and could enjoy the luxury of eating wherever I wanted, so I went to one of those fancy restaurants on the top floor of a building tall enough to give you vertigo. After having a drink I walked toward the john, trying to find an exit out onto the terrace. I wanted a few shots of the city for my personal file. I opened several doors without finding anything. Just like my life, I thought with a cynicism I sometimes miss. The rooftop terraces of all buildings are alike. A space filled with geometric forms, in shades of gray. Someone should make a living painting horizontal murals on terrace roofs with messages for the planes that fly over this city every five minutes. Though I don't know what the messages would be. What can you say to someone about to arrive except "welcome"? It's been a long time since anyone felt welcome in this city.

Someone was scrambling over an aluminum fence on the opposite side of the terrace. Maybe it was my lucky day and he was gonna commit suicide. I activated the "urgent" button inside my thigh, hoping I wasn't wrong. A little later a green indicator lit up my retina, telling me that I was on some station's monitors, though not yet on the air. The guy was standing on a cornice, looking down. He was dark and stubby; his back was to me so I couldn't see his face. I jumped over the fence and looked down, establishing the scene for the viewers; it could be edited later. The dark man turned and saw me, got nervous, and jumped. Right then a red light went on in my eye and I heard a voice tainted with static say in my ear, "You're on the air, pal!"

That night I found out that the man was named Veremundo, a fifty-four-year-old gym teacher. The suicide note they found on his body said he was tired of being useless, of feeling insignificant from dawn to dusk, and that the worst thing about his suicide was knowing it wouldn't affect a soul.

Suicides always say the same thing.

WHEN IT IS IMPOSSIBLE TO SET UP AN EXTERNAL CAMERA TO SITUATE THE ACTION, THE REPORTER SHOULD OBTAIN A FEW ESTABLISHING SHOTS—"LONG SHOTS"—TO ENSURE THAT THE SPACE IN WHICH THE ACTION TAKES PLACE IS LOGICAL TO THE VIEWERS. REPORTERS SHOULD PREPARE FIXED SHOTS FIRST, AND ONLY LATER, WHEN THERE IS ACTION, CAN THEY USE MOTION SHOTS.

Suicides don't pay very well. There are so many every day, and people are so unimaginative, that if you spend a day watching television you can see at least ten suicides, none of them very spectacular. Seems the last thing suicides think of is originality.

Only once did I try to talk a suicide out of it. It was a woman, about forty years old, skinny and worn-out. I told her that the only thing her suicide was going to accomplish was to feed me for about two days, that there was no point being just another one, that I totally understood life was a load of shit but there was no sense killing yourself just to entertain a thousand assholes who do nothing but switch channels looking for something that would raise, even just a little, the adrenaline level in their bodies.

She jumped anyway.

I returned home, and that night I watched the personal copy I'd made over and over again. Every action happened thousands of times on my monitor. I ended up playing it in slo-mo, trying to find some moment when her expression changed, the moment when one of my words might've had an effect I didn't know how to take advantage of.

I went to bed with swollen eyes, a terrible taste in my mouth, and thinking that what I'd said to that lady I might just as well have been saying to myself.

I've had enough, and I leave my house to go buy something to eat. I jump on my bike (which I use to get around near home) and just before reaching a pizza place I hear a bunch of patrol cars a few blocks away. I press my thigh to activate the controls, and the green signal goes on in my eye. I pedal as fast as I can, following the sound of the sirens. I turn a corner and see five cop cars parked at the entrance to a building. I leave my bike leaning against one of them, hoping no one'll steal it, and run toward a cop who's keeping gawkers back. I show her my press badge and she grudgingly lets me in. Tells me to go up to the third floor. When I arrive, a couple of paramedics are examining a body that's convulsing in the doorway of the apartment. I stop to establish the shots. One full shot of the paramedics, one long shot of the corridor, and I try to walk slowly and keep my vision fixed so that the movement isn't too abrupt. I stop at the doorway and slowly pan my head in order to establish the setting on thousands of monitors throughout the world. My indicator light's been red for several seconds. I approach an officer who's covering up a corpse near a TV monitor, and on the monitor they're transmitting my shot. I feel the shiver that always accompanies a hook, I begin to get dizzy, and a shooting pain crisscrosses my brain. I lose all sense of space until I turn around and spot a cop trying to be the star of the day. The cop sees the red light in my right eye and looks into it. "We got a report from some neighbors in the building, they'd heard a baby crying, and they knew that three single men lived here. You know how people are, they thought they were some kind of faggot perverts who'd adopted a baby so they could feel like they were more normal."

I interrupt the laughter of the cop who's posing for my right eye, and ask him when they were notified.

"Twenty minutes ago. We ran a check on kidnapped babies. When we got here, they'd already killed the neighbors. Seems they were monitoring all phone calls, and they began shooting at us . . ."

The officer kept on talking, and I was concentrating on getting the shot when I sensed a movement behind him. Apparently a closet door was opening. The next thing I register—and I suppose it's gonna be pretty spectacular since my shot was a close-up of his face—is a flash of light and his face exploding into pieces of blood and flesh.

I hurl myself against his body, grabbing hold of it and using my momentum to carry us toward whoever did this. Before reaching the closet I let go of the body and step back, to get a clear shot. The headless corpse of the policeman strikes another body and knocks it down. I run up quickly and stomp on the hand holding a gun. I can hear the bones as they break. Too bad I don't have secondary audio capacity so I could record the sound. I hope someone in the transmission room patches it in. The shot is a bird's-eye view of some guy's face, soaked with the blood of the cop. I can't make out his features. More cops arrive. I take a few steps back.

"It seems," I comment on the air, "that there was still one person hiding in the closet, and this carelessness by the police has cost yet another officer his life." It's always good to criticize institutions. It raises the ratings. Just then I hear a commotion at the door and quickly turn around to find a young woman crying, followed by a private security guard. She goes into one of the rooms I haven't managed to shoot yet. When I try to go in, a cop stops me and his look says I can't enter. I know he's dying to insult me, but he knows I'm on the air and it could harm the police department's image in this city, so all he says is I can't go in. I manage to get shots of the woman picking up a bundle and holding it to her breast while endlessly repeating, "My love, my baby."

"What is that, officer? Is it a baby?"

"This is a private moment, reporter, you have no right to be filming it."

"I have information rights." I lie by reflex, but I don't succeed in budging him. I try my luck with the girl who'd gone inside crying. "Can I help you in any way, miss?" Just then I realize the bundle she'd picked up is all bloody. Various police officers and two paramedics try to take away the baby, at least I suppose that's what it is, but she doesn't want to let go of it. She pats her hair and comes over to me. Hurry up, I think, the clock's running on your fifteen minutes. "You're a reporter, aren't you?" My first instinct is to nod my head but I remember that it's an unpleasant motion for TV viewers, I'm not supposed to be anything but a verbal personality, and so I answer by saying yes.

"Someone stole my baby, and now I've found him but it looks like the cops hurt him, he's been shot in the leg." The girl cries harder and harder while a paramedic tells her that all she's doing is hurting the baby more. I get confused because someone's started to shout in my ear receiver. They want me to ask the girl her name. The paramedic grabs the baby. In my head, the program directors keep talking. "We couldn't have planned this better, this is drama, just wait till you get your check, the ratings are gonna add a lot of zeros to it."

The rest is routine. Interviews, facts, versions. The fate of the baby will be a different type of reporter's job and it'll keep the whole city enthralled all this afternoon and maybe into tomorrow morning, when some other reporter tapes fresher news.

When I leave the building my bike's no longer waiting for me, and I have to walk home. I live in a world without darkness. All day long there's an indicator light in my retina telling me my transmission status. I can turn the indicator level down, but even when I'm sleeping it keeps me company. A yellow light and a buzz, a murmur. They're who I sleep with. They're my immediate family. But my eyes belong to the world. My extended family spans an entire city, though no one would recognize me if they met me on the street.

I haven't gone out for a few weeks now. My last check frees me up from having to wander around looking for news. Privacy is a luxury for a man in my condition. Several times a day a yellow indicator goes on in my right eye and I hear a voice asking if I have anything, they have some dead time and it's been days since I transmitted anything. I simply don't answer. I close my eyes and remain quiet, hoping they'll understand that I'm not in the mood.

What do I do on my days off? Well, I try not to see anything interesting. I read magazines. I look at the window of my room. I count the squares on the living room floor. And I remember things that aren't recorded on tape, while my eyes stare at the ceiling, which is white—perhaps the least attractive color on a TV screen.

THE MOST COMMON ERRORS MADE BY OCULAR REPORTERS ARE DUE TO THE REFLEXES OF THEIR OWN BODIES. A REPORTER MUST LIVE UNDER CONSTANT DISCIPLINE SO AS TO AVOID SEEMINGLY INVOLUNTARY REFLEXES. THERE IS NO GREATER SIGN OF INEXPERIENCE AND LACK OF PROFESSIONAL CONTROL THAN A REPORTER WHO CLOSES HIS EYES IN AN EXPLOSION OR A REPORTER WHO COVERS HER FACE WITH HER ARMS WHEN STARTLED BY A NOISE.

Today is not a good day. I go walking the streets, and in every store I hear the same news. Constant Electrical Exposure Syndrome, CEES for fans of acronyms, seems to be wreaking havoc. Continuous stimulation of the nerve endings, caused by electricity and an environment which is constantly charged with electricity—radiation from monitors, microwaves, cell phones—seems to have a fatal effect on some people. I stop in front of a shop window and start recording a reporter with his back to a wall of TV screens: "It seems the central nervous system is so used to receiving external electronic stimulation that when it doesn't get it, it begins to produce it, constantly sending electric signals through the body that have no meaning or function, speeding up your heartbeat and making your lungs hyperventilate. Your eyes begin to blink and sometimes your tongue starts to jerk inside your mouth. Some witnesses even say that the victims of this syndrome can 'speak in tongues,' or that this syndrome 'is what causes this type of experience in various subjects.'" They insert shots of several people speaking in tongues here.

The reporter, looking serious and trying to get people's attention, keeps walking, while images of people who suffer from these symptoms appear on the video wall. The screens fill with shots of serious men with concerned faces. Interviews with experts, no doubt.

"No one knows for certain the exact nature of the syndrome. The global scientific community is in a state of crisis. There are those who say this is just a rumor started by the media, simply another disease transformed into a media event. Some say the syndrome isn't as bad as it seems. But there are also those who believe that civilization has created a monster from which it will be difficult to escape."

The images on the monitors change. Various long shots of rustic houses, surrounded by trees. The music changes. Acoustic instruments, a flute and a guitar.

"However, there are already several electric detox centers out in the country. Rest homes devoid of electricity. This is perhaps the only possibility or hope for those who exhibit symptoms of the syndrome. As always, hope is the last thing to die in what is perhaps the most important 'artificial' disease of this century. There are those who say that what cancer was to the previous century, CEES will be to ours."

They show a few shots of these places. The patients look out the windows or at the walls, as if waiting for something they know will never arrive. As if waiting for civilization to keep a promise, yet aware that it never will, since the promise has long been forgotten.

The equipment for corporal transmission is very expensive. My father gave it to me. Well, he doesn't know what he gave me. I just received an e-mail on my eighteenth birthday saying that he'd deposited who knows how much money into an account in my name, that I had to decide what to do with it and that after spending it I was on my own. That I shouldn't seek him out anymore.

I still keep that e-mail on my hard drive. It's one of the advantages of the digital age. Memory becomes eternal and you can relive those moments as many times as you want. They remain frozen outside of you, and when you don't know who you are or where you come from, a few commands typed into your computer bring your past to the present. The problem is that when the past remains physically alive in the present, when does the future get here? And why would you want it to?

The future is a constant repetition of what you've already lived; maybe some details can change, maybe the actors are different, but it's the same. And when you haven't actually lived it, surely you saw something similar in some movie, on some TV show, or you heard something like it in a song. I keep hoping my mom will return one day and tell me it was all a joke, that she never died. I keep hoping my father will keep his promise and come see me in the orphanage. I keep hoping my life will stop being this endless repetition of days that follow each other with nothing new to hope for.

I paid for part of my operation with the money. Legally, half the operation is paid for by the company that owns the rights to my transmissions. The doctors tried to talk me out of the implant, but I was already over sixteen, so I told them to just concentrate on doing their job. I needed to earn money and I knew perfectly well that luck and necessity are strange bedfellows. Three days later the nerve endings of my eyes and vocal cords were connected to a transmitter that could send the signal to the video channels.

That was the last time I heard from my father.

The most important detail that an ocular reporter must remember is to avoid monitors when transmitting live. If a reporter focuses on a monitor that is broadcasting what he is transmitting, his sense of balance will be harshly affected and he will begin to suffer from severe headache. Exposure to this type of situation is easily controlled by avoiding shots of monitors when transmitting live. It is important to note that the reflected transmissions "hook" the reporter, and there is a change in the stimuli that travel

FROM THE BRAIN TOWARD THE DIFFERENT MUSCLES OF THE BODY. FOR THAT REASON IT IS SOMETIMES ALMOST IMPOSSIBLE TO BREAK OFF VISUAL CONTACT WITH THE MONITOR. THE ONLY WAY TO PREVENT THESE "HOOKS" IS THROUGH ABRUPT MOVEMENT OF THE BODY OR NECK AS SOON AS VISUAL CONTACT IS MADE WITH THE IMAGES ONE IS TRANSMITTING. LATEST RESEARCH REVEALS THAT LONG PERIODS OF EXPOSURE TO THESE VIRTUAL LOOPS CAUSE SYMPTOMS SIMILAR TO THOSE OF CEES. THIS INFORMATION WAS OBTAINED FROM RECENT EXPERIMENTS AND FROM THE RECORDS OF THE TOYNBEE CASE.

The Toynbee case is a legend no one in my profession can ever forget. Some anti-media extremists kidnapped a reporter and blindfolded him so that he couldn't transmit anything. Every two hours they broadcast their opinions to a nation that watched, entertained: "The media are the cause of the moral decay of our society; the media are causing the extinction of individuality; thousands of mental conditions stem from the fact that human beings can only learn about reality through the media; the information is manipulated." The whole ideological spiel, just like on one of those flyers they hand out in the streets. It's ironic to think that those extremists may be the only ones who'll survive if an epidemic like CEES wipes out humanity. They always try to avoid electricity. I don't know what I prefer, to keep hoping that this reality miraculously gets better or that some stupid extremists take over the world and impose the rules of "their" reality. The only thing you can learn from human history is that there's nothing more dangerous than a utopia.

So, as an example and metaphor of their complaints, they tied up the reporter, who worked under the name Toynbee, and put him in front of a monitor. They immobilized his head and connected his retina to the monitor. I've seen those images a thousand times. The only thing the reporter's eyes see is a monitor within a monitor within a monitor, until infinity seems to be a video camera filming a monitor that's broadcasting what it's recording, and there's no beginning, no end, there's nothing, until you remember that a human being is watching this, it's the only thing he can see and it's giving him an unbearable headache, as if someone were crisscrossing his skull with cables and wires. The images weren't enough. For those who know what it feels like to get hooked, the images were painful, but for those who'd never felt that kind of feedback they were frankly boring. The extremists—conscious that they were putting on a show and that before they'd be able to broadcast ideas they had to entertain the world—set up a video camera to tape Toynbee's face, and sent the signal to the same transmission station the reporter was connected to. At the station they knew there was nothing they could do to help Toynbee, since he was connected directly to the monitor, and they began to transmit both things: the monitors reproducing themselves until infinity, and Toynbee's face. The station executives say they would've cut the broadcast if they'd had doubts about the source of the hook, but everyone knows that's not true. Ratings are ratings.

Watching that reporter's face is quite a show. First, a few facial muscles start to move, as if he had a tic. At first he tried to move his eyes, to look to either side, but right next to the monitor was the tripod with the camera taping his face. And so on one half of the screen you could see how the loop was broken: all you saw was the partial view of a TV set, showing the image of a video camera on the right side of the screen and the real video camera on the other side, as if reality didn't have depth, only breadth. As if reality repeated itself endlessly off to the right and left. But the hook was stronger than his willpower, and gradually the reporter stopped trying to look off to the side. Sometimes the monitor showed how he tried. A very slow pan to the right or left that slowly came back again, as if the muscles of his eyes had no strength left. Toynbee began to sweat. His face began to convulse more violently, each time sweating bigger drops that struggled against gravity until, just like the reporter's eyes, they gave up and slid rapidly down his convulsing face. Each drop followed a different path. His face, lit up by the monitor, seemed to be full of thousands of monitors, since his damp skin also reflected, in distortion, the monitor he was looking at. The muscle spasms were getting stronger, and just as the sweat deformed the monitor, each convulsion moved the reporter's face one step further away from what we know as human. There were no longer moments when you could see normalcy in his face. Everything was movement and water and eyes that looked out feverishly, desperately. Sometimes, when I recall the images, the eyes even seem to be concentrating, as if they were discovering a secret that not only makes you lose your mind but causes your body to react violently, because it's something that human beings shouldn't be allowed to see.

A few minutes later his eyes seemed to lose all focus, even though they kept on receiving and transmitting light. His eyes were vacant, just like the monitors. I've always liked to think that at that moment the only thing the reporter could see was a kitschy image of his past—I dunno, the birthday party his mom threw him, or some day when he was in a play, or his first kiss, or some other idiocy of the kind that always makes us happy. There was no more willpower left in his eyes, but his eyelids were being forced open, so his body and the ghosts that occupied his body were still functioning. Several of his facial muscles atrophied and stopped working, which made the movements of his face even less natural. The shot continued until his face had no expression left, just spasms and movement, expressions that went beyond the range of human emotions, possibilities that ceased to have meaning the moment they disappeared.

Until his heart exploded.

Sometimes, when I'm bored and on the bus returning to my apartment, I begin to record everything I see. But then I stop seeing and just let the machines do their work. I go into a sort of trance in which my eyes, though open, observe nothing; and yet when I get home I have a record of everything they saw. As if it wasn't me who saw it all.

When I watch what I taped I don't recognize myself. I relive everything I saw without remembering anything. At those times it's my feelings that are on standby.

Some truths become evident when reality is observed this way.

The poor are the only ones who are ugly. The poor, and teenagers. Everyone with a little money has already changed his or her face and now has a better looking one, has already made his face or her identity more fashionable. Teenagers aren't allowed this type of operation because their bone structure is still changing. That's how you can tell economic status or age, by checking out the quality of the surgical work on people's faces. We live in an age when everyone, everyone who's well off in this world, is perfect. Perfect body, perfect face, and looks that speak of success, of optimism, as if the mind were perfect, too, and could think only correct thoughts. Today, ugliness is a problem humanity seems to have left behind. Today, as always, humanity's problems are solved with good credit.

Sometimes I like to think about the scene of my suicide. One of my options is to connect the electric camera terminals I have in my eyes to an electric generator in order to raise the voltage little by little, until my brain or my eyes or the camera explodes. It thrills me to think of the images I'd get.

Or I could prepare something cruder. Take a knife and cut out my eye. Cut it out by the roots. Sometimes I think I'd prefer not to see anything, I'd prefer a world in shades of black. Get rid of my eyes. Even if they sued me, even if I had to spend the rest of my life rotting away in jail.

And while I decide, I sit alone at home, waiting. Waiting for a promise to be kept . . .

Today I woke up with the urge to go out into the street and find something interesting. I've been walking around for a couple of hours without any destination. It's a nice day. I hear shouts at the end of the street and take off running in that direction. A drugstore. I press the button and my indicator light changes from yellow to green. I stop a few meters from the entrance and file a report. "Shouts in a drug store, I don't know what's going on, I'm going to find out." I take the time needed to establish the scene and slowly start to approach. A lot of people are leaving the drugstore, running. The story of my life. Wherever no one wants to be, there go I.

It's hard to get inside. I try to shoot several of the faces of the people stampeding each other to get out. Desperate faces. Scared faces. The red light goes on. "I'm at a drugstore, the people are trying frantically to get out. I haven't heard any shots." I have to shove several people aside until I can get through the door, and I head toward the place everyone's leaving. "Looks like someone's lying on the ground." A bunch of people wearing uniforms surround him. Probably the store employees. I stop a moment to establish the shot. I stop an employee who wants to get outside and look him in the eyes. He's so scared he doesn't even realize I'm transmitting. "What's going on?" "The guy was standing there, taking something off the shelves, when suddenly he collapses and starts to shake. He's infected . . ." The guy pushes me and jars my shot. Shit. I approach the body; there's an ever widening circle around him. I pass these people and get a full-body shot of the guy, on the floor having convulsions. He's swallowing his tongue. I approach and get down close to him. He looks at me desperately when his head's not jerking around. Toynbee. He has the same facial features. "This man was shopping in the drug store when he suffered a seizure." The guy turns to look at me, realizes there's a red light burning in my retina, and begins to laugh. His laughter starts to mix with his convulsions and before long you can't distinguish his laughter from his pain. I try to hold him in my arms, I try to touch him to calm him down, but it has no effect. I see a red light in his left eye. He's transmitting. I let go of him and his head hits the floor hard. Out of nowhere, he seems to be drowning. He shudders twice and remains quiet, looking at me. In my head I hear, "Say something, say something about CEES, *talk,* dammit, it's your job."

The reporter is motionless. The camera in my eyes records a tiny red dot that remains alive in his. Today my face will probably appear on the monitors.

Two days later my news is no longer news. It seems like every day more attacks of the syndrome are reported. Forty percent of the victims are reporters. I remember AIDS and the homophobia it awoke. Seems like it's us reporters' turn to live in fear, not just of dying, but of the fear of others. Mediaphobia? What will they name this effect?

The common citizen (and believe me, they're all common) still doesn't understand that the syndrome isn't transmitted by bodily contact. Everyone runs away when they see someone falling apart in a fit of convulsions. They still don't get it that the body is no longer the important factor. They live under the misconception that if they touch a victim they'll get infected. It's like a phantom virus that can't be located, it's in the air, in the street, it's wherever you go but in reality it doesn't exist. It's a virtual virus. And it's a sickness we're exposed to by living in this world. It's the sickness of the media, of cheap entertainment, it's the sickness of civilization. It's our penance for the sin of bad taste.

FOR ALL REPORTERS WHO TRANSMIT LIVE, CONTROL IS THE PRINCIPAL WEAPON AGAINST THE REFLEX STIMULATION CAUSED BY THE INDICATOR LIGHT. THE VIEWER CAN SEE THROUGH THE REPORTER'S EYES ONLY ONCE THE RED LIGHT IN THE RETINA GOES ON. ALL MOVEMENT, ALL ACTION ON THE REPORTER'S PART, SHOULD BE PERFECTLY PLANNED. THERE MUST BE NO MISTAKES. FRONTAL SHOTS ARE BEST. IT IS ALWAYS NECESSARY TO TAKE FACE SHOTS OF THE SUBJECT, BY MEANS OF THE CAMERA CONNECTED TO THE NERVE ENDINGS OF THE EYE, IN ORDER TO ESTABLISH IDENTIFICATION BETWEEN THE SUBJECT AND THE VIEWER. THE REPORTER FUNCTIONS AS A MEDIUM. HE/SHE IS MERELY THE POINT OF CONTACT BETWEEN THE ACTION AND THE REACTION THAT THOUSANDS OF VIEWERS WILL HAVE IN THEIR HOMES. THE REPORTER MUST BE THERE WITHOUT BEING THERE. EXIST WITHOUT BEING NOTICED. THIS IS THE ART OF COMMUNICATION.

The opening sequence of the program I usually transmit on goes like this: all the shots are washed out as if they were done in some familiar, old-fashioned style, as if done without the necessary transmission quality, that being the excuse for washing them in gray tones that'll later change to reds. First there's a subjective shot of a stomach operation; then the doctors turn and talk to the camera, and the whole world learns that the camera is the face of the person being operated on. Then there's an action sequence of a shootout downtown, till one of the people firing turns and sees the camera and presses the trigger; the camera shot jolts and seems to fall to the ground. Everything starts to flood, a red liquid's filling up the lens. The pace starts to pick up. A shot from the point of view of a driver who crashes into a school bus. A worm's-eye view of a guy throwing himself off a building (I've always thought he looks like a high-diver). The sacrifice of a cow in a slaughterhouse. The assassination of a politician. An industrial accident where some guy loses an arm. Shots of explosions where even the reporter gets blown up. A skyjacking where the terrorist shoots a passenger in the head. And so on. The images go by faster and faster until you can hardly make out what's going on, all you see is motion and blood and more motion, shapes that don't seem to have any human reference anymore, until it all begins to acquire a bit of order and you start to see red, yellow, and gray lines that dance about rapidly and leave the retinal impression of a circle in the middle of the screen where the lines meet. An explosion stops the sequence, and inside the circle the program's logo is formed: Digital Red.

Welcome to pop entertainment in the early twenty-first century.

What will I be doing in twenty years? Will I keep roaming the streets looking for news to transmit? Not a very pleasant future. Belonging to the entertainment industry gives off an existential stink. Some still call it journalism, though everyone knows the news is there not to inform, but to entertain. My eyes make me commune with the masses. Thousands of people see through my eyes so they can feel that their lives are more real, that their lives aren't as putrid and worm-eaten as the lives of the people I see. I'm the social glove they put on in order to confront reality. I'm the one who gets dirty, and I prevent their lives from smelling rotten. I'm a vulture who uses the misfortunes of others to survive.

When you get up close to a mirror you can't see both your eyes at the same time. You can see either the right or the left. The closer you get to your image the more distorted it gets and you can only see yourself partially. The same thing happens with a monitor. You're not there. You're the unknown one who moves in a way you don't recognize as your own. Who speaks with a voice that doesn't sound like yours. Who has a body that doesn't correspond to your idea of it. You're a stranger. To see yourself on a monitor is to realize how much you don't know about yourself and how much that upsets you.

If I wanted a more dramatic effect I could get myself hooked, like Toynbee. Connect myself directly to a monitor and start to transmit. See how reality is made up of ever-smaller monitors (and no matter how hard you try, you can't find anything inside those screens, just another monitor with nothing inside) and go crazy when I realize that's the meaning of life. Totally forget about control over my body.

Allow my eyes to bleed.

THE TRANSMISSION TIME OF AN OCULAR REPORTER IS THE PROPERTY OF THE COMPANY THAT FINANCES HIS/HER OPERATION. CLAUSE 28 OF THE STANDARD CONTRACT ESTABLISHES THAT SIX HOURS OF EVERY REPORTER'S DAY ARE PROPERTY OF SAID COMPANY.

A terrorist attack in a department store. I hate department stores. Almost all of them are festooned with monitors that randomly change channels. It's easy to get hooked. You have to be careful. The police are just arriving on the scene. I'm about to transmit but decide not to tell central programming. As always, I look for an emergency exit. A manager is trying to take merchandise away from customers who are capitalizing on the situation to save a few pesos. The manager is so busy that he doesn't even realize when I push him. He falls and a bunch of people quickly run out with the stuff they're stealing. A little old lady of around sixty carries a red dress in her hands and smiles pleasantly when she leaves. I enter the store and hide behind the clothes racks. I get up to the third floor via the emergency stairs, which are empty. I don't know if the terrorists are here inside or if they simply left everything in the hands of a bomb. I avoid several of the private security guards hired to guard the store, not wanting them to see me yet. One of them comes upon a shoplifter, and he and his partner kick the hell out of him. The guy's bleeding and crying. Everyone tries to take advantage of an emergency situation. The two security guards go away, leaving the customer lying there on the floor. Blessed be capitalism.

I move on to the candy department, and the smell makes me dizzy. I've never understood how they keep the flies away from the exposed candied fruit. I hear some voices and hide. I begin to hear a buzzing sound and I gently tap my head. But the sound's not coming from there. The hum is coming from my right. I crawl until I get to a box, which I open cautiously. Inside is a sophisticated device with a clock in countdown mode, rapidly approaching zero. I have a little more than a minute, so I take off running. I forget about transmitting or anything else. When I feel I'm far enough away I turn around and press a button; it's green. I see the two security guards approaching the candy section. I quickly turn my head. I'm about to shout at them to get away when I hear a voice in my ear. "Where the fuck are you? Straighten out the shot, show us something we can broadcast. Are you in the store?" I slowly correct the shot, steadying my head in a slow pan while I notice the red indicator light switch on in my eyes. I manage to spot the two security guards in the candy section. I force myself not to blink, and the bomb explodes. The fire is so hot and the colors so spectacular that for the first time in a long while I forget about the red light that lives in my head. I miscalculated. The force of the explosion lifts me up and I fly several meters through the air. I'm not a body, I'm a machine soaring through the air, whose only purpose is to record and record and record so that the whole world can see what they wouldn't want to live. The clothes burn, the display shelves fall apart, thousands of objects go flying. Some hit me but I try to keep the shot as steady as I can. All in the name of entertainment.

I slam against a wall and try to keep my head up so I can tape the fire.

For the first time I feel at home in a department store. Everything is flames, everything is ashes. The stylish dresses feed the fire, the perfumes make it grow. The spectacle is unparalleled. Civilization destroying itself. I'm in a department store, one of civilization's most glorious achievements. I see a sign that's beginning to burn; it says, "Happy Father's Day." Promises, promises . . .

I get up and my whole body hurts. I walk toward the exit. A voice in my head is shouting, "Where the fuck do you think you're going? I need fixed shots, I need you to talk; tell the world about your experience. Don't be an asshole, you don't tape an explosion every day! Where do you think you're going?"

And it doesn't stop until I'm three blocks from the attack.

Today I crossed a line. I don't know and I don't care if I killed the security guards. It's one thing to report on stuff that happens and another thing to make what happens more spectacular.

What were the security guards? They were graphic elements to liven up my shots. They were mimetic elements that the audience would be able to identify with. They were dramatic elements to make the story I had to tell more interesting. They were scenery.

Today I crossed a line and I don't want to think about anything. My whole body aches.

Situations like these make me think about the urgency of my suicide. At least that way I could decide something, and not just let destiny take the lead. Suicide is the most elaborately constructed act of the human will, it's taking control of your destiny out of the hands of the world.

Yesterday I was organizing a bunch of my tapes. I found a program about my old-time heroes, the experiential reporters. "Crazies," as the foreign media call them. I pressed the play button and sat down to watch them. There are some pretty stupid people in this world, like the reporter who, after getting himself thrown in jail, started to insult the cops so that they'd beat him. He taped everything. The shots are especially successful because half the time he's on the floor trying to make visual contact with the faces of the cops who are pounding on him. Some people consider him a hero. But whenever you see the disfigured faces of the police who are beating him up you can't help thinking how ridiculous the situation is. The reporter is there because he chose to be there. Good job, amigo, boost your company's ratings. I also watched the famous operation on Grayx, one of the martyrs of entertainment. The reporter, trying to make a commentary on the depersonalization of the body, agreed to subject himself to surgery in which they'd remove his head and connect it to his body by way of special high-tech cables. The guy outdid himself, narrating his whole operation, describing what he was feeling while they connected his head to his body with cables that allowed him to be five meters away from his head. It is probably one of the most important moments of this century. When the operation's over you can see a subjective shot of the body on the operating table as Grayx tells it to stand up. The body gets up and begins to stumble, because the head that's sending it instructions sees things from a strange perspective. The body slowly approaches the head, picks it up and turns it around so that the eyes (and the camera) can look in the direction it's walking in, and at that point the viewer no longer knows who's giving the instructions, the body or the head. The body takes the head in its arms like a baby and stands in front of a mirror where you can see a decapitated body holding its head in its arms. The head doesn't seem to be very comfortable because it's a bit tilted; the guy didn't have enough coordination to hold it straight, so all these shots lack horizontal stability. Grayx is talking about the feeling of disorientation, about the possibilities that the surgery opens up, about what would happen if instead of cables they used remote control, about how marvelous the modern world is, while his arms try to hold his head straight and he keeps looking back, his face twisted with the effort of trying to make his body do what he says, all the while failing to control it.

This program always brings me odd memories. I had sex for the first time after watching it with a girlfriend from high school. We were at her house watching the broadcast. No one was around. I don't know how many people might've had sex after the inauguration of the first lunar colony or when they broadcast the assassination of Khadiff, the Muslim terrorist leader, or at any other key moment in the televised history of our century, but I can tell you that it's an unforgettable experience. Watching a man with his body separated from his head on the same day that you become aware of how your body can unite with another and become one is something you don't easily forget. Every time I watch it I have pleasant memories.

Now Grayx is in a mental institution. Seems the technology he was helping to develop causes mental instability. Apparently people need corporal unity in order to remain sane. Grayx lost contact with reality, and they say he now lives in an imaginary world. He had so much money that he built a virtual environment and connected it to his retina, and that's the only thing that keeps him alive.

I haven't felt good ever since the explosion. I have severe pains in the pit of my stomach. Yesterday I told them to deposit the check into my account. Seems I won't be having any trouble over the security guards. To create news with your own body, like the crazies do, is perfectly legal, but make news at the expense of other people's rights and you can wind up spending the rest of your life in jail.

I go to the bathroom and start to pee. I look down and see that the water and my urine are full of blood. I start to hear voices just as a green light goes on in my retina.

"If I were you I'd go straight to a doctor. That red color in your piss don't look healthy at all."

"Leave me alone."

"I can't, you've gone two days without doing a single thing. You already know how it is with contracts. Besides, don't be ungrateful. I was only calling to tell you your check's been deposited. Maybe when you see your pay your mood'll improve. The ratings were really phenomenal."

I've gone down into the sewers of the city a number of times trying to prove one of the oldest urban legends. Thousands of rumors say there are human communities in the deepest parts of the network of underground pipes. A lot of people believe they're freaks, mutants, that their eyelids permanently cover their eyes and their skin is so white they can't tolerate the sun or even the flashlights that everyone who goes down to look for them uses. A new race, grown out of our garbage.

A society that doesn't rely on its eyes, that doesn't have to look at itself for self-recognition. Their behavior must be weird. They'd have to touch each other, they'd have to listen to each other. They wouldn't have to look like anything or anyone. A different world, different creatures.

Every time I descend on one of my exploratory trips I use my infrared glasses and carry very low intensity lights. I've gone down more than ten times and not once have I found anything. No mutants, no freaks, no subterranean race offering something new to humanity, something different from what's shown on TV.

It's just me down there.

Last night my right arm began to convulse. I couldn't do anything to stop it. My fingers opened and closed as if they were trying to grab something, to hold on to something.

Maybe I'd prefer a less sensational exit. Get a tank of gas, seal off a room and fall asleep . . .

IT IS IMPOSSIBLE FOR HUMAN BEINGS TO AVOID BLINKING, BUT IT IS POSSIBLE TO PROLONG THE PERIOD OF TIME BETWEEN ONE BLINK AND THE NEXT. REPORTERS SHOULD DO EXERCISES TO ACHIEVE THIS CONTROL. FURTHERMORE, THE OPERATION ON THEIR EYES IS DESIGNED TO STIMULATE THE TEAR DUCTS SO THAT THE EYES DO NOT DRY OUT SO EASILY, AND THUS REPORTERS CAN KEEP THEIR EYES OPEN LONGER THAN THE ORDINARY INDIVIDUAL.

WHEN MUSCLE MOVEMENT IN THE EYELIDS IS DETECTED, SPECIAL SENSORS IN THE EYE "ENGRAVE" THE LAST IMAGE THAT THE EYE HAS SEEN, AND WHEN THE EYELID THEN CLOSES THIS IMAGE IS THE ONE WHICH IS TRANSMITTED. WHEN THE EYELID RAISES, TAPING CONTINUES. THIS NECESSARY ERROR IN THE WORKINGS OF THE HUMAN BODY HAS CAUSED MICROSECONDS OF MEMORABLE MOMENTS IN THE HISTORY OF LIVE TV TO BE LOST FOREVER.

A more spectacular news story, a riskier stunt. They always want something more. More drama, more emotion, more people sobbing before the cameras, before my eyes. I don't want to think, I'm not made to think, just to transmit. But with every transmission I feel I'm losing something I won't ever recover. The only thing I hear in my head is *more, more, more.*

I could also take everything I feel some attachment for, fill a small bag, find a sewer drain, and head down it, but this time without any lights. I'd wander around for entire days, I'd have to start eating rats and insects and drinking sewer water. Maybe I'd spend the rest of my life wandering among the tunnels that form a labyrinth under this city, but at least I'd be searching for something. Or maybe I'd find a new civilization. Even if they didn't accept me, even if they were to kill me for bringing in outside influences, it'd be comforting to know that there are choices in this world. That there's someone who has possibilities the rest of us lost centuries ago. Or maybe they would accept me, and I could live for years and years without having to worry, doing manual labor and finding a new routine to my life. To be what I think I can be and not what I am.

Maybe, maybe . . .

These are the voices in my head:

"There's a fire, don't you wanna go check it out? Fires and ratings go hand in hand."

"Armed robbery, a black car with no license plates, model unknown, get some shots."

"This is good, a lovers' quarrel, she was making a cake and she destroyed his face with a mixer. The boyfriend, a little miffed, decided he was going to stick *her* in the oven instead of the cake. The neighbors called it in, but it didn't turn into anything big. Good stuff for a comedy."

"You wanna talk? The night's slow and I ain't got nothin' to do, they're broadcasting games from last season."

"Another family suicide. In the subway, a mother with her three kids."

And so on, continually.

The whole world is on TV. Anyone can be a star. Everyone acts, and every day they prepare themselves because today could be the day that a camera finds them and the whole world discovers how nice, good looking, friendly, attractive, desirable, interesting, sensitive, and natural they are. How human they are. And all day long everyone sees tons of people on screen trying to be like that, so people decide to copy them. And they create imitators. And life just consists of trying to seem like somebody who was imitating somebody else. Everyone lives every day as if they were on a TV show. Nothing's real anymore. Everything exists to be seen, and everything that we'll see is a repeat of what we've seen before. We're trapped in a present that doesn't exist. And if the transmitted don't exist, what about those of us who do the transmitting? We're objects, we're disposable. For every reporter who dies on the job or who dies of CEES, there are two or three stupid kids who think that's the only way of finding anything real, of living something exciting. And everything starts all over again.

I always try not to chat with the program directors. Normally they're a bunch of idiots. Their work is easy and they use us like remote-control cameras. Normally I don't even ask 'em their names. There's no point. Who wants to know more people? Ain't nothing new under the sun. Everything's a repeat, everything's a copy.

There's only one program director who knows me a little more intimately. His nickname's Rud, I don't know his real name. I met him (well, I listened to him) when I was drinking, that is, when I was trying to get so drunk I wouldn't have to think, wouldn't have to want anything. I wanted the alcohol to fill me so that I wouldn't have to make decisions, so that whatever decision I made would be the liquor's fault, not mine: "I was drunk."

I sure do miss booze.

Alcohol and my profession are not good friends. In my body I have equipment that belongs to a corporation, so they can sue me if I willingly damage the machinery. Besides, it's not unusual for program directors to tape your drinking sprees and then use them to blackmail you. Some even put them on the air. Once they broadcast two guys who were beating me up 'cause I'd insulted them. I remember thinking that the only good thing about it was that my face wouldn't be shown on the air, they could transmit everything I did but no one would see me, no one could recognize me. Anonymity is a double-edged sword.

Rud calls me the Cynic because he doesn't know my name either. It's easier to talk with someone that way. You avoid problems, as well as commitments. Well, it turns out he'd listened to one of my booze-induced rants. He listened to me patiently all night long, complaining, crying, laughing. I walked over five kilometers. The only thing I did was stop at liquor stores to buy another bottle. I wanted to forget everything, so each time I got a different type of booze. I don't even want to remember all the stupid things I said. Anyone with a little sense of humor would call that night "Ode to Dad" because I spent the whole time talking about him. There was even a stretch when I asked Rud to pretend to be my father and I accused him of stuff, I shouted at him and spit at him. My father was inside my head. At one point I started to beat my head against a wall. I don't have any real memories of that. Turns out Rud recognized the street I was on and called the paramedics to come take me home. They had to put eight stitches in my forehead. Not even modern surgical techniques let me get off without a scar.

Five days later I got a package with no return address, just a card that said, "Greetings, Rud." Inside was the bill from the paramedics. There was also a videocassette. Rud had taped my whole binge.

Sometimes, when I'm in the mood to drink, I play the videotape and cry a bit. That way there's no chance I can deceive myself, everything is recorded, I can't lie. It's no illusion, it's me. Sometimes, but not always, I manage to feel better after watching it.

I'd like to go up to the top of the building where I shot my first transmission. I'd set up two external cameras, one with a long shot, the other medium-range. I'd get close to the edge of the building, turning my back to the street so that the shots would be frontal, and I'd press the button in my thigh. Someone would criticize me for thinking that rooftop terraces were news, until they received the signals from the other cameras and realized what I was about to do.

Suddenly, a red light would illuminate my gaze. I would think about all sorts of things. I would want my father to be able to see this, but it wouldn't matter, a lot of people would see it from the comfort of their homes. It's the same thing. I'm everyone's son.

I would clear my throat to say something live with the broadcast, but I'd remain silent. What more can one say? What could I say that someone before me hasn't already said better?

I would look at the cameras and then up at the sky, where they say that gods who loosed plagues onto humanity once lived. In the sky I would find nothing.

The wind would begin to blow and my hair would get in the way of the camera in my eyes.

I would take one step backward and begin to fall.

And maybe, just maybe, I would forget about that buzzing sound for once.

Mauricio-José Schwarz

MEXICO

Besides being a fiction writer, Mexican-born Mauricio-José Schwarz (1955–) is a journalist, a translator, and an audiovisual media producer. He has published two collections of poems, two journalistic essays, two short story collections, and three detective novels in Spanish, and has also tried his hand at writing in English.[1] Schwarz has also collaborated on a number of anthologies and other collective volumes. His SF works include *Scenes from Virtual Reality* (*Escenas de la realidad virtual,* 1991), *Out Beyond, There Is Nothing* (*Más allá no hay nada,* 1996), and *Off the Record* (*No consta en archivos,* 1999). Furthermore, he co-edited with Don Webb the United States/Mexico SF anthology *Border of Broken Mirrors* (*Frontera de espejos rotos,* 1994).

As the author himself indicates, he has enjoyed trying out a variety of occupations, including street sweeper, TV actor, guitar player, photographer, Web page designer, translator, electrician, and researcher of paranormal phenomena. He has been living in Gijón, Spain, since 1999. His SF work has been internationally recognized since 1984, when he received Mexico's *Puebla* award for best SF short story. In 1990 he won the *Plural,* an international SF prize, and in 1994 he was a finalist in both the Argentinean *Más Allá* and the Mexican *Kalpa* competitions.

In "Glimmerings on Blue Glass" ("Destellos en vidrio azul"), Schwarz draws from his interest in the detective novel by making a fictional private eye, Jackknife Springs, a subversive influence in the life of the nameless protagonist, also a detective. The few glimpses we get of Springs's adventures cleverly delineate a contrast with our SF detective's bleak and exploitative world, one where only submissive, idiotic people have a chance to get work. Schwarz's story speaks to the potential power of popular fiction to undermine repression—in this case, from capitalism.

Glimmerings on Blue Glass

Destellos en vidrio azul, 1996

by Mauricio-José Schwarz

translated by Ted Angell

My boss looked at me with the contempt he has for everyone around him in the investigations office. Rumor has it he's an embittered man. I know it's not just a rumor. It's absolutely true.

"How much longer are you gonna take with that investigation?" he growled. His double chin trembled with each word, drawing my eye and distracting me.

"I only need to interrogate the suspect. Tomorrow I'll have the results," I promised uncomfortably. Across my boss's face flickered the closest thing to satisfaction he could feel. He lowered his eyes to his desk and picked up a few papers, showing me his perfectly shaved head. That was his way of telling me I could go.

Back at my own desk, I pretended to go over the Contero file. After all, once I talked to the guy I could write my conclusions in just a few minutes. And in the Contero folder I was hiding the new adventure of Jackknife Springs, the detective with the blue shades, which I was itching to finish reading.

Jackknife is the secret hero of the office. He's what we all once aspired to be, the original idea behind our work. Yes, we're private detectives, but that has a novel meaning inside these walls. We four men under the boss's orders regard him with bitterness, but this is one of the few jobs we can aspire to, and nobody complains out loud. Our protest is expressed in the adventures of Jackknife Springs. Rumor has it the boss also reads 'em on the sly, but that's just a rumor.

Jack was entangled in a mess of union corruption, a theme that turned out to be close to us. Before immersing myself in my reading, I looked over at the next desk. Beni Ruiz was absorbed in a file. Too absorbed: no doubt he was also living the adventures of Springs, who, while I watched, kept a silent lookout at the entrance to a food factory where the workers' leader had been murdered, a case handed to him by the dead man's coworker and bedmate: a breathtaking woman with dark skin, fervent intelligence, magnificent breasts, and scared-puppy eyes that didn't fool Jackknife. She was a hard woman, physically and emotionally. She wanted Jack to find the murderer, but not to deal with him. That was her business, and the detective with the blue shades well knew she was prepared to take care of the punishment end of things.

The door to the boss's office opened silently. He oils it personally every Monday: hinges, latch, knob. That, plus the rubber-soled shoes he wears, makes him hard to detect.

At least that's what he thinks.

The slightest breeze behind me was sufficient warning. Softly I turned the page and looked at the familiar data on Jacinto Contero. After a short pause, the boss started to walk toward the coffeemaker.

Facing Jacinto Contero, I didn't feel like a colleague of Jackknife Springs. I felt as far from being a detective as one could be without being a criminal. The man before me looked normal, except for the constantly open, slightly twisted mouth. From time to time, just before drooling, he swallowed the saliva accumulated at the corner of his mouth. Twenty-six years old, good manual ability, few problems to communicate. When someone talked to him, he listened with all the concentration of a child. At first glance he didn't have any problems, but the factory always verifies its candidates because of the danger of infiltration. In the beginning they hadn't been worried, but then there'd been an attempted strike by some who obviously were too smart for their own good.

I don't know if all the other factories have the same policy. I've heard they do, that now none of them use normal, dangerous workers. I've heard that in the past they were all like the factory where the latest Springs story took place. That's number sixteen on the list of the hundred big rumors they feed us. On the outside no one knows. Our salary is a guarantee of that. Rumor twenty-two: our salary is among the highest of all the insiders in the country.

"Jacinto Contero," I finally said. The man smiled with satisfaction and nodded his head in a wide arc. "How old are you?"

"Twelve," he said, blissfully articulating each letter.

"Please, put your hands on the table," I asked. He took his fists out of his lap where he kept them hidden, covering his genitals in a defensive pose. His hands were delicate.

"Do you cut your own hair?" He shook his head.

Why do they have us if they have social workers and psychologists? Because we can see further, draw conclusions from a multitude of details meaningless in themselves, but revealing when taken together. And also because we go out onto the street, pound the pavement, stand guard outside the houses of suspects, ask people uncomfortable questions they don't want to answer. We gather data no psychologist or social worker would be able to access in the normal course of their work. We do dirty and efficient work.

"Do you remember Doctor Fuentes?" He nodded, blushing. He liked his doctor, who'd been in charge of his therapy for years; he liked her and couldn't hide it. "Was she nice to you?"

"Yes. Very." The words tumbled lazily out of his mouth.

I looked at Jacinto Contero with intensity. I put in practice all my training, all my powers of observation. I mentally checked various apparently minor details of his appearance and attitude against what I had noted in the file. Everything confirmed that he was only a mentally retarded person with enough rehabilitation to work on an assembly line. That was why so many charitable organizations had been established, thanks to which businesses deducted from their taxes the ever more generous contributions they made, and also obtained ideal workers—who didn't get bored, didn't complain, and accepted their pay with gratitude, without bringing up the question that they might have a right to more, that their horizons could expand with original concepts like justice, equality, and solidarity. Their few necessities were covered and they didn't change, didn't grow, they didn't think about more. They were the ideal investment.

Jacinto looked like living proof of the goodness of the system. And certainly nothing gave him away as a normal guy who was pretending to be an imbecile just to get a halfway decent job.

"That's all. You can go," I said as nicely as I could.

"Where?" He asked without malice.

"Go back outside, the bus is waiting to take you back to the residence," I told him. A few live in their little apartments, but almost all of them stay forever in the group home. Actually, a good part of their salary goes straight to the place's coffers to pay part of their support, food, and other necessities. Whatever money they save, they spend in the residence's shop or on the occasional outings to amusement parks, movies, or stores. They settle for little and enjoy it a lot.

Brief conclusions. The factory has nothing to fear from Jacinto Contero. He's what he appears to be, nothing more. The boss, nearly smiling later while reading my report, assigned me another investigation. Something strange was going on with Marta Revilla, a worker in the textiles division. Someone had seen her with a book that was apparently far above her level. I went to my desk with the file and returned to the world of Jack.

On the photocopied pages, Jackknife Springs was engaged in a bloody fistfight with the hit man who had killed the union leader. When the hit man tore the blue shades off the detective's olive-skinned face, we true initiates knew the fight was almost over, Springs's fury would be unleashed like water from a broken dam. One page later, the murderer was confessing with terror the name of the mastermind of the crime, a young personnel director too zealous in his job at the food plant. Before leaving, Jackknife sprinkled him with gasoline and tossed him a box of matches. I, like all of Springs's regular readers, knew the hit man would choose self-immolation over the risk of ever seeing himself reflected again in Jack's blue shades.

In the office I thought about my brother, this Jacinto whom I'd seldom be able to see again, that lively kid who'd prepared himself from an early age to get a job and not end up on the streets, in the cycle of anguished violence, among the smell of roasted rats, fear in his eyes and the aroma of solvents used as a drug clinging forever to his nose and palate, looking for victims from whom to take wallets full of plastic rectangles, dreaming of guessing the PIN number of a stolen card and solving his life's problems in an ATM machine. We all knew that a job like mine was for one in ten thousand. I'd been lucky. If I hadn't, I'd have had to create myself a disguise like my brother's. Or live on the street.

There's no one better than me to evaluate the deception carried on by Jacinto, who in reality goes by another name. I was inflexible, he knows that. He'll survive in the factory if he's not careless like Marta Revilla appears to have been.

On my desk the detective with the blue shades took it upon himself to act as guide to blind justice.

Lifting my gaze, I could see a pair of blue shades poking out of Beni

Ruiz's coat pocket, the kind of shades that are becoming fashionable among Jackknife's readers. If the boss sees them, Beni will be in trouble. Springs is not very popular at certain levels. That's no rumor.

I've decided to give in to my curiosity. Tonight I'll buy my own blue shades.

Ricard de la Casa and Pedro Jorge Romero

SPAIN

Ricard de la Casa (1954–) was born in Barcelona. He earned his teaching degree in 1977 and taught primary school in Lérida, though he has supported himself chiefly by working in various family businesses. His deep interest in SF culminated in his cofounding the popular fanzine *BEM* in 1990. This event marked the beginning of the fruitful collaboration he has enjoyed for over a decade with fellow editor and writer Pedro Jorge Romero.

De la Casa's first short novel, *Beyond QWR Equation* (*Més enllà de l' equació QWR*), written in Catalan, was published in 1989 and translated into English in 1992. His second short novel, *Under Pressure* (*Sota pressió*), also in Catalan, was published in 1996. He is a past president of the Spanish Association of Fantasy and Science Fiction (AEFCF).

Pedro Jorge Romero (1967–) was born in Arrecife, Lanzarote, and holds a degree in physics. In 1989 he edited a nonfiction magazine dedicated to SF studies. Romero is very active in Spanish SF fandom and has published articles, commentary, criticism, and short stories in magazines such as *Pórtico, BEM, Kenbeo Kenmaro, Elfstone, Blade Runner Magazine, Parsifal,* and *Cuásar,* as well as in journals like *Diario de Avisos* and *La Gaceta*. He has also translated for the SF press Ediciones B. He is codirector of the SF collection *The Sword and the Clock* (*La espada y el reloj*), lectures on science fiction criticism, and is currently working on essays about Spanish SF and the works of Juan Miguel Aguilera and Javier Redal. He has a passion for both literature and computers, especially Windows programming.

The story we include here integrates "hard" SF concepts like wormholes and quantum theory with time-travel speculation. Written in 1997, it focuses on the historic post-Franco transition to democracy (1975–1981),[1] presenting it as a period to be cherished and protected by the collective memory of all Spaniards. It is no coincidence that the dangerous consequences time travel might have on history or our perception of it come in the form of terrorism, one of the major political and social problems of contemporary Spain.

The Day We Went through the Transition

El día que hicimos la Transición, 1998

by Ricard de la Casa

and Pedro Jorge Romero

translated by Yolanda Molina-Gavilán

"It's your turn to go through the Transition today," said the voice of the duty lieutenant in my ear.

I opened my eyes at once. The whole room was dark. A temporal alarm had gone off, so the entire building would be completely sealed off: nobody could go in or out. Ten seconds later the lights went on. Our bodies' nanosystems started to become active and control hundreds of biological processes. I could see more clearly now.

The Transition is a classic. Someone has to go through it at least once a week, and sometimes even two or three times on the same day. Why are all terrorists, from both sides, fixated on that time period? Why don't they intervene more often in the Civil War, or in that Invincible Armada affair? I suppose that the Transition is just so full of possibilities, there are so many simultaneously open paths, that every political camp or economic group believes itself capable of adjusting the process so that its particular position triumphs.

It seems to be a particularly Spanish fixation as well. Other countries also suffer from attacks by terrorists who attempt to change history to their liking, but those cases happen once or twice a year. We, however, have to manage up to thirty cases a week, and more than half of them may be placed at the Transition period. It seems that we Spaniards are so unsatisfied with our own history and are so incapable of accepting that others have triumphed in the past, that we make great efforts to change it. It doesn't matter, in any case: the work of the GEI Temporal Intervention Corps is to stop these situations from happening, and we pay particular attention to the Transition.

To tell the truth, we've become experts at it. Learning from the terrorists has provided us with an excellent understanding of that period. We have delved into all its twists and turns so much that we're able to venture into those years without any specific study or preparation.

Rudy is a specialist in temporal flux—I would say a very good one. He's capable of discerning what action will yield the best result. Marisa and I are experts in comparative Spanish history. Not only our own, but also the post-2012 main underlying branches. Isabel is an expert in both subjects at once; she is very good at connecting them.

We got up from our hard old beds immediately. I was the first one, Isabel was next, then Marisa, and finally Rudy. Isabel and Marisa were very experienced, but it was the first time that Rudy would go through the Transition since his recent recruitment. As for me, I've gone through the Transition ten times in a row: my best record.

Those of us who are on duty normally sleep with our clothes on to be ready in case we need to carry out an operation. We were soon ready; Isabel came close and stared at me. It was a confirmation of our agreement; we have been lovers on most occasions, only friends on others, but we've always been together and have supported each other. Our last relationship had been a bit unbalanced; she was not very sure of herself, but it seems that I kept trying.

"Let's go," she said to me, looking away.

"Yes," was my laconic answer. I always get up in a bad mood and don't feel like talking.

Rudy and Marisa had already left with that weird speed that characterizes them; I still haven't managed to get used to their hyperactivity. They have a strange relationship, those two; one minute they ignore each other and the next they're inseparable. Each quarantine period changes everything. Though in reality, every TIC agent has to live with that; couples like Isabel and me are rather the exception.

We ran through the hallways toward the documentation chamber. In the holographic movies, at whatever temporal line, the policeman or secret agent throws himself immediately into action, beating people up right and left, and everything is fixed. Reality is not like that at all. Unfortunately, while there is an action component to our work, first there is a need to establish precisely which change in time has occurred and evaluate the best way of correcting it. We intervene only afterward, trying to execute an operation in the cleanest and quickest way possible. And even then we still have to write the report. And God save you from having to report on a disappearance, because in that case the paperwork becomes endless and another operation is needed.

We arrived at the tubes. Marisa pressed the button that would take us to the basement. The documentation chamber is located on one of the lowest levels of the TIC General Headquarters. It's a large place, almost completely filled by six computer terminals, and underneath there's only the armored dome that contains the portal, the most watched and secure place in the TIC.

The tubular door opens directly onto the documentation chamber. During an emergency only the guards on duty—us in this case—may access the room. The tubes' electronic system reads the state of our implants to determine if we have permission to be there. In the event that one of us wasn't authorized, the tube wouldn't even move.

The support group was already there evaluating the changes. José Luis, Sara, Didac, and Sandra. They would be our substitutes if anything were to go wrong during the operation.

"I swear I'm getting fed up with so much Transition," yawned Sara as she saw us arrive.

Isabel sat down in front of one of the consoles. Marisa occupied the one that was free. The rest of us stood behind. From her seat, Isabel observed the changing images of the laborious search for the rupture point that the computers were trying to locate by historical comparison. The system is relatively simple; one just needs to begin searching back starting from 7 August 2012. At first, events differ quite a bit from history as we know it, but little by little the changes start merging toward zero and history more closely resembles the real one. Besides, in this case, we also had the advantage of knowing, through some preliminary automatic analyses, that the change had happened at the Transition. Each console is connected simultaneously to our own databases, to history as it happened, and to the external database, which allows us to compare the records.

The entire TIC General Headquarters, which in turn depends on the Spanish Intelligence Group, is enclosed in an ecstasis field. This means that we notice the changes in history only by comparing our records to those on the outside; for those of us who are inside the chamber, the change that had altered life in the outside world had not taken place and we remembered history just as it had happened. The existence of the ecstasis field means that we are virtually trapped in the building. We can leave, yes, but we cannot lead an independent life. If we were to live outside without protection, history's tidal wave would end up engulfing us. We would end up living a particular version of the universe and we would lose our effectiveness as agents. No, we may spy on the world, on outside reality, but we can't really enjoy it.

The theory that allows for time travel is probably the strangest of the whole history of physics; it's difficult to understand and it's based on an incredible number of equations. It is the basis for a great unification theory that some day will explain everything but that, for now, allows us to travel through time using reasonable quantities of energy. It is simply called Temporal Theory, or TT. Unfortunately, some of the effects caused by the theory are almost metaphysical. When it was formulated, when that young physicist finally comprehended it and conceived it pure and whole for the first time, the theory changed the nature of the universe and of reality itself. Before 7 August 2012 only one temporal line existed. There was only one history, shared by all. That August afternoon, exactly at the moment the theory was definitively formulated, time became multiple; temporal lines started to diverge as quanta phenomena were happening in the universe. There are now infinite histories, most of them almost identical, globally indistinguishable with only trivial details to differentiate them; yet others are very different. Exact copies of each human being on Earth live in many—in billions of them.

Philosophers and physicists have spent years trying to explain this, and they haven't gotten very far. It is clear, though, that the first quantum physicists were right: the observer has an effect on the observed, and the existence of intelligent beings in the cosmos alters the workings of the universe. How else to explain this situation? Five minutes before one August day there was only one history, and five minutes afterward there were millions. Furthermore, those temporal lines are real and may be visited easily. The same technology that allows time travel allows taking a trip among alternative temporal lines.

In 1955, Hugh Everett formulated what was called the "many worlds interpretation" of quantum mechanics.[1] According to him, each time a phenomenon of quantum scale occurred, the universe divided itself into as many versions as were necessary to account for all possible results. In the simplest case, there were two possibilities: on one branch the process had happened, and on the other it hadn't. But now one could say that Everett was both right and wrong at the same time. Before the summer of 2012, the universe, in the simplest, two-option case, accepted one of those phenomena and discarded the other one. But after that summer, the universe executes all the possibilities and Everett is proven correct. Since 7 August 2012, the universe divides itself into as many universes as are necessary to cover all possibilities.

The ecstasis field surrounding the Temporal Intervention Center, which is based on a weird property of what physicists call imaginary time, allows those of us inside to experience only one past. If someone changes history, we continue to remember history just as it was, which lets us perceive when it has been manipulated. Unfortunately, the ecstasis field was a late byproduct of the theory, and by the time it was developed it was already too late—although I'm not sure what could have been done differently: surround the entire universe with an ecstasis field?

One thing we can be certain about is that this theory proves we are alone in the universe. At least that there is no extraterrestrial civilization at our stage of development. If there were a more advanced civilization, their physicists would have discovered Temporal Theory before and we would now see that the temporal divergences in the universe began at an earlier date than our own discovery of the theory. Since that isn't the case, the conclusion is that we are alone, or at least, that we are the most advanced in the entire universe. It's not as surprising as it seems: someone had to be the first.

"I've got it," José Luis said out loud to get our attention.

We all crowded around his console. The computers had located the change point. On his screen was the 28 February 1977 front page of *El País*. In the version we had on our database—the version of history as it had really happened—the headlines were the usual ones for the time period. The version we had from the outside had only one headline that covered the whole first page: *Carrillo Murdered.*[2] The newspaper from the day before was identical to our version, but the one for the following day had that ominous news eclipsing all the rest.

"This is new, isn't it?" said Rudy.

Nobody acknowledged him; he really wasn't looking for an answer.

"Poor man, that was all he needed. They've done just about everything else to him." Rudy continued.

During our training they teach us many of the tricks used to change the past. Almost all of them follow the same plan, killing some well-known person. Almost invariably they're the same people: Hitler, Stalin, Kennedy. But Rudy was right: they hadn't tried to kill Carrillo during that interview, which was odd, considering the many times the Communist leader was manipulated in one sense or another.

"We'd better look some more. Return to your consoles and continue searching. This is too obvious," I said.

Each one of us tried to find data that would link Carrillo with that date. With the information from the newspaper article, and from later ones that dealt with the news, we soon had a more or less clear idea of what had transpired. But we did not find any other point of change that wasn't caused by the assassination of the Spanish Communist Party's leader.

I started to compare data. President Suárez had arranged a secret interview with Carrillo for 27 February.[3] At that time, the Communist Party hadn't been legalized yet—that was still a couple of months away—and, for the Spain of the times, to have an interview with the CP's secretary-general was to have a date with the devil himself. It seems incredible now, but back then the Communist Party had great moral weight in Spanish society, and counting on the Communists was essential for the consolidation of democracy, but acting with too much haste could bring about serious consequences. Suárez understood this, but he also knew that if he could legalize the Communist Party and celebrate free elections with the whole political spectrum, he would gain strength and prestige. For that reason he arranged that ultrasecret interview; only the king and a couple of government members were in the know. The meeting itself wasn't very important, but if it had been discovered, the still-strong Francoist structures would have forced the fall of Suárez and delayed or stopped the advent of democracy.

"That's odd . . . It's been more than three years since Carrillo wasn't murdered," said Isabel in her characteristically soft voice.

At five in the afternoon they picked Carrillo up from his apartment in the Puente de Vallecas.[4] He was driven down a hidden road. A person—a woman—took him to the Santa Ana cottage in the outskirts of Madrid, a quiet place. In real history, Suárez arrived a few minutes later and they both talked for hours about Politics with a capital "P." What the terrorists had done was very elementary. They had simply blown up Carrillo's car just before it got to the house. They were thus assured of two things: that the Bunker[5] would know of this interview and that the Communist Party would be enraged about their leader's death. Weren't government members the only ones that knew of this supersecret interview? Suspicion fell immediately on the executive branch of the government, particularly on Suárez himself, who was innocent.

From that moment on there was a flood of events. I searched for the latest Carrillo assassinations. There were only two: in both instances he had been gunned down, once as he was strolling in the middle of the street only hours before the Communist Party became legal, and the other time when he made his first public appearance. The consequences of the two assassinations were, in both cases, much less serious than this one.

This time, the authorities asked for calm in vain. The Bunker demanded immediate explanations and Suárez's instant removal from office, which the king was forced to agree to only a few days later. Meanwhile, the Communist Party took to the streets. The previous month, faced with the Atocha Street lawyers' murders, the Spanish Communist Party had shown some savoir faire by leading silent protests, but back then they had Carrillo as their guide and trusted the democratization process, if only minimally. Now Carrillo was no more and nobody trusted the government.

From the short list they presented to the king, the Francoists forced the election of a harsh president who ordered a charge on the protesters. Civilians were confronting the police all around the country. Gradually, other democratic forces began to join the demonstrations. The democratization process had been definitely lost, but the worst was yet to come.

A week later there is a coup d'état. The king loses all his effective powers and a state of emergency is declared throughout the country. Nobody respects it. The clashes continue, and it soon becomes clear that Spain is immersed in another civil war: what no one wanted, what everyone would have liked to avoid. Cataluña and the Basque Country take advantage of the confusion to declare themselves independent, Morocco occupies the Canary Islands, invoking its sovereignty, but at least the Canary Islanders escape the worst of the war. Barcelona is besieged and completely razed. Nobody knows how many sides are involved in the fighting. In the capitals, snipers shoot at anything that moves, and a stunned international community witnesses a civil war in Europe. Spain in 1997 was what Yugoslavia was in the 1990s: a land of mass murders, exterminations, rapes, war crimes . . .

All types of weapons are used, biological, chemical . . . millions of people die, even more when a nuclear explosion destroys Madrid. Nobody knows who has detonated the device or where it has come from, everyone points fingers at each other. That proves to be too much. United Nations forces occupy Spain and impose a precarious peace. After five years of fighting, the country is ruined, destroyed, devastated, having lost almost one-third of its population, with refugees and survivors who hardly have anything to eat. There is no parliament anymore, there is no monarchy—the royal family died with Madrid—there is nothing worth fighting for. The wounds will take time to heal. Reconstruction will take years, and no one knows how long it will last. Its echoes still resound in 2032.

I must admit that as a terrorist plan it was a very good one, better than most. I've seen them in all colors. Sometimes they prolong Franco's life and that delays the whole democratic process. In some versions, democracy arrives with Franco still alive and in command of the army. On other occasions, they avoid the death of Carrero Blanco,[6] who becomes president of the king's first government and manages to stop the opening-up process. Others also plot to assassinate the king and create a republic. And at times they conspire for Juan Carlos not to succeed Franco; his place is then filled by another candidate to the throne, one who continues the dictator's work. But as far as number of effects per minimal cause is concerned, nothing matched this case. Who could imagine that the murder of one man in circumstances that later would be recorded as only a historical footnote could have such huge consequences?

Causing a change in history after 2012 would not have the slightest consequence; such a thing would simply make a new version of history that would coexist with those already in existence and with those constantly produced by quantum mechanics. But TT prohibits the simultaneous existence of more than one history before 7 August 2012. Thus, the preexisting history gets replaced by the one resulting from the change. Many times I've asked myself why we insist on correcting history; after all, who cares? The only answer I have been able to find is that history just as it was, good or bad, happy or unfortunate, is ours and nobody has the right to manipulate it according to who-knows-what murky interests.

All that aside, once the junction point has been located, we must fix it. This is the most delicate moment. Normally the true instigators don't expose themselves directly; they hire the necessary personnel to carry out the action and they, in turn, subcontract other menials wherever they want to intervene. So in general all we find are some poor devils who barely know anything. On the other hand, we have the names of those highly specialized in temporal jumps, who need to be apprehended. We try to scare the former to death so that they don't become repeat offenders, but we can't do much more. The latter are very difficult to surprise. They, like us, have all the time in the world at their disposal, and we do not have the necessary equipment to invest in costly and lengthy field research. Therefore, when we run into them, more out of luck than anything else, we aren't usually very considerate.

We took the tube and went to the Transition chamber. That period is visited so often it occupies a whole wing of the main basement. Wardrobe and props are stored there; likewise our weapons, disguised as everyday objects in that time period. We use those clothes so much we need to replace them quite often.

We changed for the time period and the season. We left and got in the tube again. We passed new security controls, even stricter ones, and arrived at the underground dome where the portal is kept.

When one visits it as often as we do, it ends up losing all its charm; it becomes one more piece of the armored dome's surrealist decoration.

The structure is a type of cube. It's really taller than it is wide and it isn't solid—it consists only of the lines that form the structure. It's called the Visser Portal and is made of negative mass.[7] When you get close you start to feel a strange repulsion, because instead of attracting matter, negative mass repels it. Therefore, it's impossible to touch it, but that isn't necessary. The structure is about five meters wide and we all fit in perfectly.

The portal is completely inactive as is. To make the trip one has to find an adequate quantum wormhole, one that connects our time period in a natural way with the temporal point we want to travel to. It seems that, at a sufficiently small scale, the space-time is not a plane but a foam where anomalous structures are constantly being formed. Some of these structures are tunnels that connect two separate regions—for example, a point from 2032 with another one in 1977. Those structures are formed and destroyed so many times that we don't have to wait very long to find the right one. When we do, the technicians feed it with energy in order to make it grow to macroscopic size, big enough so that we can cross it. But it isn't safe yet, the negative mass structures need to be attached to the Visser Portal so they become stable. First the one next to us is connected, then a similar one, a little smaller, is sent through the tunnel so that the other end is also stabilized. At that moment, if the wormhole's chosen longitude is small enough, one can go across almost instantaneously. You simply see the image from the other side, take one step and there you are.

Before 2012 they knew that such a thing was possible, but they believed the necessary energies were so great that no government on Earth, not even all of them together, would have been able to provide the energy required to open a portal. Besides, the portals must be huge, about five kilometers in diameter, in order to guarantee a successful crossing and, in that case, we were talking about several times the mass of the sun. TT changed all that. All of a sudden, minimal quantities of energy could be used to expand a tunnel between two regions of the space-time continuum or between two different space-times.

The technicians were now prepared for the jump. Located in a control room above was our support team, in case we needed additional information or in the event there were any last-minute changes in the continuum.

"Everyone ready?" Isabel asked. As the veteran of the group, it fell to her to be the leader.

Everybody checked the equipment they carried. We'd put on those clothes so many times, we no longer noticed how strange we looked. With a bit of luck we wouldn't have to go undetected for long; if everything went as planned, it would be a simple in-and-out job. Everyone seemed to have the equipment in order. Rudy was the last one to finish. He was looking at his wrist as if one of the readings didn't quite convince him. Finally he lowered it and said yes.

"All set," he said.

Good, that was it. Now or never, as always. Marisa, the daring one, was the first one to approach the portal. She stood right at the edge. She must have been feeling all the tension. The structure's negative mass combines with the positive mass of the tunnel, and that's why the sum could have either a negative, a positive, or a null net mass. The technicians always hope to get a null mass, but they're satisfied if the combined mass isn't too big in absolute terms. That way, in theory, you shouldn't feel anything when you approach, but in reality, the negative mass is closer to your body than the tunnel is, and it's normal to feel a slight pressure that pushes you forward.

Marisa disappeared and was followed by Rudy. I stopped myself at the threshold. I have never liked going through the portal. Our tunnels are normally less than twenty centimeters long, so that it's just a matter of taking one step to cross it. However, they're long enough so that you feel the peculiar effects caused by their geometry. If you look briefly toward the tunnel's wall, you will see your own image there, being repeated ad infinitum. Of course, at the other end you see the outside landscape, but that's exactly what makes it more disconcerting.

I turned to Isabel and kissed her on the lips.

"Good luck," I said.

"Good luck," she said back. She glanced at me for a moment but then looked away and approached the tunnel as well.

Each time I cross the portal old memories of how I was recruited for the TIC come to mind.

I remember mixed emotions, nostalgia and innocence, just like when someone watches a stale disk of images and movies. Everything has that blurry patina that makes defects disappear and makes you believe those times were better than they really were.

Once a week after class I used to join my friends at the La Granja Park to chat, work out, and, eventually, spend the night partying. That spring day they had canceled my historical perspective class and I arrived earlier than usual, something that of course was part of the plan.

Wearing my shorts and a pair of red shoes Isabel would later tell me were horrible, I laid down on the grass to kill time. Some things never change, and it seems my bad taste in clothes is quite known.

She approached me. It was Isabel, of course, but I didn't know that yet. She sat down next to me, close enough so as to make sure her presence was noticed, but not so close that I thought she was after me. She was wearing the light blue dress I liked so much, the one I had given her as a present. Her hair was down and she wore almost no make-up, very natural. Everything carefully thought out, everything researched. Is there anything we haven't analyzed? She had a copy of History Reviews, a journal I was in the habit of reading. I stared at her while she did her best to keep her eyes glued to the page. Suddenly, she lifted her face, saw me, smiled, and buried her face in the journal again.

I got up and approached her.

"Have you read Martinson's article on Carthage?" I asked her. "The one that says it didn't really exist, that the Romans built it so they could later say they had destroyed it?"

She kept silent and still while looking at me for seconds that seemed an eternity. Her expressive eyes suggested more than I needed to know and more than she wanted to display. Something about her, something indefinable, seduced me right then; it was as if a shiver ran up and down my body. I suppose at that moment she was already playing with me.

"Well, excuse me for approaching you like this," I continued. "I saw the journal you're reading and it just so happens to be my specialty. My name's Mikel, and I teach at Logroño's UniCentral."

I shifted my body trying not to look too ridiculous. I decided to sit down next to her.

"Hi," she said, a little doubtful. "I'm Isabel. I've read the article . . ." She paused while her lips outlined a hint of a smile. "To tell you the truth, I think it's totally moronic."

I was completely taken aback. I was expecting many replies, but not that one. She sat there, looking at me, calm, serene, waiting. It was obviously a provocation, and it took me a while to realize it.

"Don't listen to me," she said with an open smile. "I had a bad day yesterday, that's all. Now I'm trying to put the pieces back together."

I had lost the initiative. The feeling that overcomes you at times like these is one of impotence, of being left out of the game. The problem is I still didn't know that from the moment she had appeared we were playing with marked cards.

"Although . . . we could discuss the subject," she added without giving me time to even think of an answer. "I warn you that I'm not easy to convince."

Her voice sounded much better this time. Later I knew why: it had been a shock for her to see me, to hear me again.

"Me either," I said regaining my control somewhat.

We got up and started walking. I didn't know that from that day on I'd never see my friends again.

Of course we didn't talk about Martinson, or Carthage, or anything like that, nor did we need to. We chatted about trivialities, work, and dreams. Isabel let her true mission be lost in a limbo of gestures and anecdotes. We wandered aimlessly from here to there, we had dinner at some strange but quiet place, we ended up in my apartment.

It was at five in the morning, after having made love for the second time, that she told me. She gave me the same old speech. Why pretend? I would find out sooner or later. One needs to have a great capacity to absorb what they tell you and I admit I didn't understand it too well. What was all that about time travel, changes in history and parallel universes? She told me as well that she had been in love with me for years although, according to my own temporal experience, we'd only met that morning. I fell back asleep from shock and the peace that comes from not understanding.

I woke up first, got up, and walked toward the window; I needed to think. Outside, one of those blue days that predicts the arrival of the heat blinded me with its light.

She stirred in bed, looking for me.

"What are you thinking about?" she asked with eyes closed. She knew I was there. She knew what I was thinking, what my doubts were.

I had been meditating. The terrible reality of what she had told me had been settling in my mind, and a question was steadily buzzing about my brain.

"Do I have any option that isn't joining the TIC?" I asked her, in a somewhat sad voice.

"Of course," she answered me. "You may stay here."

"Is that what you want?"

Isabel didn't lie to me. She knew I needed her to be sincere, or at least to appear to be.

"No."

"What's our future like?"

Her answer was a nail in the coffin of my hopes. Her tone, however, gave her away.

"We don't have any future," she said.

I didn't get all the implications of her answer. Even now I discover new sides to her short but intense response.

We had lunch together that day, we went for a walk, chatted, tried to be as honest as possible. I was sincere; she only needed to be persuasive. The portal appeared in the afternoon and I crossed it for the first time to go to the TIC. We arrived seconds after Isabel left to look for me. I went through the formalities of recruitment. It was confusing to realize everybody knew me and was happy to see me again. It was as if I had always been there, and in a sense that was true. My old colleagues greeted me and took me to the accelerated instruction booths. That was the day my life started again.

We were near the place and it was still early. Everything seemed calm; it was sunny and warm for February. What we were really hoping for was to see the unsuspecting bombers appear. Usually that's the best way to go: the meeting was so secret that there were no security devices. Who would trust a police force inherited from the Francoist system?

Each one of us had a preassigned mission, so we all knew what we had to do. We headed toward the action point.

"I think they're coming," announced Marisa, who was watching the road.

"Rudy, be on the outlook for any Extras," said Isabel, and added: "Marisa, cut them off from behind. Mikel, you're with me. We'll use stunners as defense. That will be enough."

We're always afraid some Extra may show up, some stranger from the future, that is. Someone who'd come to ruin the plan. It's a bit dumb, but it works sometimes. So the best thing to do is not to lower one's guard.

We've studied terrorist bomb attacks so well that we can almost fix them with our eyes closed. It's a matter of blocking their way naturally, while we prepare our stunners. Normally we don't want to kill anybody, only stop the attempt. If any Extra appeared, of course, we wouldn't hesitate to kill him.

The van was approaching. They were calm. The place they had chosen for the bombing was still a few kilometers away. There were three of them, young, probably recruited in some Madrid neighborhood like Tresaguas or Horcasitas. I almost pitied them.

When they had almost reached us Isabel sent us the signal to begin. The moves were balletlike. Somehow I seemed to be flying above the place, supervising the operation. I saw myself moving, Isabel stopping them and me stunning the first one, Isabel the second one, me the third, seizing the bomb. Marisa was behind us observing, on guard. Rudy was a bit further out, checking out everything around us. He has something special that makes him sensitive, a sixth sense that allows him to anticipate danger.

I looked at the device; it was a common bomb, powerful enough to reach its target. Incredibly crude. I looked it over twice. Simple, I corrected myself, like the operation, and that was something I didn't like. I looked to Rudy for a sign, but he was still calm, so I tried to relax.

Only a few seconds had gone by and everything was over.

The simplest thing was left to do, but it was the trickiest: all those people need to be moved away from there, the road needs to be cleared for Carrillo, the bomb must disappear and those men need to forget the affair. Nobody must find out.

We can hang around to make sure there isn't a back-up team or another bomb, but that's just wasting time. Carrillo will never know he owes us his life, nor do we care. It's simpler to return and make sure everything is back in its original place.

We get in the van and begin the return trip to Madrid. We abandon it in Vallecas, a good place for it to disappear without a trace. We inject the three of them with a solution that will make them forget even their names. They will have to go back to school. We take the bomb, their weapons, and all their documents back to our own time period. Nobody will know who they are or what happened to them.

We stop somewhere with little traffic. We make them get out and give them a little push so they start to walk. They are three zombies by then. We start the car, they get lost in the crowd. Soon they'll be noticed.

We leave the van in an open field and look around for a discreet place to await the portal. It'll be a few minutes until they find an adequate quantum tunnel. I start to relax.

The bad thing about traveling through time is that you get completely disconnected from your own time. There's no way to communicate with it; you're left to your own devices and can only count on your own team for help.

When I saw the familiar sight of the dome I sighed in relief.

"Complete success," Isabel informed us.

Didac was gesturing at us from above.

"Tune to channel four, I think Didac wants to give us some bad news," I remarked.

"Hello everyone, I'm happy to see you," said Didac, waving a greeting. "I believe the worst is over, but there are still serious deviations in the course of events."

Marisa swore.

"Meeting in the documentation room in five minutes," said Isabel, stoically accepting that the operation had been a failure.

"What's our current situation?" asked Isabel as soon as she came in.

José Luis motioned toward the terminals without a word.

The problem was still simple. The meeting had been broadcast by radio when it was being held, and Suárez had been exposed. His position had been weakened and his enemies had taken advantage of the situation to the fullest. There was no war, everything seemed to be going well, but Suárez had been forced to negotiate with the Francoists and the

Transition had been delayed. The temporal line showed clearly now how a few special groups had benefited. I thought I understood.

"An interesting simulation exercise," I said raising my voice so that everyone could hear me. "They create a deviation we must resolve; I suspect our arrival is the cause they were waiting for so they could trigger a new effect, precisely the one they really wanted. The first one was nothing but bait. Effective."

The ability to intervene in time is not unlimited. You cannot continue to put patches over other patches forever. Someday everything may explode in our faces if we keep on fixing history. We're already beginning to have problems with forgetful people.

Isabel and the rest of the group looked at me. They had all understood the trap that had been set for us. We were the fuse for the true historical manipulation.

"Don't be so Machiavellian," Rudy remarked. "They knew we were going to intervene, so they planned everything out. We've only corrected an anomalous situation for them, one that makes room for a beneficial one. They're sophisticated, but I've seen worse."

"We have to go back," said Marisa.

We all looked at each other. Nobody likes to go back to the same place we're already at; it's just nerves. It's been proven we can coexist with ourselves in the same place and time, even though I don't know anyone who likes doing it. We couldn't ask the back-up team to go, either; it was our mission and we had to fix it ourselves.

Isabel transmitted the new data to Operations Control and requested another delivery. Meanwhile, the rest of us focused on looking for a new inflection point.

We located it: a radio station had been tipped off about something that was going to occur at that location. They had sent a camouflaged car and none of us had taken notice. That's the problem with the huge quantity of variations, ours or theirs, that can get caught up in a mission. Intelligent and simple. They never get tired, but they don't realize we don't get tired either.

We got ready again. We hadn't changed clothes, so this time everything went faster. We entered the tube and there we were again. It was still that ominous afternoon. We were one kilometer further down, at a point midway between our first action and the country house where the conversations were to be held.

The first warning came, as was normal in these cases, from Rudy.

"Danger!"

We were all more calm and relaxed, since there was no reason for this to be dangerous or complicated. Except that this time nothing went well. They were waiting for us. They knew we would go and, unfortunately for us, they had even guessed where we would enter that continuum. That's our worst moment, since we're always dazed for a few minutes.

They were shooting at us but we didn't see anybody. They were Extras, of course; the weapons they were using left no doubt. Rudy had detected them, but not fast enough. We all tried to cover ourselves and spread out. What mattered was to locate the source of the shots. Marisa set up a scanner as soon as she found the source, and we all started to return fire.

There were two of them, and they were placed at an angle so as to catch us in crossfire. Rudy was already positioning himself to catch them from behind while Marisa moved in on his left. I was shooting like a madman to cover them while Isabel, the most daring, was advancing straight toward them, covering herself as best she could. With luck there wouldn't be any traces of the raid left. We were all shooting with plasma pistols—they don't make any sound and affect only the ecstasis field that surrounds us; that's enough.

I didn't have time to think. I heard a scream and a red light lit up on my console. I didn't want to find out whose it was. We had just suffered a casualty. The three of us who were left coldly bore down on them; we were already in position and didn't give them any kind of a chance. They knew they would never have one. It was as if a light went off, only you don't stay in the dark.

We became tense, serious. Suddenly everything was quiet; it was time to worry about the rest of the world and about ourselves. I didn't need to look at the console to know which one of us was gone. What a euphemism! I felt a sharp pain and I let it show.

"It's Isabel," Marisa's voice pierced my ears.

I approached her body. Her head was smashed. I held her right wrist and read what her control panel said. It indicated a massive brain failure. Our nanosystems can repair many wounds, but not even all the technology of the twenty-first century could reconstruct a shattered brain.

"We've got a job to do," Rudy declared. He's usually the most practical and coldest among us.

We divided up the work. This time we were more conscientious. We checked that nobody had witnessed the little battle, then prepared the bodies to take them back to the future with us.

When we finished, we simply waited for the transmitter people to arrive. Rudy and Marisa kept watch just in case any other Extra showed up trying to spoil the plan.

Isabel's memory hit me at regular intervals, as if it had installed itself in my heart. Each beat gave me life, each beat killed me.

The transmitter people arrived, very discreetly, in a car without any identification and parked two hundred meters from the house. I didn't even give them time to get out of the car. I went straight to them. I blurted out what we had prepared: I pretended I was lazy and sold them the information they wanted to hear. I sent them to Arganda. The information was good, I told them. Some of their colleagues had already come and gone when they got the new tip; at the last minute, the meeting of several Francoist factions had moved to the old Institute in Arganda del Rey, on the road toward Valencia. They still had time to get there, since it had been delayed for two hours because of the move. If they hurried, they would still arrive in time.

It was best to muddle up places, times, and characters. Besides, Arganda had been a communist domain during the first decade of the Transition. It was perfect for the Francoists. The car started up again and made its way down the road. We didn't see them again.

We were checking everything around us. The hours seemed like flagstones slowly falling down on us. Right on time, Carrillo passed by us and went inside the house. That time there was no strange movement. The leader of the Communist Party didn't even see us as he went by. We had saved his life, but he would never know that.

We checked around for the last time and waited for the portal to go back to our time. When we returned it was a relief to verify that history was back to being the original one, at least for now. Somebody, somewhere, would be plotting some new way to change it. The technicians took the bodies away.

As the second most senior member, I tackled the difficult duty of filling out the paperwork. Rudy and Marisa offered to help, but I preferred to do it alone. The bureaucrats, those who are safe in their offices, want to know everything about everybody. They don't leave anything to chance.

When I was finished, the orders for the second operation flashed on the console screen before me.

Isabel lied to me. I don't bear her any grudge. We know everything about ourselves; there are too many possibilities about the future. The truth is there are so many futures that knowing anything about them simply stops being interesting. That's why she didn't tell me the truth, and I'm grateful to her for that; it's a bit overwhelming to begin to glimpse all of the implications of belonging to the GEI.

Before crossing the portal I have consulted every available file about Isabel. So now I know everything about her. Not firsthand. It was the first time she was recruited in this life, so I have lots of information about her previous enlistments, but they are cold reports, without soul, without conscience, without respect for her. That's why I've decided to be my own memory. I think I must have considered doing it more than once, writing to leave myself the story of my experiences with Isabel, the only thing that really matters to me. It's clear I'll always be here, so I'd better have some good notes about my own emotions and feelings. Maybe someday I'll get tired and erase them, but that will be the decision of another Mikel, not me. Perhaps I'll get Isabel to collaborate. All the Mikels that follow me will always have the opportunity to access what I'm writing.

I am walking around the halls of the university where Isabel studies. I am going to find her. Before getting here I've had to evaluate what my feelings toward Isabel are at this moment. I try to be as impartial as possible so that they don't interfere with the operation, which absolutely must be successful. It's odd how Isabel has categorically refused to be recruited some times; it happened to me once and I believe I know why, even though I haven't told anyone. I've discovered that the first hours are crucial to her subsequent behavior toward me, so the first thing I had to do was establish exactly what it was I wanted, this time, from her. We are like little gods deciding the lives of others, returning over and over again to make the same decisions. One has to be careful, since what we are sure of is that at some time things will be reversed, and therefore one must work and behave honestly so that later you may be treated likewise.

According to the records, I have already explored some variations with Isabel, not only about kinds of relationships, but even with regard to age. I have three particular moments in which I'm completely certain about her behavior. The first one is when she is twenty-three and a bit wild, but her intuition and self-assurance are brilliant. The second is when she's twenty-six. It's her best moment: she's just over a failed relationship, disillusioned with her work and with men, she's decided to take refuge in her studies, her best qualities aren't lost yet. The third one is when she's thirty-two, which is when I personally like her best. She's much more serious, poised, and her character has lost much of the harshness that irritates me when we fight. I've never gone beyond them. In many of the temporal lines, Isabel begins a lasting relationship at thirty-three, and I've never felt like exploring much further from that point.

This time I've chosen the hardest of the three Isabels I prefer. She's twenty-six and she'll look at me with mistrust. She's withdrawn into herself since her last companion let her down. It's clear I won't get anything today. That's what I prefer; at this point sex doesn't interest me. I think I would be unable to tell her how much I love her, unable to explain to her what a tremendous temporal mess we've gotten ourselves into. As she stands before me, Isabel wouldn't be able to understand why I complain. She would remind me too much of that other Isabel, so familiar and close, who has just kissed me and wished me luck before entering the portal. We both have to go through a period of mutual adaptation—well, only I have to this time; everything will be new, and thus attractive, for her.

I have three days ahead of me to talk to her. Isabel will miss her classes, I've already reserved a table at the Gorría Atemparak in Barcelona for tomorrow. We'll go to the theater and go see *Aïda* again. According to the records, I've seen it countless times, but it'll be the first time for both of us. We'll take a walk along the beach and, little by little, I'll unravel the threads of the huge skein I'm hiding. Maybe at the end we'll wind up in bed, maybe not. That's one of the few things I don't dare to predict.

I'm getting closer, all I have to do is go around a corner and I'll have her in sight. I vow I'll take care of myself and her, of us both. I don't want to go through this, it's very hard on me.

There are people, many people in the hallways, they're coming out of class. For a moment I doubt I'll be able to see her. I'm not afraid, I know she's there, waiting for me to come and tell her I'm sorry.

None of the records, none of the tapes have prepared me for her dazzling appearance. She is over there, at the exact place and at the right time. She has that cheerful, happy look, her shining eyes seem to give off light. Her lips form a smile that is a never-ending invitation. She's looked at me from afar without recognizing me, she has no reason to, she's talking to a classmate and they would continue if I didn't get in their way. She doesn't know who I am yet, she doesn't avert her eyes until she's right next to me. I've simply bumped into her and she has dropped her books. All I could do was smile and hide my face. I'm telling her that I'm sorry and she listens to a simple apology, in reality I'm asking her forgiveness for what I'm doing to her, for uprooting her from her temporal line, for loving her, for taking her far away and maybe for killing her over and over again, but I cannot do anything else. What better team than the one already formed? The one whose members' reactions are all known, and whose value and ability have been proven. Who's to stop us from continually recruiting the same agents when there are millions of almost identical copies of them in millions of similar worlds?

I speak but I don't listen to myself; I only have ears for her. I recite a song learned too long ago.

I close my eyes. I finally understand what she felt when she came toward me in the park. I desperately look for time to recover, I let her smell envelop me.

The situation is somewhat poetic. Isabel is here again, she has always been here, she never left. I only need to hand her the memories she has lost, so that she becomes herself again.

It's hard to realize it, when you finally understand you want to forget it, you would like not to even suspect it, but this moment arrives and you bump right into bitter reality. Now I know we are immortal, we don't have any future, but what does that matter when an eternal present is ours? Millions of Isabels await me. All of them are within my reach. All of them are waiting for a fraction of their own eternity.

Pablo A. Castro

CHILE

Pablo A. Castro (1974–) is an up-and-coming young writer who has been publishing science fiction for only a few years. Castro went to school at the French language–immersion school Alianza Francesa and subsequently was accepted into the literature program at the Universidad Católica de Chile. He later switched majors to political science and graduated with a degree in that field in 2001.

Castro's literary career began in 1997 when his first story, "Game Over," was published in *El Mercurio,* Chile's foremost newspaper, which has gone on to publish several other stories by him. In 2000 he entered *Fixión 2000,* Chile's first national SF competition. The jury, which included Chile's grand master of SF, Hugo Correa, was unanimous in awarding first prize to Castro for "Exerion," the story we have included here.

"Exerion" demonstrates brilliantly how SF can be used to explore the personal and social consequences of authoritarianism in Latin America. Video-arcade games figure prominently in Castro's fiction, and in this story the game becomes an extended metaphor for the trauma suffered by thousands of Chileans during the brutal military dictatorship of General Augusto Pinochet (1973–1989). In the futuristic landscape and language of the high-stakes data storage and retrieval world popularized in cyberpunk, the bitterly ironic "Exerion" captures the desperate feel of the search for information undertaken by families and friends of the "disappeared" in Chile. The main character's addiction to computer games bespeaks his emotional emptiness and estrangement from reality in the wake of his father's violent abduction, and the Gibsonesque finale suggests the self-sacrifice and potentially endless state of suspension risked by those who demand truth and justice in a totalitarian world.

Exerion

Exerión, 2000

by Pablo A. Castro

translated by Andrea Bell

He had about one hour left before they killed him, and of all the things he could do he thought that perhaps the most fitting would be to let the terminal screens fill up with the landscape of some old video game. He looked for one special one. In truth all of them were special, though Exerion seemed the most appropriate. He started it up, took over the controls, and turned down the basement lights until it was almost dark.

Part of his features were reflected on the screens, and the stimulating lights of the game mixed with the blackness of the visor that covered his eyes and most of his face. His features disappeared as his vision focused on the flashing graphics and the tiny ship that fired as it evaded its enemies.

Exerion wasn't a difficult game. The ship you command moves all over the screen, eluding birds and little butterfly-ships and circle-ships that descend in a row, just so that you can destroy them in that order. The firing style is up to you: shot by shot or a steady automatic stream. The only problem is that you run out of bullets, but if you can maintain the necessary kill level you can resupply. A real closed circle.

As a game, Exerion is definitely prehistoric. Up to twenty years ago it was possible to copy it, but now it was impossible to find it anywhere and it was stored only on the hard drives of some fanatics. Besides, it wasn't any fun for terminal junkies; none of the games from that era were. Most addicts spent their time fighting online, annihilating real enemies stationed in other parts of the world, or simply falling victim to an ambush in some hypernet suburb. Sometimes he let himself be seduced by the vertigo of being in several places at the same time, fighting, but too much skill and energy were needed to stay alive, and he always lacked those.

Still, back around 1985 Exerion had been a real addiction for him. Those were the days when games lived on screens similar to those of old

TV sets, housed in black cabinets decorated with space drawings that represented the different games. Underneath the screens were a joystick and a pair of buttons, enough to move the ship around and to fire. The game was activated by a token you bought at the entrance to the arcade. After a while, never very long, the game became familiar to you, and if you got into it enough you could always rack up an incredible score that would stay lit up on the screen along with your initials. Then you knew that there was something you were the best at, or simply better than the rest.

He became obsessed when he was barely ten years old. Maybe younger. Now he was fifty-five, of that he was sure, though at times he felt twice as old. His body lay almost inert in a hydraulic chair that moved all around the room, while his one arm served as a hook. His legs didn't reach the ground, because he no longer had any. Sometimes he tried to remember what it was like to feel them but he quickly came back to his senses, focusing on the screens of his terminal or on something even more attractive. But only the screens seemed real enough, active enough, to reanimate him. Cables extended from them that connected to him via small jacks installed in his head and in the stump of the arm he didn't have either.

He remembered those times when he was totally caught up in the game, just like he would be with computers and terminals later, though that memory sensation was harder to recall. Sure, all he need do was activate the neural recovery program and his memories would come back in more recognizable forms. They would again seem a bit clearer, like transparent dreams with something to say. But the program was becoming more and more inadequate as the invisible and indestructible nanoraser devoured faces and places, covering over the gaps with a nebulous and dreamlike void that wasn't enough to gestate any feeling or emotion awaiting its chance. But he was sure that something still trembled within his soul, a place where the subatomic electro-eraser couldn't reach, and even if it could, whoever had programmed it hadn't taught it to make pieces of something that was essentially immaterial disappear.

But the memory of Exerion had survived the nanoraser, and he sometimes believed it was the only thing that was going to stay in his mind. He remembered small and significant details: the time he learned the trick of the basic maneuvers with which to throw his enemies off his trail; the time he reached the first challenge stage before his classmates did; the day he managed to get further than the rest of them, the rest being schoolkids (from the best schools), unknowns, university students, and nonstop players. When he recorded his initials and made his way through the throngs who were waiting their turn he felt something that might have been happiness or a strange satisfaction, like when he'd scored a goal and his teammates ran after him to congratulate him. Then he went home, and he was never the same after that. They had taken his father away.

The house was a mess, as if a wind had blown in and rearranged the objects and faces. His mother was talking on the phone, and he could still remember her features deformed with anguish, frightening him. It seemed like her warm and comforting face had been lost, or had never existed. Later his brothers and sisters arrived, asking what had happened and trying to calm his mother down, as little by little other people showed up to find out what had happened. He saw familiar faces and others he thought he knew only at a distance, he saw lots of other things and nothing at all, but never did he believe or feel that he was a part of them. He was watching a movie, a disturbing movie that never seemed to end and was threatening to become even more terrifying. So he just watched, trying to do something with hands that were capable only of destroying enemies in Exerion and not of helping out with what was happening at home. But when night fell, his sister hugged him and he felt her tears, which wanted to pour forth, though she held them back with difficulty. For several days he would witness each one of them collapse into stifled sobs as time passed and their father became a blurred or unfamiliar figure.

He still remembered some of those things. He remembered his family's faces, their features, although the memory wasn't very strong and at times it turned into a dream. Had it been like that? Had his sister really hugged him? Had his brother's perpetually ironic smile, which always reminded him of his father, disappeared? Was his mother the one who had caressed him one night when both had discovered that they couldn't sleep?

Had he really played Exerion that day?

Sometimes, when he awoke to nights darker than others, things became confused and he came to doubt that his father had ever been taken away. Maybe, he thought, it wasn't him but his mother, or maybe it *was* his father but they'd let him go and he was still alive, or probably very sick and waiting to die. Maybe he had already died and he didn't remember that. Maybe after a long period of suffering his father had passed away, and he, wholly indifferent and feeling nothing, had withdrawn.

Then he would shake himself in desperation and try to make everything fit together and assure himself that none of this had happened, his father really hadn't returned nor had his body been found. That's when he would believe he could close his eyes once more, but already the true memories were exploding forcefully and he would have to face them without going back to sleep, while he groped around in the darkness to turn on the screens of his terminal and activate the connections.

Within half an hour they're going to find him and they're going to kill him. When he'd realized this five years ago, he'd thought of how he could escape and save himself. But then he'd understood it wasn't worth it, and that when the time came he would think of something. Well, he'd thought of Exerion. Not bad. Although it had been on the disk for a long time, he hadn't dared start it up and play it. Not because of the memories, but because they could liquidate him very quickly and then his fifty-five years would once again feel very real and heavy. In his mind's eye he could see that time when he'd gone into an arcade, discovered the game in a corner, and inserted a token; he'd lasted only a few minutes. His hands had been incapable of agile maneuvering and his ships had been destroyed far too easily, over and over again, above the reflection of his already aging and skeptical face.

But now he had three big birds after him, and as he filled them with bullets and their colors changed until they exploded, he felt he could be ten years old again.

"The first thing would be to deactivate all of the computer links," he thought, as if he were explaining it all to someone in particular. And not only that. He'd also have to cut the electric current (sometimes they used an electronic flow detector), cover himself with a heat-diffusion blanket, and pray that the ultrasound signals of the metropolitan satellite would get lost in a storm. Really, the best thing would be to abandon the place and quickly escape. When they set off an IIP (Intrusion in Progress) alarm and when that got upgraded to a "neural fugue" (theft of classified data), those guys went in with everything, except a detection order. He knew what happened to people who challenged the security systems. They disappeared completely. They were impossible to recover, even in the hypernet.

He noticed the time. He still had time. It was still possible to get a long way into Exerion . . .

They never heard from him again. The house was never the same again, either. And of course they had to go through the whole unavoidable routine of those years: first the menacing fear that led them to abandon the house and live with relatives, all piled together in one room. Later on they left Santiago for a long while until things calmed down. Then came rage, manifesting itself in his brother who swore he'd blow up a barracks or kill someone someday, while his mother helplessly contemplated how hatred was threatening to destroy them all. Afternoons when his mother would return home from another painful scrutiny of the lists. Hopeless accusations and never-ending lawyers who knew better than anyone that nothing could be gained. Long trials. Rulings against them that could wipe out in a day all that was left of them. The ghostly black-and-white photos of his father on posters that drove away the memory of his enthusiastic, ironic, paternal face. Joint marches. Midnight vigils.

And when he distanced himself from all that, when he got bored and turned halfway around, he was all alone.

Alone, he thought, just when, through carelessness, some missiles were destroying him. The same as with his family . . . and him not feeling a thing. For years he had asked himself why, how had he reached such an alienated state? Where had the pain gone, the hurt, the fury, and the desire for vengeance? The impotence? Something, something much more powerful than the electronic eraser virus that infested his head, had devoured everything, everything that should have come from his heart, leaving him thus, like a skeptical doll that hoped for nothing and gave nothing, only shots fired at virtual enemies and entire nights spent in front of the screens. But at the beginning, at the start of the routine, he had stayed by his family's side. He had worn his sad and lost face, trying not to be out of step with everyone else's feelings, until he couldn't take it anymore.

He distanced himself, yes, and the rest of the family never forgave him. No one did. But they were wrong. He loved the old man. He loved his father. But everything had happened so quickly, had been so overwhelming and suffocating that he felt they had also taken away his sensitivity and the possibility of still believing. That afternoon, when he came home it, too, had disappeared. It seemed to him like he was still in front of Exerion and that he hadn't run out of tokens. That person, that ten-year-old child, was there somewhere, and while he destroyed a column of circle-ships he thought that over the years he had turned into a clumsy and bewildered continuation or elderly imitation of that kid, simulating being present and alive.

The child kept firing and eluding ships with surprising skill.

They would arrive in about fifteen minutes. They didn't have an official name, but around here they were known as the mindtracers. They were from Computer Intelligence, a special division that brought together personnel from all the branches of the armed forces. They had been formed after an Argentinean student had neutralized the limited early warning system during the Ushuaia crisis. In time they came to assist the police in detecting minor crimes, and they also illegally infiltrate the homoneural nets. Sure, there was never any shortage of daredevils who'd wander around inside the military files, and the intrasecurity laws were very clear about that one: twenty-five years. Of course the unwritten law was even clearer: five bullets in the head or a high-power molecular disintegration laser.

He fired some fifty bullets into a flock of birds that were bombing him relentlessly. The birds were blasted into pieces that instantly disappeared when another flock replaced them. He executed a basic maneuver, then rose to the upper edge of the screens and waited for them to attack again. They never made it. He shot them to bits in order as he descended, then they disappeared. He smiled.

He still had three lives in reserve and the indicator showed 356 bullets. At that rate he would get really far. How far could you go? He had no idea. There was a guy who claimed to have scored 2,897,056 points. He could prove it. And even if it were a lie he believed him, thinking that someday he would reach that score, just from the sheer desire to feel he had done it. But even with that, there came a point where the old games became as repetitive and wearying as a routine. No matter how many new levels you reached it'd always be basically the same.

Looking for his father had always been the same. And how could everyone else understand that, for him, pursuing all that no longer meant anything? How could he explain to them that he felt nothing, and that nothing is worse than not being able to feel anything when you know you have to? That some men should come to your house, grab your father, take him to some place where they just about fry him, where they get their kicks out of torturing him and then end up tossing him like a sack of potatoes or a bag of garbage into some freezing half-dug hole, into the dark sea, or . . . something even worse that you don't know about but that, by intuition, makes you shudder. How could you feel cut off from that?

When they hired him as a tactical consultant and he helped them protect files and taught them how much they could do via the interactive networks, less than 10 percent of the population still remembered the events. Were they all as insensitive as he was? At some point everyone forgot what had happened, what could happen again, what sometimes happened and what hadn't yet been found out, not because they were bad people or anything, but because they lived in a constant and deliberate state of omission. Sometimes he would look at the city and wonder how many of the people who lived there had no one or were nothing, pretending to have a life that no one knows for sure really exists. How many good and special people walked among the crowds, people who, if they were to disappear, wouldn't be missed by anyone? How many stars were there in that cold galaxy that went unnoticed by the thousands of skeptical observers when they burned out? The world was a field of the disappeared. But wasn't it possible to recover something, with a little bit of willpower and some empathy? As an intelligence officer from the Chilean Air Force had told him, "We have the names and the possible whereabouts. Not all of them, naturally. But we can recover and store that information, of course. Information doesn't disappear, it only changes . . . and we can't ignore it or erase it, even if we wanted to."

Then he found him, he found them all, and it wasn't all that hard. There was a long list of them, and for each of them there was a file and a possible destination. There were a lot of names. People as forgotten as a movie's final credits. And there *he* was, among the other names. He read and repeated it several times in order to feel that it was his father's name. And as he slowly spelled it out, the memories returned, some real and others that he believed he remembered, disarrayed fragments, blurred images covered by dark borders, a smile . . . a walk through the plaza . . . a midafternoon caress . . . worn hands offering him some money for metal game tokens.

He went back years, while the information blinked across his face. He believed he felt himself once again part of something, part of a family that no longer existed and that would never be one again. But his father's name and information were there, and it was just a matter of penetrating the files again and maybe he would have something important to offer the rest of them, those others who still awaited some truth, something that proved he wasn't what they had thought and that he was indeed a part of them even though they were no longer there.

But no tactical consultant could emerge unscathed after being inside the nerve center of the military system. Sure, they weren't going to kill him, that was too obvious. But a few electronic viruses, a nanoraser in his head . . . they could slowly do away with someone and make him disappear without needing to dig a hole or fly over the deep, dark ocean.

When he managed to detect them the viruses had already clogged the arteries in his extremities and he was able to save only his right arm. The nanoraser didn't make itself known until much later. It had removed the names of his family and most of their faces. He recovered something with the neural program but the nanoraser remained, changing itself into part of his life and of his insensitivity.

They would be here very soon, but he didn't care. Everything was ready and he couldn't avoid it. For years he had calculated the exact amount of time they would take to find him after he extracted the information. But in all that time he hadn't been able to find a way to escape and save his life. His life, the fifty-five years he carried in his body. His mutilated body. All those years . . . what had happened during them? Was it the void on top of voids that diluted time and changed it into nothing but reference numbers? He thought maybe it was because of the nanoraser, which was still in action, which deleted a little bit here, a little bit there before he was able to notice it, or else because of the electronic viruses that had left him like a mutilated doll. But very soon he understood that it was something more. Something, a feeling he couldn't erase and that was able to pierce through feelings and memory. Sometimes it was loneliness, sometimes an endless night in front of the screens. It was an insipid and exhausting job, or a New Year's Eve spent staring at the clock without moving. It was walking among the inexpressive and hostile masses before he lost his legs, or just the hydraulic chair that sometimes got stuck. It was a heart that each day gets a bit colder, that loses its shape and color . . . a too-common name buried among thousands of common names, one man in a city of 10 million beings who know or know of something that you lost. It was the uselessness of the nets that couldn't carry him back to that much-needed past. It was an arm reaching out in bed and not finding anyone, caressing a body that's only imagined and that leaves its shape outlining a feeling of anguish.

He understood then that it wasn't worth the trouble to escape. After all, they wouldn't come to kill him, or to make him disappear. He was no longer there. Maybe he never had been. Life had made him disappear like a hologram that loses its source of energy and light; powerful life pulsed out there from which all others seemed to drink, except him.

To escape . . . to escape from them made no sense. There was no place to go. The files with the data about the dead and the possible places where they could be found, or merely what had happened to them, were lying there waiting to be activated. They would reach all conceivable terminals. Everyone would be able to access them. That would be enough. He thought of signing his name but then changed his mind. Somehow he felt that he couldn't erase the years by being one of the missing. Then he signed as *Exerion,* and that felt good. If anyone really cared, they would go to the trouble of finding out who was behind that strange name.

Victor Morales. He had designed the personality program, copying what still remained in his brain, inserting facts about his life, his family, and all those things that can give shape to someone. During those last years that work was what had allowed him to keep on living. An interactive program that, once activated, would be like being inside his mind, a somewhat inert and diminished mind, but enough to give an idea of who he was. Whoever activated it would feel who he had been, who he still was, and then someone could at last understand. In any case, it wasn't anything new. The hypernet was full of those programs, copies of people who were trying to live on beyond their ended or disappeared lives, trying to give shape to existences that seemed to be nothing but meaningless, unrecognized pieces. Out there were millions of voices and faces seeking each other without being part of any real connection that truly united them. And there they were, waiting for someone to penetrate them and feel like them, strange ghosts rocked by an ocean of information that grew larger every minute, every frenetic second, diluting and alienating the fragments that were becoming increasingly remote and distant, losing themselves.

His personality program was in suspension, just like the stolen files, and waiting.

He felt they were near. He looked at the score. Then he focused his strength on the game and began to destroy without hesitation, finishing everything off quickly. He fired, maneuvering with expert skill while the giant birds and the butterfly ships appeared and disappeared in succession. And suddenly, almost without noticing, he saw that he had passed the goal and had easily scored 3,000,000 points. He leaned back and a smile emerged, a little, rejuvenating smile that could send him back to 1985, leaving him completely weightless in a strange state of suspension that brought things to his mind, penetrated his soul, and eluded the nanoraser. Maybe it was the shape of his past, or perhaps his mother's eyes, his brother's or sister's smile, her hair, or maybe all the family together in some snapshot or during a peaceful Christmas. Maybe it was just him, in front of a machine in an arcade of old games, using up his last tokens, inputting his initials and watching a bunch of people's faces reflected on the screen as they witnessed his achievement.

His one arm abandoned the controls and allowed the enemy to destroy him over and over again until the screens turned fuzzy and he inscribed part of his name. Then he felt that something was coming back to him. He wasn't sure, maybe it was just a tingling sensation, but it was real and it made something inside him shiver.

Perhaps the nanoraser faltered, or maybe it was only his past reconstructing itself in a matter of seconds, rebuilding him in pieces that recognized and embraced each other with a strange and beautiful joy. He couldn't be certain, maybe it was only a shudder . . .

I felt again.

He launched the capsule with the data files and the still inactivated personality program. Both of them moved away from the terminal and lingered there, just on the other side of the screens, which blinked in the darkness of the basement, lighting up a strange body that remained connected to them, waiting in silence or maybe only silencing the wait.

One minute later a high-powered laser penetrated the wall of the room and pierced his head. The lifeless body collapsed while other shots destroyed the screens and everything was blanketed in darkness.

I was launched in the midst of a vertigo I could hardly understand, although I was already in suspension enough to be able to be part of what was happening out there beyond the screens. I wasn't activated. I can see and have seen myself for an hour, though it was hard to recognize myself. Or maybe years have passed . . . I'm not sure. Here it always seems to be yesterday or tomorrow. I am Exerion . . . I am Victor Morales . . . I am also voices and eyes getting lost on diffuse screens . . . a boy playing . . . an unrecognizable mother . . . a father whose face does not exist and who is only outlines and kindness. I am a waiting program, waiting to be found so that I may be reborn . . . or disappear forever. I am a game. A copy that floats in a galaxy of copies and awaits its chance. I could be even more alive and speak with clarity, but I need someone out beyond my reach to insert my code name. It will be a long wait. Who could make the connection between me and a report about the dead and the disappeared? Who cares if, in the hypernet, that report is me?

Is there anyone who has played Exerion and who remembers its name like a certain boy used to, a boy whose memories seem to tremble inside me?

Michel Encinosa

CUBA

Michel Encinosa Fú (1974–) resides in Havana, the city of his birth. He holds a degree in English language and literature from the University of Havana, and works as a researcher at the Provincial Center on Books and Literature (Centro Provincial del Libro y la Literatura) and as a journalist for the magazine *Somos Jóvenes*. He has been publishing for only a few years, but has to his credit one epic fantasy novel, *Black Sun* (*Sol negro,* 2001), and a handful of SF/fantasy stories published in anthologies in Cuba, Mexico, Argentina, and Italy. His second novel, the quasi-cyberpunk *Paths* (*Veredas*), and a short story collection, *Neon Children* (*Niños de neón*), are scheduled to be published in Cuba shortly.

"Like the Roses Had to Die" ("Como tuvieron que morir las rosas") illustrates how a highly literary style does not preclude plot advancement through action and suspense. The story's energetic pace coexists with a Lezamaesque[1] vocabulary brimming with neologisms that enrich the genre. The main theme of Encinosa's well-crafted tale underscores a central SF concern at the turn of the twenty-first century: human beings choosing to create their own alienness. As a well-recognized metaphor for difference, alienness here is persecuted in the name of purity or uniformity. But it would be simplistic to see the story as a straightforward paean to individuality (and the lurking figure of Castro as a menace to it), since—as the reader will notice—there is also an implicit denunciation of the illusion of choosing one's own singularity.

Like the Roses Had to Die

Como tuvieron que morir las rosas, 2001

by Michel Encinosa

translated by Ted Angell

Others died, but that happened in the past,
which is the most propitious season (who could doubt
  this?) for death.
Is it possible that I, a subject of Yakub Almansur,
will die like the roses and Aristotle had to die?
—Diván Almotásin the Maghreb (twelfth century)[1]

"Yes, you heard right. I said, 'Mastín is,' not 'Mastín was.' You're pretty sharp, as always. I'll bring him to you now."

Baphomet creeps out of reach of the Wolf's eyes, as the latter turns onto her rigid back with a grunt. If the fever of her eyes could kill, that bastard would be nothing but an unrecyclable slag heap. Now he brings in Mastín, dragging him by one leg. He leaves him barely a meter from the Wolf, who looks at her inert companion with damp eyes, without the strength to even stretch out her arm and touch him.

Baphomet tilts his head.

"You break my heart. You can't imagine. The son of a bitch weighs a ton, by Mitra," he says, prodding Mastín with his foot. "Hey, someone's here to see you."

Mastín opens his eyes, returning from the abyss, and all his muscles tense up when he sees the Wolf. They tense up, but there is no movement at all.

"I've doped him up with anilatine," explains Baphomet. "It was better than having him jump on me and tear out my throat."

"That can still happen," mutters the Wolf. "Something is going wrong with your plans. According to what you said, I should be dead by now."

"Nothing's wrong. Quite simply, the process makes you immune. Which will call for due correction in time," Baphomet draws a revolver from his clothing. "But not yet. Not until the miracle becomes manifest.

Make an effort. Somewhere you should have a reserve, even if it's minimal. So, how are you going to get it out? No problem. A little honest rage will suffice."

Having said this, Baphomet aims with premeditated slowness and shoots Mastín in one foot. The howl of pain deafens the Wolf's ears. And the Wolf, in delirium and clinging to the edge of reality with cracked nails, slides into the void, wrapped in an aura of rage, of hatred, of desperation.

The Wolf was waiting for the Wizard beneath the Portals. The day was splendid in the Walled Zone. A little bleak for the Skaters, since the Benefactor of the moment had set two dozen extra lasers in the towers that covered the perimeter. In any event, the Dailies were having a great time with some Iberian immigrants from whom it was rumored they'd bought half the floating stocks of Top-Gen in Micronesia, in addition to the fallout from speculations in the decadent Pro-Mars. It was midmorning, and the Wolf occupied a table under the blue awnings of the Portals, sipping a Ganímedes and admiring the synthetic marble Doric columns that guarded the main entrance of the unfinished Olympic stadium project, which about five years back had become the decorative pandemonium of the asphalt market of Ofidia. Its high walls, which had never held spectators, gave it its name. It was market day. A full tapestry.

She perked up her ears when three law enforcement turbocopters flew overhead hunting a child in a turbopack. They fired a couple of buzzard missiles and showered his remains over the stands on the north side. The vendors shook their helpless fists at the offending police vehicles and cleaned off their merchandise.

"Damn, one of these days those uniformed scuzzballs will have the gall to butt in here fully geared, shooting at random. What is Baphomet up to?" said the neighbor at the next table over from the Wolf, a sexagenarian Escapee with the muscles and skin of a baboon implanted on his arms and legs over the originals. They looked at each other, and the baboon licked his chops.

"Want a banana, pretty face?"

"I don't chew vegetables," she growled, showing two rows of lily-quartz canines. "And I don't go with half-wit simian chemaddicts either."

The baboon growled something to himself, and the Wolf switched tables. From the corner of her eye, she noticed a laser fix on a Skater from its tower and cut the Skater in half with a sweep. The others moved away, cautious, and descended as a mob on a Porsche that, forewarned, had entered the perimeter with its windows closed. The fingernails of the Skaters scraped little bits of paint off the roof. The Wolf sighed and ordered another Ganímedes, which tasted more insipid than the first. And then she saw the Wizard.

He came crossing the perimeter, on foot. Always so stubborn. The Skaters didn't hesitate to charge. A potential victim, without any apparent protection, just that white cloak with a hood. He seemed not to see them while they surrounded him and two positioned themselves behind to come at him with plenty of momentum. How pleasant it would be for them to leave in his flesh the fine red furrows of their fingernails, carriers of the latest version of the Worm virus. The Wizard walked slowly, not worried about getting quickly to the terrain covered by the protective lasers. Two or three guys jeered from atop the walls above the Portals. Others, seated below the awnings, turned their seats in order to better see the spectacle. The Skaters were irate, having suffered more than twenty casualties since sunrise. They wouldn't be content with just inflicting a pair of scratches to inoculate the Worm. They would come at him in pairs, in tens, ripping through clothing and skin, they would knock him to the ground and stomp him with their turboskates. The man's indifference further inflamed them. The two situated behind the Wizard charged, in silent and burning rage.

Barely two meters from him they were enveloped in a white cloud. Nothing could be distinguished within that milky sphere that no breeze could dissolve. A dozen Skaters came close and, after making a couple of rounds, entered with fingernails extended. A green flare-up began within the center of the white sphere, mixed in with it, and then the sphere imploded, while silvery lightning flashed in its interior and truncated shrieks split the air. The cloud finally faded away, and the Wizard continued his leisurely walk toward the Portals, leaving behind him a circle of ash-covered ground, where fifteen corpses lay gashed by multiple sharp weapons, their faces green and smoking.

The Wolf finished her Ganímedes and ordered two apple juices, without moving her gaze from the tall, white figure approaching her. Yes, one had to admit that the Wizard managed his daily survival pretty well, but he wasn't her type. Too neutral, too priestly. Too mysterious.

No, the Wolf didn't want a frigid man, a sphinx, an enigma. She wanted one capable of laughing, raging, of being touched. Who sweated honey or acid, but who sweated. A man who was an expert at biting. Because anyone could grit his teeth, but few knew how to do it the way the Wolf liked. Teeth that went to the tendon without leaving a mark on the flesh, lips that searched for the flavor of the nerve and not of the epidermis, a tongue that touched the marrow of the bone, not wet or dry, not dull or probing. A man who understood the language of grunts to the fifth degree and who couldn't care less about breaking the moon into bits with the cry of orgasm. That was the man the Wolf wanted. It was what she did have, finally, after a long search. And that was what she was about to lose forever, unless the Wizard agreed to help.

And anyway, why would he refuse? They were friends. Well, friends as much as a Veteran of the Solar System and ex-aerospace fighter pilot could be to an androgynous CyberGandalf of uncertain age and race. Nobody knew what goals the Wizard had in his life, if you could call it a life. Confined thirty-six hours a day in his grotto, twenty levels below the asphalt, only occasionally allowing himself to be seen on the streets. For the benefit of his personal legend, the Wolf would swear. She always intuited in this esoteric and sybaritic misanthrope a repressed exhibitionist. Or a devil without any known scruples or discernible ambitions. The type of person that one always treasures in one's private gallery of friends, leaving the rest green with envy. But this wasn't the case. The Wolf appreciated the Wizard, more than anything because he was sincere and had guts. And because he knew many things, the kind of things it's good to know if one is dedicated to trafficking in orbit-made electrodrugs in the Low Town of Ofidia, the megaurban capital of the world, and if one pays no protection to any of the Families that govern the tide of blood and credit on the asphalt.

The long shadow of the Wizard fell across the surface of the table, and the sharp nose evinced an expression of intense derision under the hood, where the face was shadows, and the eyes two tiny, silvery flares:

"Beautiful sky, isn't it? Clean, like the conscience of few."

The Wolf's only response was to motion to the glasses. The Wizard sat down, sniffed the two juices and tasted one. He savored it pensively and said:

"They've raised the dose of LK. It's almost addictive now. Extract of cannabis two thirteen, São Paulo, I think." He took another sip. "São Paulo, yes, no question about it, not as acidic as the stuff from Caracas and almost as sweet as the stuff from Novo Velázquez. And the usual alkaloids. Not bad, though. At least not for someone who has his personal biochemistry well balanced and protected." He emptied the rest on the floor and wiped his lips with the sleeve of the gray robe he was wearing under the cloak.

The Wolf contemplated the pantomime and the monologue without saying a word. The Wizard tossed the hood back over his shoulders, offering his high and pallid cheekbones and his perfectly shaven skull to the sun. His sharpened chin pointed to the Wolf's forehead:

"Well, what have you got? I hope it's important. You've ruined an experiment of mine. I was . . ."

"Later," the Wolf cut him off. If the Wizard started to describe one of his hallucinatory odysseys of techno-alchemy, it would take half a year. "It's about Mastín."

"Ah. Intoxicated with designer proteins again?" the Wizard betrayed a trace of derision in his eyes. "Hormone shock from abusing speed steroids? Cellular self-consumption from playing with his synthetic glands? Hangover from homemade vodka?"

"In a credit cage, with Wendy's Cossacks."

"Ah. But they operate in border zones. Why this rendezvous in the Walled Zone? Just to see how I squash some children on turboskates, or how they squash me?"

"You could have come through the tunnels."

"Today I woke up feeling claustrophobic. I dreamed about my mother."

"Are you going to listen to me?" she scratched one paw with the other.

"No. I'm going to count to zero, then leave. Speak."

"I only know that the money wasn't his. He never deals in that volume," seeing the Wizard's interrogating eyebrows, the Wolf sighed. "Two hundred megacredits."

"That stinks. Cash, stocks, basic bonds, washed-up securities? What circles was your hubby hunting in?

"Dammit, no." The Wolf slammed her fist on the table. The other glass fell over, drenching the Wizard's sleeve, who acknowledged it obliquely and kept his eyes on the Wolf.

She took a deep breath:

"Dammit, no," she repeated. "He doesn't get involved in those things. He's a jungle hunter, not a bird of prey. He has more neurons than you'd like to think."

The Wizard let out a skeptical "hmm," and nothing else.

"It was cash," said the Wolf. "Frozen payroll, backup memory crystals, in a briefcase with pupilar, vocal, and gene scanning locks."

"Big business, indeed," the Wizard showed his teeth. "I didn't know Wendy's Cossacks could aim that high. Who hired them and why?"

"Who, I don't know. Why . . . well, do you know what happened in the Scarlet District?" she furrowed her brow and scratched one thigh.

"Two square kilometers of real estate blown into the stratosphere with military explosives. Hard not to notice. So the Cossacks did it. Strange. It's not normal to hire mediocre urban mercenaries for a blast like that."

"The explosion was the contractor's thing. The Cossacks were there to erase footprints."

"Two square kilometers?" the Wizard twisted the corner of his mouth, with his trademark skepticism. "Fine, let's say it's so. We touchy types are a separate subspecies within the human race. And how does Mastín enter into the mix?"

"He was the payment link. He was assaulted on the way. They took the briefcase from him. He arrived at the Cossacks' too unharmed for his own good. They suspected him. And they've got him detained, to see if he'll squeal on his accomplices. I knew it wasn't him. He's a warrior, too naive for these maneuvers. I know they've got him here, somewhere in the Walled Zone. One of the Cossacks owes me a favor, and he left me a note in a telematic mailbox on the NET. Nothing else. I want to get him out."

"Wendy has him." The Wizard looked at his hands. "Raw meat to chew."

"Mediocre mercenaries, you said." The Wolf showed her canines, with sad derision.

"That's what bothers me. The mediocre ones are sloppy, unpredictable . . . DUCK!"

She obeyed without a word. A burst of lead swept the table, causing splinters, pieces of plastic, and apple juice to rain down on the neighboring tables.

The Wizard grabbed the Wolf and dragged her behind him, weaving in between the tables and the feet of the alarmed customers, who fled screaming or took cover and drew arms.

The Wolf wasn't surprised when the Wizard disappeared before her eyes, nor when she found herself invisible. A piece of cool, friendly cloth covered her. The uproar remained behind, in the Portals, toward which three squads of armored security guards were running. She and the Wizard dragged themselves along, sensing the stomps and kicks, until they got to the Green Plaza.

"That's it, very good, that's how you do it. Give me more of that, I need it for my Genesis," and Baphomet shoots again, this time at Mastín's thigh.

Mastín only trembles slightly, his gaze fixed on the ceiling. He doesn't even look at the Wolf. Pride, resignation. The Wolf closes her eyes again.

The fugitives snuck into the Forest and took cover behind a baobab.

"We lost the first play," declared the Wizard, taking the cloak off the Wolf.

"Chemoarsenal, holocamouflage in your robe and cloak," she shifted her head. "Don't you have a turbopack too? A pocket-size fission bomb? Or an instant Earth-Moon shuttle—'Just add two drops of water'?"

"I have something better," the Wizard touched his temple.

"Oh, I see," She patted her armpits, waist, and calves. "U-Colt 45, submachine gun, vibrating dagger, glowworms. And a Fury 30 shotgun, short stock. That's what I have, and that's what I'm going to use. So . . ."

"So you think it's too big for the lobby, dear?" the Wizard passed his hand through the trunk of the tree. "But it would go better next to the pool. We'll put a barbecue underneath . . ."

The Wolf had also heard the footsteps in the brush.

"Not a barbecue. It would damage it."

"It's a blessing to meet someone who loves trees," the salesman's eyes studied them. "This baby takes root in any climate or soil. High tendency toward metabolic mutation, without visible phenotypic disorders."

"As a matter of fact, I wanted something simpler. An algae grove, for example," smiled the Wolf, throwing her arms around the Wizard's neck. "Pocket Atlantis in the sauna. Say yes. Yes? Come on, don't be mean."

"Women always change the world to their liking, don't they, pal?" the salesman smiled at the Wizard knowingly. "You're in luck. My cousin, behind the Sahara, sells marine landscapes wholesale."

"Thanks a million," grumbled the Wizard, and left the hundred-square-meter forest behind the Wolf, crossing the holobarrier that maintained the illusion of being lost in an infinite Amazon.

Outside, they shoved and elbowed their way through the tide of ramblers, hawkers, dust jockeys, thousand-mile kids, tribals in poly-carbon exoskeletons, caravan neoyuppies, idle gypsies, and cyborgs, all of them strolling within the archipelago of stands, where all types of provisions, weapons, clothing, parts, tools, and products in general were being offered at severely competitive prices—stolen, discarded, recycled, second- or thirdhand, in any case of more than doubtful qual-ity or guarantee.

Nevertheless, it wasn't wise to move very quickly, which could give them away. Therefore they stopped from time to time in front of one or another comic tableau of marginal subculture, and they pretended to pay close attention to the declamations of a Poet of Martyrdom whose bio-lenses threatened to laser-blind whoever dared to look straight at him. They levitated randomly from the stands of homemade molecular cos-metics to those selling porosylon garments handwoven in the Taoist set-tlements of the Yukon. They let themselves be dumbfounded by the countless bacterial radiation posters, where the benefits and advantages of buying a condominium in installments in Machu Picchu National Re-serve were extolled, along with the ultimate novelty in random interface sex software or a set of pheromonal dermoimplants fashionable among the elite Nymphs of Oz division. They avoided an altercation between cadets from the Cybrion Foundation and technicians from Mirage Plus-Prodigy, Inc., later taking cover in the relative refuge offered by a per-formance of historic holopresences, taking a place in a scene of a really neat parody: a hypothetical meeting of all the generations of the Tudors and Borgias in a trucker bar. The audience was delighted.

Leaving the Tudors and Borgias behind, they snuck into a little carni-val of exotics. Here the Wolf felt at ease, in her natural habitat, and her confidence returned. She was among brothers. She didn't see a single ac-quaintance, but that didn't make any difference. There were wonders she had never seen before. A young man with seven pairs of dove wings along his back, and braided blond hair down to his nude hips. A woman bordering on obesity had traded her breasts for wax-gel hives, and she rolled back and forth on a skateboard, satisfied and serene, in harmo-nious and symbiotic communion with the cloud of bees that surrounded her. A ring surrounded two naked girls in a duel, each one displaying the finest of her mobile or bas-relief holotattoos. Exotic whores jumped from one potential client to another, exhibiting their vegetable implants, their patches of synthetic transparent skin, their extra breasts or vaginas in the most imaginative places on their bodies. A gang of gray-haired thugs rocked around a campfire to the rhythm of ritual drums, creaking back and forth on their metallic and rusty prosthetic arachnid limbs. A mermaid clumsily guided her aquarium on tracks, threatening to run over her crowd of suitors. In fact, a massive return to mythological classics was being displayed, an abundance of fauns, fairies, chimeras, elves, and harpies, each one its own personal design and combination of animal, vegetable, and artificial parts, taken from the natural, cultivated to order, or even warped at the level of molecular fusion, according to the originality of the version or the money at stake. The Wolf found a two-headed Gorgon charming: Siamese twins joined at the chest, with live snakes implanted in their skulls. Cobras—cloned ones for sure, since those things were so expensive—hissed continuously, eager to sink their sharp fangs into the flesh of some unwary soul.

"Madness," muttered the Wizard, behind the Wolf. "A Ferris wheel of freaks. Why so much illusion, so much vexation of the ego, so much mutilation of the spirit and the flesh?"

"It's not mutilation, but liberty," protested the Wolf. "Stress of the individual pattern. Every primitive man had his own design of body painting, with ashes or dyes. I am me, and no other."

"Exterior vanity," he snorted.

"Not everyone has your level of terabytes and mystic or philosophical hierarchies in neurons," she replied. "They're simple people. You also are an exotic, in a way. We all are. Just by living in the world, in this epoch. You are what you do, nothing more than that."

"Humph." The Wizard lowered his head and fell silent.

They emerged into a corridor. From the opposite side rose a fence with electrified barbs, isolating more select markets, with local customs duties.

"I need a high place," decided the Wizard. "The steps."

The markets, restaurants, and private function rooms of the steps were the most expensive. Paying one toll after another, crossing barriers, they arrived at one of the viewpoints, the only places at the top of the walls of the architectural complex not off-limits to the common people. Along the rest of the upper ground were installations for security troops, towers for defensive lasers, skydromes for armed vehicles or visiting VIPs.

Without delay, the Wizard got hold of a rented telescope and pointed it toward the interior of the Walled Zone. The Wolf, at his side, sipped a soda and thought about Mastín.

"There are seven interesting, distinct groups, scattered throughout the crowd. They might or might not have to do with us. They just finished sticking their swords five times into a vendor on the west side. A security squad just put some shoplifters out for the Skaters to eat. We have a few minutes here, I think," declared the Wizard, setting down the telescope. "Next play?"

"Go with the Benefactor," suggested the Wolf, not very convinced. "He's the maximum authority here. He knows who moves under his shadow. If the Cossacks are here, he'll know where, how, and why."

"Good morning, would you do me a favor, thank you very much?" smiled the Wizard. "Forget it. Nobody looks the Benefactor in the eye. Only his secretaries. And the Cossacks are now part of the security of this place, I've seen them. Maybe this same Benefactor is holding your hubby. And the place is big underneath. Cellars, storerooms, parking lots, rest rooms, tunnels. Castle of termites. Hey, stop biting your nails and listen to me, do you mind?"

"Listening to you isn't going to solve anything. I want to get Mastín out. I have to. Damn!" She stuck a paw under her clothing and scratched herself with sudden frenzy. "Nerves. It's nerves."

"Don't look behind you," whispered the Wizard. "On the count of three, dive. Try to land on your feet. One. Two. Three!"

They jumped over the railing and fell, with a laser beam searing their heels. One, three, six meters. Just over the necks of some elegant diners, sitting at a banquet fit for a king. A bite, a swipe of the claw, a dagger plunged into the chest of a bodyguard, a bullet grazing the skin of her thigh. A shout, when the Wizard opened his cloak and a cloud of gases spread out over the scene. The Wolf fled, throwing punches left and right. A half-open door. Hallway empty. She ran, until she felt the footsteps of the Wizard behind her.

They stopped. The Wizard glanced at her thigh:

"Do you think it was a poison bullet?"

"I hope not. If it was, we'll know when I turn green. Now what?"

"Down, terra firma," he replied. "Look for an exit. Outside's better."

"Mastín must be inside here, somewhere."

"Underneath for sure."

"Underneath, then," she urged.

Calmly, the Wizard got down on his knees and spread out on the floor his runes carved in bone:

"Ehwaz, parallel with Thurisaz and Dagaz. Movement, entrance, and advance. Othila and Nauthiz, separation and repression; face down. Odin, the unknown, over Berkana, the evolution. Stinks. Let's see. Uruz and Gebo, strength and company, tangent on the line of Jera and Kano, harvest and beginning. Who could tell? Otherwise, Sowelo opposed to Perth. Total achievement aligned with initiation. Huh. Yeah, it could be."

"And so?"

"Downward, then," he agreed, gathering his runes. "Might as well. The wasp's nest is already stirred up. Maybe we'll get lucky." He trotted down the hallway behind her. "Have you tried a liniment of peppermint with pesticides? It must be fleas."

The Wolf didn't respond, and kept running, scratching her head at short intervals.

Mastín's blood soaks the leg of his pants and flows through the hole burned in his boot. The Wolf blinks, trying to clear her eyes, and spits out:

"I'm going to kill you seven times, you son of a bitch! You'll never get away with this! Never!"

"Forget it," replies Baphomet. "First of all, you can't even kill a fly. And my project is safe, within me," he pats his body. "Organic cases, cryogenized. Each and every one of my cultures. All the documentation. Being a leader teaches you not to trust anybody. I am my own scientist, lab technician, and secretary. So you're shit out of luck."

Another shot, at Mastín's hand. He lets out a shout and turns his head toward the Wolf. Now his eyes are not those of the virile martyr, but those of the friend, of the lover who pleads for hope. But the Wolf cannot do anything but hate, hate, hate, and immersed in the vortex of this devastating hatred she looks away and closes her eyes, wishing for a jump backward in time and fortune, wishing.

They'd descended as much as a hundred meters below the asphalt, or at least that's what the Wizard's sensors indicated. Hallways, service corridors, stairs, elevators, descent tunnels, double doors, ventilation conduits. They'd wasted a dozen of the Benefactor's henchmen, and a lot of alarms had gone off in hysteria. The Wolf felt intoxicated with action, pushing for a fight, and encouraged by the presence of the Wizard, very encouraged. In fact, there was nobody like the Wizard to pull tricks out of his sleeve at the right moment, to get by alarms and intrusion countermeasures, to tell a worn-out, idiotic joke and let out a snicker at the right moment just before she succumbed to despair. The Wolf was thankful for his alliance, his unselfish sacrifice. But without telling him, of course. It wasn't necessary. For his part, the Wizard kept making fun of the itching the Wolf felt all over her skin, attributing it to a blight common to domestic pets or to poisoning from some filet of beef or lamb, which the Wolf liked to eat raw and bloody.

The Wolf's weapons had lost all their ammunition, and she had to get rid of them and pick up weapons from the fallen thugs. The Wizard never used weapons, at least not in the regular sense. Somehow he managed things so that the competitive body count went in his favor. "I like to do things big, really big," he said.

In spite of the heat of success, the Wolf lost neither caution nor sight of reality. Trackers were on their trail, they had to be. Entire squads following their steps from above, others trying to cut them off in their path, and even more below, waiting in ambush. There was no way of knowing if their subterranean course was being monitored or not; the Wizard might have overlooked many things, in the hurry and the fright. These ideas whipped up the Wolf's paranoia, and she was forced to advance more cautiously, to fear the next intersection, the next turn, any shadow in the corner of her eye, the slightest current of air on her cheeks. The frenzy of the battle became a tightening of the belly, bristled hair, erect tail. Her heart was heavy. Her senses began to play tricks on her.

Even the Wizard became an additional reason for apprehension, always behind her, silent, most of all in the last few minutes, his shadow gliding across the walls, even when the Wolf couldn't make out her own. Also, although she moved forward in a crouching position, in small quick hops, with nervous irregularity, the Wizard went in uniform steps, confident and deliberate, upright behind her as if in reality it were he and not the assassins scattered throughout that underworld who was planning to erect a hunting trophy from the Wolf's remains. But the Wolf didn't say anything. He was doing enough by helping her, and didn't need to put up with her fears, like those of an overgrown child. So she went forward, with her stomach in her throat and her temples throbbing, scratching herself continuously. Her fingernails were red; she had made herself bleed. And the unrelenting itching kept getting worse, taunting her. Another torture for her nerves, which were already very close to breaking down.

They stopped in a dead-end corridor, next to a metal stairway that went up the wall and disappeared into the darkness of a hole in the ceiling. The Wizard shrugged his shoulders.

"There's nothing down below. I suggest we go up. At any rate, ever since we got into this we've known that finding Mastín is a crapshoot. But I would bet on going further up."

"I don't like it." She looked into the hole. "It could lead anywhere."

"We've been anywhere for the past hour," he yawned.

The Wolf, envying his calm, opened her mouth to say something nasty, but instead she ducked and took cover behind some containers. The Wizard did the same.

The floor trembled as the armored men passed by, about twenty of them. Few weapons could take down an armored mercenary with a single shot, and they didn't have any of those that could. Twenty armored gorillas against two fools. The Wolf went up first, with the breath of the Wizard on her heels.

About twenty meters, she guessed. Then her head ran into something hard.

"A grating," she told him below. "Dark outside, but the locks are open. Just one second . . ."

She pushed with all her strength. Nothing. She wheezed, went up two more stairs, and pushed with her back until the texture of the metal was impressed on her flesh. She groaned.

"What's wrong?" asked the Wizard.

"I can't. Damn." She let out a falsetto laugh. Her muscles trembled.

"Let's both push," he decided, coming up to her height.

Each one put one foot on a step, the other on the opposite wall of the conduit, and strained as if possessed. The grating hesitated, then finally opened. The Wizard went out first, sniffing his surroundings, and the tail of his robe brushed across the Wolf's face, who had enough spirit to comment, in a whisper:

"Hey, don't you ever wear underwear?"

"It's bad for the circulation," he answered, and extended a hand to her.

"Well, at least I know you have everything intact. Curiosity satisfied. So, do you use it? A girl I know saw you once and asked me . . ."

"Shhh," he hissed. "Look. This isn't just any dirty room."

Her lupine eyes quickly recognized the plastisteel military containers. Seals intact. Weapons, equipment, campaign rations.

"The hit on the Charles Manson Army-Police Station," she muttered, looking at the seals closely. "So this is where they wound up. I saw it on the pirate news. The corporate news didn't say shit about it."

"Are you going to report it?"

"I've never been a model citizen," she said, and suddenly she leaned heavily against a box.

The Wizard came to her side immediately.

"What?"

"Very weak," she responded. "And hungry. Divine Fenrhir, I am so hungry! And cold. Really cold." Her teeth chattered. "And this itching, damn. Even my bones itch."

"You're burning," the Wizard observed, touching her. "Great day to catch a cold."

"It's not a cold. I don't know what it is." She rubbed her eyes. "I keep getting dizzy."

"You're not pregnant? Just a joke. Hey, the way you are right now, I don't think that . . ."

"I came here for Mastín," she stressed every word. "I'm not leaving without him."

"Is it your heart or your libido talking? I imagine he's very good at performing miracles in of lubricious concupiscence, but . . ."

"Fuck you."

"After you," he moved aside, cheerfully, and let her pass. "There's a door there," he pointed. "It's open. When you get ready to faint, just tell me."

Return. Return to a bloody Mastín. Return to a victorious Baphomet, who absently scratches his backside:

"And if you think that being a spiritual guide makes me conceited, well, you're crazy. It's a job for pariahs. I don't even get a salary. Ha. I had to play a lot of tricks to dispose of the previous Benefactor and occupy his place, and then restructure the chain of command. But it was worth it. Here I move the credit necessary for my alchemy tricks. That's no little thing. Technology is expensive. You can imagine."

And he pulls the trigger. Right in the center of Mastín's cheek, crosswise, without damaging his teeth, crossing the face from side to side.

The Wolf screams, howls, cries.

The soldier eluded the swipe of the claw, but he wouldn't have escaped the Wizard's fist if the Wolf hadn't stepped in to intervene.

"Stop!" She faced the man, who grasped his submachine gun too late. "It was you, isn't that right, Santo? The message on the NET?"

"It was me," he admitted, and shuffled his feet nervously. "Are you getting out? I am. Somewhere away from here. C'mon, c'mon . . ."

"Not yet. What about Mastín?"

"I don't know. Over there somewhere," he waved a hand. "I don't like the stuff going on. Too ugly."

"What?" the Wolf queried. "What's going on?"

The Wizard looked at the man, frowning.

"Really ugly. Too ugly," the man whispered.

"Damn," she said.

"Designer virus," he said, reluctantly. "I heard them talking about it. Selective pandemics."

"Tell me the whole thing."

"It's to wipe out the exotics. Say you're an exotic with reptile skin implants, or fern branches. That biomodification forces your organism to express a particular trait. Enzymes, hormones, whatever. They give you the virus, and the virus learns those traits. It reproduces. Your body begins to spread it that way. Say you have birch bark implants. That's the virus's marker. It'll kill everyone who has birch bark. You give it to someone, and with that you kill all the rest of their type. The virus by itself doesn't do anything. You have to inoculate it first so it can replicate. That's how it works. If I were a neuroburnt, a know-it-all, I could explain it to you better. But I'm not a know-it-all. I'm just scum, and I wanna vanish. It all sucks. I have implants, y'know? Dolphin skin, on my back. I don't wanna die, at least not so soon. I'm going to the Moon, to Asimov Town. Maybe the thing will take a while to get there. From there I'll go to Mars. I worked in the Red Mines before. I know what it's like. I can put up with it."

"Who's behind this shit?" Every hair on the Wolf's body was now standing on edge, and her itching had intensified. She had to muster all her willpower in order not to rub up against the wall. She clenched her teeth. She felt dizzy, from hunger and nausea.

"There's this group. Silver Race, they call themselves. A bizarre syncretism. Nietzsche, Amon, Mabuya, Saint Peter, I'm not sure. They have worship services. An insane liturgy. Fanatics. The Immaculate Man, the Clean Man, they preach that. The Pure Man, the Man without Subterfuges and Artificial Vanities. That kind of shit."

"And Baphomet, the Benefactor of the Walled Zone, is he in on this?"

"Yeah, he is, of course he is. He's a complete and clean human. Just like Wendy's Cossacks, who don't allow exotics in their ranks and like to hunt them for fun. Everyone knows it. That's why he hired them. Now there isn't a single exotic in the security personnel of the Walled Zone. I have this stuff on my back, no one knows about it, no one has seen it. A few days ago I had to blow a kid's head off, just because he had the same implant I did. White dolphin skin. Pretty as anything. But they were watching me, the others. I had to do it. So I did it. Shit. Let's go."

"What does Mastín have to do with this?" The Wolf shook him by the collar of his jacket.

"I don't know! Nothing, I think. It's something else. Something about the money they say he stole from us. They think you're in on the game, and that you're coming to look for him. That's why they almost got you now. If I were you I wouldn't go that way," he pointed to the corridor that the Wolf and the Wizard were heading for before they ran into him. "But if we go to the level above, there's a buried hangar. Turbocopters. We run like hell, and then adiós."

"You go," the Wolf let go of him. "We'll just keep going the way we were."

"Each has his own way to die," he said, sadly.

"Over there at the turn there's an ascending air conduit. It should take you to where you need to go. Come on, I'll show you," offered the Wizard.

The Wolf leaned against the wall and closed her eyes, her ears down. She felt dull. But still, she couldn't stop scratching herself, although with less rage than before. She didn't have enough strength even for that. The Wizard returned:

"May Mitra protect him."

"What do you think about what he said?"

"Huh. It wouldn't be the first or the last selective pandemic in this vapid era of metahumanity. A lot of private viral design agencies make their living that way: Pandora, Firstborn, Temple of Fear. But still . . ."

"He was really terrified. And I know him. He's a tough guy, not a storyteller."

"He's a vulgar mercenary. If there is something, who knows what it could be."

"He sounded really convincing."

"Terror makes any of us sound convincing."

"And if it were true? I remember a kid I met at the Borodino Aerospace Station, geostationed over the Indian Ocean. We were cadets. And he looked like an old man. When the Apology VII was released, the selective pandemic that killed only adolescent males with 80 percent Caucasian biotype, the vaccine was designed and put in circulation in two months. Millions died. And millions were saved. But the ones who were saved suffered an increase in epidermal metabolism, a side effect of the vaccine. They looked like old men. That's what happened to that kid I met. Eventually, they had to get rid of their skin and use synthetic implants or mass-produced cloned tissue. I don't know what became of him . . ."

"And I don't know why you're telling me all this," protested the Wizard. "It would be better to . . ."

"I feel like it. And a couple minutes' rest will do me good. I also remember the day I was eating sushi in a floral club in the Crystal Ephebes district, and the rose in the vase in front of me, in the middle of the table, dried up, fell apart, and turned to dust, in less than five seconds. It was the Aphrodite ST9, the pandemic designed in South Africa. Took three days to go all around the world. Goodbye to the roses. Who worried about that? Flowers don't pay taxes, they don't go into the corporate field, they don't invest or buy stocks, they don't race in the Grand Prix of MegaConsumption. Who cares about them? The same thing happened with the gladiolas, lilacs, and water lilies. The water lilies, think about that; more than one samurai must have cried looking at the denuded rivers. Someone just decided to be nasty and did it. Others did away with who knows how many animal species. A few philanthropic ecologists isolated some specimens in time, and made big money out of that. It's sickening. And the brainiacs paid by pious funders keep on shattering their own neurons, redesigning DNA chains, polymerizing genes, killing themselves to create cheap substitutes of what nature took eons to dream, conceive, and give birth to . . ."

"Melodrama isn't your strong suit."

"And then, human beings themselves. By age ranges, by race, by telemetry of profession or hobbies. By mere whim. All the vaccines are invented in a rush, and they all have side effects. But at least they save a profitable percent. That's encouraging. And now? The exotics. Wow. The human race should be homogeneous, OK, let's purify it. Just for having tastes outside the gestalt, a free and audacious corporal aesthetic—

BAM. You're a pagan, an outcast, a corpse. And it's just implants! Your genetic map is as 'clean' as anyone's. Exoticism is not inherited."

"It's inherited, in social terms," the Wizard said, pedantically. "Sociological evolution. Darwin a step beyond the organic world."

"And so what? If it's evolution, then it's evolution. And that's it. Anyone with half a brain would respect that."

"Not everyone has half a brain. A quarter, at the most."

"Try to see further. We exotics are a fraction of humanity. A fraction divided in many fractions, then subdivided into countless variants. Yes, there are millions of us, but how many of each type are classifiable by specific standards? Five thousand, ten thousand at the most. The variety is staggering. Do you think the Corporate Counsel, or some subsidized pharmacological power, is going to spend megacredits on developing a vaccine to save a few thousand people, half of whom would be dead by the time the drug hits the market? A dead patient doesn't pay. It's not profitable. Forget it."

"You have to accept that if this thing is serious, the idea isn't bad. I mean," the Wizard hurried to clarify, "it's intelligent. A host virus is enough, and it replicates itself. Really, it would be a labor worthy of Confucius to inoculate a specimen of each type, but I don't consider that a major problem for the mastermind running this show."

"Damn," the Wolf looked at him with disdain and suspicion. "You would be willing to shake hands with that pig."

"On the intellectual plane, yes."

"And on the ethical? Say one word, and I'll bite you."

"Easy there. Keep in mind that the exotics are one of the most prolific sources of social and economic disorder there are. Carousel of imposters, parade of excesses. Think about how much credit is moved in the exotic subculture, in the traffic and consumption of narcotics."

"No more than in the rest of the marginal subcultures."

"But they're the most obvious. Anyone with talent in viral engineering, without much global analytic vision and who's fanatically religious besides, would make that decision in a heartbeat."

"Cut the speech, I'm not in the mood for your crap."

"And I'm not in the mood for musings."

"You're the esoteric; you're the one who's musing."

"I don't evoke aged young people or dead roses, when I have who knows how many armored and armed goons gunning for my ass."

"Just to see it there, turned to dust right in front of me," the Wolf shuddered. "I couldn't finish the sushi. I gathered up the dust and put it in a little box. I don't remember what corner of the house I have it in now . . ."

"*Anemone verborum*," grumbled the Wizard. "Cut it out. Mastín. Remember?"

"Mastín," the Wolf winced. "We have to keep moving. Mighty Fenrhir! Experimental subject, culture broth, or reluctant Judas?"

"We got nothing yet," said the Wizard. "We need to keep going. How do you feel?"

"As if I were going to explode," she breathed deeply, very deeply, and started walking down the corridor. Dizziness, fever, itching, hunger. And rage. Plenty of rage. If they'd done that, whatever it was, to him, to Mastín, a lot of blood was going to flow through the holes in that fiend. The Wizard followed her silently.

The Wolf is a whirlwind of stone. Her skin burns. Her bones burn. Her rage burns.

"Almost. One more push, little fanged princess. I'll help you," Baphomet shoots Mastín in the shoulder. Splinters of bone and flesh splatter on the Wolf's face.

"You won't deny that I have a good sense of the dramatic," gloats Baphomet, and whistles an old, irritating bolero.

She was slow. Too slow. And too slack. It took her four blows to knock out the assassin. Another threw himself upon her and twisted her arms behind her. The Wolf threw herself down, relying on her body weight, and got loose as best she could. The man fell upon her and the Wolf found herself suddenly waving her arms like a hysterical little girl, without even scratching the face of her rival, who burst out laughing and thrust a knee into her chest before beginning to strangle her. It was the fool she was making of herself that finally annoyed the Wolf, and she got free of those hands with a well-trained move in order to quickly sink her sharp lily-quartz fangs into the man's neck. When she sat up, her face red and dripping, she received an electric blow in her back. She jumped, turned in the air, and faced the new enemy. The woman's muscles burst the seams of her shirt. One feint, then another, with the cudgel in front of her. The Wolf jumped, ducked, seized the woman's forearm and broke it in a ninety-degree angle. The blood splattered on her fur. Her rival, without flinching, attacked again. Doped with Aprotamine Zen, or some other neuronal chaos-inducing drug. Or nervous tissue removed or burned. It was all the same. The Wolf trapped her again and broke her spine, for good measure. Two more, the last ones in the group, attacked together. She concentrated, waited for the blows, and struck first. A swipe of the claws. Jugular cut. Elbow strike. Nose buried in the brain. She fell to her knees, her energy spent, unable to move a finger.

She could move only her eyes, and her vision took in a dirty floor, gray walls, and nine corpses. She and the Wizard had been taken by surprise, like children. Luckily, the henchmen wore no armor. The Wizard . . . over there, somewhere. She thought she remembered having heard him shout in the distance. It couldn't have been very far, if it was he who was now crouched at her side.

"I found Mastín, Wolf. Not far from here. Let's go, I can't carry him alone."

She tried to move, but she had no strength left whatsoever. She could barely hear herself mumble.

"I can't get up, Wizard. You get him out, if you can. Leave me here."

"Do you still itch?" inquired the Wizard. "Tell me, do you still itch?"

She indicated "no" with her eyes, confused.

"Perfect," the Wizard clapped his hands. "You just need a little push. A little push."

She blinked her eyes, not understanding.

"It's really dark, don't you think? We need a bit of light here. I told you that I woke up feeling claustrophobic this morning," the Wizard moved away and touched something on the wall.

A panel slid open, and the Wolf closed her eyes, blinded by the light. When she opened them, she recognized the sky. An immense and open sky without clouds.

"You hear that?" the Wizard came to her and whispered in her ear. "Can you hear it?"

The shouts. The commotion. The marketplace in the Walled Zone. Outside, from the other side of the window. High noon over the city. And the light from outside illuminated her thoughts: "Baphomet."

"I've had worse nicknames," remarked the Wizard, or rather, Baphomet. "For your moral peace, your husband didn't steal anything. It's easy to get street rumors started. That blown-up part of the Emerald District, well, I had to try out a new explosive. I have a buyer now. Can you guess who? The Corporate Council, the World Government itself. It's not a mystery to anyone that the Lower Towns of the big cities are the favorite culture broth and proving grounds of the powers of the world. The live test of a brand-new explosive is well worth a few thousand lives in a marginal district that has been in decline for a while and doesn't bring in any commerce. As far as the pandemic, well, I would be lying if I said the Council knew my game and supports it, but it wouldn't be risky to bet they would support it if they knew about it. Nobody has figured out the real percentage of exotics in the world's population. If everything goes well for me, and there are no reasons to fear otherwise, we'll discover that there is much more living space for the clean people. Does 'living space' ring a bell? It's a shame that apostle never surpassed mediocrity. The limited vision of his times, I suppose. Or lack of adequate charisma."

"You . . . Mastín . . ."

"You still don't get it. Itching, fever, nausea, hungry as a bear? This is not just any designer virus. It learns from you, it learns to kill you, it learns to kill the likes of you. It turns your body into a laboratory, and it doesn't waste anything until it drains all your energy. And adrenaline is the ideal catalyst. Paranoia, shooting, full-contact fights. The perfect recipe. Of course, now I'm the paranoiac. Could I have other exotics hidden in my troops, like that little buddy of yours? May Mitra devour him. And to think he was the very one I allowed to leave you a clue in the NET. Divine chance. The ways of purification are inscrutable. At least I left a dagger plunged in his forehead. If you want something done right, do it yourself."

"You're a savage."

"You offend me. You're the savage . . . The virus? I gave it to you during the first fracas, in the Portals. No more than an accidental touch. Why not tie the subject to a cot, inoculate him and dope him with catalyzers, instead of putting on this make-believe hunt? I could tell you that I had to test the subject's strength, his survival factor, and such trivia. But no. It's the fun, you get it? Just for that it was worth sacrificing some of my best soldiers."

"Die, dammit!" The Wolf saw circles before her eyes. "When did you start? How many so far . . . ?"

"None yet. You're the first live experiment. Like blowing up the Emerald District. You aren't itching now. Good. The neutral version of the virus has sucked you dry, it has learned how to kill whom it should, and it's ready to reproduce its expansion version. The plague will come out of you, and you won't even know it. You just need a little push. Do your part. A little more juice in the kettle, and everything will be done. It's time to eat, and my stomach is rumbling. You can do it, I know you can. That's why I picked you . . . By the way, Mastín wouldn't have worked; he's nothing but a skirt-chasing blowhard, and his visceral bio-chemistry is a mess. He would have died on me halfway through the process. Not you. I wonder now, what exotic pseudospecies will I proceed with, after you extremist canines? Reptiloids? Parasitoids? Electromechanical prostheses . . . ?"

"You said 'Mastín is.' Is he alive? Is he alive?!?"

"Yes, you heard right. I said 'Mastín is,' not 'Mastín was.' Pretty sharp, as always. I'll bring him to you now."

And he brought him, doped and defenseless. And said so many horrible things. And drew his revolver. Five shots. Five bloody holes in that beloved skin. Five heretical novas in the devout firmament of that shimmering fur. Five lashes of rage and impotence . . .

How many seeds of moments would be necessary to procreate the jungle of the eternal? Biopsy of rage, leisureology applied to barbarity, orgasms of atrocity around each corner.

Mastín is unconscious. Doped, losing blood. His skin, underneath his fur, ashen and dry. His breath is a tenuous, confined hiss. The calm of his face resembles, disturbingly, the look on his face during postorgasmic drowsiness; confidence, completeness, a fable at rest. But one detail belies the image, and that detail is his temples, beating to the rhythm of his ever weakening heart. The Wolf believes she's hearing the pumping of that heart, and she can't bear it.

Suddenly, the Wolf sits up halfway, resting on one elbow, panting, the world spinning around her.

"Wonderful," marveled Baphomet. "Just the right individual, I told you so. Hmm, it should have happened by now, but my sensors aren't picking up any viral emission. Maybe you're not in the best of shape, and I may have gotten a bit carried away. Another little push, I think, to see if we can finish this little game."

Baphomet aims. No, not Baphomet. The Wizard. The Wolf makes herself see him as the Wizard. Someone tangible, known for long years. The Wizard aims.

"Sloppy. Unpredictable. Like all mediocrities."

"Huh?" the Wizard, as if driven down from the clouds to the earth, takes his finger off the trigger. "What's that? What do you mean?"

"You got a little carried away. Sloppy. Just a bag of tricks. Unpredictable. A equals B, B equals C, therefore C equals A. Mediocre. You said it."

"The essence of genius lies in its imperfection, otherwise there is no development of aptitudes for the correction of errors and for learning. Vulgar dialectics. Don't equate milk with butter. Theorem refuted," he points at Mastín again.

"And then what? Only you are left. That's what it's about, right? The king of the exotics. Alone and without competition. The species of a solitary individual."

"You keep insisting on that stupid idea," the Wizard shakes his head and moves closer. "Can you explain it in a short paragraph? For my archives of nonsense."

"All the basic principles of exoticism have their triumph in you. Wild aesthetics. Overstressing of the ego. Breaking with the standards of social conduct. Radical posture. Propaganda personified. And everything else. You don't need implants. You are, in yourself, no more than an attractive implant, attached to the social organism."

"The archives thank you," the Wizard makes a gesture of reverence and aims again.

"And as far as the psychopathies proceeding from sexual impotence . . ."

"Filthy Mitra!" the Wizard goes to her and stops at her side. "Let's get this straight. In case you don't know, I always wanted to have you, as blasphemous as it was for my doctrine. And you talking to me constantly, Mastín this, Mastín that, as if I were your little sister and you wanted to shock me. That was one of the reasons I chose you two for this. It's that simple. Without all that Freudian complication. As to whether my equipment works, I'll tell you I do it every day and with clean women."

"Nothing more to say?"

"Nothing."

"Good-bye, then."

The Wolf launches a kick, prepared with all her pent-up rage, at the

Wizard's knee, and he falls to the floor. The revolver fires and the bullet disappears into the sky. The Wolf throws herself upon the Wizard, and thanks only to her weight she manages to control him.

"Stupendous, hail Mitra!" shouts the Wizard at the top of his lungs. "I told you, girl! You're magnificent!"

Mastín lets out a weak groan, a couple of meters from them.

The Wolf's eyes blaze.

"Bingo! There it is! The dawn of purification! I see it in your pupils!" shouts the Wizard, his own pupils those of the genocidal fanatic, the one who has broken all his limits.

Slowly, he manages to extend his arm out of the Wolf's control. The revolver seeks out Mastín's body. His face. His throbbing and bare temple.

"Dammit, no!!!"

The teeth sink into the flesh. Gurgling. Convulsions. The Wizard rolls his eyes and pulls the trigger.

"How does it look?"

"The one on the shoulder is bad, but there's no infection. You'll be breaking bricks with this arm again."

"And you?"

"No fever. I ate normally."

"Do you think . . . ?"

"No. Just some lethargy. It's there, in my body, all throughout. Embryo of pandemia. But the son of a bitch went overboard, and what energy I had left wasn't enough to finish the process."

"And still, you fixed him."

"I was running on pure anger. But now that I'm better, the embryo can develop fully. You'll have to treat me with a lot of tenderness. I shouldn't go to such extremes of excitement or anger. I'm dangerous if that happens. Very dangerous. Enough to annihilate my entire species."

"I still can't believe that he would be such an idiot, after everything. Who's ever seen a revolver with seven shots? And you, you were already there, there . . ."

"Don't even remind me of it. Open his organic cases, cram his mediums and documentation in the first fission incinerator I find, pick you up, get you out of the Walled Zone, bring you home, patch you up. Like the dead man said, it's no small shit."

"I'm still amazed. Him, of all people . . ."

"Do things on a big scale. That's what he said. There must be total chaos right now in the Walled Zone. Heads rolling. Power struggles. I'm not going back there for at least a week, when nobody will remember what happened."

"On a big scale. Ha! Holy Cabal! Messianic delusions . . ."

"Everyone measures his greatness in his own way. You're all the grandeur I need. Damn, how I've missed you. Come here . . ."

NOTES

INTRODUCTION (PAGES 1–19)

1 We gratefully acknowledge the editors of *Science Fiction Studies* for permission to reprint ideas and information taken from articles previously published in that journal (see bibliography for full citations).

2 Considered the first Mexican SF story, "Syzygies and Lunar Quadratures" ("Sizigias y cuadraturas lunares") was written in 1773 by Friar Manuel Antonio de Rivas in a Mexico still under Spanish dominion. See Fernández Delgado 1996. An anonymous manuscript entitled *Sinapias* is an example of utopian writing during the Spanish Enlightenment. See Winter 1979.

3 The Spanish literary canon insists on limiting nineteenth-century literature to the realist and naturalistic modes, thereby ignoring a rich body of fantastic and science fictional works. This, in turn, has meant that unlike its French and English counterparts, Spanish early SF production is very little known internationally. Santiáñez-Tió notes, for example, that Enrique Gaspar's "The Anacronopete" (1887) is the first Western novel to include a time machine, anticipating H. G. Wells's famous work (1994: 283).

4 See Molina-Gavilán et al. 2000.

5 The bibliography cites a number of monographs on these and other early SF works. See, for example, studies by Bell, Dendle, Fernández Delgado, Hahn, Holmberg, Kason, Moreno, Pestarini, Ricco, and Said Cidoncha.

6 This movement—generally dated between 1885 and 1915 and led by Rubén Darío and José Martí—originated in Spanish America and later spread to Spain. Drawing on French Parnassian and Symbolist currents, Spanish American modernist writers created a literary aesthetic that prized an embellished and mannered language. *Modernismo*, then, is not to be confused with the European and U.S. modernist movement associated with James Joyce, Ezra Pound, and T. S. Eliot (Stavans 1994: 14; Lindstrom 1994: 7).

7 *Coronel* is the Spanish word for "colonel." The *Ignotus*, named after this writer's pseudonym, is now Spain's most important SF prize.

8 The series has enjoyed a renewed interest lately with the publication of the essay "Travels of the Aznar" ("Viajes de los Aznar," 1999) by Carlos Saiz Cidoncha and Pedro Alberto García Bilbao, and with current plans to reedit the series.

9 Although Colombian by birth, Rebétez was an enthusiastic promoter of Mexican SF during the 1960s.

10 Neither Adolph, Britto García, nor Berroeta are primarily SF writers, though each has contributed significant works to the genre.

11 *Minotauro* later had a second run of eleven issues (1983–1986).

12 The following works exemplify this trend: José Emilio Pacheco's *Medusa's Blood* (*La sangre de Medusa*, 1958), José Agustín's *Near the Fire* (*Cerca del fuego*, 1986), Carlos Fuentes's *Christopher Unborn* (*Cristóbal Nonato*, 1987), Gerardo Cornejo's *To the North of the Millennium* (*Al norte del milenio*, 1989), and Homero Aridjis's *Doomsday's Grand Theater* (*Gran teatro del fin del mundo*, 1990).

13 This magazine promoted Spanish-language SF, publishing Latin American and Spanish authors alike.

14 The *Puebla* has been devoted to the Mexican SF short story since 1984, with but a few interruptions. In 2001 its name was changed to the *Concurso Nacional de Cuento Fantástico y de Ciencia Ficción* (National SF and Fantasy Story Contest). The Cuban Writers' Association created a special SF category for the *David* national literary prize in 1979; currently, however, it is in hiatus because of Cuba's economic struggles. The multiple-category *Más Allá*, named in honor of the magazine, began recognizing excellence in regional SF in 1984; due to factionalism in the main Argentinean fan club, CACFyF, the *Más Allá* has been temporarily suspended, though there has been some talk of reviving it. The *Prêmio Nova* was awarded from 1989–1996.

15 The *Ignotus* and the *Gigamesh* are awarded by the Spanish Science Fiction Association (AEFCF). The *Alberto Magno* is sponsored by the University of the Basque Country, and is open to stories written in Spanish and Basque. The *UPC Award* is given yearly by the Polytechnic University of Catalonia and is an international contest open to works written in English, Spanish, Catalan, and French.

16 Another high quality Argentinean SF magazine that published anglophone as well as Argentinean works was *El péndulo*, which had three runs (1979, 1981–1982, and 1986–1987), for a total of nineteen issues (Hassón, n.p.).

17 E-zines are notoriously unstable; however, the list of Web sites in the bibliography (which is incomplete and does not include personal Web sites) was valid as of June 2002. Some of the bigger e-zines, such as *Axxón, Gigamesh*, and *BEM*, have useful links to other interesting sites as well.

18 The International Publishing House Web site, which has world SF in English, plus author and translator contacts, is located at iph.lib.ru. To subscribe to RGP, send an e-mail message to Roberto de Sousa Causo at rscauso @yahoo.com.br.

19 A good example of Mexican-style cyberpunk is *The First Street of Solitude* (*La primera calle de la soledad*, 1993), by Gerardo Horacio Porcayo.

20 See Molina-Gavilán 2002 for further discussion (in Spanish) of the characteristics of "soft" SF.

21 For an in-depth look at the New Socialist Man in Cuban science fiction, Spanish-speaking readers may consult Juan Carlos Toledano's recent doctoral dissertation (2002), "Ciencia ficción cubana: El proyecto nacional del

hombre nuevo socialista" (Cuban science fiction: The national project of the New Socialist Man).

22 Two other traditional Latin American narratives are the search for El Dorado, which associated the region with the fast and easy acquisition of fortune, and Caudillismo, the practice of rule by a political boss or military strongman, which perpetuated the perception of a sharp division between the "military people" and the "revolutionaries."

23 See De Bella's *Más Allá* winner, "Amoité" ("Amoité," *Axxón* 48). For Chavarría, see his story "Chronicle of the Great Reformer" ("Crónica del gran reformador") in *Beginnings of Uncertainty* (*Principios de incertidumbre*, 1992) and his 1997 novel *The Myth of the Black Mirror* (*El mito del espejo negro*).

24 A sampling of such texts might include Daína Chaviano's *Fables of an Extraterrestrial Grandma* (*Fábulas de una abuela extraterrestre*, 1988), Rosa Montero's *Tremor* (*Temblor*, 1990), Elia Barceló's *Natural Consequences* (*Consequencias naturales*, 1994), and Lola Robles Moreno's *The Rose of Mist* (*La rosa de las nieblas*, 1999).

25 A bibliographic study by Dolores Robles Moreno of the Biblioteca de Mujeres in Madrid lists women writers in Latin America and Spain. This study may be obtained by writing to the Women's Library, Barquillo 44, 20 Izda, 28004 Madrid, Spain; phone: 34 91 319 3689.

26 Miquel Barceló has declared that if Elia Barceló wrote in English and had been published in the United States, she would be as famous as Ursula K. Le Guin, Joanna Russ, or Vonda McIntyre (1989: 7).

27 We can mention, for example, Boullosa's novel "Earth's Heavens" (*Cielos de la tierra*, 1997) and Esquivel's *Law of Love*, 1996 (*La ley del amor*, 1995.)

28 E-mail to Yolanda Molina-Gavilán, 19 December 1998.

JUAN NEPOMUCENO ADORNO (PAGE 23)

1 For more about the author, see Fernández Delgado 1999.

"ON THE PLANET MARS" (PAGES 37–43)

1 This word still does not appear in any dictionary, but I hope that the Royal Academy of Language will be able to publish this or a similar definition:

TELEFOTEIDOSCOPE (from Gr. *tele*, far; *phos*, *photos*, light; *eidos*, image; and *scopeo*, I see or I examine). Device that reproduces images on a mirror via electric wires, regardless of the distance between the images and the device itself. [Author's note.]

"MECHANOPOLIS" (PAGES 48–51)

1 *Erewhon*, an anagram for "Nowhere," is a satirical novel on Victorian England published in 1872 by Samuel Butler (1835–1902). The protagonist, an explorer, travels to the remote land of Erewhon, where physical illness is considered a crime but moral lapses like thefts and murder invoke condolences

and medical treatment. In the passage Unamuno cites, an alert Erewhonian convinced his fellows to ban most machinery before it could take over completely. [Translator's note.]

ERNESTO SILVA ROMÁN (PAGE 52)

1 For more about the author and this work, see Bell and Hassón 1998.

JUAN JOSÉ ARREOLA (PAGE 58)

1 A Catholic counterrevolutionary insurrection in Mexico during the late 1920s, the Cristero Wars began when President Calles outlawed the Catholic Church.

2 We would also direct readers to an English translation of some of these texts, *Confabulario and Other Inventions* (1964).

ÁNGEL ARANGO (PAGES 63–64)

1 All quotes taken from e-mail correspondence with Andrea Bell, September 2002.

"THE CRYSTAL GOBLET" (PAGES 69–85)

1 DOPS stands for the Departamento de Ordem Política e Social (Department of Political and Social Order), a police force created by the military regime that controlled Brazil from 1964 to 1985. It was notorious for committing egregious human rights violations, including the torture of prisoners, and was abolished in 1983.

2 "Miguelzinho" is the Portuguese diminutive of the name Miguel.

3 A coastal town southeast of São Paolo.

"ACRONIA" (PAGES 93–108)

1 In English in the original.

2 Yves Tanguy, French surrealist painter (1900–1955).

3 In the Spanish original this metaphor is conveyed with the word *bolillero*, which Capanna describes as a type of bingo tumbler that used to be commonly employed during oral examinations in Argentinean schools. The teacher would select a disk or ball from the *bolillero*, and the unlucky pupil to whom it corresponded was thus called upon to answer the test question. (E-mail to Andrea Bell, June 2001.)

4 This and subsequent verses are from "The Hollow Men," by T. S. Eliot.

5 In the Old Testament, these same words mysteriously appeared on King Belshazzar's palace walls during a feast. Daniel interpreted them to mean Belshazzar's days were numbered and his kingdom in jeopardy, for God had weighed him and found him wanting (Daniel 5:25–28).

EDUARDO GOLIGORSKY (PAGE 109)

1 1976 was the year of the military coup against Isabel Perón and the beginning of Argentina's infamous period of state-sponsored repression known as "The Dirty War" (1976–1983).

2 The American Mickey Spillane (1918–)—pseudonym of Frank Morrison Spillane—is known for his "hard boiled" style of detective fiction that includes substantial doses of sex and violence.

3 Souto 1985: 54. [Translation ours.]

"THE LAST REFUGE" (PAGES 110–115)

1 The streets mentioned in this story indicate that Maidana is traveling east through the San Nicolás neighborhood of Buenos Aires, heading toward the dockyards of Puerto Madero. San Nicolás has long been prime real estate in the thriving commercial and cultural heart of a world-class city; however, Goligorsky's descriptions of deserted streets and abandoned, weed-choked ports accurately depict Puerto Madero in the 1960s.

"POST-BOOMBOOM" (PAGES 117–122)

1 As the reader shall soon see, the book in question is titled *The Corpuscle: What a Piece of Junk!* This is Vanasco winking at his local readership, as just about every Uruguayan and Argentinean would have recognized the title as that of a compilation published by a Uruguayan primary schoolteacher, José María Firpo (*¡Qué porquería es el glóbulo!*, 1963). The volume and its sequels were a collection of wild and often hilarious observations and misunderstandings about science offered up by Firpo's young pupils over the years. Thus the irony of Vanasco's characters using the book as an unimpeachable scientific reference, and the more tragicomically misguided their efforts to pass humanity's knowledge on to their children. [With the editors' thanks to Norma Nélida Dangla.]

MAGDALENA MOUJÁN OTAÑO (PAGE 123)

1 "Gu Ta Gutarrak" is also the name of a poem by Pedro Mari Otaño published in 1899 that became very famous among the Basque diaspora in the Americas. For a full text of the poem in Basque and Spanish, see www.buber.net/Basque/Diaspora/bertsol_pampa.html (accessed 11 July 2001).

2 For a deeper analysis of this aspect of the story, see Molina-Gavilán 1999b.

"GU TA GUTARRAK (WE AND OUR OWN)" (PAGES 124–135)

1 The battle of Roncesvalles between Franks and Basques in the year 788 when Charlemagne crossed the Pyrenees to reconquer Barcelona. The Franks were attacked in a narrow mountain pass.

2 Lit. "The Lord who is above." [Author's note.]

3 *Euskalerria* in the original.

4 This refers to the accident that occurred in Spain in the 1960s when a U.S. Strategic Air Command plane fell to the sea carrying hydrogen bombs. [Author's note.]

5 The Basque language.

6 "Thanks to God" in Euskera. [Author's note.]

7 "Mother and Father" in Euskera. [Author's note.]

8 In English in the original.

9 "Good-bye" in Euskera.

10 "Inquisitive snout." [Author's note.]

11 Elcano was a Basque sailor and explorer who led the final leg of Magellan's historic voyage around the world.

12 "Forgive me, Mother" in Euskera. [Author's note.]

13 "Butterfly" in Euskera. [Author's note.]

14 "Good-bye gentlemen. Gentlemen, good-bye. Good-bye and a half." [Author's note.]

15 A war cry or a cry of jubilation. [Author's note.]

16 From "txistu," a whistle, those who play music with a txistu. [Author's note.]

17 The Lord of the Forest, in Basque mythology. [Author's note.]

18 Reference to the elephants that Hannibal used to cross the Alps during the First Punic War (264–241 B.C.E.) and to Flaubert's novel *Salambó*, which is set in Carthage. [Author's note.]

JOSÉ B. ADOLPH (PAGE 153)

1 All quotes in this introduction are from Andrea Bell's conversations with Adolph in Lima, Peru, in August 2000.

"THE FALSIFIER" (PAGES 154–157)

1 Lands and their inhabitants granted to conquistadors by the Spanish crown.

2 Pedro Cieza de León, *The Second Part of the Chronicle of Peru*, trans. and ed. Clements R. Markham (New York: Burt Franklin, 1883), 5–7.

ANGÉLICA GORODISCHER (PAGE 158)

1 See www.gigamesh.com/libros.html, "Títulos publicados" (accessed 5 October 2002), for Gorodischer's bibliography as well as additional biographical information in Spanish about the author.

2 For a deeper analysis of this story, see Molina-Gavilán 1999a.

"THE VIOLET'S EMBRYOS" (PAGES 159–193)

1 We have chosen not to translate these two terms. It is important to note, however, that in the original Spanish, *matronas*—a feminine noun meaning "matrons" or "midwives"—is preceded by the masculine article "los," thereby creating a semantic anomaly difficult to reproduce in English. Car-

ita Dulce (literally, "little sweet face") is a character's name. [Translator's note.]

2 In Spanish, "Sleeping Light Three." [Translator's note.]

3 A ship's name, the "Niní Paume One." [Translator's note.]

4 Saint-John Perse is being quoted here.

FEDERICO SCHAFFLER (PAGE 208)

1 For a Spanish-language biography and bibliography that includes the author's e-mail address, please consult www.quintadimension.com/literarea/biofede.html.

"A MISCALCULATION" (PAGES 209–211)

1 The reference is to the 1925 essay "The Cosmic Race" ("La raza cósmica") by the Mexican writer and cabinet minister José Vasconcelos. In the essay, Vasconcelos rejects a Eurocentric blueprint for Mexico's future, celebrating instead his country's native cultures and the "cosmic race" that will result from fusing Mexico's distinct ethnic groups.

GUILLERMO LAVÍN (PAGE 223)

1 Large, usually foreign-owned assembly plants that have proliferated in Mexico's free-trade zones, maquiladoras are often criticized for their harsh working conditions.

"REACHING THE SHORE" (PAGES 224–234)

1 Juan Cortina (1824–1892) was a rancher who has become legendary in Mexican-American folklore for his armed resistance to U.S. abuses in the border provinces. He raised a small army and for months carried out a series of military raids, the most famous of which was his capture of Brownsville, Texas, in 1859. Judith, the cantina singer, is an invention of the author's.

ELIA BARCELÓ (PAGES 235–236)

1 This personal opinion and other professional information was sent by the author to Yolanda Molina-Gavilán in e-mail dated 13 July 2001.

2 Excerpted and translated from e-mail sent to Andrea Bell, 8 October 2002.

MAURICIO-JOSÉ SCHWARZ (PAGE 265)

1 Some of his English-language stories have appeared in *Ellery Queen Mystery Magazine*, *Fiction International*, *Literary Review*, and the *Alabama Fiction Review*.

RICARD DE LA CASA AND PEDRO JORGE ROMERO (PAGE 271)

1 The death of Franco (20 November 1975) and the accession of Juan Carlos I

as king opened a new era: the peaceful transition to democracy by means of the legal instruments of Francoism.

"THE DAY WE WENT THROUGH THE TRANSITION" (PAGES 272–292)

1 Dr. Hugh Everett III (1930–1982) was a Princeton-educated physicist and formulator of quantum mechanics' "relative state," or "many worlds" theory.
2 Santiago Carrillo was the secretary-general of the Spanish Communist Party from 1960 to 1982 and a key figure during the years of transition to democracy after Franco died in 1975.
3 Adolfo Suárez was prime minister of Spain from July 1976 until January 1981 and secretary-general of the National Movement, the reformed party once led by Franco and known as the Falange.
4 A working-class Madrid neighborhood.
5 The reactionary forces.
6 Admiral Luis Carrero Blanco was appointed by Franco as his successor in June 1973, but a squad of commandos from the Basque separatist group ETA blew up his car and assassinated him on 20 December the same year.
7 Matt Visser is a mathematics professor at the University of Wellington (New Zealand) who has published on wormhole physics.

MICHEL ENCINOSA (PAGE 305)

1 José Lezama Lima (1910–1976) was one of Cuba's foremost writers. Lezama's use of language, rich in metaphors and neologisms, has become synonymous with a neo-baroque style of prose in Latin American letters.

"LIKE THE ROSES HAD TO DIE" (PAGES 306–330)

1 Thank you, Borges. [Author's note.]

SELECTED BIBLIOGRAPHY

SELECTED PRIMARY SOURCES

Acosta, Óscar, ed. 1970. *Primera antología de la ciencia-ficción latinoamericana.* Buenos Aires: Rodolfo Alonso Editor.

Adolph, José B. 1972. El falsificador. In *Hasta que la muerte.* Lima: Moncloa-Campodónico Eds.

Adorno, Juan Nepomuceno. 1851. *Introduction to the Harmony of the Universe; or Principles of Physico-Harmonic Geometry.* London: J. Weale.

Aguilera, Juan Miguel, and Javier Redal. 1994. *El refugio.* Barcelona: Ediciones B.

———. 1988. *Mundos en el abismo.* Barcelona: Ultramar.

Aguimana de Veca, Tirso. 1870–71. *Una temporada en el más bello de los planetas.* Published serially in *Revista de España* 13–18.

Agustín, José. 1986. *Cerca del fuego.* Mexico City: Plaza y Janés.

Arango, Ángel. 1964. *¿Adónde van los cefalomos?* Havana: Revolución.

———. 1966. *El planeta negro.* Havana: Granma.

———. 1967. *Robotomaquia.* Havana: Unión.

Aridjis, Homero. 1990. *Gran teatro del fin del mundo.* Mexico City: J. Moritz.

Arreola, Juan José. 1952. Baby H.P. In Trujillo Muñoz 1997.

———. 1964. *Confabulario and other inventions.* Trans. George D. Schade. Austin: University of Texas Press.

Bajarlía, Juan-Jacobo, ed. 1967. *Cuentos argentinos de ciencia ficción.* Buenos Aires: Merlín.

———. 1969. *Historias de monstruos.* Buenos Aires: La Flor.

———. 1970. *Fórmula al antimundo.* Buenos Aires: Galerna.

———. 1972. *El día cero.* Buenos Aires: Emecé.

Barceló, Elia. 1989. La dama dragón. In *Sagrada.* Barcelona: Ediciones B.

———. 1994a. *Consecuencias naturales.* Madrid: Miraguano.

———. 1994b. Estreno. *Cyberfantasy* 6: 41–44.

Belevan, Harry, ed. 1977. *Antología del cuento fantástico peruano.* Lima: Universidad Nacional Mayor de San Marcos.

Bignami, Ariel, ed. 1980. *Fantásticos e inquietantes.* Buenos Aires: Grupo Editor de Buenos Aires.

Bioy Casares, Adolfo. 1940. *La invención de Morel.* Buenos Aires: Losada.

Blixen, Carina, ed. 1991. *Extraños y extranjeros: Panorama de la fantasía uruguaya actual.* Montevideo: Arca.

Britto García, Luis. 1970. Futuro. In *Rajatabla.* Havana: Casa de las Américas.

Borges, Jorge Luis, Adolfo Bioy Casares, and Silvina Ocampo, eds. 1940. *Antología de la literatura fantástica.* Buenos Aires: Sudamericana. Published in English in 1988 as *The book of fantasy.* New York: Viking.

Boullosa, Carmen. 1997. *Cielos de la tierra*. Mexico City: Alfaguara.

Braceras, Elena. 2000. Póslogo LyC. In *Cuentos con humanos, androides y robots*. Buenos Aires: Colihue.

Buiza, Carlos, ed. 1970. *Antología social de ciencia ficción*. Madrid: Zero.

Capanna, Pablo. 1968. Acronia. In *Los argentinos en la luna*, ed. Eduardo Goligorsky. Buenos Aires: La Flor.

———, ed. 1995. *El cuento argentino de ciencia ficción*. Buenos Aires: Nuevo Siglo.

Cardona Peña, Alfredo, ed. 1966. *Cuentos de magia, misterio y horror*. Mexico City: Finisterre.

Carneiro, André. 1997. *A máquina de Hyerónimus e outras histórias*. São Carlos: Editora da UFSCar, Clube Jerônimo Monteiro.

Carón, Carlos María. 1968. La victoria de Napoleón, in *Los argentinos en la luna*, ed. Eduardo Goligorsky. Buenos Aires: La Flor.

Castellote, Miguel, ed. 1972–73. *Antología de la ciencia ficción en lengua castellana*, vols. 1 and 2. Madrid: Castellote.

Castillo y Mayone, Joaquín. 1832. *Viage somniaéreo a la Luna, o Zulema y Lambert*. Barcelona: Librería de M. Sauri y Compañía.

Castro, Pablo. 2000. Exerión. In *Fixión 2000*. Santiago: W&W Ediciones.

Causo, Roberto de Souza, ed. 1994. *Dinossauria tropicalia*. São Paulo: Edições GRD.

Chavarría, Héctor. 1992. Crónica del gran reformador. In *Principios de incertidumbre*, ed. Celine Armenta, José Luis Zárate Herrera and Gerardo Porcayo Villalobos. Puebla: Gobierno del Estado de Puebla.

———. 1997. *El mito del espejo negro*. Mexico City: Grupo Editorial Vid.

Chaviano, Daína. 1983. La Anunciación. In *Amoroso planeta*. Havana: Letras cubanas, 1983.

———. 1988. *Fábulas de una abuela extraterrestre*. Havana: Letras cubanas.

Cócaro, Nicolás, ed. 1960. *Cuentos fantásticos argentinos*. Buenos Aires: Emecé Editores.

Cócaro, Nicolás, and Antonio Serrano, eds. 1976. *Cuentos fantásticos argentinos: Segunda serie*. Buenos Aires: Emecé Editores.

Collazo, Miguel. 1966. *El libro fantástico de Oaj*. Havana: Unión.

Cornejo Murrieta, Gerardo. 1989. *Al norte del milenio*. Mexico City: Liga Literaria.

Correa, Hugo. 1959a. *Alguien mora en el viento*. Santiago: Alerce.

———. 1959b. *Los altísimos*. Santiago: Editorial del Pacífico.

———. 1971. *Cuando Pilato se opuso*. Santiago: Ediciones Valores Literarios.

Cuentos argentinos de ciencia-ficción. 1967. Buenos Aires: Ed. Merlín.

De la Casa, Ricard, and Pedro Jorge Romero. 1998. El día que hicimos la transición. In *Cuentos de ciencia ficción*, ed. Juan Miguel Aguilera. Barcelona: Bígaro.

Encinosa, Michel. 2001. Como tuvieron que morir las rosas. Unpublished story.

Esquivel, Laura. 1995. *La ley del amor*. Barcelona: Plaza & Janés. Published in English in 1996 as *Law of Love*, trans. Margaret Sayers Peden. New York: Crown.

Fabra, Nilo María. 1890. En el planeta Marte. In Santiáñez-Tió 1995.

Fernández Delgado, Miguel Ángel, ed. 2001a. *Visiones periféricas: Antología de la ciencia ficción mexicana*. Mexico City: Lumen.

——, ed. 2001b. *Relatos mexicanos de ciencia ficción del siglo XIX*. Mexico City: Goliardos/CIFF/Angelito Editor.

Fixión 2000. 2000. Santiago: W & W Ediciones.

Fuentes, Carlos. *Cristóbal Nonato*. Mexico City: Fondo de Cultura Económica, 1987. Published in English in 1989 as *Christopher Unborn*, trans. Alfred MacAdam and Carlos Fuentes. New York: Farrar, Straus & Giroux.

Gandolfo, Elvio, ed. 1981. *Cuentos fantásticos y de ciencia ficción en América Latina*. Buenos Aires: Centro Editor de América Latina.

Gaspar, Enrique. *El anacronópete*. Barcelona: Daniel Cortezo y Cía., 1887.

Gaut Vel Hartman, Sergio, ed. 1987. *Fase uno: Relatos de ciencia-ficción*. Buenos Aires: Sinergía.

Goligorsky, Eduardo. 1967. En el último reducto. In Souto 1985.

——, ed. 1968. *Los argentinos en la luna*. Buenos Aires: La Flor.

González Morales, Antonino, ed. 1969. *Antología española de ficción científica*. Madrid: Prensa Española.

Goorden, Bernard, and A. E. Van Vogt, eds. 1982. *Lo mejor de la ciencia ficción latinoamericana*. Barcelona: Ediciones Martínez Roca.

Gorodischer, Angélica. 1973. *Bajo las jubeas en flor*. Buenos Aires: La Flor.

——. 1978. Los embriones del violeta. *Los universos vislumbrados. Antología de la ciencia ficción argentina*. Ed. Jorge A. Sánchez. Buenos Aires: Andrómeda.

——. 1979. *Trafalgar*. Buenos Aires: El Cid.

——. 1990. *Opus dos*. Barcelona: Ultramar.

Grassi, Alfredo Julio, and Alejandro Vignati, eds. 1968. *Ciencia ficción: Nuevos cuentos argentinos*. Buenos Aires: Calatyud-DEA.

Guzmán Wolffer, Ricardo. 1993. *Que Dios se apiade de todos nosotros*. Mexico City: Consejo Nacional para la Cultura y las Artes.

Henríquez, Bruno, ed. 1999. *Polvo en el viento: Antología de ciencia ficción cubana*. Buenos Aires: Ediciones Instituto Movilizador de Fondos Cooperativos.

Hernández, Vladimir. 1999a. *Nova de cuarzo*. Havana: Ediciones Extramuros.

——, ed. 1999b. *Horizontes probables*. Mexico City: Lectorum.

Holmberg, Eduardo Ladislao. 1875. Viaje maravilloso del señor Nic-Nac: En el que se refieren las prodigiosas aventuras de este señor y se dan a conocer las instituciones, costumbres y preocupaciones de un mundo desconocido. Buenos Aires: Imprenta de *El Nacional*.

Hurtado, Oscar, ed. 1971. *Introducción a la ciencia ficción*. Madrid: M. Castellote.

Lavín, Guillermo. 1994. Llegar a la orilla. In *Frontera de espejos rotos*, ed. Mauricio José Schwarz and Don Webb. Mexico City: Ediciones Roca.

Llopis, Rogelio, ed. 1968. *Cuentos cubanos de lo fantástico y lo extraordinario.* Havana: UNEAC.

Lugones, Leopoldo. 1926. *Las fuerzas extrañas.* Buenos Aires: M. Gleizer. Published in English in 2001 as *Strange Forces,* trans. Gilbert Alter-Gilbert. Pittsburgh: Latin American Literary Review Press.

Martí, Agenor, ed. 1988. *Aventuras insólitas.* Havana: Letras Cubanas.

Menén Desleal, Álvaro. 1969. *Una cuerda de nylon y oro y otros cuentos maravillosos.* San Salvador: Dirección General de Cultura del Ministerio de Educación.

————. 1972. *La ilustre familia androide.* Buenos Aires: Ediciones Orión.

Miralles, Francisco. 1886. *Desde Júpiter: Curioso viaje de un santiaguino magnetizado.* 2d ed. Santiago: Imprenta Cervantes.

Mond, F. [Féliz Mondéjar]. 1983. *Con perdón de los terrícolas.* Havana: Letras Cubanas.

Monteiro, Jerônimo. *3 meses no século 81.* Rio de Janeiro: Livraria do Globo, 1947.

————. 1969. O copo de cristal. In *Tangentes da realidade.* São Paulo: Livraria 4 Artes Editora.

————, ed. 1959. *O conto fantástico.* Rio de Janeiro: Civilização Brasileira.

Montero, Rosa. 1981. *La función delta.* Madrid: Debate. Published in English in 1991 as *The Delta Function,* trans. Kari Easton and Yolanda Molina-Gavilán. University of Nebraska Press.

————. *Temblor.* Barcelona: Seix Barral, 1990.

Moreno, Horacio, ed. 1993. *Lo fantástico: Cuentos de realidad e imaginación.* Buenos Aires: Ediciones Instituto Movilizador de Fondos Cooperativos.

Mourelle, Daniel Ruben, ed. 1986. *Parsec XXI.* Buenos Aires: Filofalsía.

Mouján Otaño, Magdalena. 1982. Gu ta gutarrak. In *Lo mejor de la ciencia ficción latinoamericana,* ed. Bernard Goorden and A. E. van Vogt. Barcelona: Martínez de la Roca. Reprinted in *Ciencia ficción argentina,* ed. Pablo Capanna. 1990. Buenos Aires: Aude.

Nuño, Juan, ed. 1988. *Fantasmas computarizados.* Caracas: Bexeller.

Olvera, Carlos. 1968. *Mejicanos en el espacio.* Mexico City: Diógenes.

Pacheco, José Emilio. 1958. *La sangre de Medusa.* Mexico City: Librería de M. Porrúa.

Porcayo, Gerardo Horacio. 1993. *La primera calle de la soledad.* Mexico City: Consejo Nacional para la Cultura y las Artes.

————, ed. 1997. *Los mapas del caos: Breve antología de ciencia ficción mexicana.* Mexico City: Ramón Llaca y Cía.

Reloba, Juan Carlos, ed. N.d. *Juegos planetarios.* Havana: Ed. Gente Nueva.

————. 1988. *Contactos.* Havana: Ed. Gente Nueva.

Rivera Saavedra, Juan, ed. 1976. *Cuentos sociales de ciencia-ficción.* Lima: Editorial Horizonte.

Robles, Lola. 1999. *La rosa de las nieblas.* Madrid: Kira.

Rocha Dórea, Gumercindo, ed. 1961a. *Histórias do acontecerá*. Rio de Janeiro: Edições GRD.

———, ed. 1961b. *Antologia brasileira de ficção científica*. Rio de Janeiro: Edições GRD.

Rodrigué, Emilio, ed. 1966. *Ecuación fantástica: 13 cuentos de ciencia ficción por 9 psicoanalistas*. Buenos Aires: Hormé.

———. 1967. *Plenipotencia*. Buenos Aires: Minotauro.

Roman, Ernesto Silva. 1929. El astro de la muerte. In *El dueño de los astros*. Santiago: La Novela Nueva.

Rojas, Agustín de. 1990. *El año 200*. Havana: Letras Cubanas.

Rojas-Murphy, Andrés, ed. 1988. *Antología de cuentos chilenos de ciencia ficción y fantasía*. Santiago: Andrés Bello.

Rojo, Pepe. 1996. *Ruido gris*. Serie Narrativa 1. Mexico City: UAM.

———. 2000. *Punto cero*. Mexico City: Times Editores.

Saiz Cidoncha, Carlos, and Pedro Alberto García Bilbao. 1999. *Viajes de los Aznar*. Madrid: Silente.

Salazar, Alí, and Justo Vasco, eds. 1988. *Recurso extremo*. Havana: April.

Santiáñez-Tió, Nil, ed. 1995. *De la luna a Mecanópolis. Antología de la ciencia ficción española (1832–1913)*. Barcelona: Quaderns Crema.

Santos, Domingo, ed. 1982. *Lo mejor de la ciencia ficción española*. Barcelona: Martínez Roca.

Sanz, José, ed. 1969. *SF Symposium/FC Simpósio*. Rio de Janeiro: Instituto do Cinema.

Sasso, Roberto, ed. 1996. *C.R. 2040*. San José: Editorial Universidad Estatal a Distancia.

Schaffler, Federico. 1983. Un error de cálculo. In Trujillo Muñoz 1997.

———, ed. 1991. *Más allá de lo imaginado: Antología de ciencia ficción mexicana*, vols. 1 and 2. Mexico City: Consejo Nacional para la Cultura y las Artes.

———, ed. 1993. *Sin permiso de Colón: Fantasías mexicanas del quinto centenario*. Guadalajara: Universidad de Guadalajara.

———, ed. 1994. *Más allá de lo imaginado: Antología de ciencia ficción mexicana*, vol. 3. Mexico City: Consejo Nacional para la Cultura y las Artes.

Schwarz, Mauricio-José. 1991. *Escenas de la realidad virtual*. Mexico City: Claves Latinoamericanas.

———. 1996. Destellos en vidrio azul. In *Más allá no hay nada*. Serie Narrativa 108. Mexico: UAM.

Souto, Marcial, ed. 1985. *La ciencia ficción en la Argentina: Antología crítica*. Buenos Aires: EUDEBA.

———. 1988. *Historia de la fragua y otros inventos*. Buenos Aires: Ultramar Editores.

Tavares, Braulio. 1989. Stuntmind. In *A espinha dorsal da memória*. Lisbon: Caminho.

Torres, Raúl, ed. 1972. *Antología española de ciencia ficción*, vols. 1 and 2. Madrid: PPC.

Trujillo Muñoz, Gabriel. 1997. *El futuro en llamas: Cuentos clásicos de la ciencia ficción mexicana*. Mexico City: Grupo Editorial Vid.

Unamuno, Miguel de. 1913. Mecanópolis. In Santiáñez-Tió 1995.

Uribe, Augusto, ed. 1985. *Latinoamérica fantástica*. Barcelona: Ultramar.

Urquizo, Francisco L. 1934. *Mi tío Juan*. Mexico City: Editorial Claret.

Vanasco, Alberto. 1967. Post-bombum. In *Adiós al mañana*, ed. Alberto Vanasco and Eduardo Goligorsky. Buenos Aires: Minotauro.

Vanasco, Alberto, and Eduardo Goligorsky, eds. 1966. *Memorias del futuro*. Buenos Aires: Minotauro.

Veríssimo, Erico. 1962.*Viagem à aurora do mundo*. 2d ed. Rio de Janeiro: Editôra Globo.

Viage de un filósofo a Selenópolis, corte desconocida de los habitantes de la Tierra, escrito por él mismo, y publicado por D.A.M. y E. 1804. Madrid: Gómez Fuentenebro y Compañía.

Visiones: Un panorama de la ciencia ficción argentina, hoy. N.d. Diskette. Buenos Aires: Ediciones Axxón.

Yoss, [José Miguel Sánchez], ed. 1999. *Reino eterno: Cuentos de fantasía y ciencia ficción*. Havana: Letras Cubanas.

Zaluar, Augusto Emilio. *O doutor Benignus*. Rio de Janeiro: Typ. do Globo, 1875.

Zárate Herrera, José Luis. *Xanto: Novelucha libre*. Mexico: Planeta, 1994.

SELECTED SECONDARY SOURCES

Arango, Ángel. 1984. La joven ciencia-ficción cubana (Un lustro dentro del concurso David). *Unión* 23: 128–138.

Balboa Echevarría, Miriam, and Ester Gimbernat González. 1995. *Boca de dama: La narrativa de Angélica Gorodischer*. Buenos Aires: Feminaria.

Barceló, Miquel. 1989. Presentación. In *Sagrada*, by Elia Barceló. Barcelona: Ediciones B.

———. 1990. La ciencia ficción en España. In *Ciencia ficción. Guía de lectura*. Barcelona: Ediciones B.

Barceló, Miquel, and M. Jakubowski. 1993. Spain. In *The Encyclopedia of Science Fiction*, ed. John Clute and Peter Nicholls. London: Orbis.

Bell, Andrea. 1998. Prelude to the Golden Age: Chilean science fiction, 1900–1959. *Science Fiction Studies* 25: 285–299.

———. 1999. Current trends in global SF: Science fiction in Latin America: Reawakenings. *Science Fiction Studies* 26: 441–446.

Bell, Andrea, and Moisés Hassón. 1995. *Desde Júpiter:* Chile's earliest science fiction novel. *Science Fiction Studies* 22: 187–197.

Capanna, Pablo. 1966. *El sentido de la ciencia ficción*. Buenos Aires: Columba.

———. 1979. Humor y ciencia ficción. *Suplemento de Humor y Ciencia Ficción* 1: 8–11.

———. 1985a. Prestigios de un mito. *Minotauro* 9: 76–88.

———. 1985b. La ciencia ficción y los argentinos. *Minotauro* 10: 43–56.

———. 1990. Estudio preliminar. In *Ciencia ficción argentina*. Buenos Aires: Aude.

———. 1992. *El mundo de la ciencia ficción: Sentido e historia*. Buenos Aires: Letra Buena.

———. 1995. Ciencia ficción: La penúltima ideología. *Razón y fe* 231: 481–493.

Carneiro, André. 1967. *Introdução ao estudo da science-fiction*. São Paulo: Conselho Estadual de Cultura.

Causo, Roberto de Souza. 1994a. SF in Brazil. *Locus* 402: 47.

———. 1994b. SF in Argentina. *Locus* 402: 48–49.

———. 1995. SF in Brazil. *Locus* 411: 35–38.

Chaviano, Daína. 1984. La ciencia ficción en Cuba. *Plural*.

———. 1986a. Un día de otro planeta: Carta de presentación. *Unión: Revista de la Unión de Escritores y Artistas de Cuba* 1: 79–80.

———. 1986b. Veinte años de ciencia ficción en Cuba. *Unión: Revista de la Unión de Escritores y Artistas de Cuba* 1: 119–130.

———. 1987. Para una bibliografía de la CF cubana. *Letras cubanas* 6: 273–280.

Ciencia ficción en la Argentina. 1985. *Suplemento Cultura Diario Tiempo Argentino*, 29 December.

Cisternas Ampuero, Cristián. 1998. "Las cartas olvidadas del astronauta," de Javier Campos: Una propuesta de lectura desde/para la ciencia/ficción. *Revista chilena de literatura* 53: 87–105.

Cócaro, Nicolás, and Antonio Serrano. 1960. La corriente literaria fantástica en la Argentina. In *Cuentos fantásticos argentinos*, ed. Nicolás Cócaro. Buenos Aires: Emecé.

———. 1976. Introduction to *Cuentos fantásticos argentinos: Segunda serie*, ed. Nicolás Cócaro and Antonio E. Serrano Redonnet. Buenos Aires: Emecé.

De Ambrosio, José. 1989. ABC de la ciencia ficción argentina. *Cuasar* 21: 90–103.

———. 1997. Borges y la ciencia ficción. *Cuasar* 28: 49–50.

Dellepiane, Angela B. 1985. Contar = mester de fantasía o la narrativa de Angélica Gorodischer. *Revista Iberoamericana* 51: 627–640.

———. 1987. Critical notes on Argentinian science fiction narrative. *Monographic Review/Revista Monográfica* 3: 19–32.

———. 1989. Narrativa argentina de ciencia ficción: Tentativas liminares y desarrollo posterior. In *Actas del IX Congreso de la Asociación Internacional de Hispanistas*, vol. 2, ed. Sebastian Neumister. Frankfurt: Vervuert.

Dendle, Brian J. 1987. Spain's first novel of science fiction: A nineteenth-century voyage to Saturn. *Monographic Review/Revista monográfica* 3: 43–49.

D'Lugo, Martin. 1975. Frutos de los "frutos prohibidos": La fantaciencia rioplatense. *Otros mundos, otros fuegos: Fantasía y realismo mágico en Iberoamérica*. Conference proceedings of the XVI Congreso Internacional de Literatura Iberoamericana. East Lansing: Michigan State University Latin American Studies Center.

Ferman, Claudia. 1997. Mujeres, cuento fantástico y ciencia ficción: Los poblados márgenes de "la" literatura argentina: Una entrevista con Angélica Gorodischer. *Osamayor* 4: 45–54.

Fernández Delgado, Miguel Ángel. 1996a. A moon voyage inside an astronomical almanac in eighteenth-century Mexico. *New York Review of Science Fiction* 97: 17–18.

———. 1996b. A brief history of continuity and change in Mexican science fiction. *New York Review of Science Fiction* 99: 18–19.

———. 1997a. El primer cuento de ciencia ficción mexicano. *Asimov Ciencia Ficción* 9: 9–16.

———. 1997b. "Más allá de lo imaginado": La antología que hizo historia. *Memoria de la III Convención Nacional de la Asociación Mexicana de Ciencia Ficción y Fantasía.* Reprinted in *Yubai* 6 (1998): 14–18.

———. 1997c. Páginas olvidadas de la historia de la ciencia ficción mexicana. *Memoria de la III Convención Nacional de la Asociación Mexicana de Ciencia Ficción y Fantasía.*

———. 1998. Borges y la ciencia-ficción: Obras de imaginación razonada. *Artifex* 17: 30–32.

———. 1998–99. Hacia una vindicación de la ciencia ficción mexicana. *Artifex* 20–21: 25–30.

———. 1999. Juan Nepomuceno Adorno y la poesía intuitiva o ciencia ficción mexicana del siglo XIX.*Umbrales: Literatura Fantástica de México* 41: 2–21.

———. 2000. Las crónicas lunares de Amado Nervo. *Umbrales: Literatura Fantástica de México* 44: 2–7.

Ferreras, Ignacio. 1972. *La novela de ciencia ficción: Interpretación de una novela marginal.* Madrid: Siglo XXI.

Font, María Teresa. 1970. La sociedad del futuro en Pérez de Ayala, Huxley y Orwell. *Revista de estudios hispánicos* 41: 67–83.

Foster, David W. 2002. Preface to *Ciencia ficción en español: Una mitología moderna ante el cambio,* by Yolanda Molina-Gavilán. Lewiston, N.Y.: Edwin Mellen.

Galván, Delia. 1996. Alicia Yañez Cossio en ciencia ficción. *Letras femeninas* 22: 65–75.

Gandolfo, Elvio E. 1978. La ciencia ficción argentina. In *Los universos vislumbrados: Antología de la ciencia ficción argentina,* ed. Jorge A. Sánchez. Buenos Aires: Andrómeda.

———. 1985. Una utopía latinoamericana. *Minotauro* 9: 96–104.

———. 1998. Volver al futuro. *Los inrockuptibles* 26: 16–19.

Gaut vel Hartman, Sergio. 1986. Ciencia ficción en la Argentina. *Gigamesh* 3: 69–75.

Goligorsky, Eduardo, ed. 1968. Foreword to *Los argentinos en la luna.* Buenos Aires: La Flor.

Goligorsky, Eduardo, and Marie Langer. 1969.*Ciencia-ficción, realidad y psicoanálisis.* Buenos Aires: Paidós.

González-Cruz, Luis F. 1982. Oscar Hurtado's *The Dead City of Korad:* A unique experiment in Cuban science fiction poetry. In *Literatures in Transition: The Many Voices of the Caribbean Area: A Symposium*, ed. Rose S. Minc. Gaithersburg, Md.: Hispamerica.

Goorden, Bernard. 1985. De algunos temas originales en la ciencia ficción española y latinoamericana en el siglo veinte. Trans. Margarita Cervantes Deras. *Plural* 163: 38–43.

Gorodischer, Angélica. 1987. Narrativa fantástica y narrativa de ciencia ficción. *Plural* 188: 48–50.

Hahn, Oscar. 1978. *El cuento fantástico hispanoamericano en el siglo XIX: Estudio y textos.* Mexico City: Premia.

Hassón, Moisés. 1987. Ciencia ficción religiosa en Chile. *Vórtice* 7: 38–43.

———. 1994. *Indice: Revistas de Ciencia Ficción, 1947–1989,* vol. 1. Santiago: [Moisés Hassón].

Holmberg, Luis. 1952. *Holmberg, el último enciclopedista.* Buenos Aires: Colombo.

Kason, Nancy. 1987. The dystopian vision in *XYZ* by Clemente Palma. *Monographic Review/Revista Monográfica* 3: 33–42.

———. 1997. *Horacio Kalibang o los autómatas:* A Nineteenth-Century View of Artificial Beings. In *The Dark Fantastic: Selected Essays From the Ninth International Conference on the Fantastic in the Arts.* Contributions to the Study of Science Fiction and Fantasy, no. 71, ed. C. W. Sullivan III. Westport, Conn.: Greenwood.

Kreksch, Ingrid. 1997. Reality transfigured: The Latin American situation as reflected in its science fiction. In *Political Science Fiction*, ed. Donald M. Hassler and Clyde Wilcox. Columbia: University of South Carolina Press.

Larson, Ross. 1973. Fantasy and imagination in the Mexican narrative. Ph.D. diss., University of Toronto.

———. 1974. La literatura de ciencia ficción en México. *Cuadernos hispanoamericanos* 284: 425–431.

Lefebvre, Alfredo. 1968. *Los españoles van a otro mundo.* Barcelona: Pomaire.

Lindstrom, Naomi. 1994. *Twentieth-Century Spanish American Fiction.* Austin: University of Texas Press.

Lojo de Beuter, María Rosa. 1990. Dos versiones de la utopía: "Sensatez del círculo" de Angélica Gorodischer y "Utopía de un hombre cansado" de Jorge Luis Borges. In *Mujer y sociedad en América: IV Simposio internacional*, vol. 1, ed. Juana Alcira Arancibia. Northridge [Westminster, Calif.]: California State University, Northridge.

Mauso Villarubia, Pablo. 1988 and 1991. Ciencia ficción en Brasil. *Nadir* 10: 8–10 and 11: 2–10.

Miranda, Álvaro. 1994. *La poética del espacio: Estudios críticos sobre ciencia ficción.* Montevideo: Editores Asociados Academia Uruguaya de Letras.

Molina-Gavilán, Yolanda. 1996. La ciencia ficción hispana: Un estudio de casos argentinos y españoles. Ph.D. diss., Arizona State University.

————. 1998. Science fiction. In *Encyclopedia of the Novel*, ed. Paul Schellinger. London: Fitzroy Dearborn.

————. 1999a. Alternate realities from Argentina: Angélica Gorodischer's "Los embriones del violeta." *Science Fiction Studies* 79–26: 401–411.

————. 1999b. Magdalena Mouján Otaño's "Gu Ta Gutarrak (We and Our Own)": A science fictional look at the Basque nationalist myth of pure racial origins. *Romance Language Annual* 10: 600–605.

————. 2002. *Ciencia ficción en español: Una mitología ante el cambio.* Lewiston, N.Y.: Edwin Mellen.

Molina-Gavilán, Yolanda, Miguel Ángel Fernández Delgado, Andrea Bell, Luis Pestarini, and Juan Carlos Toledano. 2000. Cronología de CF latinoamericana, 1775–1999. *Chasqui: Revista de literatura latinoamericana* 29(2): 43–72.

Mora, Gabriela. 1994. "De repente los lugares desaparecen" de Patricio Manns: Ciencia ficción a la latinoamericana? *Revista Iberoamericana* 60: 1039–1049.

Mora Vélez, Antonio. 1994. Daína Chaviano y el humanismo de la ciencia ficción latinoamericana. *Universidad de Córdoba* 6: n.p. Reprinted in *La ciencia y el hombre: Revista de la Universidad Veracruzana* 25 (1997): 65–70.

Moreno, Horacio. 1999. El nacimiento de la ciencia ficción argentina en el siglo XIX. *Cuasar* 31: 41–44.

Morillas Ventura, Enriqueta, ed. 1991. *El relato fantástico en España e Hispanoamérica.* Madrid: Quinto Centenario.

Mosier, Patricia. 1983. A communicating transcendence in Angélica Gorodischer's *Trafalgar. Chasqui: Revista de literatura latinoamericana* 12(2–3): 63–71.

————. 1988. Women in power in Gorodischer's *Kalpa Imperial.* In *Spectrum of the Fantastic*, ed. Donald Palumbo. Westport, Conn.: Greenwood.

Nascimento, R. C. 1985. *Quem é quem na ficção científica.* São Paulo: Scortecci.

Negrete, Javier. 1998. Evolución convergente. In *Cuentos de ciencia ficción*, ed. Juan Miguel Aguilera. Barcelona: Bígaro.

Núñez Ladeveze, Luis. 1976. *Utopía y realidad: La ciencia ficción en España.* Madrid: Del Centro.

Oropesa, Salvador A. 1992. *La obra de Ariel Dorfman: Ficción y crítica.* Madrid: Pliegos.

Pérez, Genaro J. 1984. Cultivadores, temas y motivos de la ciencia ficción actual en España. *Romance Notes* 25(2): 102–108.

Pessina, H. R., and Jorge A. Sánchez. 1978. Esbozo para una cronología comentada de la cf argentina. In *Los universos vislumbrados.* Buenos Aires: Andrómeda.

Pestarini, Luis. 1998. El primer cuento argentino de ciencia ficción. *Cuasar* 30: 3–4.

Planells, Antonio. 1990. La literatura de anticipación y su presencia en Argentina. *Revista iberoamericana de bibliografía* 40: 93–113.

Rebétez, René. 1966. *La ciencia ficción: Cuarta dimensión de la literatura.* Mexico City: Secretaría de Educación Pública, Cuadernos de Lectura Popular.

Remi-Maure. 1984. Science fiction in Chile. Trans. Lynette Stokes, Laird Stevens, and Robert M. Philmus. *Science Fiction Studies* 11: 181–189.

Risco, Anton. 1990. Los autómatas de Holmberg. *Mester* 19(2): 63–70.

Rodríguez, Antonio Orlando. 1999. ¿Milicianos versus extraterrestres? Apuntes sobre la ciencia ficción en Cuba. Paper presented at the session Cuba y la ciencia ficción: Un género popular en el márgen, at the second CRI Conference on Cuban and Cuban-American Studies, Florida International University, Miami, 19 March.

Saiz Cidoncha, Carlos. 1976. *Historia de la ciencia ficción en España.* Madrid: Sala Editorial.

———. 1988. *La ciencia ficción como fenómeno de comunicación y de cultura de masas en España.* Madrid: Editorial de la Universidad Complutense.

Sánchez Arce, Claudia. 1993. *Los temas de la ciencia ficción en Trafalgar.* Mexico City: Universidad Autónoma del Estado de México.

Sánchez Durán, Fernando, and Antonio Campaña. 1991. *Narrativa chilena ultrarealista.* Santiago: Zona Azul.

Santiáñez-Tió, Nil. 1994. Nuevos mapas del universo: Modernidad y ciencia ficción en la literatura española del siglo XIX (1804–1905). *Revista Hispánica Moderna* 47(2): 269–88.

Scari, Robert M. 1964. Ciencia y ficción en los cuentos de Leopoldo Lugones. *Revista Iberoamericana* 30: 163–187.

Schwarz, Mauricio-José. 1984. Los cubanos en la CF. *Excelsior,* 8 April.

Serra, Emilio. 1986. Sobre la ciencia ficción argentina. *Gigamesh* 4: 96–102.

Sociedad Chilena de Fantasía y Ciencia Ficción. 1989. *Fantasía y ciencia ficción: Cinco conferencias de literatura de fantasía y ciencia ficción.* Santiago: Depto. de Cultura.

Souto, Marcial. 1985. *Introduction to La ciencia ficción en la Argentina,* ed. Marcial Souto. Buenos Aires: Eudeba.

Stavans, Ilan. 1994. Introduction: Private eyes and time travelers. *Literary Review* 1: 5–20.

Tavares, Braulio, ed. N.d. *Fantastic, Fantasy, and Science Fiction Literature Catalog.* International Publications Series 2. Rio de Janeiro: Fundação Biblioteca Nacional.

Toledano, Juan Carlos. 1999. Influencias de la revolución en la literatura cubana de ciencia ficción: F. Mond y Agustín de Rojas. *Romance Language Annual* 10: 848–852.

———. 1999. SF in Cuba. *Locus* 43: 42–43.

———. 2002. Ciencia-ficción cubana: El proyecto nacional del hombre nuevo socialista. Ph.D. diss., University of Miami.

Trujillo Muñoz, Gabriel. N.d. La ciencia ficción latinoamericana. In *Piedra de toque,* ed. Raúl Navejas Dávila. Mexicali: Universidad Autónoma de Baja California.

———. 1991. *La ciencia ficción: Literatura y conocimiento.* Mexicali: Instituto de Baja California.

———. 1999. *Los confines: Crónica de la ciencia ficción mexicana.* Mexico City: Vid.

Urraca, Beatriz. 1995. Angélica Gorodischer's voyages of discovery: Sexuality and historical allegory in science fiction's cross-cultural encounters. *Latin American Review* 23: 85–102.

Vaisman, Lus A. 1985. En torno a la ciencia ficción: Propuesta para la descripción de un género histórico. *Revista chilena de literatura* 25: 5–27.

Vasquez, María Esther. 1983. Angélica Gorodischer: Una escritora latinoamericana de ciencia ficción. *Revista Iberoamericana* 49: 571–576.

Verrecchia, Juan Carlos. 1987. *Hombres del futuro:* La revista olvidada. *Vórtice* 7: 44–50.

Vinelli, Aníbal. 1977. *Guía para el lector de ciencia ficción.* Buenos Aires: Convergencia.

Weinberg, Félix. 1976. *Dos utopías argentinas de principios de siglo.* Buenos Aires: Solar/Hachette.

Winter, Sylvia. 1979. A utopia from the semi-periphery: Spain, modernization, and the Enlightenment. *Science Fiction Studies* 6: 100–107.

SELECTED INTERNET SOURCES

Many of these sites have links to other resources for Spanish- and Portuguese-language sf.

A Quien Corresponda: aquiencorresponda.spedia.net (Mexico)

Ad Astra: dreamers.com/adastra (Spain)

Asociación Española de Fantasía y Ciencia Ficción: www.aefcf.es (Spain)

Axxon: www.giga.com.ar/axxon/axxon.htm (Argentina)

BEM: www.bemmag.com (Spain)

Ciencia Ficción Mexicana: www.ciencia-ficcion.com.mx (Mexico; an online encyclopedia)

Cuasar: quintadimension.com/cuasar (Argentina)

Espora: www.egroups.com/subscribe/espora (Spain)

El Guaicán Dorado: www.cubaliteraria.cu/guaican/index.html (Cuba)

Gigamesh: www.gigamesh.com (Spain)

International Publishing House: iph.lib.ru (Russia)

Laberinto: members.tripod.com/~nexus30/laberinto.htm (Mexico)

¡Nahual!: www.geocities.com/nahualzine (Mexico)

QuintaDimensión: www.quintadimension.com (Argentina)

Realidad Cero: members.tripod.com/~realidadcero/rco.htm (Mexico)

ABOUT THE CONTRIBUTORS

Ted Angell, a native of southern California, studied Spanish and translation at Interpretes y Traductores Salamanca in Salamanca, Spain. He currently resides in southern Brazil and is a student at Yorktown University in Yorktown, Virginia.

Andrea Bell received her Ph.D. in Spanish from Stanford University. She has published and presented on science fiction from Latin America and is an active member of the International Association for the Fantastic in the Arts. She is an associate professor in the Modern Languages Department at Hamline University in St. Paul, Minnesota.

Casandra Griffith, Laura Wertish, and Rena Zuidema are all graduates of Hamline University's College of Liberal Arts. Each undertook a literary translation as part of a collaborative research project within the Spanish major.

Patricia Hart holds a Ph. D. from the University of North Carolina at Chapel Hill and is a professor of Spanish at Purdue University. She has published extensively in the areas of peninsular Spanish twentieth-century literature, Catalan literature, and translation, as well as film in Spain and Latin America. Her works include fiction (*Little Sins*, 1980); literary criticism (*The Spanish Sleuth: The Detective in Spanish Fiction*, 1987; *Narrative Magic in the Fiction of Isabel Allende*, 1989); and translations from Catalan (*A Corpse of One's Own*, 1993; *Júlia*, 1998, both by Isabel-Clara Simó).

Sara Churchill Irausquin graduated from Hamline University with degrees in Spanish and anthropology. Her interest in Spanish language and cultures led her to study in Chile, and she has traveled widely throughout Latin America.

Yolanda Molina-Gavilán was born and raised in Madrid, Spain, and holds a Ph.D in Spanish literature from Arizona State University. Her research centers on science fiction literature in the Spanish-speaking world and on contemporary Spanish cinema. She is an associate professor of Spanish at Eckerd College in St. Petersburg, Florida.

Joe F. Randolph has been studying foreign languages and translating them into English for over thirty years. In addition to Portuguese, he can read and translate Catalan, Galician, German, Italian, Norwegian, Russian, Spanish, and Swedish, and has a passing acquaintance with some others. Working in different fields has provided him with a broad vocabulary that has proven useful in translation.

Roberta Rozende is a recent graduate of Eckerd College of Liberal Arts.

David Sunderland holds advanced degrees in Spanish and Portuguese from Middlebury College and has traveled extensively in Spain and Latin America. He has been teaching Spanish and Portuguese language and culture since the mid-1970s. His disciplinary interests include professional and advanced language application and U.S. Latino literature.

Juan Carlos Toledano, assistant professor of Hispanic studies at Lewis and Clark College in Portland, Oregon, works on the fantastic in Hispanic narrative. He has written a dissertation on the New Socialist Man in Cuban science fiction (University of Miami) and has published various articles on the topic.

Library of Congress Cataloging-in-Publication Data

Cosmos latinos : an anthology of science fiction from Latin America and Spain /
    translated, edited, & with an introduction & notes by Andrea L. Bell & Yolanda
    Molina-Gavilán.
        p. cm. — (The Wesleyan early classics of science fiction series)
        Includes bibliographical references.
        ISBN 0-8195-6633-0 (cloth) — ISBN 0-8195-6634-9 (pbk.)
        1. Science fiction, Latin American—Translations into English. 2. Latin
    American fiction—20th century—Translations into English. 3. Science fiction,
    Spanish—Translations into English. 4. Spanish fiction—20th century—
    Translations into English. I. Bell, Andrea L., 1960–   II. Molina-Gavilán,
    Yolanda. III. Series.

PQ7087.E5C67 2003
863'.087620898—dc21   2003041182